THE [illegible]

FOUNDER ED[illegible]

Rober[illegible]
Betty [illegible]

Eugène Labiche was born in 1815. He was the author, sometimes in collaboration, of more than 150 farces, and his work was consistently well received from his first play in 1838, to the seventies. His most famous plays include *Un Chapeau de paille d'Italie*, in collaboration with Marc Michel (1851), *Le Voyage de Monsieur Perrichon*, with Édouard Martin (1860), and *La Cagnotte* (1864). In 1864 he was invited to write a piece for the Comédie Française, and in 1880 he was made a member of the Académie. He died in 1888.

Victorien Sardou, born in 1831, was one of the most successful exponents of the 'well-made play'. For some time he was Sarah Bernhardt's favourite contemporary dramatist, and wrote a series of dramas for her, including the spectacular *Théodora impératrice de Bizance* (1884). He was also the author of a number of comedies, including *Les Pattes de mouche* (1860) and *La Famille Benoiton* (1865). He died in 1908.

Georges Feydeau, born in 1862, was probably the most brilliant and well-known writer of bedroom farce. His output was vast, stretching through from the *belle époque* to the 1920s. Among his best works are *Le Dindon* (1898), *La Puce à l'oreille* (*A Flea in Her Ear*) (1907), and *Occupe-toi d'Amélie* (1908). He died in 1921.

Frederick Davies is well known as the translator of the comedies of Carlo Goldoni, nine of which have been published and performed throughout the United Kingdom and abroad. In 1969 he was elected to a Schoolmaster Fellow Commonership at Churchill College, Cambridge. His previous work includes two novels for children, critical essays on the work of John Cowper Powys, W. H. Auden and Simenon, and translations of two plays by Labiche. His translations of *Four Comedies* by Goldoni have been published in Penguin Classics.

THE HAPPIEST OF THE THREE

EUGÈNE LABICHE

and

Edmond Gondinet

LET'S GET A DIVORCE!

VICTORIEN SARDOU

and

Émile de Najac

GET OUT OF MY HAIR!

GEORGES FEYDEAU

Translated and introduced

by

Frederick Davies

PENGUIN BOOKS

Penguin Books Ltd, Harmondsworth, Middlesex, England
Penguin Books Inc., 7110 Ambassador Road, Baltimore, Maryland 21207, U.S.A.
Penguin Books Australia Ltd, Ringwood, Victoria, Australia

—

Published in Penguin Books 1973

—

Made and printed in Great Britain by
Cox & Wyman Ltd, London, Reading and Fakenham
Set in Monotype Fournier

—

CONTENTS

à GEORGES SIMENON,
Romancier du monde: Homme du cœur

INTRODUCTION

Eugène Labiche: 1815–1888
Victorien Sardou: 1831–1908
Georges Feydeau: 1862–1921

Eugène Labiche was born in Paris on 6 May 1815. Between 1837 and 1877 he wrote 173 plays. A collected edition of fifty-seven of them was published, in ten volumes, in 1878. In 1880 he was elected to *l'Académie française*. He died in 1888. Of the three writers of French farce represented in this book he is the only one to have been ranked by some critics with Molière.

Up to the age of thirty-seven, however, when he had already written over sixty plays, he was still no more than one of a number of successful writers of vaudeville. Then, in 1852, with the coming of Napoleon III and the Second Empire, his plays began to increase in range of comic observation and in depth of social criticism, and gradually he raised French farce to the level of the comedy of character and manners. There is little doubt that this achievement was the result of the violence of his reaction against his own class, the bourgeoisie.

Labiche was born into this class of merchants, lawyers, doctors and civil servants who began to assert their power under Louis-Philippe and consolidated it under the Second Empire. His father was a prosperous manufacturer of glucose. To the age of sixteen Eugène was educated at the Lycée Bourbon, obtaining his *baccalauréat ès lettres* in 1833. In 1834, he made a six-months tour of Switzerland, Italy and Sicily with two friends who were later to number amongst his collaborators. On their return to Paris, he adopted the carefree life of a boulevardier, frequenting cafés and theatres and writing articles for the smaller journals. In 1837 he wrote his first play in collaboration with Marc Michel and Lefranc and it was performed in 1838. In 1839 he published a novel but withdrew it from circulation within a few months. He had made his choice: the theatre. Three more plays were written and performed in 1839, and another three in 1840. Then came a second journey to Italy, followed by a stay in Holland, and in 1842 Labiche married Adèle Hubert. They went to live at 37 rue de la Caumartin in Paris, and apart from the time he spent at the farm he later acquired in the Sologne Labiche never moved from that address, dying peacefully there on 22 January 1888.

By August 1851 Labiche had written another forty-eight plays. Then, on 14 August 1851, he presented *Un Chapeau de paille d'Italie* at the Palais-Royal. The overwhelming success of *An Italian Straw Hat* marked the beginning of Labiche's gradual elevation of farce from the knock-about buffoonery of vaudeville to a portrayal of character and manners. But it was not until 1860, with *Le Voyage de Monsieur Perrichon*, that he succeeded in combining both comedy of manners and comedy of character in the same play.

Perrichon is a man of his time, one of the bourgeoisie who, like Labiche himself, had welcomed the liquidation of the Second Republic and the seizure of power by Louis-Napoleon. But Perrichon is no longer the caricature of farce. He is the first of a long line of characters who belong not only to their own time but to all time, who give the feeling that they have existed in their own right before they make their entrance on the stage, who are no longer stock types but human beings. Labiche achieves this by means of numerous little nuances aimed at revealing the lack of self-knowledge of people ostensibly so sure of themselves and of their own importance. Beneath the jovial vanity of the petty bourgeoisie, Labiche reveals the pettinesses and cowardices of men who are hardly conscious of their true natures.

It is clear that Labiche knew very well what he was doing: making people laugh at themselves – without realizing it was themselves they were laughing at. When talking about his plays he now frequently used the phrase 'donner le change'. His aim was now to 'put people on the wrong scent'. The majority of the main characters in his plays of the next fifteen years are not only mean, petty mediocrities: they are tricksters, egoists and hypocrites. They deceive themselves, their families and their business associates. Their one object in life is to get the better of their rivals. Yet they are cowards. They love money and fear change. In order to keep what they possess, they distrust everybody. Like the world of Balzac, the world of Labiche is a world distorted by the vision of its creator. Yet, like Balzac's, it is an authentic world, a world which exists in its own right, complete and often horrifyingly credible. However extraordinary the situations in which Labiche places his characters, they themselves remain real and credible. They are not caricatures but portraits of certain aspects of human nature drawn with exact observation and ruthless realism. Labiche is a portrait painter who spares neither his models nor himself, whom he sees reflected in them. He neither accuses nor excuses. He paints what he sees without offering any moral. He leaves it to his audience and, more easily, to his reader to draw their conclusions. For it is easier for the discerning reader than for the involved audience, ensnared in the art which is putting them on the wrong scent, to see the bitter indictment hidden under the surface farce.

Labiche uses laughter, and the obsessive speed of farce, to disarm his audience and – to use his own words – to put them on the wrong scent. He knew very well that if he failed to make his audiences laugh at his characters, they would recognize themselves and be furious with him. So he does not allow his audiences the time to say to themselves: 'But that's me!' His swift farce masks the frequent cruelty of his dialogue. The dialogue of his plays, read in cold blood, often reveals a bitter melancholy which justifies Flaubert's exclamation after seeing a performance of *Le Prix Martin*: 'But this ranks with Molière!' Labiche emphasizes the absurdity of his characters so that the laughter they arouse will hide the truth that they – and we – and he – are absurd, profoundly, senselessly and, to Labiche, terrifyingly, absurd.

It should be remembered that the world of the bourgeoisie which Labiche portrayed in his plays was the world which sickened Baudelaire and disgusted Daumier. Labiche shared their nausea and disgust, but unlike them he was able to adjust himself to the world of the bourgeoisie through his ability to laugh at it and make others laugh at it. 'I have never been able to take mankind seriously', he wrote to Émile Zola. If he had, he would not have been able to live the comfortable bourgeois life that he did. The guiding principle of his life was *le bon sens*. He uses this phrase almost as much as Carlo Goldoni did in his *Memoirs*. And like Goldoni, by using his common sense, and laughing at what he saw in himself and others, he saved himself from being overcome by bitterness and disillusion. He enjoyed being mayor of the village in the Sologne where in 1853 he bought a château and a farm, yet, when he ridicules the pretentious pomposities of petty bourgeois village politics in his one-act masterpiece *La Grammaire*, it is himself he is poking fun at more than anybody. Later he told the Goncourt brothers that he had been nominated as mayor because he had let the authorities know that he was the only person in the district who used a handkerchief and not his fingers. This habit of laughing at himself was the secret of the success both of his plays and of his own adjustment to the bourgeois world, whose vanities and values he saw through so clearly.

After the tremendous success in 1851 of his vaudeville-type farce *Un Chapeau de paille d'Italie*, Labiche knew he could now write whatever he pleased so long as he did not allow his audiences to realize they were seeing themselves in the characters on the stage. This was brought home to him just over a year later when he presented *La Chasse aux Corbeaux*, an obvious satire on the financiers and speculators which the change of régime had proliferated. The play was a complete failure. Labiche realized his mistake: he had not only put on the stage characters whose originals were in his audience; he had allowed them to realize this; he had allowed them to become conscious of the aggression which Freud was later to show to be so essential a part of the successful functioning of farce. This became part of the service his collaborators rendered him: to warn him when he was allowing the bitter, cruel and aggressive undercurrent to show itself too obviously.

Thus, like the plays of Anouilh, those of Labiche can be divided into his *pièces roses* and his *pièces noires*. The former are his plays of pure farce such as *Un Chapeau de paille d'Italie*. From his comedies of character and manners beginning with *Le Voyage de Monsieur Perrichon*, there developed his *pièces noires*, such as *Célimare le Bien-Aimé* and *La Cagnotte*. His masterpieces, however, can be interpreted *en noir et en rose*. Such a one is *Le Plus heureux des trois*.

The Happiest of the Three (1870) was Labiche's reply to a challenge by Sarcey, the greatest dramatic critic of nineteenth-century

France. Sarcey had complained that three quarters of the plays then performed dealt boringly with the subject of adultery since their authors treated the subject so very seriously. He had added that a writer of farce, if he were truly a master of his genre, would be able to arouse laughter from such subjects which in real life can have dreadful consequences. Labiche accepted the challenge and with Gondinet as collaborator produced *Le Plus Heureux des Trois*. It can be interpreted *en rose et en noir*. One interpretation is: "It is terrible to be deceived." The other is: "It is ridiculous to attach so much importance to anything like that." Its success led Labiche to write two more plays on the same theme, *Doit-on le dire?* and *Le Prix Martin*. The last of this trilogy, which caused Flaubert's exclamation, was withdrawn after only twenty performances. Its failure with the public was probably what made Labiche decide to write no more plays and to retire from Paris to his farm in the Sologne.

Finally, mention must be made of Labiche's collaborators and their function. Of his 173 plays, only six were written without a collaborator. Many of Labiche's collaborators, whose names are given next to his on his plays, were well known in the theatre of the time: Delacour, Martin, Marc Michel, Augier, Gondinet. Those critics who have questioned the claim made by others that Labiche ranks with Molière have also sometimes questioned how much of Labiche's plays were written by him and how much by his collaborators. They can best be answered in the words of Émile Augier, who was Labiche's collaborator in *Le Prix Martin*:

> The distinctive qualities which gained a lasting popularity for the plays of Labiche are to be found in all the comedies written by him with different collaborators and are conspicuously absent from those which they wrote without him.

And in the words of Philippe Soupault, who has written one of the most perceptive studies of Labiche (1964):

> It seems that Labiche's collaborators were mostly critics who were expected to present objections, to play the role of first reader, to be the public. Labiche used to try out ideas, judge their effect by observing the reactions of these friends who were closely in touch with Parisian life and with the changing tastes of the public. Some of them, no doubt, sugges-

ted ideas which pleased Labiche. Others contented themselves with making corrections, shortening lines, suggesting modifications. The creator was Labiche.

The name of the man who contributed more than any of Labiche's collaborators appears on none of the title-pages of his plays. He was Jean Marie Geoffroy, the actor who played most of the great leading roles in Labiche's plays: Marjavel in *Le Plus heureux des trois*, Perrichon in *Le Voyage de Monsieur Perrichon*, Chambourcy in *La Cagnotte*, Caboussat in *La Grammaire* and many others.

Geoffroy impersonated the main bourgeois character in Labiche's plays not only to the public but to Labiche himself. There can be no doubt at all that when writing his plays Labiche could mentally see and hear Geoffroy acting the main character. The result was that the words Labiche wrote were dictated by his knowledge of how they would be spoken and interpreted – briskly, fussily and pompously – by Geoffroy.

Perhaps no better summary could be made than that made by Gilbert Sigaux at the end of his preface to a selection of Labiche's plays published in 1960:

> Let us repeat again: Labiche ought not to be considered only as a writer of farce: farce was for him only a means. His portrayal of character is scathing in its irony, deeply serious in the midst of the maddest of his inventions ... The best of Labiche is that which puts him, by means which were the right ones for him, among the great moralists.

*

Victorien Sardou was born in Paris on 5 September 1831. The number of plays he wrote between 1834 and 1907 is not known since he destroyed many, especially during his early career when many were rejected, or accepted and not performed. The collected edition of his plays, however, reached a total of fifty plays with the publication of the fourteenth volume in 1959. In 1878, the same year as Labiche, he was elected to *l'Académie française*. He died in 1908.

Sardou's name has been coupled with Scribe's in so many denigratory references to the 'well-made play' that it is difficult to gain any idea of his achievement when there is so much to prejudice one beforehand. The 'well-made play', which had such a great vogue during the nineteenth century, depended for its success more upon situation and action than upon portrayal of character. In all drama, however, there has always been until recently a tendency to emphasize action at the expense of character. The very word 'drama' comes from the Greek meaning 'a thing done or acted'. Even in Greek drama and in Shakespeare's tragedies, although we know the hero to be noble, to be capable of both good and evil, the action is always emphasized throughout to show the evil he is capable of rather than the good. There is no doubt that Scribe and Sardou emphasized action at the expense of character, and provoked the reaction of the Naturalists, such as Hauptmann and Chekhov and – under the influence also of modern psychology – of Pirandello.

The ideal play would doubtless contain a well-balanced combination of action and character, but to elevate Chekhov simply because his plays emphasize character and are almost static in action, and to denigrate Sardou simply because his plays emphasize action and are almost static in their development of character is a form of literary snobbery which ignores assessment of many other qualities.

Perhaps Hofmannsthal put the issue better than anyone:

> Sardou, the heir of Scribe, created a type of play the ingredients of which were entirely dynamic; action took the place of all else; and for twenty years Sardou dominated the stages of Europe . . . This was the type of play in which the characters were never guilty of any 'irrational' exhibition of character: they were fixed units in a sharply outlined plot, manipulated by the skilled hand of the playwright.

Sardou declared that his type of play expressed 'life through movement'. His opponents, the Naturalists, claimed that 'movement through life' should be the aim of the artist. Sardou plotted the action and situations of his plays with immense care; he grouped his characters according to a prearranged plan of development, and the dénouement always led up to a 'big' scene.

The danger in such craftsmanship was that it could turn the characters into manipulated puppets. It was this danger that Bernard Shaw reacted against, not the plotting of a well-constructed play, something which Shaw himself showed he recognized the importance of in his own plays.

Many of Sardou's comedies give entertainment of a very high order. In others we can too easily feel the hand of the dramatist manipulating his characters. The great merits of the former should not be ignored because certain dramatic critics have chosen to make a division between plays which are good 'literature' and plays which are 'theatre' – to the detriment of the latter.

Sardou's father had owned an estate planted with olive trees near Cannes. A night's frost killed all the trees and the family was ruined. His father came to Paris and earned a living in various employments. Victorien grew up learning to fend for himself and to make his way in the world as best he could.

When he was twenty-two he had his first play produced at the Odéon. *La Taverne des étudiants* ran for five nights and was then withdrawn. Then followed disappointment after disappointment. Play after play was rejected. A few were accepted but never performed. He was found eventually by a friend, Mademoiselle de Brécourt, in a garret, without food, surrounded by his rejected manuscripts, and dying of typhoid fever. She not only nursed him back to health but persuaded the actress, Mademoiselle Déjazet, to read his plays. She asked him to write a play for her.

Although the first play he wrote for Mademoiselle Déjazet was banned by the censor, Sardou's luck had turned. He wrote three more for her and all were performed with successful and long runs. Then, in 1860, the same year that Labiche had his outstanding success with *Le Voyage de Monsieur Perrichon*, Sardou achieved his outstanding success with *Les Pattes de mouche*, with the great actor Coquelin playing the main part. He soon ranked with Augier and Labiche, and for the next twenty years he wrote play after play ridiculing some aspect of social or political life. In *Nos intimes* he ridiculed the bourgeoisie; in *Les Vieux garçons* he ridiculed the gay life of elderly bachelors; in *Séraphine* he ridiculed religious hypocrisy, rivalling Molière's *Tartuffe*; in *Nos Bons villageois* he ridiculed the craze for country life; in *Les Ganaches* he ridiculed over-conservative political beliefs; in *Le Roi Carotte* he ridiculed over-radical political beliefs; and in 1880, in *Divorçons!* he ridiculed the impending divorce laws.

Then, at almost the same time that Feydeau abandoned his broad style of comedy and turned to writing his more subdued one-act plays, Sardou abandoned comedy altogether and began to write romantic historical plays. These are the plays which have caused too many dramatic critics to relegate Sardou to a too minor rank among dramatists. Most of them were written for some famous actor or actress. *Robespierre* was written expressly for Sir Henry Irving. *La Sorcière* and others were written to order for Sarah Bernhardt. Sardou became a poorer dramatist through his association with Bernhardt. Bernhardt often sacrificed the play to her own immense personality, to the detriment of both the play and her own art. Her world-wide reputation as an actress was achieved largely in Sardou's plays. For many years Eleanora Duse was her greatest rival. And it was Duse, incidentally, who played the part of Cyprienne in *Divorçons!*

Sardou married Mademoiselle de Brécourt after she had nursed him back to health and success. After they had been married only eight years she died. In 1871 he married again. He died in Paris on 8 November 1908, having lived to a greater age and become a wealthier man from his plays than either Labiche or Feydeau. Very few indeed of his plays were written in collaboration with anyone else. But like Labiche and Feydeau, he had a collaborator whose name appears on none of his plays: Virginie Déjazet, who played the lead in so many of Sardou's comedies, was one of the most charming actresses of the nineteenth century and the delight of Paris for many years.

Sardou's success rested on the popularity with his audiences of the 'well-made play', which depended upon superb craftsmanship in the construction of plot. The Naturalists reacted against this and stood for the rejection of plot. They carried Naturalistic dialogue to such an extreme that their plays became documentaries. This caused another revolt: Expressionism, which, however, still wanted a drama without plot, without a story. Plot was reinstated for the drama of this century by Bertold Brecht with his Epic Theatre. When one remembers these reactions of mood and taste, one realizes that Max Beerhohm, who was by no means an admirer of Sardou, may have been right when he wrote on the death of Sardou in 1908:

Sardou never had any ideas except for 'situations' and in the whole course of his vivid and honourable career created not one human character. When he wrote historical plays the heroes or heroines of history became as lifeless as the creatures of his own fancy – mere wheels for the grinding of 'situations'. Fashion veers. Perhaps before the present century has run its course Sardouism will have as great a vogue as it had in the 'seventies and 'eighties of the century that is past. Meanwhile, peace to the ashes of a brilliant man who had long survived our interest in him.

*

Georges Feydeau was born in Paris on 8 December 1862. Between 1883 and 1916 he wrote more than forty plays. A collected edition of thirty-seven of them, in nine volumes, was not published until 1948. He died in 1921.

Unlike Labiche and Sardou, Feydeau was never elected to *l'Académie française*, although his plays achieved as great success with the public as theirs. Nor has he since received the serious critical attention they have. However, since the Second World War six of his plays have been added to the repertoire of the *Comédie française*, an increasing number of them has been performed in translation in Britain and America, and, in his introduction to Feydeau's collected works in 1948, the French critic Marcel Achard hailed him as 'the greatest French comic dramatist after Molière'.

Feydeau was a direct descendant of a Marquis de Feydeau de Marville. His father, Ernest Feydeau, was a novelist of repute under the Second Empire. He was a friend of Flaubert and Gautier, and encouraged his son's passion for the theatre which showed itself first as an ambition to be an actor. After completing his education at the Lycée Saint-Louis, Georges became an habitué of the salons of Parisian society and gained a reputation as an amateur writer and speaker of humorous monologues. In 1883, when he was twenty-one, he had his first comedy performed. This decided him to abandon his ambition to become an actor, even though he had just been offered a contract by the director of the Vaudeville theatre.

He then undertook his period of military service and it was while serving with his regiment that he wrote his first full-length play, *Tailleur des dames*. After some difficulty in finding a theatre to accept it, it was finally performed in 1887 with phenomenal success. Feydeau immediately wrote another six plays in rapid succession, some in collaboration with his friend Maurice Desvallières, hoping no doubt to repeat the success of *Tailleur des dames*. They were all performed with varying degrees of success but none received the tremendous public acclaim given to *Tailleur des dames*.

During the next two years, from 1890 to 1892, Feydeau deliberately wrote nothing. He spent the time studying closely the works of other writers of farce in an attempt to discover how he had achieved such success with his first full-length play. He studied the plays of Labiche, especially Labiche's development of the comedy of character. He studied the comedies of Hennequin as models of the well-made play. From the latter he learnt the rules of logical construction which were to give his later plays the precision of machines. He himself formulated the rule that when two characters should under no circumstances ever meet each other, they must be thrown together as quickly as possible. There would then follow with inexorable logic all the absurd results which would have been avoided by keeping them apart.

Nearly two years later Feydeau took up his pen once more, and success never again left him. All but two (*Le Ruban* and *La Main passe*) of the plays he wrote between 1892 and 1916 can be divided into three groups according to their type of leading female character.

There are no outstanding female roles in Labiche's plays, apart from Madame Bonacieux in *Permettez, Madame*; all Labiche's heroines resemble each other. All Feydeau's plays, on the contrary, are dominated by their leading female character. From 1892 until 1908 he rang the changes on two types of heroine. Firstly, there are the plays, such as *Monsieur Chasse*, *La Puce à l'oreille* and *l'Hôtel du Libre-Échange*, whose heroines are young women of impeccable bourgeois upbringing. They have not committed adultery, but they dream of doing so. They are charming and slightly mad. In many ways they are similar to Labiche's young women. They think it a shame that they cannot take a lover without having to deceive their husbands. Yet, though they dream of deceiving their husbands, they cannot bear the idea of being deceived themselves.

This type of heroine preponderated at first. Success followed success. With success came a great deal of money. Feydeau began to play the stock market. At first he was lucky. Then, after an unexpected panic on the market, he found himself in debt to the sum of several million francs. Like Scott and Balzac, forced to write more and more novels, Feydeau found himself forced to write more and more plays to pay off his debts. As he was essentially lazy by nature, it is most probable that many of his masterpieces of farce would never have been written but for these material pressures. Towards the end of his life he said: 'They tell me I earned millions. I never saw more than fifty thousand francs.'

Gradually Feydeau's second type of heroine became more prominent in such plays as *La Dame de Chez Maxim*, *Un Fil à la patte* and *Occupe-toi d'Amélie*. These are the cocottes, the young women of easy virtue, the *dégrafées*, or the undressed, as they were called at the time. They are amusing and self-assured, witty and determined. In their wake follow a horde of cosmopolitan spongers, rakes, and layabouts. And because these heroines have no standards of value save their own impulse and pleasure, they are prone to all kinds of madnesses. This tendency of theirs provides Feydeau with the mainspring for his mechanism of lunatic logic. They are likely to say anything, do anything – including bringing together the kind of people who should be kept apart. Their main delight is in possessing jewelry. They blossom like exotic flowers in situations which are suffocatingly painful to everybody else. Because they have charm, wit and beauty and nothing to lose, they feel themselves the equal of any lady of society, bourgeois or aristocratic.

The third and last period consists entirely of the plays dominated by leading female characters who are nagging shrews. It is also the period of his masterpieces, his series of one-act plays. In these plays Feydeau introduces two characters, a man and his wife, engaged in a frustrating war of nerves. He now abandoned for good the lunatic logic of his mechanized farce, concentrating his sense of the farcical upon a weak and rather stupid man in the clutches of a fascinating but pitiless shrew. The characters are again caught up in a network of circumstances and these conjugal comedies are no less perfectly constructed, but the humour arises more from the conflict of character: they contain a psychological dimension lacking in his previous plays and which can only have been drawn directly from life. If Feydeau had not subjected these ill-mated couples to the distortion of his sense of humour, they would convey the pathological horror of the husbands and wives in Strindberg's plays.

With this change in style and pace came a change in language. The language in which the characters of these last plays express themselves is not the eloquent French of Labiche nor the serviceable prose of Sardou. It is an abrupt and chaotic language, and it changes with the class and occupation of the character.

These changes have been the subject of speculation. What made Feydeau abandon his broad style and concentrate on these shorter, more subdued and yet more highly concentrated comedies which in many ways anticipate the plays of Becket, Ionesco and Pinter? He had probably sensed that with the decline in popularity of vaudeville towards the end of the nineteenth century, the genre of farce which he had made his own might also begin to lose its hold on the public. More likely is the fact that with the enthusiastic reception given to his one-act plays, he found he could succeed with far less effort. But more likely still is that he wrote these plays, which tread a razor's edge between farce and tragedy, in an attempt to avoid the mental breakdown which finally overwhelmed him. There is some evidence that Feydeau himself was undergoing marital difficulties. At the time he began writing these last plays, of which the most famous are *Feu la Mère de Madame*, *On Purge Bébé* and *Léontine est en avance*, he left his wife and family and went to live alone in a Paris hotel. He remained there until 1919 when he was taken to a sanatorium at Rueil where he died in 1921.

The first critical biography of Feydeau, written by Jacques Lorcey, has since been published in France, to mark the fiftieth anniversary of Feydeau's death. Lorcey's brilliant analyses of Feydeau's plays and his access to hitherto unpublished documents and letters confirm my own judgement of Feydeau as a writer of comedies of manner deeply penetrating in their psychological and moral discernment and as a man far more complex than he allowed his contemporaries to realize. It is now clear that Feydeau's happy marriage foundered on the rocks of his unlucky speculations on the Stock Exchange. Gradually, over the years, quarrels between himself and his wife became more and more bitter and violent until 'in September, 1909, after a quarrel more violent than any before,

Feydeau fled from his home, with a comb, a toothbrush and pyjamas, and took refuge in the Hotel Terminus, near the Gare Saint-Lazare'. His apartment there was to remain his only home for the next ten years.

At the height of his success a critic had wondered how a mind could give birth to such madness – such feverish acceleration of pace – without bursting, and predicted that its owner would end his days in a mental hospital. Feydeau's mind did actually give way – perhaps when he found he could no longer laugh at the madness he saw within and around him.

Like Labiche, Feydeau wrote most of his plays in collaboration, mostly with his friend Desvallières. As with Labiche it is almost impossible to discern how much of any play is Feydeau and how much Desvallières. But as with Labiche and his collaborators, the plays Feydeau wrote by himself were just as successful as those he wrote with Desvallières and others. Desvallières and the others, however, never wrote a successful play by themselves or with any other collaborator. We may assume that Feydeau, like Labiche, was the creator.

Also like Labiche, Feydeau probably owed more to somebody whose name appears as collaborator on none of his plays. This was the actress, Armande Cassive, whom he depended upon to interpret most of his female roles, sensual or shrewish – and whom like Labiche with Geoffroy he must have been able to see and hear mentally playing the part as he wrote it.

Finally, Feydeau always insisted that his plays should be rehearsed for three months. Long and careful rehearsals were necessary to obtain the precision of timing and the acceleration of pace. For these reasons also he insisted that his stage directions were as important as the dialogue. A play by Feydeau contains more numerous and more detailed stage directions than plays by any other dramatist including Shaw. Every movement, gesture, position of every character is carefully indicated. For this reason a play by Feydeau is more difficult to cut than a play by any other dramatist. To try to do so would result in the precise mechanism failing to function just as a watch would not work if the slightest part were removed.

*

All great plays, whether tragedy, comedy or farce, have the same aim: self-knowledge. Tragedy achieves it by a direct arousing of sympathies and antipathies; comedy and farce achieve it indirectly by irony and ridicule. Ramon Fernandez in his *La Vie de Molière* says: 'Molière teaches us the unspeakably difficult art of seeing ourselves in spite of ourselves.' The same could be said with equal truth about these great writers of farce: Labiche, Sardou and Feydeau. By means of laughter they reveal the truth that we may not only be mistaken in ourselves but the cause of mistakes in others. The writer of farce shows us that by deceiving ourselves we deceive our fellow men. They are our benefactors not only for this but also because they perform such an unpalatable task, not with condemnation, but with gaiety.

THE HAPPIEST OF THE THREE

by

EUGÈNE LABICHE

and

Edmond Gondinet

CHARACTERS

ALPHONSE MARJAVEL

KRAMPACH

JOBELIN

ERNEST JOBELIN

HERMANCE

BERTHE

PÉTUNIA

LISBETH

ACT ONE

A drawing-room in MARJAVEL*'s house.*

On the left, towards the front of the stage, is a fireplace. On the mantelpiece is a clock above which is a stag's head. Back-stage a small pedestal table. A large cuckoo-clock right. There is a door back left and a door back right. In the middle of the stage is a divan, which opens, and a basket of flowers. Back centre, another door. On either side of this door is a portrait. The one on the right has a woman's face painted on either side of it. The portrait on the left is that of MARJAVEL. *There is a small table beneath each portrait. On the right, towards the front of the stage, is a window opening on to a balcony.*

When the curtain rises, PÉTUNIA *is dusting the divan.*

PÉTUNIA [*to the audience*]: I ask you, what is the sense in dusting a room? You simply send the dust from one armchair on to another. Moving it round, that's all! [*She moves right and dusts the portrait; turning it round she sees the portrait of another woman on the back of it.*] Well, look at that! Madame's portrait! And on the back of it, the portrait of another woman!

[MARJAVEL, *in the middle of shaving, appears at door back left, with a towel round his neck.*]

MARJAVEL: Pétunia!

PÉTUNIA [*replacing the portrait as it was*]: Monsieur?

MARJAVEL: Isn't Ernest here yet?

PÉTUNIA: No, Monsieur.

MARJAVEL [*disappointed*]: No? [*Giving a sigh*] Ah, well! [*He disappears.*]

PÉTUNIA [*alone, coming centre*]: He's like a lost sheep, without his Ernest! Went and fetched him to Paris himself – and installed him in the summerhouse at the end of the garden. Looks like a law of nature: husbands are always the last to suspect their wife's got a lover!

[HERMANCE *enters back right, carrying a small parcel.*]

HERMANCE: Pétunia! [*She holds out the parcel.*]

PÉTUNIA: Yes, Madame?

[*She takes the parcel from* HERMANCE *and puts it on the little table right.*]

HERMANCE: Has Monsieur Ernest not arrived yet?

PÉTUNIA: No, Madame.

HERMANCE: No? [*Giving a sigh*] Ah, well! Take my hat off, will you? And you needn't do any more in here.

PÉTUNIA [*taking the hat and putting it in the divan*]: Very well, Madame. [*She goes out back right.*]

HERMANCE [*alone, she runs quickly to the stuffed stag's head above the mantelpiece and opens it like a box*]: Our secret hiding-place! [*Looking into the box*] Nothing! He's not written! Oh, these men! They don't know how to love! [*She takes a letter from her pocket and puts it in the box which she closes.*] Every day I send him a letter ... but today I've told him what I fear ... about that cab-driver I've seen prowling about outside the house.

MARJAVEL [*putting his head in, door back left*]: Hasn't Ernest come yet?

HERMANCE: No ... that is, I've not seen him.

MARJAVEL: What on earth's he doing? It's gone ten o'clock!

HERMANCE: You want him for something?

MARJAVEL: No, no! It's just that I like to see him about the place ... he amuses me. He's so ... naïve! D'you know, somebody was talking yesterday about some married woman who ... well, wasn't all she should be. And d'you know what Ernest said? He said 'Is it really possible? Are there really married women who deceive their husbands?' He's a child, still! A child!

HERMANCE [*laughing*]: Oh, completely!

MARJAVEL: One day I'll amuse myself and tell him a thing or two.

HERMANCE [*quickly*]: Indeed you won't! What's it to do with you?

MARJAVEL: No, no, I was only joking. Don't worry, I won't. Oh, yes, there's something I knew I had to tell you.

HERMANCE: What?

MARJAVEL: I've engaged a new man-servant.

HERMANCE [*astonished*]: Really? Well, it's a good idea.

MARJAVEL: And his wife.

HERMANCE: Ah!

MARJAVEL: Steady people ... the sort I like to have about the place ... I'm having them sent from Alsace.

HERMANCE: From Alsace?

MARJAVEL: Yes, I wrote to my agent: 'Find a steady fellow ... marry him to a steady girl ... and send them to me.' They're arriving today.

HERMANCE: But ... what about Pétunia?

MARJAVEL: I think it's more than time we got rid of her. You don't want to keep her, do you?

HERMANCE: No, not at all!

MARJAVEL: Oh, she's not a bad girl, but she's always got a fireman in the kitchen.

HERMANCE: Yes, I had noticed that ...

MARJAVEL: It makes me jumpy ... I'm always thinking the house must be on fire.

HERMANCE: Then you'll tell her to go?

MARJAVEL: No ... not me ... you ...

HERMANCE: What for?

MARJAVEL: Domestic affairs ... they're your concern. That's what my first wife always said – dear Mélanie, her portrait's on the back of yours – I didn't want to separate you both.

HERMANCE [*dryly*]: Thanks very much!

MARJAVEL: Ah, if you'd only known her, you'd have loved her ... everybody loved her. Ask Jobelin, Ernest's uncle. He knew how to appreciate her. Well, whenever a servant had to go, she used to say to me, 'Alphonse, aren't you going to take a little walk to your café?' I used to go. And when I got back, it was done.

HERMANCE: All right. I'll do it.

MARJAVEL: Of course, if you'd rather wait for Ernest ... he could do it.

HERMANCE: No, that wouldn't do!

MARJAVEL: As a matter of fact, there's something else I want him to do.

HERMANCE: What? Can't I ...

MARJAVEL: No, one of the drain-pipes seems to be loose. He's young; he can climb up. It will give him some exercise.

HERMANCE: But that's dangerous!

MARJAVEL: I know that! I wouldn't climb up that pipe for a

thousand francs! If somebody said to me – here's a thousand francs, I wouldn't do it!

HERMANCE: Well then!

PÉTUNIA [*outside*]: Yes, at once.

MARJAVEL: Tut! There's Pétunia now! Be firm! I'll go! [*He goes out left.*]

PÉTUNIA [*entering back right*]: Has Madame any orders for me?

HERMANCE: Yes, I want to speak to you. I am going to have to do without your services.

PÉTUNIA [*stupefied*]: Madame is dismissing me?

HERMANCE: That oughtn't to be such a surprise.

PÉTUNIA: No, I should have guessed ... I've not been fortunate enough to please Monsieur Ernest.

HERMANCE [*astounded*]: Please him? What have my domestic affairs to do with Monsieur Ernest?

PÉTUNIA: Oh, I just meant ... that Monsieur Ernest is Monsieur's friend ... and yours, Madame.

HERMANCE [*to herself*]: She knows something!

PÉTUNIA: Madame will give me a week's notice?

HERMANCE: Certainly.

PÉTUNIA [*weeping*]: It won't be easy for me! I'd become quite fond of Madame and of Monsieur Marjavel! And of Monsieur Ernest as well!

HERMANCE: Well ... since you've become so attached to us ... and so discreet ...

PÉTUNIA: Ah, Madame!

HERMANCE: I will see my husband. I'll speak to him. I ought to tell you he's very annoyed by this fireman you invite into the kitchen.

PÉTUNIA: Well, I can't very well invite lords and dukes. He's my guardian.

HERMANCE [*to herself*]: She's laughing at me. [*Aloud*] All right, that will do. I'll send for you when I want you.

PÉTUNIA [*going towards the door back and stopping*]: That dress that Madame was wearing yesterday is very old. Was Madame thinking of throwing it away?

HERMANCE: No, you can have it.

PÉTUNIA [*with effusion*]: Oh, I will never leave Madame! Never! [*She goes out back.*]

HERMANCE [*alone*]: She's got me! We're in her hands! And Ernest isn't here yet!

MARJAVEL [*entering*]: Isn't Ernest here yet?

HERMANCE [*forgetting*]: No, I'm waiting for him.

MARJAVEL: Me as well, dammit! Eleven o'clock! I bet he's still dressing himself. If he thinks I've invited him to my country house to sit waxing his moustache! . . . It will finish by my coming to a decision!

HERMANCE: What?

MARJAVEL: I'll invite someone else!

HERMANCE: You're not being fair. Yesterday he watered your garden for you until nine o'clock in the evening – while you smoked your cigar.

MARJAVEL: You know I can't do it – it's bad for my lumbago. Anyway I played that game of his – bézique – afterwards to reward him.

HERMANCE: You mean your game!

MARJAVEL: Why mine rather than his?

HERMANCE: Because he detests the game!

MARJAVEL: Does he? Then why does he say to me every evening: 'Well, papa Marjavel, aren't we going to have our little game?' You sit near us doing your embroidery . . . then his eyes light up . . . shine . . .

HERMANCE [*quickly*]: At the sight of the cards.

MARJAVEL: Rather! Don't think I haven't noticed it all too well! D'you know what I think! Ernest is a card-player! He doesn't like horses, he doesn't like eating, he doesn't like women . . . at least I've never noticed it . . .

HERMANCE: Nor I, neither!

MARJAVEL: So – he's a card-player! That means he'll come to a bad end! I'll have to warn his Uncle Jobelin. But never mind that now! Have you seen Pétunia? Have you . . .

HERMANCE [*to herself*]: What shall I say? [*She runs and picks up the little parcel that Pétunia put on the small table.*] Wait, dear! Guess what this is?

MARJAVEL: What is it?

HERMANCE [*unwrapping the parcel and giving him a smoking-room skull-cap*]: Today's your Saint's Day – Saint Alphonse!

MARJAVEL: A smoking cap!

HERMANCE [*quickly pulling off the ticket which is hanging from it*]: I embroidered it all myself – secretly.

MARJAVEL [*embracing her*]: Ah, my dear! How good you are!

HERMANCE: Because you often get a cold in the head in winter.

MARJAVEL: That's true . . . it makes my nose swell.

HERMANCE: I've padded the inside with eiderdown.

MARJAVEL [*beaming with happiness*]: With eiderdown! She surrounds me with eiderdown! My word! I must be the happiest man who ever lived! It was the same with my first wife.

[HERMANCE *puts the cap back on the table.*]

Exactly the same. [*Tenderly*] Hermance! . . . [HERMANCE *comes near to him.*] You will find I am not ungrateful, and, tonight . . . I will come and read my newspaper in your bed.

HERMANCE [*lowering her eyes*]: Don't talk like that!

MARJAVEL [*teasingly*]: Don't you want me to come and read my newspaper in your bed? Say it, then! Say it! Ah! You do, don't you!

HERMANCE: Now, stop it . . . Marjavel . . . stop being so silly.

MARJAVEL [*exclaiming loudly*]: Good heavens!

HERMANCE: What is it?

MARJAVEL: If today's my Saint's Day, we'll be having visitors! Jobelin – with his flowers – he never misses – and little Berthe, his niece – and my sister, Isaure.

HERMANCE: Well?

MARJAVEL: What are we going to do? Our two Alsatians haven't arrived and you've got rid of Pétunia. There's only Ernest left.

HERMANCE: No, I haven't sent Pétunia away.

MARJAVEL: Ah, all the better. It can wait till tomorrow.

HERMANCE: That girl is in a very interesting position.

MARJAVEL: Just as I thought! That fireman!

HERMANCE: No, no! You misunderstand. I mean very worthy of our interest.

MARJAVEL: She is? How?

HERMANCE: I made her talk about it . . . She is bringing up all on her own, out of her small wages, two orphans, in an attic.

MARJAVEL: No?

HERMANCE: And she's giving them a very good education . . . by doing without things herself.

MARJAVEL: Well, you don't say! Who'd have thought that!

HERMANCE: Hers is a life of self-sacrifice . . . of devotion . . . She has renounced everything for them.

MARJAVEL: But that's wonderful! . . . Wait – what about the fireman?

HERMANCE [*at a loss*]: The fireman . . . he's their father.

MARJAVEL: Then they aren't orphans.

HERMANCE [*smiling*]: Oh, a fireman . . . that's not being a father – he's always out at fires!

MARJAVEL [*moving to the little table right on which there is a bell*]: That's true. I am very touched indeed to hear of Pétunia's conduct. I shall keep her. [*He rings the bell.*]

HERMANCE: What are you doing?

MARJAVEL: I'm ringing for her. I shall say a few words to her.

[PÉTUNIA *enters.*]

Approach, Mademoiselle, approach.

PÉTUNIA: Monsieur?

MARJAVEL: I know all. Continue, Mademoiselle, to tread this path of abnegation and sacrifice which you have undertaken.

PÉTUNIA: Pardon?

MARJAVEL: The orphan brings good luck. [*He passes in front of her.*] Continue, Mademoiselle, continue; the orphan brings good luck. [*He goes out left.*]

PÉTUNIA [*going quickly to* HERMANCE]: What orphan?

HERMANCE [*softly, to* PÉTUNIA, *as she goes to door*]: Keep quiet – if you want to stay here! [*She goes out by the same door as her husband.*]

PÉTUNIA [*alone*]: She knows how to fix things, I'll say that for her. She's even got her husband paying me compliments now!

JOBELIN [*entering back, carrying a bottle and a bouquet of roses*]: Is Marjavel at home?

PÉTUNIA: Yes, Monsieur Jobelin! I'll go and tell him you're here. [*She goes out back left.*]

JOBELIN [*alone; he puts the bouquet and the bottle on the couch*]: Yes, this coming to give my good wishes to Marjavel on his Saint's Day is a habit I contracted in the time of his first wife. And I can't even now enter this room without feeling moved. I'll allow myself just one melancholy look at the portrait of poor Mélanie. [*Speaking to the portrait of* HERMANCE] Ah yes, you have been replaced, poor Mélanie! How quickly they forget . . . only one year and three days. [*Going closer to the portrait, looking at it.*] But here am I, and I do not forget . . . [*Stopping.*] Tut-tut! This is the second one . . . [*He turns the portrait round showing Mélanie.*] Here I am! Come to perform my pious pilgrimage . . . dear Mélanie! . . . we were indeed very guilty. [*Speaking to the portrait of* MARJAVEL, *on the other side*] We deceived you, Marjavel! You excellent man! You perfect man! You most admirable man! Yet I feel no remorse, because I have repented . . . [*He comes back centre.*] And if I've repented, it's because she's no longer here . . . Poor Mélanie! And it was I who suggested to Marjavel the idea of hanging her portrait behind the other . . . The last time we came back together, we were in a cab . . . she had a fear . . . quite charming . . . of being recognized . . . so she used to hide behind a fan which she thought had been won in a lottery. Poor child! I was the lottery! Ah, how everything here recalls her to me. [*He sighs as he looks at the divan and then goes to the mantelpiece.*] And it was I who had the machiavellian idea of giving Marjavel this stag's head . . . on his Saint's Day. It was in there we used to hide our letters to each other. [*He opens it.*] Good heavens! There's still one of our letters here! [*He opens the letter, coming centre.*] How imprudent of her! Written in a trembling hand . . . yes . . . she was always trembling. [*Reading aloud*] 'A terrible misfortune menaces us! That cab-driver has recognized us . . . he is spying on us . . . his number is 2114. Try to see him. I have a presentiment that that cab will bring us misfortune.' [*Speaking*] She was like a child with her presentiments! . . . I remember once she dreamed of a black cat . . . and she made out it was the Superintendent of Police.

PÉTUNIA [*entering*]: Will you come this way, Monsieur Jobelin? Monsieur Marjavel is waiting for you. [*She goes out right.*]

JOBELIN [*taking up his bottle and bouquet*]: Ah, well, I'll go and give him these roses and this bottle of 1789 rum. There isn't another bottle of 1789 left anywhere. Yes, this is the only one. [*He goes out.*]

[ERNEST *enters back right carrying a bouquet of roses and a bottle of rum.*]

ERNEST [*alone*]: I come to give my good wishes to Marjavel on his Saint's Day: some roses and a bottle of 1789 rum – the only one left. I've pinched it from my uncle Jobelin. Damn, that lumbago again. That brute Marjavel made me water the garden till nine o'clock last night. [*Looks at door left.*] Poor Hermance! It was all for you! And there is your dear portrait. [*Speaking to the portrait*] Ah, we were indeed very guilty. [*He puts the bottle and his bouquet on console table right, then, seeing it is the portrait of Mélanie.*] Tut! it's the other one! Who is always turning the old one round? [*He turns the portrait round to show* HERMANCE'*s portrait*] Yes! We have indeed been very guilty! [*Speaking to* MARJAVEL'*s portrait*] We have deceived you, Marjavel! You excellent man! You perfect man! You most admirable man! Yet I feel no remorse ... because I do not repent! Not at all! [*He comes centre.*] The day before yesterday I went a most delicious drive with Hermance. This morning I found the number of the cab in my pocket. [*He takes it out.*] 2114. I shall keep it as a memento of our love. Let's see if Hermance has left anything for me in the stag's head. [*He opens it.*] It was very convenient, finding this hiding place for our letters. [*He looks in.*] Nothing! [*He puts the head back on upside down, with the horns pointing downwards.*] Oh, damn this lumbago! It'll take me days to get rid of it!

HERMANCE [*entering quickly, left, very agitated*]: Ah, there you are! I've been waiting for you all morning ...

ERNEST: What's the matter?

HERMANCE: I've only a minute ... and there's so much I've to tell you! Somebody's coming.

[*They separate quickly.*]

ERNEST: No, it's all right! Go on!

HERMANCE: Oh, dear ... I don't know where to begin. First of all, my maid suspects!

ERNEST: Pétunia?

HERMANCE: Monsieur Marjavel was wanting to dismiss her. I've arranged for her to stay.

ERNEST: Good! It's best never to dismiss a maid who suspects...

HERMANCE: And he's hired two servants from Alsace – steady people he calls them – to spy on us I'm sure...

ERNEST: Oh, what an idea!

HERMANCE: Somebody's coming!

[*She sits quickly on the left end of the divan.* ERNEST *sits quickly on the right end. He takes out his watch trying to put on an unconcerned air.*]

ERNEST: No, it was only a cab.

HERMANCE [*getting up*]: A cab! That reminds me! Beware of that cab-driver!

ERNEST [*getting up at the same time as* HERMANCE]: What cab-driver?

HERMANCE: And if they want you to go up the drain-pipe – don't! It's very dangerous.

ERNEST: What drain-pipe?

HERMANCE: There! I'm forgetting the most important thing. I left my fan in the cab – it was a present from my husband.

ERNEST: But I have it. I found it. I've put it in the pocket of my overcoat.

HERMANCE: Then, quick, give it me...

ERNEST: Later. I called at my uncle's on the way here – to borrow something – 1789 – and I've left my overcoat there.

HERMANCE: Somebody will find it! We're lost!

ERNEST: You're always trembling. You mustn't. [*He puts his arm round her waist.*] I'm prudent! I'm discreet!

[*The cuckoo from the clock makes a long, loud call and then strikes slowly two o'clock.*]

HERMANCE [*pushing him away*]: Somebody's coming!

[*She sits quickly on a chair left near the mantelpiece.* ERNEST *sits quickly on chair right.*]

ERNEST [*after a pause*]: It wasn't your husband – it was the cuckoo.

HERMANCE [*getting up*]: I'll stop that thing! Frightening me like that!

ERNEST: What's the point in doing that! It's not as if we can be here together every day of the week!

HERMANCE: No, we can never be alone together!

ERNEST: Last night, I wanted to surprise you ...

HERMANCE: How?

ERNEST: I climbed – without making a noise – up the trellis under your balcony. I thought I'd got to your window ... I knocked three times ... and a deep voice said 'Who's there?'

HERMANCE: It was my aunt's room! We're lost! [*She moves quickly right.*]

ERNEST: No! I dropped quickly to the ground – and everything was quiet. So I'll come back again tonight.

HERMANCE: Tonight! It's impossible! I forbid it!

ERNEST: Why?

HERMANCE: It's Monsieur Marjavel's Saint's Day and ...

ERNEST: Well?

HERMANCE: Oh, nothing.

ERNEST: Listen ... if it should be possible ... leave the window of this room open ... [*He points to the window.*]

HERMANCE: No ... it won't be possible ... you must go now. We mustn't be found together. Come back in five minutes.

ERNEST: All right ... in three minutes. Oh, I was forgetting! [*He picks up his bouquet and the bottle of rum.*] Oh, I'm so happy!

[*He goes out back as* MARJAVEL *enters arm in arm with* JOBELIN.]

HERMANCE [*to herself*]: Just in time! [*She goes right and pretends to be looking for something.*]

JOBELIN [*as he enters, holding his bottle*]: Yes, this rum was produced in 1789 by a cousin of Lafayette. His nephew bequeathed it to my uncle's grandfather – it's the only bottle left in the world.

MARJAVEL: Dear old Jobelin! There's a friend for you! [*As he passes his wife.*] Isn't Ernest here?

HERMANCE: I haven't seen him.

JOBELIN: When I left, my niece Berthe was getting ready to come and visit you ... She has a little something for you as well.

MARJAVEL: Ah, dear Berthe! So she has thought of me as well! But what on earth can Ernest be doing? I mean – I should have thought – today of all days ...

PÉTUNIA [*at door, announcing*]: Monsieur Ernest!

[ERNEST *enters with his bouquet and bottle.*]

ERNEST [*bowing ceremoniously to* HERMANCE]: Madame ... my dear Marjavel ... [*He gives him the bouquet.*]

MARJAVEL [*severely*]: Monsieur Ernest, I should prefer less of the flowers and a little more haste.

ERNEST: Excuse me ... I had to go out of my way this morning in order to get you ...

MARJAVEL: What?

ERNEST [*giving him the bottle*]: This bottle of 1789 rum. It's the only one in the world.

JOBELIN [*to himself*]: I recognize that!

ERNEST: It was produced by a cousin of Lafayette.

MARJAVEL: Then he produced two of them ...

[*He shows the bottle given by* JOBELIN, *takes* ERNEST'*s and the bouquet and puts them all on the console table left.*]

ERNEST [*softly, to* JOBELIN]: You had two of them?

JOBELIN [*softly*]: I got them from Paris last week, you fool!

MARJAVEL [*returning centre*]: My dear friends ... I thank you ... and to show how much I value your kind presents ... these two bottles ... I shall drink them myself. I'll not give any to anyone.

JOBELIN [*protestingly*]: But ...

MARJAVEL: No, do not thank me!

JOBELIN [*to himself*]: I wouldn't have minded a tot now! [JOBELIN *sees* BERTHE *entering back and goes to meet her.*]

JOBELIN: Ah! Here is my niece.

BERTHE [*holding in her hand some braces wrapped in paper, to* HERMANCE]: Good morning, Madame. [*Going to* MARJAVEL.] Monsieur Marjavel, may I give you ...

JOBELIN [*quickly, interrupting her*]: The work of her own little hands ... I watched her making them.

MARJAVEL [*who has unwrapped the parcel*]: A pair of braces ... thank you, dear child ... I promise to wear them myself ...

JOBELIN [*to himself*]: Braces, yes! But the rum?

BERTHE [*to* ERNEST]: Good morning, cousin. You left your overcoat at uncle's ... and this fell out of the pocket. [*She takes out the fan.*]

HERMANCE [*to herself*]: My fan!

ERNEST [*to himself*]: The little fool!

MARJAVEL: Let's see? Mm ... very nice!

ERNEST [*softly, to* HERMANCE]: He'll recognize it!

HERMANCE [*softly to* ERNEST]: We're lost!

[BERTHE *moves left.*]

MARJAVEL [*taking the fan over to* ERNEST]: You're a dark horse, you are! Fans dropping from your overcoat pocket!

JOBELIN [*to himself, following the fan with his eyes*]: That's very like the one Mélanie had!

ERNEST: Monsieur Marjavel, you don't think that...

MARJAVEL: I think that this fan belongs to somebody's wife – but what's certain, it doesn't belong to mine!

HERMANCE [*forcing a smile*]: That's true!

ERNEST [*laughing nervously*]: Ha, ha! Very funny!

JOBELIN [*taking the fan out of* MARJAVEL*'s hands*]: Will you allow me? [*Explosively*] It is! I recognize it! It's...

ALL: What?

JOBELIN [*curbing himself*]: It's... it's the fan of Anne of Austria.

ERNEST: Which I've just bought to give to my cousin Berthe.

BERTHE: To me? Oh, how nice! [*Softly, to* JOBELIN] You see, he does love me!

JOBELIN: I can't believe it!

BERTHE: Why's it so unbelievable?

JOBELIN: No, I mean... it's unbelievable it should be so like one I gave...

BERTHE: To whom?

JOBELIN: To Anne of Austria!... Oh, I don't know what I'm saying any more!

[BERTHE *and* JOBELIN *move backstage.*]

MARJAVEL: My friends, we shall spend the day together! I have a plan! [*He rings the bell. Then, seeing the head of the stag upside down, utters a cry.*] Oh!

ALL: What is it?

MARJAVEL [*going to the mantelpiece*]: Somebody's been touching my head!

HERMANCE: No!

ERNEST: No!

JOBELIN: No!

MARJAVEL: Yes! The horns are upside down!

JOBELIN [*to himself*]: Clumsy of me!

ERNEST [*to himself*]: I must take care!

MARJAVEL [*examining the head with his hands*]: It turns round!

HERMANCE [*softly, to* ERNEST]: Did you take my letter?

ERNEST [*softly, to* HERMANCE]: No!

HERMANCE [*softly, to* ERNEST]: We're lost!

MARJAVEL: Yes, it opens! There's a letter-box inside!

HERMANCE [*softly, to* ERNEST]: The letter can't be there!

ERNEST [*softly, to* HERMANCE]: Somebody's taken it!

HERMANCE [*softly, to* ERNEST]: Pétunia!

JOBELIN [*to himself, taking the letter out of his pocket and looking at it*]: A good thing I happened to get there first!

MARJAVEL [*closing the stag's head*]: That's quite ingenious . . .

PÉTUNIA [*entering right*]: Did you ring, Madame?

HERMANCE [*softly, to* ERNEST]: Here she is!

ERNEST [*softly, to* PÉTUNIA]: Here's twenty francs! Burn it!

PÉTUNIA [*astonished*]: What?

MARJAVEL [*near the mantelpiece still looking at stag's head, to Pétunia*]: Go and fetch a cab. A large one. There are five of us.

PÉTUNIA: Certainly, Monsieur. [*She goes out back.*]

MARJAVEL: We're all going to dine at Doyen's. I shall treat you all – to celebrate my Saint's Day.

BERTHE: Oh, how nice! I've never dined in a restaurant before!

ERNEST [*softly, to* HERMANCE]: At Doyen's! There's a shrubbery there!

HERMANCE [*softly, to* ERNEST]: Be quiet!

ERNEST [*softly, to* HERMANCE]: Why not? To celebrate his Saint's Day?

[PÉTUNIA *returns back right carrying a small plaque in her hand.*]

PÉTUNIA: The cab's waiting below . . . number 2114. [*She gives the plaque to* MARJAVEL.]

HERMANCE, ERNEST and JOBELIN [*all uttering an exclamation on hearing the number of the cab*]: Oh! Good heavens!

MARJAVEL: Why, what's the matter?

HERMANCE: Nothing! Something pricked me.

JOBELIN: I bit my tongue!

ERNEST: One of my shoes is too tight!

[MARJAVEL *moves backstage to put on his overcoat, and* BERTHE *to tidy herself.* PÉTUNIA *helps her.*]

HERMANCE [*softly, to* ERNEST]: 2114. That's the number of our cab!

ERNEST [*softly, to* HERMANCE]: I know that!

HERMANCE [*softly, to* ERNEST]: He's recognized us!

ERNEST [*softly, to* HERMANCE]: No, no, he can't have!

HERMANCE [*softly, to* ERNEST]: I'm positive!

ERNEST [*softly*]: Oh, damn!

HERMANCE [*softly, to* ERNEST]: Hide yourself! Cover your face! [*She picks up her hat-veil from the divan and, folding it, makes a mask of it.*]

ERNEST [*to himself*]: What the devil can I put round my face? [*He notices a little white curtain by the window. He pulls it down, rolls it round making it into a muffler which he wraps round his face below his eyes.*]

JOBELIN [*to himself, coming forward*]: It's not likely this cab-man will recognize me after a year ... but it's best to make sure ... [*Seeing the spectacles on the mantelpiece*] Marjavel's spectacles ... [*He puts on a pair of blue-tinted spectacles.*]

ERNEST [*to himself, after having put on the curtain*]: That should do it!

MARJAVEL [*looking at them*]: What the devil's the matter with you all?

HERMANCE: It's because of the dust.

JOBELIN: The sun's too strong for me.

ERNEST: I can't stand the draughts. [*To himself*] What the hell am I to do with this rod?

BERTHE [*to* ERNEST]: A muffler in August!

ERNEST [*softly*]: Shut up and give me your arm! [*He shoves the curtain-rod down his trouser-leg.*]

MARJAVEL: Pétunia! [PÉTUNIA *comes forward.*] If two people from Alsace arrive asking for me ask them to sit down and wait. You can bring that wicker chair in from the kitchen for them.

PÉTUNIA: Very good, Monsieur.

[MARJAVEL *takes his wife's arm while* BERTHE *moves forward towards* ERNEST.]

MARJAVEL: Let us go!

JOBELIN [*to himself*]: I can't see a damn thing!

[*He collides with* HERMANCE.]

ERNEST [*to himself*]: Damn this curtain rod!

[*They all go out back, except* PÉTUNIA.]

PÉTUNIA [*alone*]: Have a good time! That leaves me mistress of the house! There's only me – and Monsieur's sister, Mademoiselle Isaure. But she never comes out of her room – and she's been dyeing her hair this morning and now she's drying it.

[KRAMPACH *and* LISBETH *appear back centre. They both carry comical-looking parcels. Lisbeth holds a cast-iron pot in her hand. Both are in Alsace national costume.*]

KRAMPACH: Guten Tag mein Fräulein ... Wohnt hier Herr Marjavel? Ein Mann, welcher einen grossen Bauch und Reichtum hat ...

PÉTUNIA [*astonished*]: What is it? What d'you want?

KRAMPACH: Ah, she does not understand. Is it here that lives Monsieur Marjavel, a man who has a big belly and much money?

LISBETH: Ja, a big belly and much money!

PÉTUNIA [*to herself*]: I'll bet these are those Alsatians! [*Aloud*] Are you the Alsatians?

KRAMPACH: Ja!

LISBETH: Ja!

PÉTUNIA: They don't look all there, to me.

KRAMPACH [*coming centre*]: Wir sind diesen Morgen ... [*correcting himself*] We have left this morning at four o'clock.

PÉTUNIA: Oh, you *can* speak French?

KRAMPACH: Ya ... a leetle bit ... not much ... [*He slaps himself on the thigh.*] You leetle devil! [*To* PÉTUNIA] But my wife, she has been more to school than I – I have not been at all. [*He slaps himself on his thigh.*] Leetle devil!

PÉTUNIA [*to herself*]: What's he hitting his leg for? [*To* LISBETH] Then you speak French?

LISBETH: Ja.

PÉTUNIA: And you've come to work for Monsieur Marjavel?

LISBETH: Ja!

PÉTUNIA [*pointing to* KRAMPACH]: And ... he's your husband?

LISBETH: Ja!

[PÉTUNIA *sees* KRAMPACH *seating himself on the couch and makes him get up.*]

PÉTUNIA: No, not there! I'll go and get you a wicker chair. Give me your parcels. [*She takes them from him.*]

KRAMPACH: It is kind of you.

PÉTUNIA [*to* LISBETH]: And yours? [*She takes them from her.*]

KRAMPACH: Not the pot! A wife must never part from her pot!

PÉTUNIA: Oh, don't worry yourself! I don't want your pot! [*She goes out leaving the pot with* LISBETH.]

KRAMPACH [*hitting himself on various parts of his body while* LISBETH *moves right, looking at him*]: There! There! There! You leetle devil!

LISBETH: What *is* the matter with you?

KRAMPACH: It is like this since this morning – before we left home – I had to go to the bottom of the garden. And ever since, there is a beetle in my trousers.

LISBETH: A beetle?

KRAMPACH: Since we left Mulhouse – it scratches me, it bites me. [*Slapping himself again*] There! There! There!

LISBETH: Why do you keep it then?

KRAMPACH: Keep it? On the train ... with ladies ... it is not possible to take off one's trousers. The railway people would not like it.

LISBETH: You could have got off at a station.

KRAMPACH: That is what I try to do ... but the train starts again too quick. [*Slapping himself*] The leetle devil moves quick – from place to place. Hit me on the back! Quick! Quick!

[LISBETH *puts down her pot and hits him on the back.*]

He goes down again! He goes down! It is no good! I will have to take them off! [*He makes as if to undo his braces.*]

LISBETH [*who has picked up her pot again after having slapped him on the back with both hands*]: No, no! You can't.

KRAMPACH: There's no one here!

LISBETH: What about me?

KRAMPACH: You – you are one of the family! Keep a look-out. If somebody comes, warn me!

LISBETH [*moving back-stage and turning her back*]: Hurry up, then!

KRAMPACH [*going towards mantelpiece whilst making as if to take off his trousers*]: If you knew what it is like to have a beetle inside your ...

LISBETH [*coming forward*]: Quick! Somebody's coming!

PÉTUNIA [*enters, carrying a wicker chair*]: There's a chair for you ... [*She puts it in front of the couch, shaking her hand.*] And now I've got a bit of wood down my nail!

KRAMPACH: That's bad.

LISBETH: It is not good.

KRAMPACH: But I know a remedy ... you cover it with some soft cheese ... and then you get a hen to lick it ...

PÉTUNIA: Fool!

KRAMPACH [*going to the chair*]: Word of honour! [*To himself*] If I could sit on it! [*He sits. To* LISBETH] If you're tired, sit on your pot.

LISBETH: No, my bonnets are in it.

KRAMPACH: It's got a lid, hasn't it?

LISBETH: No, I don't want to.

KRAMPACH: Please yourself.

PÉTUNIA [*returning from tidying the mantelpiece*]: You're a fine one, you are! Why can't you let your wife sit down?

KRAMPACH: Standing up is good for a wife who has something to think about.

PÉTUNIA: What's that?

KRAMPACH: Tcha! She made a mistake before her marriage.

PÉTUNIA: With you?

KRAMPACH: With me it would not have been a mistake.

LISBETH [*crying*]: You had promised me you would never speak of it.

KRAMPACH: I won't ever speak about it ... I have sworn I won't! But it is all right for me to tell Mademoiselle – who doesn't know about it. [*He makes several jumps as he sits and finishes by scratching himself and saying, to himself*] This can't go on! It's getting worse!

PÉTUNIA [*to herself*]: He's at it again! What's the matter with him?

KRAMPACH: When I married Lisbeth, she was a skinny little scarecrow. Her father came and found me in the field pulling up the mangel-wurzels. He said to me: 'Krampach, you're an honest man. My daughter has made a mistake. You can marry her.'

PÉTUNIA: What a nice way to put it.

KRAMPACH: I replied with a smile of incredulity ... like this ...

which meant . . . 'Herr Schaffouskraoussmakusen, I realize what an opportunity you are offering me, but I prefer to be the first in Rome than the second with Lisbeth.'

PÉTUNIA: Ah! You have your pride?

KRAMPACH: Ya . . . a leetle.

PÉTUNIA: But you overcame it?

KRAMPACH: I did. Because she had five thousand francs which came from her mother . . . Frau Schaffouskraoussmakusen.

PÉTUNIA: Then it was for her money?

KRAMPACH: Ya . . . it was invested with Kuissermann.

LISBETH: He breeds leeches.

KRAMPACH: Be quiet . . . you can't speak . . . you have made a mistake! The money was put with Kuissermann, breeder of leeches, at twenty-two per cent which he hasn't paid. It is a good interest.

PÉTUNIA: But if he hasn't paid it . . .

LISBETH: It aquimilits.

KRAMPACH [*not understanding*]: Aquimilits? What aquimilits? [*Understanding*] Oh, yes, it accumulates. But just as it was to be paid, he left for Paris, with all of it.

PÉTUNIA: Then you were robbed?

KRAMPACH: Ya . . . but I will find him again.

PÉTUNIA: Oh, Paris is a big place.

KRAMPACH: Never mind, I have a plan. Every Sunday I will wait in the market square. He will have to come there some time.

[*The bell rings.*]

PÉTUNIA: Somebody's ringing . . . I'll be back!

[*She goes out.*]

KRAMPACH: Ach! That leetle devil! It has woken up! She's gone – so I can take them off. [*He begins to take off his braces.*]

MARJAVEL [*entering back followed by* HERMANCE *and* PÉTUNIA]: Where are they? I want to see them!

PÉTUNIA [*pointing to* KRAMPACH *and* LISBETH]: There they are.

MARJAVEL: Good day, my friends! Did you have a good journey?

KRAMPACH: Thank you, it was not too bad. [*He holds out his hand to* MARJAVEL.]

MARJAVEL: Ah, no! There's no need to shake hands. [*Seeing* KRAMPACH *fastening his braces*] And as much as possible you will refrain from adjusting your dress in this drawing room. [*To his wife*] They look steady folk.

HERMANCE: But they're just peasants!

MARJAVEL: They'll adapt themselves. [*Aloud*] It is late. Pétunia will show you your room. We will talk tomorrow.

KRAMPACH [*nodding*]: Goodnight, Monsieur and Madame.

LISBETH: Goodnight, Monsieur and Madame.

MARJAVEL [*to himself, looking at* LISBETH *who has come forward near* PÉTUNIA]: Yes, she's quite good-looking.

[LISBETH *and* PÉTUNIA *go out left.*]

KRAMPACH [*to himself, making to follow them*]: This time, I will be able to get them off.

MARJAVEL [*calling him back*]: Krampach!

KRAMPACH: Monsieur?

MARJAVEL: Wait. Since you are to be my valet, you will help me undress. Light the candles.

KRAMPACH [*to himself, lighting two candles*]: Aren't I ever going to be able to be alone?

MARJAVEL [*to his wife*]: I'd better have him near me. I don't feel too good.

HERMANCE: What's the matter with you?

MARJAVEL: I ate two slices of melon.

HERMANCE: I've told you often enough about that.

MARJAVEL: I can't understand it. One slice is all right. But a second is fatal.

HERMANCE: Then why d'you *take* two?

MARJAVEL: Why d'you think – it is my Saint's Day, isn't it? I suppose you never make mistakes.

HERMANCE [*quickly*]: I didn't say that . . . dear.

MARJAVEL [*holding his stomach and moving right*]: It's getting worse! Devil take that second slice! It's stifling in here! [*Calling*] Krampach!

KRAMPACH: Monsieur?

MARJAVEL [*sitting on chair near little table right*]: Open the window.

HERMANCE [*to herself, in alarm*]: Oh good heavens! That's Ernest's signal! [*Aloud*] No! Don't open it!

MARJAVEL: Open it!

HERMANCE [*to her husband*]: You'll catch cold!

MARJAVEL: There's no danger, open it. I'm well wrapped up.

[KRAMPACH *opens the window, then returns to the mantelpiece.*]

Ah, that's better!

HERMANCE [*to herself*]: Now he'll be climbing up the trellis! [*Aloud*] Dear, if you're not feeling well, you'd better go to bed.

MARJAVEL: Do you think so?

HERMANCE: Oh, yes, there's nothing better than bed.

MARJAVEL [*getting up*]: Goodnight then. [*He kisses her.*] Tomorrow night, I'll come and read my newspaper in your bed.

HERMANCE: Yes. Hurry up.

MARJAVEL: Krampach, come with me!

KRAMPACH: Yes, Monsieur.

[*He thumps himself on the back two or three times and follows* MARJAVEL *out with the candle and the fire-tongs.*]

HERMANCE [*alone*]: Quick! Let's shut that window!

[*She goes towards the window.* ERNEST *appears on the balcony. He carries a piece of drain-pipe in his hand. She recoils.*]

It's him!

ERNEST [*entering*]: Yes! I saw the signal. And here I am – panting with love!

HERMANCE [*seeing the piece of drain-pipe*]: What on earth have you got there?

ERNEST: It's a bit of the drain-pipe. It came loose as I was climbing up. I couldn't let it fall, because of the noise, so I brought it with me – Hermance, I arrive panting with love!

HERMANCE: You'd better hide it – if my husband finds it . . .

ERNEST: I didn't intend keeping it in my hand. Where shall I put it?

HERMANCE: I don't know. [*Pointing to the divan which she opens*] Put it in here.

ERNEST: Oh, that opens, does it? [*He puts the drain-pipe in the divan which he shuts.*] Hermance, I arrive panting with love.

HERMANCE: You'll have to go.

ERNEST: Why?

HERMANCE: My husband is in there . . . in bed.

ERNEST: That won't worry me . . . [*Passionately*] Hermance, forget heaven and earth! We are alone in the world! This is Juliet's balcony and I am Romeo.

HERMANCE: Not so loud!

ERNEST: One kiss! Just one! [*He makes as if to embrace her.*]

VOICE OF MARJAVEL [*off-stage*]: Hermance!

[HERMANCE *recoils quickly.*]

ERNEST [*to himself*]: That man's becoming a nuisance – he won't give me a moment's peace.

VOICE OF MARJAVEL: Hermance!

HERMANCE: He's coming! Fly!

ERNEST: The balcony . . . that's best! [*He goes towards the balcony and suddenly stops.*] No, that's no good!

HERMANCE: Why?

ERNEST [*softly, to* HERMANCE]: Your aunt's at her window . . . drying her hair!

HERMANCE: Oh, good heavens – where then?

VOICE OF MARJAVEL: Hermance!

HERMANCE [*opening the divan*]: Here! Get in here!

ERNEST: With the drain-pipe? [*Getting into the divan*] I can't stay long in here!

HERMANCE: Hurry! [*She closes the divan and goes quickly to the chair right where she sits and pretends to take up some work from the table.*]

MARJAVEL [*entering, followed by* KRAMPACH]: Didn't you hear me, dear?

HERMANCE [*rising and going to him*]: No, I didn't hear anything.

KRAMPACH: Monsieur has the stomach-ache. [*He gives himself a slap on the thighs and puts the fire-tongs back in the fireplace.*]

MARJAVEL [*to* KRAMPACH]: And you slapping yourself all the time doesn't help! Oh, I don't feel well. [*He sits on the divan.*]

HERMANCE [*to herself*]: That's fine! One on top of the other!

MARJAVEL: Somebody go and find Ernest quickly!

HERMANCE: That's no use . . .

MARJAVEL: Yes . . . I want to see Ernest. [*To* KRAMPACH] Go on . . . in the summerhouse at the end of the garden. If he's asleep, wake him up.

KRAMPACH: At once, Monsieur. [*To himself*] I'll find a bush to get undressed behind. [*He goes out back.*]

MARJAVEL [*seated*]: I'll get Krampach to sleep on this divan.

HERMANCE [*to herself*]: Oh, heavens!

MARJAVEL: So that if I need him ...

HERMANCE [*to herself*]: He'll suffocate in there! [*Aloud, taking hold of her husband's hands*] You're feeling better, aren't you?

MARJAVEL: No, it's still just as bad.

HERMANCE: Oh good heavens, your hands are like ice! You're freezing cold!

MARJAVEL [*frightened*]: Do you think so?

HERMANCE: You must walk about! Quickly!

MARJAVEL: Yes, yes – to get the circulation going!

[*They begin to pace backwards and forwards across the stage.*]

HERMANCE: Further! Further! Go through all the rooms!

MARJAVEL: You're right! I'll go right round, and come back. [*He goes out right, taking long steps and counting.*] One ... two ... three ...

HERMANCE [*opening the divan*]: Quick! Get out!

ERNEST [*raising his head out of the divan, looking very pale*]: I'm suffocated! A glass of water! Sugared water!

MARJAVEL [*outside*]: ... twenty-three ... twenty-four ...

ERNEST: Aaah! [*He drops back into the divan.* HERMANCE *closes it and sits on it.*]

MARJAVEL [*entering right and crossing the stage*]: Twenty-five ... twenty-six ... twenty-seven ...

[*He disappears left.* HERMANCE *rises and lifts the divan top.* ERNEST'S *head appears again.*]

ERNEST [*continuing*]: Sugared water! With a touch of orange in it!

HERMANCE: There isn't time! He'll be back!

ERNEST [*getting out of the divan*]: That drain pipe has cut my face.

HERMANCE: He'll hear you! Go! Come back in five minutes!

ERNEST [*rushing out back*]: All right! [*To himself*] What one does for love! [*He disappears back.*]

MARJAVEL [*entering, counting his steps*]: ... fifty-one ... fifty-two ... I've taken fifty-two paces. [*To* HERMANCE] Isn't Ernest here yet?

HERMANCE: Not yet.

MARJAVEL [*falling on to the divan*]: I'm exhausted ... all that walking. I did fifty-two steps. [*Two little discreet knocks are heard on the door.*] Come in!

[ERNEST *enters.*]

HERMANCE: Monsieur Ernest!

MARJAVEL [*sulkily*]: And about time too!

ERNEST [*pretending eagerness*]: You sent for me? Is something the matter?

HERMANCE: My husband is not too well . . . I am going to make him some tea. And a poultice. Light the fire. [*She goes out right.*]

MARJAVEL [*to* ERNEST]: Light the fire!

ERNEST [*to himself, lighting the fire*]: Very nice, I must say!

MARJAVEL [*groaning on the divan*]: Oh! Oh!

ERNEST [*going to him and taking his hand*]: Poor fellow! How d'you feel?

MARJAVEL: Very weak. I thought you were never coming.

ERNEST: I was in bed. I had to get dressed.

MARJAVEL: If I had a sick friend, I wouldn't bother about how I looked.

ERNEST [*feeling his pulse*]: It's nothing much . . . a little exhaustion, that's all.

MARJAVEL: What did you say!?

ERNEST: You're just a little exhausted.

MARJAVEL: Then it's nothing dangerous?

ERNEST: No, no.

[HERMANCE *returns carrying a cup of tea and a little saucepan which she puts on the floor near her.*]

HERMANCE [*to* MARJAVEL]: Here you are, my dear, a cup of tea. [*She sits on his right,* ERNEST *on his left.*]

MARJAVEL [*putting the cup to his lips*]: Thank you . . . it's too hot.

[HERMANCE *and* ERNEST *both blow on the tea in the cup.*]

It's exhaustion I have . . . [*He drinks.*] It's nothing dangerous.

HERMANCE [*picking up the saucepan*]: You make the poultice, Monsieur Ernest. [*She gives him the saucepan.*]

ERNEST [*getting up, very surprised*]: Me? [*He goes to the fireplace.*]

HERMANCE [*taking the cup and putting it on the small table right*]: Yes . . . stir it, stir it!

ERNEST [*to himself, stirring with the spoon furiously*]: And I arrived panting with love!

MARJAVEL: Ah, that's better ... it's going ... Hermance come and sit by me.

[HERMANCE *moves the chair a little further away from* MARJAVEL.]

ERNEST [*to himself*]: Does he forget I'm here? [*He knocks with the spoon on the saucepan.*]

MARJAVEL: No! Nearer!

HERMANCE [*sitting on the divan*]: Here I am, dear ...

MARJAVEL [*putting his arm round her*]: Ah, what an angel you are! I'll never know how to thank you. [*He kisses her hands.*]

ERNEST [*to himself*]: This is going too far! [*He bangs loudly on the saucepan.*] He's taking no notice! [*He kicks over the fire-tongs and shovel in the fireplace.*]

MARJAVEL [*to* HERMANCE]: You do love your big lovey-dovey so much! [*He kisses* HERMANCE *on the cheek.*]

ERNEST [*to himself*]: It's not just his stomach that's wrong with him! [*Holding out the saucepan*] Here's the poultice! [*He pushes it into* MARJAVEL*'s hand.*]

MARJAVEL *yells as it burns him.*

HERMANCE *jumps up.*]

CURTAIN

ACT TWO

A drawing-room in the summerhouse where ERNEST *is living. Country cottage furniture. Doors upstage left and right. Fireplace back-stage. Mirror. Writing-desk.*

Back-stage right, a small table; down-stage right, two doors. Centre stage, a larger table. Left, in front of a small couch, is an armchair. There is another chair left of the fireplace.

When the curtain rises ERNEST *is found asleep in another armchair right of the fireplace. He holds a piece of drain-pipe in his arms. A knock is heard at the door right. He does not waken.* JOBELIN *enters, followed by* BERTHE.

JOBELIN: Nobody here. [*To himself*] This summerhouse upsets me. Mélanie and I came here sometimes. Memories everywhere...

BERTHE [*after walking round the room examining it, she discovers* ERNEST]: Uncle! My cousin's here!

JOBELIN: Asleep!

BERTHE [*lowering her voice*]: What's he holding so tightly?

JOBELIN: It's a piece of drain-pipe.

BERTHE: Holding it to his heart?

JOBELIN: It reminds me how I fell asleep myself once in that armchair – with an aquarium in my arms.

BERTHE: You?

JOBELIN: But I had a reason...

BERTHE [*indicating* ERNEST]: Look at him, uncle – doesn't he look sweet?

JOBELIN: Well – he's certainly having a good sleep.

BERTHE: And so peaceful!

JOBELIN: That's hard to tell.

BERTHE: I bet he's dreaming of me.

JOBELIN: Why?

BERTHE: Because he's in love with me.

JOBELIN: But he's never told you he is.

BERTHE: That makes no difference ... didn't you see how he blushed when he gave me the fan yesterday?

JOBELIN: Mm ... that's true!

BERTHE: So why don't you speak to him about your marriage plan?

JOBELIN: Firstly – it's not my plan – it's yours ...

BERTHE: Not at all! You said to me the other day: 'I think Ernest will make a good husband ...'

JOBELIN: Yes – but it wasn't you I was thinking of ...

BERTHE: Well, I like that! And to tell me so, as well!

JOBELIN: There's one objection. I'm his guardian. And you've more money than he has.

BERTHE: But don't you see? That's why he doesn't say anything! Oh you just don't understand!

JOBELIN: You're sure that's it?

BERTHE: Yes!

JOBELIN: You're absolutely certain?

BERTHE: Yes!

JOBELIN: Then, leave us ... I'll speak to him.

BERTHE [*going towards door right*]: Oh, you are good, uncle! Thank you!

JOBELIN: Go for a walk in the garden. I'll call you.

BERTHE [*going out right*]: Oh, he will be so happy!

JOBELIN [*putting his hat on the table*]: This little chat will have to be a serious one. [*He moves the chair left of fireplace, puts it in front of* ERNEST *and sits.*] My dear Ernest, look into your heart and tell me what you see there ... of course, he's asleep! I'll have to wake him.

[*He taps lightly several times on the drain-pipe.* ERNEST *grunts but does not waken.*]

That sounds as if he'll be in a bad temper if I waken him – and negotiations might fail. I'd better wait. [*He rises and comes centre.*] Yes, I slept like that once, with an aquarium in my arms. But I had a reason. The aquarium had come from Mélanie. I'd been foolish enough to admire the fish as we passed the lake in the Tuileries. The same evening I received my aquarium. Mélanie had a flair for little things like that! Poor Mélanie! We were very guilty!

[ERNEST *moves the drain-pipe from nestling in his right shoulder so that it nestles in his left shoulder – without waking.*]
Ah – he's waking! No, he's off again! [*Looking at* ERNEST] He seems to be sleeping very soundly.

[KRAMPACH *enters right, hastily, with a letter in his hand.*]

KRAMPACH [*to himself, as he enters*]: I wonder why there's no address on it?

JOBELIN [*going to him*]: Ssh! Can't you see my nephew is asleep!

KRAMPACH [*examining the drain-pipe*]: What is it? A new kind of gun?

JOBELIN: Don't be a fool! It's a drain-pipe. It collects the water which falls from the sky.

KRAMPACH [*looking up and holding out his hand to see if it is raining*]: I don't feel it!

JOBELIN [*going centre*]: What is it you want?

KRAMPACH: The concierge gave me a letter.

JOBELIN: Give it me then.

KRAMPACH: One moment . . . is it for you, is it for him, or is it for the person who knows cab No. 2114?

JOBELIN: The cab? It's for me! Speak lower!

KRAMPACH: I'm not saying anything. [*He gives* JOBELIN *the letter.*]

JOBELIN [*opening the letter and, to himself*]: [*Reading*] You big booby! [*Speaking*] He recognized me! In spite of my blue spectacles! Mélanie's forebodings were right! [*Reading*] You big booby!

[*He realizes* KRAMPACH *is listening and pushes him away.* KRAMPACH *goes over to the fireplace and examines* ERNEST.]

So I've found you at last! [*Speaking*] And after a whole year! [*Reading*] When you go out in a cab with someone else's wife, you should tip the driver more than twenty-five centimes. [*Speaking*] I thought I gave him thirty. [*Reading*] I could cause you a lot of trouble. But I'm an honest man. So I'd rather borrow five hundred francs from you . . . [*Speaking*] What's this? [*Reading*] I will wait for them under the seventh lamp-post. If I don't get them within an hour I'll make it a thousand. Signed. No. 2114. [*Speaking*] There'll be a scandal! He'll tell Marjavel! [*Going through his pockets*] I must act at once! [*To* KRAMPACH] Have you five hundred francs on you?

KRAMPACH [*going through his pockets*]: I'll see ... I've twenty-five centimes and thirteen sous in my trunk ... [*He moves back to fireplace.*]

JOBELIN [*very agitatedly*]: Keep them! [*To himself*] What's to be done? In an hour he'll want a thousand! Ah! That would be the simplest solution! I could borrow it from Ernest. I needn't wake him! [*He goes to the writing desk.*] The same old writing desk – how well I know it! Yes, the same broken lock – all you've got to do is give it a knock. [*He taps the lock and the desk opens.*] There! The exact amount! A five hundred franc note! [*He shuts the desk, calling.*] Krampach!

KRAMPACH: Monsieur?

JOBELIN [*very softly*]: You will find a cab ... No. 2114 ... under the seventh lamp-post ...

KRAMPACH [*also very softly*]: A cab under a lamp-post? Right!

JOBELIN: You will give the driver this money. You will say it's from the young man ...

KRAMPACH: What young man?

JOBELIN: Me!

KRAMPACH: All right! There was no harm in asking, was there? [*He goes out right.*]

JOBELIN [*alone*]: It's blackmail, that's what it is! This cabby is out to blackmail me! And he's got me where he wants me, worse luck! Mélanie's posthumous honour is in my hands – and there's Marjavel, as well. He'd challenge me. It would mean a duel! Of course, I wouldn't defend myself. No, I'll just have to smile and pay up! Oh, I've gone all hot and thirsty! I'd better get a glass of water in the next room. [*He opens door left.*] Good God! The aquarium's still here! Ah, Mélanie, if you only knew what you are costing me!

[*He goes out door down left.* HERMANCE *enters cautiously through door up left, shutting it after her. She goes over and shuts door right. After taking a look round, she runs to the armchair and shakes* ERNEST *vigorously.*]

HERMANCE: Ernest!

ERNEST [*wakening with a jump, dropping the drain-pipe*]: Eh? What? The poultice? Here's the poultice!

HERMANCE: Ernest! Wake up!

ERNEST [*picking up the drain-pipe*]: Oh, it's you!

HERMANCE: I've got away for a moment. My husband's trimming his beard. He's much better today.

ERNEST: I might have known that!

HERMANCE: Yes, his pain is gone.

ERNEST: So it should have – I made enough poultices for him.

HERMANCE: You've had a bad night.

ERNEST: Oh, no, excellent! You can congratulate yourself on giving me a splendid night – first on your divan – and now with this drain-pipe! What d'you want done with it?

HERMANCE: Hide it! Get rid of it! [*Becoming tender*] Darling!

ERNEST [*hiding the drain-pipe under armchair left*]: Madame?

HERMANCE: He was in such pain! I've been up all night in his room.

ERNEST: Yes, I could hear your conversation from the divan.

HERMANCE [*a little uneasily*]: You heard?

ERNEST: Everything! At five-past two, what did you say to your husband?

HERMANCE: But – how should I know?

ERNEST: You said to him: 'Oh my great big lovey-dovey, if you die, I'll never survive you.' D'you think I liked hearing that?

HERMANCE [*embarrassed*]: I had to prevent him suspecting...

ERNEST: And then at four o'clock...

HERMANCE: What?

ERNEST: I heard the sound of a kiss. D'you think I liked hearing that?

HERMANCE: It wasn't my fault! I had to prevent him...

ERNEST: Suspecting... Well, I think you were overdoing it.

HERMANCE [*leaning on his shoulder*]: But you know it's you who has all my love...

ERNEST: I may have... but it's him who seems to profit from it.

HERMANCE [*offended*]: Are you by any chance jealous of my husband?

ERNEST: I like that! They've got a lot to complain about – husbands!

HERMANCE: Oh!

ERNEST: Oh, yes, I know they have one slight disadvantage – but since they don't know about it, what's that matter? Apart from that, what've they got to complain about? We take care of them, we make a fuss of them, we coddle them . . . they are fat, spoilt, arrogant . . . while we lovers are timid, jealous, fearful, trembling . . . as if we were thieves.

HERMANCE: Ernest!

ERNEST: For them the table is always laid, they're in possession, they can lord it over everyone . . . while we, we hide behind the furniture, we hang on to drain-pipes . . . just to pick up their crumbs . . . when they feel like leaving us any! Why do they have to make us suffer so! [*He sits on the little chair left.*] And, to crown it all, your husband thinks I'm stupid . . . but devoted . . .

HERMANCE [*going towards him*]: He didn't say that!

ERNEST: I beg your pardon, but at exactly twenty-seven minutes past three . . . my watch keeps excellent time. [*He feels for it in his pocket and does not find it.*] I must have left it in my bedroom . . . Stupid but devoted. And you didn't contradict him! Oh, no! Far from it!

HERMANCE [*sitting on the armchair near* ERNEST]: Now, look . . . calm yourself! Why do you think I've come to you now . . . happy . . . trusting . . .

ERNEST [*who has been groaning to himself now turns slowly and falls on his knees before* HERMANCE]: Ah . . . yes! This must be the first time . . . for over two months . . . that I have been alone with you. [*Holding her round the waist*] Well?

HERMANCE: What?

ERNEST: We must talk . . . yes, the time has come to talk . . .

[JOBELIN *is heard coughing in the next room.*]

HERMANCE [*recoiling, terror-stricken*]: Heavens! There's somebody there!

ERNEST: Oh, this is perfect!

[JOBELIN *can be heard sneezing and blowing his nose.*]

HERMANCE: It's my husband! I'd know that cold of his anywhere!

ERNEST: Hell!

HERMANCE [*desperately*]: He's spying on us! We're lost! Deny everything! Everything! [*She goes out back right.*]

ERNEST [*alone*]: So this is it! A duel! Well, I'd prefer that to this never knowing where one is! [*Imitating* HERMANCE*'s voice*]

We're lost! We're lost! [*He goes to door left and opens it.*] Monsieur, I am at your disposal.

JOBELIN [*entering, carrying an aquarium*]: Thank you. That's very kind of you.

ERNEST: Uncle!

JOBELIN: So you've woken up?

ERNEST [*to himself*]: He's heard nothing!

JOBELIN: These poor little fish! They're almost starving! I'll get some biscuits. [*He puts the aquarium in* ERNEST*'s arms.*]

ERNEST: Where d'you want me to put it?

JOBELIN [*going to table left and opening drawer*]: I always kept some in here. Yes, there's still some there.

ERNEST: So this is what you want to see me about?

KRAMPACH [*entering right*]: That was a bit of luck!

ERNEST: What was?

JOBELIN [*going quickly in between them*]: Yes, Krampach, I'll attend to you in a minute!

[*He pushes* ERNEST *left and* ERNEST *puts the aquarium on the table left.*]

KRAMPACH [*to himself, coming forward, as* ERNEST *and* JOBELIN *give biscuits to the fish, left*]: I found him! That thief Kuissermann! He's the cab-driver – No. 2114! I was just going to give him the five hundred franc note when I had a better idea – quite honourable! I said to him: 'There's no reply!' And I kept the five hundred franc note myself – on account of what he owes me.

JOBELIN [*coming back to* KRAMPACH]: Well? What did he say?

KRAMPACH: He said: 'It's like that, is it? Then I'll be back.'

JOBELIN: What! He'll be back?

KRAMPACH [*pulling an old notebook from his pocket*]: I must do my accounts!

ERNEST [*busy with the fish, turning*]: What are you doing, uncle?

JOBELIN: Me? Nothing! [*To himself*] He'll be back! I'd better go to my bank! Quickly! [*Aloud*] Good-bye! [*He goes out back left.*]

KRAMPACH [*to* ERNEST]: Monsieur, may I ask a favour of you? Because you are a capable man . . .

ERNEST: Capable of what?

KRAMPACH: You are capable.

ERNEST: All right, all right, what is it?

KRAMPACH: Five thousand francs less five hundred francs plus the interest over one year six months and twenty-three days – plus one day's interest on account of what's gone of today . . .

ERNEST: What the hell are you talking about?

KRAMPACH: I will begin again. Five thousand francs . . .

ERNEST: Oh, get out of here . . . you're boring me.

KRAMPACH: You might as well not be capable! [*He goes out doing his accounts.*] Five thousand francs less five hundred francs . . . plus the interest . . . that is what I cannot do . . .

[ERNEST *gives him a push out through door left.*]

ERNEST [*seeing* BERTHE *enter right*]: Berthe!

BERTHE: Have you seen uncle Jobelin?

ERNEST: He's just left me.

BERTHE: Aah! [*She lowers her eyes coyly and comes forward.*]

ERNEST [*to himself*]: What's she looking so coy about? Have I said something I shouldn't?

BERTHE [*suddenly*]: Well! I thought, monsieur, I'd see you looking happier than that!

ERNEST [*astonished*]: Me? Oh yes! I'm delighted! Enchanted!

BERTHE: And you don't want to take me in your arms?

ERNEST: Oh yes! Rather! I'll do that. Like this! [*He embraces her. To himself*] It's not her Saint's Day, is it?

BERTHE: It's about time too! My uncle actually thought you weren't in love with me.

ERNEST: He did! Oh, how stupid of him!

BERTHE: What?

ERNEST: Stupid . . . but devoted. [*To himself*] Like Marjavel said.

BERTHE: But it was quite obvious to me. You remember that walk we had in the zoo?

ERNEST [*trying to remember*]: In the zoo?

BERTHE: The day I fed the ostrich.

ERNEST: Oh yes! Marjavel made me carry four loaves of bread all the way there – to feed the bears.

BERTHE: Well, it was there that I saw you loved me.

ERNEST: In front of the bears?

BERTHE: No, no! In front of the ostrich.

ERNEST: Ah!

BERTHE: The horrid beast had snatched my glove with the cake I was giving it . . . it was going to swallow it when you fearlessly thrust your arm through the bars . . .

ERNEST [*with pride*]: That's right . . . I did have the courage . . . alone against an ostrich . . . I got hold of the end of your glove – which was just about to disappear – I pulled – the ostrich pulled.

BERTHE: And you fell!

ERNEST: Holding your three fingers . . . They were all I could save!

BERTHE [*sadly*]: Everybody laughed . . . but I knew that day that I would be your wife.

ERNEST: My wife! You! [*With a double-take*] You!

BERTHE: Hasn't uncle told you?

ERNEST: No.

BERTHE: Oh! Then you've not understood anything I've been saying! Let me go!

ERNEST [*holding her back*]: No, wait! Me – a husband? In my turn? But that's happiness! That's deliverance! [*Throwing himself on his knees*] Oh, it's wonderful! You're an angel!

BERTHE: Get up!

ERNEST: But I love you!

BERTHE: Let me go! You must ask my uncle! Then we'll see! [*She escapes and runs out right.*]

ERNEST [*on his knees*]: Me married! Oh, if only I could I'd be free! The chains which enslave me would be broken!

HERMANCE [*entering, to herself*]: My husband's at home. [*Seeing* ERNEST *on his knees*] What on earth are you doing there?

ERNEST [*embarrassed, without rising*]: Me? I . . . I was waiting for you!

HERMANCE: On your knees?

ERNEST: Yes . . . when I wait for you I get on my knees . . . it seems the right thing to do . . . I'm all ready for you . . .

HERMANCE [*letting him kiss her hand*]: What a child you are!

MARJAVEL [*entering right, seeing* ERNEST *on his knees before his wife*]: Monsieur! What is the meaning of this?

HERMANCE: My husband!

ERNEST [*to himself*]: Caught! [*Aloud*] Stay where you are! Don't walk any further! [MARJAVEL *draws back, scared.*] Have you found it?

MARJAVEL [*advancing a step*]: What?

ERNEST: The diamond Madame has lost!

HERMANCE: The diamond from my ring has fallen out . . . and Monsieur is being kind enough to look for it . . .

MARJAVEL: Good heavens! The diamond! We must look for it! [*He gets down on his knees. To* ERNEST] Especially as the house isn't safe. Somebody took some of the drain-pipe last night! You haven't found it?

ERNEST: No.

HERMANCE: I valued it all the more because it was you who gave it me, dear. It is such a . . .

MARJAVEL: Damn it! Will you stop walking about! [*He gets up.*] I'm going to get a little broom. [*To* ERNEST] In there – in your bedroom. Don't walk about! [*He goes out left.*]

ERNEST [*getting up*]: We've got out of that all right.

KRAMPACH [*entering with a letter similar to the one he gave to* JOBELIN]: It's for the gentlemen who knows cab No. 2114.

HERMANCE: The cab!

ERNEST [*quickly*]: It's for me!

HERMANCE: What can he want? Have a look! Quick!

ERNEST [*reading*]: 'You big booby! . . .'

KRAMPACH: He's said that already.

ERNEST: What did you say?

KRAMPACH: I said: 'He's said that already.'

[*As he is about to go on reading,* ERNEST *sees* KRAMPACH *listening and pushes him away.* KRAMPACH *goes to the fireplace and tidies it, then comes back and leans on the desk still doing his accounts.*]

ERNEST [*reading*]: 'So you think you can go out with somebody else's wife and only give the cab-driver a twenty-five centime tip?' [*Speaking*] I thought I gave him fifty. [*Reading*] 'If you don't send me a thousand francs within half-an-hour, I will demand three thousand.' [*Speaking*] The miserable wretch! Where's my stick?

HERMANCE: What d'you mean? You must pay! At once!

ERNEST: But it's blackmail.

HERMANCE: Would you rather have a scandal?

ERNEST: No!

[*He goes to the desk and pushes* KRAMPACH *away.* KRAMPACH *returns to the fireplace.*]

I don't know if I've got that much. [*He turns the key of the desk then gives it a knock with his fist. The desk opens and he searches through the drawers. To himself.*] But I did have a note in here. Somebody has opened this desk. Somebody who knows the trick.

HERMANCE: Well?

ERNEST [*coming back to* HERMANCE, *taking some coins from his pocket*]: I've only twenty-three francs.

HERMANCE: Oh, heavens! [*Opening her purse*] And I've only ten!

ERNEST: That makes thirty-three. [*To* KRAMPACH] Have you nine hundred and sixty-seven francs on you?

KRAMPACH [*feeling in his pockets, very gravely*]: I'll have a look.

HERMANCE [*softly*]: My husband!

ERNEST [*softly*]: Marjavel! [*To* KRAMPACH] It's all right – later will do.

MARJAVEL [*entering left*]: I can't see the broom anywhere. [*To* ERNEST] Have you found it?

KRAMPACH [*replying to* MARJAVEL]: I have twenty-five centimes and thirteen sous in my trunk.

MARJAVEL [*pushing him away*]: What's that got to do with it?

KRAMPACH: It's for Monsieur ... there's somebody waiting.

ERNEST: Oh, it's nothing! Just a bill somebody is pressing me to pay.

KRAMPACH: Nine hundred and sixty-seven francs.

ERNEST [*to* KRAMPACH]: All right ... I'll pay later.

MARJAVEL: Why later? Who is it?

KRAMPACH: It's Kuissermann.

ERNEST [*quickly*]: A tailor. [*To* KRAMPACH] Tell him I'll send it on. I haven't the sum on me.

MARJAVEL [*pulling out his wallet*]: All right, I'm here, aren't I?

ERNEST: You? Oh, no! No, I couldn't!

MARJAVEL: Ernest. [*Clapping him on the shoulder*] Don't make it awkward for me. You're my friend aren't you?

ERNEST [*embarrassed*]: Oh yes, yes, of course, but ...

MARJAVEL: Well, then, don't act like a child! [*He goes over and gives a note to* KRAMPACH.] There! Take that to this tailor.

ERNEST [*to himself*]: It's hard for a gentleman to permit it!

KRAMPACH [*to himself*]: This will join the other one. [*Writing in his notebook*] Five hundred francs ... plus one thousand francs ... plus the interest ...

MARJAVEL [*to* KRAMPACH]: What are you doing there?

KRAMPACH: I'm going, Monsieur. I'll take it to him. [*To himself*] I'll never work out this account. [*He goes out right.*]

MARJAVEL: Well, did you find it?

HERMANCE *and* ERNEST: What?

MARJAVEL: The diamond.

HERMANCE: No, not yet.

ERNEST: We were looking for it when ...

MARJAVEL: We'll have to find it. Don't walk about. [*He bends down. To* HERMANCE] You look over by the fireplace.

[HERMANCE *moves back to fireplace.*]

ERNEST [*bending down also, to himself*]: It's a nuisance – looking for a diamond that isn't lost.

JOBELIN [*entering left*]: I've just been to my bank ... [*Seeing them on the floor*] Good lord! What are you doing down there?

MARJAVEL: My wife has just lost a diamond ... the one Mélanie used to wear ...

[KRAMPACH *enters right.*]

JOBELIN: Mélanie! Let's look for it then! [*He throws himself on to the floor and begins searching.*]

MARJAVEL [*to* KRAMPACH]: Krampach, you help as well.

KRAMPACH: Help what?

MARJAVEL: A priceless diamond; look for it.

KRAMPACH [*getting on his knees and searching*]: Once, I found a beetle ... but I knew all the time where it was. [*To himself, crawling front stage*] I've just seen Kuisserman. I said to him: 'There's no reply!'

ERNEST [*seeing* KRAMPACH *and crawling over to him*]: Well? What did he say?

KRAMPACH: He said: 'It's like that, is it? Then I'll be back.' [KRAMPACH *goes on searching and moves extreme left where he stretches out full length and begins to do his accounts.*]

ERNEST [*to himself*]: What! He'll be back?

JOBELIN [*on his knees, near* ERNEST]: While we're here, here's the five hundred francs I borrowed from you. [*He gives him a note and moves back-stage.*]

ERNEST [*on his knees*]: So it was you! [*To himself*] He knows the trick of opening the desk! [*He crawls over to* MARJAVEL.] I say!

MARJAVEL: Have you found it?

ERNEST: No, but while we're here, here's five hundred francs of what I owe you. [*He gives him the note.*]

MARJAVEL [*on his knees*]: It's not that urgent...

ERNEST: I've just had something paid back...

MARJAVEL: Keep looking! Keep looking!

KRAMPACH [*lying on his stomach, has pulled out his notebook and is doing his accounts*]: Two times three makes nine... three times six makes eight... [*To himself*] I make it that he owes me eighty-four thousand francs – that seems too much...

MARJAVEL: Aren't you looking, Krampach?

KRAMPACH: Yes, Monsieur! As you see, Monsieur! [*He swims across the floor and takes a look under the armchair left.*]

ERNEST [*to himself*]: Are we going to play at this all day?

KRAMPACH [*with his head under the armchair*]: I have found something!

ALL [*getting up*]: What? Let's see!

KRAMPACH: Why this – under there? [*He shows the piece of drain-pipe hidden by* ERNEST.]

ERNEST [*to himself*]: Imbecile!

HERMANCE [*coming forward*]: Oh – good heavens!

MARJAVEL: My drain-pipe! [*To* ERNEST] What's it doing here?

ERNEST [*embarrassed*]: Really – it's quite simple – it was very windy last night – a west wind.

MARJAVEL: Well?

ERNEST: And the west wind's always blowing down drain-pipes and gutters.

MARJAVEL: That's true.

ERNEST: Well, I found that in the garden and so I brought it in so it wouldn't get lost.

MARJAVEL: Thank you, Ernest. [*To himself*] Stupid – but devoted. [*He gives the drain-pipe back to* KRAMPACH *who puts it behind the armchair and stays hidden there himself doing his accounts.*]

JOBELIN [*softly, to* HERMANCE]: He's methodical – he'll make a good husband.

MARJAVEL [*sitting in armchair left*]: Don't let's give up. [*To himself.*] My lumbago's started again. [*Aloud*] Keep on looking.

HERMANCE [*going to* MARJAVEL]: It's no use looking here, dear, I've just remembered – it must have been in the garden I lost it.

JOBELIN: The devil! We'll never find it in the soil and the sand out there.

MARJAVEL: Ernest has good eyes. Come along! Let us look! Let us look!

ERNEST [*to himself*]: A walk round the garden will suit me fine. [*To* JOBELIN] You take the right side. [*To* HERMANCE] We'll go left. Let's take a good look!

[HERMANCE, ERNEST *go out left,* JOBELIN *goes out right.* KRAMPACH *gets up and makes as if to follow them.*]

MARJAVEL: Don't trample on the flowers! [*Recalling* KRAMPACH] Krampach!

KRAMPACH [*holding the drain-pipe in his hand*]: Monsieur?

MARJAVEL: If they don't find this diamond, then after dinner this evening, you can sweep out this room. Put all the dust on one side and we'll pass it through a sieve. Well, are you happy here?

KRAMPACH: Oh yes, I am happy ... but there is one fly in the ointment.

MARJAVEL: Oh? What is that?

KRAMPACH: I will tell you ... no, I dare not tell you!

MARJAVEL: Go on, go on! What is it?

KRAMPACH: Yes, Monsieur. [*He moves back-stage, puts the drain-pipe on the chair by the fireplace and comes back again.*] Monsieur?

MARJAVEL: Well?

KRAMPACH: I will dare to tell you ... the fly in the ointment is my wife. If I may make so bold, I'd be grateful if you'd keep an eye on her from time to time. You have my permission.

MARJAVEL: What? You want me to keep an eye on your wife? Is she pretty?

KRAMPACH: Not bad ... Oh, Lisbeth is not wicked – but she has a certain nature ... and there's been trouble before.

MARJAVEL: Trouble?

KRAMPACH: She made a mistake.

MARJAVEL: She broke something?

KRAMPACH [*laughing*]: Ah! No, Monsieur! [*He gives him a slap on the shoulder.*]

MARJAVEL: That's enough of that! You're not at home now.

KRAMPACH: Don't you understand ... a mistake! With some fancy fellow.

MARJAVEL: Oh, bah! [*To himself, gaily*] Well! Well! Well! [*Aloud*] And you attach importance to that?

KRAMPACH: Oh I do and I don't. It's the sort of thing that happens everywhere. We're not the only ones ...

MARJAVEL: What d'you mean – *we're* not?

KRAMPACH: I meant it happens to others – in my country.

MARJAVEL [*laughing*]: And in Paris as well! [*He gives him a slap.*]

KRAMPACH [*convulsed with laughter*]: And in Paris as well! [*He slaps* MARJAVEL *on the shoulder.*]

MARJAVEL: Stop that ... you're the servant – you don't slap. I'm the master and I can slap. [*He slaps him on the shoulder and* KRAMPACH *roars with laughter. To himself*] Well, he certainly takes things lightly.

KRAMPACH: It was before we were married ... I was warned about it.

MARJAVEL: And you married her all the same?

KRAMPACH: It was a matter of conscience ... of five thousand francs. But there is one thing which nags me ... I would like to know the name of her seducer. [*He pronounces the word with difficulty.*]

MARJAVEL: Her seducer?

KRAMPACH: Ja.

MARJAVEL: What good would that be?

KRAMPACH: I am afraid that he was not all he should be – some common fellow – but I did not know him.

MARJAVEL: You can't always be lucky.

KRAMPACH: I have asked Lisbeth ... she does not want to tell me.

MARJAVEL: Well, what is it you want me to do?

KRAMPACH: If you would ... I mean, a master is like a father ... she has confidence in you ... make her talk ... make her tell you the whole thing.

MARJAVEL: Well! What a strange idea!

KRAMPACH: Say something like this: 'So you have made a mistake?' 'Who – who told you, who told you?' 'My little finger told me.' Say something like that and then let her go – without seeming to – and come and tell me – without seeming to . . .

MARJAVEL [*to himself*]: So he's enrolling me in his little police force.

KRAMPACH [*seeing* LISBETH *coming right*]: Here she is! Without seeming to!

[LISBETH *enters, a lighted candlestick in her hand and a basket of bottles under her arm.*]

LISBETH [*to* MARJAVEL]: Is it you who goes to the cellar?

MARJAVEL: Yes . . . but there's plenty of time. [*To himself, looking at her*] She looks a bold little hussy.

KRAMPACH [*softly, to his wife, arranging her shawl*]: Tidy yourself a bit. Monsieur is going to question you.

LISBETH [*to* MARJAVEL]: You speak to me?

MARJAVEL: Yes . . . my child . . .

KRAMPACH [*to* LISBETH]: And don't hide anything from him! A master is like a father . . .

MARJAVEL [*to* KRAMPACH]: Leave us.

KRAMPACH [*out of the corner of his mouth, to* MARJAVEL]: Without seeming to. [*Aloud*] I'll go and do the bedroom of the young man. [*To* LISBETH, *as he goes*] Speak with Monsieur! Speak with Monsieur! [*To* MARJAVEL] Without seeming to . . . [*Aloud*] I'll go and do the bedroom of the young man. [*He goes out back left.*]

LISBETH: What is it you want me for, Monsieur?

MARJAVEL: Put down your candlestick and your basket.

[*She puts the lighted candle on the basket and both on to the chair right near the little table.*]

[*To himself*] Yes, she looks as though she could make a mistake, and sweep it under the carpet.

LISBETH [*going up to him*]: Here I am, Monsieur.

MARJAVEL: Ah, yes, good! [*To himself*] How the devil am I to get her to talk about it? I'll have to find the right approach. [*Aloud*] Straighten the armchairs; this room's very untidy.

[LISBETH *tidies the room on the left only. Then to the audience, after watching* LISBETH *and moving right stage*]

It's a funny thing – but I can't remain faithful myself. I'm just not made that way. I've a charming wife, good, gentle – who adores me! If I were to die, she wouldn't survive me. Ah well, in spite of that, I've always some little affair on the go. I've a wandering eye. It was the same with Mélanie – I'd have two on the go at the same time – but I was younger then . . .

LISBETH [*returning*]: That is done, Monsieur.

MARJAVEL [*to himself*]: I still can't think of the right approach. [*Aloud*] Very good! Now wipe the candlesticks. Rub them hard!

[LISBETH *goes back to the fireplace.* MARJAVEL *sits in chair left, then, while watching* LISBETH, *addresses the audience*]

Like last week . . . I went to this rather naughty dance-hall at Mabille . . . really it was silly of me to go . . . I keep saying I won't go there any more but I still do. Well, I picked up this young Polish girl called Ginginette – quite adorable – it seems she's connected with some of the best families in Lithuania. We had two little meetings, that's all . . . I can say that for myself – I don't let these things go on for too long . . . Ah, well . . . [*He gets up.*]

LISBETH [*having wiped the candlesticks, comes forward right*]: Here I am, Monsieur.

MARJAVEL [*to himself*]: Yes, now, let us approach the matter delicately. [*Aloud, and suddenly*] So! You made a mistake, eh?

LISBETH: Who told you that?

MARJAVEL: My little finger.

LISBETH: It didn't. It was Krampach.

MARJAVEL: What's it matter? Come, tell me how it happened.

LISBETH: Oh no!

MARJAVEL [*taking hold of her hand*]: You haven't enough confidence in me . . . and that is not good. [*Caressing her arm*] A master is like a father.

LISBETH [*laughing*]: Hee, hee, hee!

MARJAVEL: What?

LISBETH: You're tickling me.

MARJAVEL: What superb teeth she has! Look at me! Yes, what superb teeth! [*He kisses her.*]

KRAMPACH [*entering with a lamp in his hand*]: Monsieur, how do the lamps work?

MARJAVEL: Ask Ernest.

KRAMPACH [*softly*]: Have you his name?

MARJAVEL [*softly*]: Not yet . . . but I'll get it.

KRAMPACH [*moving to door*]: Good! Carry on – I'll go and do the room of the young man. [*He goes out back left.*]

MARJAVEL [*to* LISBETH]: Well, my child, how could you let such a thing happen?

LISBETH: It wasn't my fault. I have a heart which loves too easily!

MARJAVEL [*laughing*]: Ah! That is very well put! Look at me . . . [*He kisses her.*] He was very handsome then, this stranger?

LISBETH: Oh yes!

MARJAVEL: Young?

LISBETH: Ja.

MARJAVEL: About my age?

LISBETH: Don't be silly! I said he was young!

MARJAVEL: And what did he used to say to you?

LISBETH: Oh, you know!

MARJAVEL: Tell me, all the same!

LISBETH: He used to look at me sideways – out of the corner of his eyes.

MARJAVEL [*giving her a side-long glance*]: Like this?

LISBETH: Oh, much better!

MARJAVEL: And then?

LISBETH: Then . . . he gave me two oranges.

MARJAVEL [*to himself*]: What a country – Alsace! A glance and two oranges! I'll get in a supply. [*Aloud*] And then? Don't hide anything from me!

LISBETH [*lowering her eyes*]: Oh, *you* know . . .

MARJAVEL: Tell me all the same.

LISBETH [*lowering her eyes*]: The next day . . .

MARJAVEL: Ah! You're going on to the next day? You're cheating.

LISBETH: He promised to marry me. And he went to get his papers.

MARJAVEL [*to himself*]: Ay-ay!

LISBETH: I waited three years for him . . . and, as he didn't come back, I married Krampach.

MARJAVEL: And you never heard of him again?

LISBETH: Yes . . . he sent me a watch . . . made of silver.

MARJAVEL: Can I see it?

LISBETH: Oh, I haven't got it any more. Krampach said it was as if I was carrying the symbol of my dishonour about with me.

MARJAVEL: Very good.

LISBETH: So he wears it.

MARJAVEL: Not so good!

LISBETH: But even that annoys him – because the watch goes slow.

MARJAVEL: I'll give you another – if you'd like one.

LISBETH: Oh, I would!

MARJAVEL [*kissing her*]: Made of gold.

LISBETH: Oh, I'd like that!

MARJAVEL [*teasing her*]: I'll see it keeps the right time – with some oranges.

[*He clasps her in his arms. She struggles near to the chair on which are the lighted candle and the basket.* KRAMPACH *appears.*]

KRAMPACH [*entering and surprising* MARJAVEL]: Oh!

MARJAVEL [*clutching* LISBETH]: She's burning! Fire! Your wife's on fire!

KRAMPACH: Eh?

MARJAVEL: The candle fell on her. Some water, quickly! Some water!

KRAMPACH: Fire! Water! Hold her tight!

[*He runs out left.* MARJAVEL *leaves* LISBETH *and moves a little left.*]

LISBETH [*laughing*]: You're a one, you are!

MARJAVEL: Quick! Tell me the name of your seducer – that will calm Krampach!

LISBETH: Like hell it will!

MARJAVEL: Do I know him?

LISBETH: Do you! Ha! He's a friend of yours! It was you who brought him to Alsace.

MARJAVEL: To Alsace? Who the devil? . . .

ERNEST [*entering left*]: Monsieur Marjavel!

LISBETH: Ah! [*She throws her arms round* ERNEST'*s neck.*]

ERNEST: Oh!

MARJAVEL [*understanding*]: Ernest!

KRAMPACH [*entering quickly with a jug of water*]: Here's some water.

MARJAVEL: She's burning worse than ever! Throw it!

[KRAMPACH *empties the jug of water on* ERNEST'*s head which frees him.* LISBETH *moves upstage.*]

ERNEST [*soaked*]: Hell! What the devil was that for?

KRAMPACH [*very astonished*]: I'll be damned! It's another one! [*He moves back near his wife, putting his jug down right near the table.*]

ERNEST [*to himself, as he wipes himself*]: Lisbeth in Paris! It only needed that!

[LISBETH *and* KRAMPACH *move right.*]

MARJAVEL [*softly to* ERNEST, *mockingly*]: So you've conquered Alsace – what about Lorraine?

ERNEST [*softly*]: Not so loud!

KRAMPACH [*returning to* MARJAVEL, *softly*]: Did she give you the criminal's name?

MARJAVEL [*softly*]: She was just going to ... when she went on fire. But I'm not discouraged. I'll carry on with the interrogation when I come back from the cellar.

KRAMPACH [*softly*]: A good idea! [*Aloud*] Lisbeth, get your basket and candle, and go with Monsieur to the cellar.

LISBETH: But that's just what ... [*She picks up the basket and candle and moves to door right.*]

KRAMPACH: Go! And be sure you do not hide anything from him.

MARJAVEL [*to himself*]: I'll have to buy some oranges. [*To* LISBETH] Come along, child! [*Aloud*] Krampach, I have a pair of new boots which are too tight for me. You can have them! [*He goes out with* LISBETH.]

KRAMPACH [*to himself*]: How good Monsieur is! He has promised me a new livery and now he gives me a pair of new boots that are too tight! When I think of the little game his wife is up to! He must be blind not to see it. I'll have to open his eyes for him. [*Aloud*] Eh! Pfft! Pfft! You, young fellow!

ERNEST [*by the fireplace, overcome with astonishment*]: What! Is it me you mean?

KRAMPACH: Come over here.

ERNEST [*to himself, going to him*]: He's a bit familiar!

KRAMPACH: I tell you a confidence ... a secret ... which you must not tell anyone ... because if you do ...

ERNEST: It wouldn't be a secret.

KRAMPACH: Right! I think that Madame Hermance ... is that how you call her?

ERNEST: Madame Marjavel.

KRAMPACH: I think that she is playing tricks on her husband.

ERNEST: Eh? Don't be ridiculous!

KRAMPACH: A man was seen climbing up the trellis under her window.

ERNEST: No! It's not possible! [*To himself*] The idiot!

KRAMPACH: I am not a child. I know what I'm talking about. This poor old man ... [*moved almost to tears at the thought*] ... who has promised me a livery and new boots ... tight ones ... so I said to myself: 'I must open his eyes for him.'

ERNEST: Open his eyes?

KRAMPACH: Tell him about her little game.

ERNEST [*to himself*]: Oh, this is too much! [*Aloud*] But you mustn't think of doing such a thing! First of all, it's false ... and it will upset him!

KRAMPACH: If it's false, it can't upset him.

ERNEST: Well, no, but ...

KRAMPACH: If it's not false – we must open his eyes. Let us go to the cellar and tell him.

[*He takes* ERNEST *by the arms and turns him round.*]

ERNEST [*to himself*]: He's going to do it! [*Aloud*] But you don't *do* this sort of thing! Look, suppose the same misfortune happened to you and someone came and told you –

KRAMPACH: Somebody did tell me.

ERNEST: Eh? Well? What happened?

KRAMPACH: I was annoyed – but I knew I could not do anything about it.

ERNEST: So, you see, then ...

KRAMPACH: That is not the point. Come, we go to the cellar and tell him. [*He takes him by the arm again.*]

ERNEST: No!

KRAMPACH: Yes!

ERNEST: He'll be coming back here. He needn't be told in front of Lisbeth. Let's wait for him.

KRAMPACH: Let us wait for him, then. [*He sits on chair, front right.*]

ERNEST [*to himself*]: If I could only trap him somehow! [*To* KRAMPACH] Well, what d'you think you're doing there?

KRAMPACH: I'm waiting for Monsieur.

ERNEST: My room isn't done.

KRAMPACH: I swept it this morning.

ERNEST: What about the liqueur cabinet?

KRAMPACH: The what?

ERNEST: The box on the table with four carafes in it: rum, brandy, cordial, kirsch.

KRAMPACH [*rising by degrees as he hears the name of each liqueur*]: Gorr!

ERNEST: Before you clean them, you'll have to finish them off.

KRAMPACH [*joyously*]: You mean – drink them?

ERNEST: Well, of course! [*To himself*] There's enough there to knock him cold. [*Aloud*] Afterwards, put some water in them and shake them.

KRAMPACH: Rinse them. In Alsace we say rinse. [*He picks up his jug of water which he had put near the table right.*]

ERNEST: Yes, yes! Go! Go!

KRAMPACH: We must open his eyes, remember.

[ERNEST *pushes him out and double-locks the door.* HERMANCE, *entering left, witnesses this.*]

HERMANCE: Why are you locking him in?

ERNEST [*coming forward quickly centre*]: He saw a man climbing on to your balcony. He wants to tell Monsieur Marjavel.

HERMANCE: Oh, good heavens! You must speak to him – you must pay him to keep quiet!

ERNEST: Yes, that's the only thing you can think of! Go and hurry your husband in here – and leave the rest to me.

HERMANCE: What are you going to do?

ERNEST: I've started him off on the liqueurs in there. In five minutes, he'll be flat on his back.

HERMANCE: But tomorrow?

ERNEST: Tomorrow can take care of itself. The important thing is to get your husband out of the way.

HERMANCE: You're right! I'll go . . . [*She is moving back-stage and finds herself face to face with* MARJAVEL.] It's him!

[MARJAVEL *enters followed by* LISBETH. *He is carrying the basketful of bottles and the candle.*]

MARJAVEL [*to* LISBETH *as they enter*]: Come along, chucks! [*Seeing* HERMANCE] My wife! [*Aloud*] We've just been to the cellar with Lisbeth. [*He hides the basket and the candle behind his back.*]

HERMANCE [*very taken aback*]: Yes ... I see ... dear ...

[LISBETH *takes the basket and the candle.*]

ERNEST [*also very taken aback*]: What a good idea ... Lisbeth ... the cellar ...

MARJAVEL: I've brought up a bottle of Burgundy. It's beginning to turn ... we'd better drink it.

HERMANCE [*perturbed*]: Yes ... we'd better ...

ERNEST [*uneasy, pulling at the covering on the chair and rumpling it without realizing what he is doing*]: Of course ... because the Burgundy ... as long as it's not turned yet ...

MARJAVEL [*to himself*]: What've they been up to? [*To* LISBETH] That basket is too heavy for you; call your husband.

LISBETH [*calling*]: Krampach! [*She puts down the basket and the extinguished candle and goes to door back right.*]

HERMANCE [*quickly*]: I thought you'd sent him out for something.

MARJAVEL: Me? Certainly not! He was here before!

LISBETH [*shouting at the top of her voice*]: Krampach! Krampach!

MARJAVEL [*calling also*]: Krampach! Krampach!

ERNEST [*to himself*]: That's done it!

[*The voice of* KRAMPACH *can be heard off-stage singing in German.*]

MARJAVEL: He's singing!

LISBETH [*opening the door*]: Come in, love!

[KRAMPACH *appears, very unsteady on his feet and roaring out his German song.*]

ALL: He's tight!

ERNEST [*to himself*]: He's tight! What luck!

KRAMPACH [*entering*]: Here I am, Monsieur, and I have something to tell you.

MARJAVEL: So've I!

[KRAMPACH *tries to speak but* MARJAVEL *interrupts him.*]

Allow me to speak! Monsieur Krampach, I do not need to

remind you that sobriety is the sister of temperance, but if you continue to behave in this disorderly and incontinent way, I shall be forced to deprive myself of your services. Now you may speak!

KRAMPACH: Well, it's like this, Monsieur, there's a man who climbs up at night into your wife's room.

MARJAVEL: A man?

ERNEST [*quickly*]: Don't listen to him ... he's drunk.

HERMANCE [*to* MARJAVEL]: Take no notice of him.

KRAMPACH: I have proof.

MARJAVEL [*going to him*]: Proof? What proof?

KRAMPACH [*pulling from his pocket a watch and chain*]: The chain of this watch had caught on the trellis.

ERNEST [*to himself*]: My watch!

HERMANCE [*to herself*]: We're lost! [*She collapses on to armchair left.*]

MARJAVEL [*examining the watch and the chain*]: But I know this. How did this come to be found on the trellis under my wife's window? Speak! Where were you going?

ERNEST: I was going ...

MARJAVEL: Where were you going?

ERNEST: I was going to the window above ... to Lisbeth's.

[*He moves upstage.* MARJAVEL *moves near* HERMANCE.]

LISBETH: You didn't tell me.

MARJAVEL: To Lisbeth! [*He gives a loud roar of laughter.*]

ERNEST [*laughing also and addressing* KRAMPACH]: Yes, to Lisbeth.

KRAMPACH [*sobering up*]: To my wife!

ERNEST: What? You mean – she's your wife?

KRAMPACH [*hurling himself at him*]: Ah! You leetle devil!

MARJAVEL [*holding him back and placing himself in front of* ERNEST]: Don't touch him! He is my friend!

CURTAIN

ACT THREE

A garden, with benches to the right and rustic chairs to the left. There is a large flowerbed in the centre of the stage, and another on the left of which only part appears on the stage. Empty flowerpots back-right. At the back of the garden, part of the house can be seen on the right.

ERNEST, *disguised as a gardener, with a watering can in each hand, is watering the centre flowerbed.*

ERNEST [*turning to the audience*]: She said eight o'clock, under the elm tree! So here I am! [*With a sigh*] Yes, here I am, disguised as a gardener. I've disguised myself, because after what happened yesterday, we can't be too careful. Poor Hermance! I've been trying to think all night of how to tell her. 'But, good heavens, Hermance, haven't you had enough of this existence? Let us return to the path of duty. Let us arrange a marriage with my cousin Berthe.' No! She would never understand that, never! Damn! It's my legs I'm watering now! [*He moves left and waters the other flowerbeds.*]

HERMANCE [*entering back right*]: Pierre, have you some melons for this evening? [*Seeing* ERNEST] Ernest!

ERNEST [*put-out*]: You recognized me?

HERMANCE: I guessed. Give me a watering can. Then we can talk at a distance, so as not to be surprised.

[*They continue watering,* ERNEST *on the left,* HERMANCE *centre.*]

HERMANCE: I asked you to come here because I'm too frightened we shall be caught.

ERNEST [*coming centre*]: So am I!

HERMANCE: Ernest, we must end it all!

ERNEST [*sadly*]: Part? – forever?

HERMANCE [*sadly*]: Do not say that word.

ERNEST: Ah, Hermance!

HERMANCE: Ah! Ernest!

ERNEST: I shall always be your friend.

HERMANCE: No I can't bear it! Ernest, you must get married.

ERNEST [*forgetting himself*]: Yes, I'd thought of it.

HERMANCE [*astounded, putting down her watering can*]: You'd thought of it?

ERNEST [*putting down his watering can*]: I'd thought that you were going to make this horrible suggestion. [*With tears in his voice*] After what I wrote to you only a week ago!

HERMANCE: I still have your letter next to my heart!

ERNEST: And yet you want me to take a wife?

HERMANCE: It is necessary, dear.

ERNEST [*hypocritically*]: Who d'you suggest?

HERMANCE: My aunt.

ERNEST: The old woman?

HERMANCE: She will be so happy!

ERNEST: I can well believe it!

HERMANCE: I've thought it all out. You will marry my aunt – she's not pretty, but then she never has been, and anyhow, what does that matter?

ERNEST: Oh! Nothing ... only, well, she's rather old, isn't she?

HERMANCE: What about it?

ERNEST: While we're at it, I think we'd do better to find a younger one.

HERMANCE [*quickly*]: Ugly, then.

ERNEST [*with indifference*]: Ugly or pretty.

HERMANCE: Pretty, never!

ERNEST: Let's think of the ugly ones then. It's all the same to me. What about my cousin?

HERMANCE: Berthe?

ERNEST: That would please my uncle.

HERMANCE: She's very pretty!

ERNEST: Pouf! I don't care for these so-called beauties, myself – and then, you know, I knew her when she was little. She hadn't a tooth in her mouth! She looked frightful! I'll always have that in my mind.

HERMANCE: I'd rather you married my aunt.

ERNEST: I'd rather be killed by Marjavel.

[*The cracking of a whip can be heard.*]

HERMANCE [*picking up her watering can*]: What's that?

ERNEST [*picking up his and moving away quickly*]: It's that cab-driver. He's left the seventh lamp-post – to move in front of the front door.

HERMANCE: But you gave him what he asked for?

ERNEST: He may be out for more. We're at the mercy of that man.

HERMANCE: I can't go on living like this. [*She puts down her watering can, near the bench left.*]

MARJAVEL [*off-stage, left*]: Krampach, fetch me that gardener, dead or alive!

ERNEST: It's Marjavel. He's speaking to Krampach! [*He puts down his watering can, back right.*]

HERMANCE [*frightened, coming centre*]: Marry your cousin today, immediately!

ERNEST: I'll write to my uncle.

HERMANCE [*moving to the flowerbed centre with* ERNEST *following her*]: And I will announce the news to my husband.

ERNEST [*holding out his hand*]: Good-bye!

HERMANCE [*taking his hand*]: Good-bye!

ERNEST [*with tears*]: So all is over?

HERMANCE [*weeping also*]: All.

ERNEST [*to himself, as he separates himself from* HERMANCE]: At last! I breathe again!

HERMANCE [*to herself, moving left*]: Now, I can stop worrying.

MARJAVEL [*entering*]: Ah! There he is! [*To* ERNEST] Hey, you there, what d'you think you're up to? [*To* HERMANCE] This fellow's found out that a diamond's missing, so he's been raking the paths!

HERMANCE: He was watering the flowers, dear.

MARJAVEL: I saw him raking, from Ernest's room. Come here, you lout!

[ERNEST *moves towards him backwards.*]

I've asked you time and time again to move this tub, these pots and these benches.

[ERNEST *picks up an empty shrub-tub and puts it over his head so that he is hidden down to his shoulders.* MARJAVEL *places in his arms two empty flowerpots and overburdens him with a chair which he puts on the top of the tub.*]

Have you nothing to say, you lazy lout? [*He gives him a push left and* ERNEST *moves off murmuring*.]

HERMANCE: You expect him to do too much.

MARJAVEL: Him? Don't be silly! He's as strong as an ox!

[ERNEST *goes out tottering*.]

And he'll make good yet!

HERMANCE: Well, aren't you even going to say good morning to me?

MARJAVEL: I'm sorry, I've been preoccupied since yesterday.

HERMANCE: What about, dear?

MARJAVEL: The loss of your diamond.

HERMANCE: Oh, it could be worse.

MARJAVEL: I can't help feeling it may have been stolen. The servants are trustworthy, but the house could be easily broken into. The wind's already taken a drain-pipe. I got up early this morning, ran down to the summerhouse, had Krampach sweep it out and put all he brushed up through a sieve.

HERMANCE: It's quite useless.

MARJAVEL: It was worth trying. D'you know whether Ernest has gone out yet?

HERMANCE: Monsieur Ernest must have a lot to do at the moment. I believe he's thinking of getting married.

MARJAVEL [*astounded*]: Ernest – getting married?

HERMANCE: You'll certainly be the first to be told about it.

MARJAVEL: I am not selfish by nature. I don't complain at losing a friend – on whom I've heaped countless favours – on whom we've both heaped countless favours.

HERMANCE: He's thirty-two – he's got to think of the future.

MARJAVEL: Everybody thinks only of themselves today. I've got used to Ernest. He's never done much for me – but he was devoted. Oh, he's every right to get married. It's just that I feel he had the makings of an excellent bachelor and that he'll make a detestable husband.

HERMANCE: You may find you are wrong!

MARJAVEL: I know him – he's plenty of faults, but as his friend I ought to speak only of his good points. If he's got any, I don't know them. Do you?

HERMANCE: Well!

MARJAVEL: Anyway who's he marrying?

HERMANCE [*with indifference*]: His cousin, I believe. Mademoiselle Berthe.

MARJAVEL: Poor child! It's Jobelin who's fixed that. Ernest hasn't any money. Berthe has plenty. Poor child!

HERMANCE [*to herself*]: It's funny! It's him who's all upset! [*Aloud*] They're waiting for me about lunch. I will see you later. [*She goes out left.*]

MARJAVEL: But who is forcing him to get married? Aren't we quite happy as we are?

KRAMPACH [*entering, solemn and dignified, in livery*]: Monsieur, I come to ask you for an audience.

MARJAVEL [*surprised*]: An audience?

KRAMPACH: I have something to tell you.

MARJAVEL: Hurry up then.

KRAMPACH: Will you be my witness?

MARJAVEL: Your witness? But if you're married –

KRAMPACH: It isn't for that. I am going to fight a duel.

MARJAVEL: With whom?

KRAMPACH: With the young man who has seduced Lisbeth.

MARJAVEL: You mean Ernest?

KRAMPACH: I mean Ernest!

MARJAVEL: But why?

KRAMPACH: How d'you mean – why?

MARJAVEL: Look, your wife made a mistake, but you overlooked it.

KRAMPACH: Yes, I overlooked it.

MARJAVEL: So, it's past and done with. And so you can't do this to Ernest.

KRAMPACH: You think so? But I want him to respect me.

MARJAVEL: Doesn't he respect you?

KRAMPACH: No . . . I found a letter addressed to my wife.

[*He pulls from his pocket a piece of paper burnt at one end and along the edges.*]

MARJAVEL: A letter?

KRAMPACH [*with the paper in his hand*]: It was among the things I swept up. I don't read French unless it is written in German.

But – that doesn't matter – I have read these words which worry me . . . There! [*He gives him the paper.*]

MARJAVEL [*glancing down the paper*]: It's a rough draft.

KRAMPACH [*reminding him*]: There! 'Your husband is a . . .' The rest is burnt.

MARJAVEL [*to himself*]: Yes, it's Ernest's handwriting.

KRAMPACH: Is a what?

MARJAVEL: 'An imbecile' . . . it looks like.

KRAMPACH [*happily*]: Is that all?

MARJAVEL: That or something like it. But this isn't to your wife. [*Reading*] 'What need have you to fear this excellent man?'

KRAMPACH [*joyfully*]: It's certainly me!

MARJAVEL [*continuing*]: 'He is naïve . . . conceited and gullible.'

KRAMPACH [*delighted*]: Yes, it's me!

MARJAVEL [*aloud, to himself*]: Naïve . . . conceited and gullible! I know people like that myself.

KRAMPACH [*without understanding*]: Yes . . .

MARJAVEL [*continuing*]: 'Let us think only of our love. That alone exists.' Is he having an affair with some married woman?

KRAMPACH: Lisbeth!

MARJAVEL: Don't be ridiculous! To Lisbeth he would have just written: 'Oranges for prudence.' No: 'Oranges and prudence!' This is to a woman of the world.

KRAMPACH: Then I can look on Ernest as a friend?

MARJAVEL: It's your duty to.

KRAMPACH [*with resolution*]: My duty? Then it shall be done!

MARJAVEL [*glancing down the letter and moving away*]: Oh, but what fire! What passion! It burns! It flames! [*As if inspired*] Ernest cannot get married! We must keep him to ourselves!

LISBETH [*approaching from the right and holding an orange in her hand which she pretends to be eating*]: Dinner is served.

KRAMPACH [*quickly*]: What's that you're eating?

LISBETH: This? It's an orange.

KRAMPACH: Who gave it you?

MARJAVEL [*softly, to* LISBETH]: Don't say!

LISBETH: It was the master.

MARJAVEL [*to himself*]: The little devil. [*Aloud*] Yes . . . I happened to have a little orange in my pocket.

KRAMPACH: If it was the master – then I'll say nothing.

MARJAVEL [*to himself, moving right*]: What fools some husbands are! Fools like him should never get married!

[*He goes out right.* LISBETH *goes to follow him but* KRAMPACH *pulls her back.*]

KRAMPACH [*bringing her centre*]: Now you can do some explaining. Yesterday I'd had a bit too much to drink – but today...

LISBETH: But I told you!

KRAMPACH: Shut up! You're the one who made the mistake! Why did you have the nerve to tell me you'd never even noticed the young man?

[LISBETH *begins to reply.*]

Shut up! Speak!

LISBETH: I told you I'd seen nobody in my room except mice.

KRAMPACH: Mice don't wear watches.

LISBETH: How d'you know?

KRAMPACH: I know because they don't.

LISBETH: Well! So what?

[KRAMPACH *and* LISBETH *continue arguing in German.* LISBETH *has the last word.*]

KRAMPACH [*after speaking in German*]: All right, all right! Why couldn't you have told me to begin with that you'd been – wronged – by a man of the world?

LISBETH: It wasn't anything to do with you.

KRAMPACH [*with pride*]: Nothing to do with me? Haven't I got my self-respect?

LISBETH: Nein!

KRAMPACH: Ja!

LISBETH: Nein!

KRAMPACH: Ja! [*With dignity*] All right, my lady. If that's the way you feel – I'll enter a petition for a separation.

LISBETH [*softening*]: Oh! Krampach!

KRAMPACH: And for permission to have mistresses myself – pretty ones – with pink hats – pretty ones!

LISBETH [*pleadingly, and then with more passion*]: No! Krampach! Don't you see – since you've had a livery – I adore you!

KRAMPACH [*a little fatuously*]: That's women for you! They're all the same! Just because one pays a little attention to one's appearance ...

LISBETH: Oh, it makes you look so handsome! [*She throws her arms round his neck and kisses him.*]

KRAMPACH [*defending himself but laughing with pleasure*]: You're crumpling me! You're crumpling me!

LISBETH: There! There's my orange ... [*She kisses him.*] You're an angel! [*She goes out left.*]

KRAMPACH [*alone, to himself*]: Everything's happening to me all at once! I have the orange ... my wife adores me and Kuissermann is paying me ... everything's happening at once. [*He moves left.*]

ERNEST [*entering right without seeing* KRAMPACH, *to himself*]: I've just been to arrange for publication of the banns.

KRAMPACH: Ah! The little fellow! [*He pretends to be arranging flowers on the left, then moves gradually centre.*]

ERNEST [*to himself*]: My uncle is coming to announce the great news – that I'm to be married in my turn – that Ernest will no longer have any friends. [*Seeing* KRAMPACH, *to himself*] Oh, lord, there's the other one – the other husband – Marjavel number two! He'll be demanding more explanations. I'd better get away!

[*He makes to leave, but* KRAMPACH *stops him.*]

KRAMPACH [*leading him back centre, with emotion and dignity*]: We have both known what it is to be in love!

ERNEST: Oh, now look! Propinquity! Springtime! You know – the young man's fancy turns to.

KRAMPACH: It was you who made the mistake. But I have overlooked it. So, it no longer exists. So I am not able to challenge you to a duel.

ERNEST: Oh I say, that's fine! That's very reasonable of you!

KRAMPACH [*insistent*]: I am not able to challenge you. But for that, I would return the watch to you. [*He takes out his silver watch.*]

ERNEST: The watch! Oh, yes ... I remember ... [*To himself*] So he wears it! [*Aloud*] Keep it.

KRAMPACH: It loses. It waddles along.

ERNEST: Oh well – if one's not in a hurry ...

KRAMPACH: It was supposed to be guaranteed for three years.

ERNEST: You want me to get it regulated?

KRAMPACH: Yes, and at the same time please have a bell put on it.

ERNEST: A bell?

KRAMPACH: At home, the inspector of police had a watch with a bell.

ERNEST: Well, you don't say!

KRAMPACH: Yes! When it is three o'clock, it goes: 'Ding! Ding! Ding!' When it is four o'clock, it goes: 'Ding! Ding! Ding! Ding!' When it is five o'clock...

ERNEST: Yes... and so on until midnight. [*To himself*] He wants an alarm clock – well, he's not asking a lot. [*Aloud*] You shall have it.

KRAMPACH [*holding out his hand*]: Let us be friends.

ERNEST [*to himself, a little put-out*]: Cheek! Oh well, there's nobody here. [*Shaking hands*] The best of friends! [*To* KRAMPACH] Go and find Marjavel.

KRAMPACH [*going out*]: Yes. Let us be friends.

ERNEST: Yes, yes, but go and find him. [*To* HERMANCE *who enters right*] Madame, here comes my uncle. [*Going up to* JOBELIN] My uncle and my cousin!

JOBELIN [*entering left with* BERTHE, *to* HERMANCE]: Madame! [*Looking around for* MARJAVEL] My dear old friend! Oh... he's not here. [*Taking up a position*] Madame, I wish you to be the first to be informed of a happy event which is about to take place. Monsieur Ernest Jobelin, my nephew, is to marry Mademoiselle Berthe Jobelin, my niece.

HERMANCE [*to* BERTHE]: I am so pleased, Mademoiselle. Please accept my best wishes.

ERNEST [*to himself*]: It's all going perfectly.

HERMANCE [*to* BERTHE]: You may rest assured that your future happiness will be very close to me.

BERTHE [*naïvely*]: Oh, Madame, I'm so happy!

HERMANCE [*drawing her a little nearer*]: Your cousin has been in love with you for a long time?

BERTHE: He'd never told me, Madame. What d'you think of that?

HERMANCE [*joyfully*]: Ah!

JOBELIN: He's too timid.

HERMANCE [*to herself*]: He doesn't love her.

MARJAVEL [*running in, happily*]: Somebody's asking for me? Oh, it's you Jobelin – and all dressed up – black coat, yellow gloves! Had we better go into the drawing-room?

JOBELIN: We are doing splendidly here beneath this verdant canopy.

MARJAVEL [*going to* BERTHE *and kissing her effusively*]: Poor child! [*Beginning to kiss her again*] Poor child!

BERTHE [*astonished*]: What's he kissing me for?

JOBELIN [*taking up a position again*]: My dear old friend, I wish you to be the first to be informed ...

MARJAVEL [*softly, to* ERNEST]: Don't worry, I'll get you out of this ...

ERNEST: Eh?

MARJAVEL [*shaking him heartily by the hand*]: Count on me!

JOBELIN [*who has gone up to* MARJAVEL *to finish his sentence*]: ... to be informed of a happy event ...

MARJAVEL [*softly*]: Get your niece out of here.

JOBELIN [*continuing*]: ... which is about to take place.

MARJAVEL [*softly*]: Get her out of here!

JOBELIN: I have the honour ...

MARJAVEL [*softly*]: Use force if necessary!

JOBELIN: Oh! [*To* BERTHE] Berthe, my dear my old friend Marjavel gives you permission to pick a bunch of his flowers.

BERTHE [*going to* MARJAVEL]: I'm being sent away ...

JOBELIN: It appears that that will be more convenient.

MARJAVEL: We will call you back. [*He kisses her effusively again.*] Poor child!

BERTHE [*going away regretfully*]: What *is* the matter with Monsieur Marjavel? [*She goes off left.*]

JOBELIN: Now, may we continue? [*Taking up a position again*] My dear old friend, I wish you to be the first to be informed ...

MARJAVEL: That's enough! You've come to tell me of Ernest's marriage?

JOBELIN [*astonished*]: Yes ...

MARJAVEL: It's out of the question.

ERNEST: Eh?

HERMANCE: What?

JOBELIN: Why?

MARJAVEL: Ernest cannot marry.

JOBELIN: Why?

MARJAVEL: He's not in love with his cousin.

ERNEST [*protesting*]: Now, look here . . .

MARJAVEL [*softly, to* ERNEST]: Leave it to me! [*Aloud*] He's having an affair . . .

JOBELIN: Eh?

ERNEST [*protesting*]: Oh, I say, dammit all . . .

MARJAVEL [*to* ERNEST]: It's better to get it over and done with quickly! [*To* JOBELIN] He is having one of those affairs which happen once in a lifetime.

JOBELIN: My nephew?

ERNEST: You're mistaken!

MARJAVEL [*continuing*]: He's in love with a married woman!

ERNEST *and* HERMANCE: Oh!

[*They look at each other and then glance away.*]

JOBELIN [*expostulating*]: Oh no! Oh no!

MARJAVEL: Yes, his is a guilty love – even if he prefers to treat it as a matter of little importance – a love which can only be pardoned on account of its overwhelming passion . . .

JOBELIN: But are you sure?

MARJAVEL [*pulling the burnt paper from his pocket*]: You can judge for yourself. [*Trying to read*] What have I done with my spectacles? Hermance!

HERMANCE: Yes dear?

MARJAVEL [*giving her the paper*]: You shall hear how well she reads such sentiments. [*To* HERMANCE] Read it – aloud!

HERMANCE: Me?

MARJAVEL: Yes . . . and don't hurry it.

HERMANCE [*reading*]: 'Your husband is a . . .'

MARJAVEL: Never mind that – it's burnt.

HERMANCE [*reading*]: 'What need have you to fear this excellent man?' [*To herself*] Oh, my God!

ERNEST [*to himself*]: It's my rough-draft!

MARJAVEL [*joyfully*]: Go on!

HERMANCE [*to herself*]: Oh, this is terrible! [*Aloud, reading*] 'He is happy, naïve, conceited and gullible . . .'

ERNEST [*excusing himself*]: Oh you know how it is ... I wrote that when ...

MARJAVEL: There's nothing wrong in being like that. As a matter of fact, I'd very much like to meet him. [*To* HERMANCE] Go on ...

HERMANCE: Is it really necessary, dear?

MARJAVEL: Of course it is! The end is heart-rending – overwhelming! Listen to it, Jobelin.

HERMANCE [*reading, coldly*]: 'Let us think only of our love. That alone exists. The rest is nothing.'

MARJAVEL [*to* HERMANCE]: Put more life into it! More fire! You read it as if it were a chapter from a cookery book. [*Lyrically*] 'Let us think only of our love. That alone exists! The rest is nothing.' [*To* ERNEST] The rest, that's the husband ... the imbecile! Go on!

HERMANCE [*continuing and letting herself insensibly be overcome by emotion*]: 'No obstacle can keep us apart, no power can ever separate us ...'

MARJAVEL [*radiantly*]: There's passion for you!

HERMANCE [*continuing*]: 'I think of you always! I dream of you always! I shall live for you always!'

ERNEST [*to himself*]: Is he out of his mind – making her read this?

MARJAVEL: Yes, yes! And the rest?

HERMANCE [*with increasing emotion*]: 'I love you for your beauty, for your grace, for that elusive charm which is driving me mad with delight ...'

JOBELIN [*to himself, pulling out his handkerchief, overcome with emotion*]: Just how I used to write to Mélanie!

HERMANCE [*reading, with sobs*]: 'I get married? Can you have thought of such a thing ever happening? Do you think I would not know how to resist? Ah, if I could only have some of the tears you have wept!'

[ERNEST *pulls out his handkerchief.* MARJAVEL *pulls out his.* HERMANCE *pulls out hers, her voice shaking with sobs. Emotion overcomes* ERNEST, JOBELIN *and* MARJAVEL. *All three begin weeping and blowing their noses violently.*]

MARJAVEL: This is ridiculous! I'm crying like a child!

JOBELIN: I also!

ERNEST: I also!

[MARJAVEL *consoles* ERNEST *and moves back-stage.* HERMANCE *turns to* ERNEST *and weeps on his chest.*]

ERNEST [*softly to* HERMANCE]: Be careful, for heaven's sake!

HERMANCE [*softly and quickly to* ERNEST]: Break off your marriage! We can't make such a sacrifice! [*She goes off quickly left to hide her emotion.*]

ERNEST [*with despair*]: Good! So it's going to begin all over again!

MARJAVEL [*to* JOBELIN]: Well? Are you convinced?

JOBELIN: Completely! This marriage is out of the question!

MARJAVEL [*to* ERNEST]: I told you I'd get you out of it.

ERNEST: Thanks – but I've arranged for the banns to be published.

MARJAVEL: And you want me to have them stopped? I'll go at once!

ERNEST: No!

MARJAVEL: Yes!

ERNEST: No!

MARJAVEL: Yes! The sixteenth arrondissement – wait for me – I'll be back. [*Softly*] But for me, this fool Jobelin would have sacrificed you! [*He goes off left.*]

ERNEST: You're going to let him go? You won't stop him?

JOBELIN [*reproachfully*]: A married woman! Oh Monsieur! I forbid you to speak to me.

ERNEST: But, good heavens, uncle – one has to sow some wild oats!

JOBELIN: Yes – a widow, perhaps.

ERNEST: Widows! There aren't enough to go round! The world is short of widows! That's why it's in the state it is!

JOBELIN: And I suppose you know her husband?

ERNEST: Yes, I know him – oh, yes, I know him all right!

JOBELIN: You're his friend?

ERNEST: Have been for years! But it's all over. It's finished. You can give me Berthe without any fear.

JOBELIN: Never, Monsieur! Never!

[*A dispute can be heard off-stage and then the sound of a slap.*]

VOICE OF KRAMPACH [*off-stage*]: Eeeh!

LISBETH [*entering and speaking into the wings*]: Caught! That'll teach you a lesson!

JOBELIN: What is it?

LISBETH: I've just given Krampach a good slap on the face. [*Giving some money in notes to* ERNEST] There's your money!

ERNEST: What money?

LISBETH: The money Krampach should have given the cab-driver – but he kept!

ERNEST *and* JOBELIN [*together – in terror*]: He kept the money?

LISBETH: Because Kuissermann owes him money – but I didn't know about it! I'm an honest woman, I am!

JOBELIN: But what about the cab-driver?

LISBETH: He's at the front door now – furious.

ERNEST *and* JOBELIN [*together*]: Good lord!

LISBETH: He asked me for the name of the husband who lives here.

ERNEST *and* JOBELIN [*together*]: Marjavel! But why?

LISBETH: He wants to write to him.

ERNEST *and* JOBELIN: Oh, good heavens! We must run and stop him! [*They move back-stage with* LISBETH.]

LISBETH: Oh, that's no use . . . his letter's gone.

JOBELIN *and* ERNEST: Gone?

[LISBETH *goes out right.*]

JOBELIN: Ernest!

ERNEST: Uncle!

JOBELIN: You understood?

ERNEST: You have guessed?

JOBELIN: In this cab was . . .

ERNEST: Madame Marjavel.

JOBELIN: Yes.

ERNEST: Oh, Hermance! } [*Together*]
JOBELIN: Oh, Mélanie! }

[*They stare at each other.*]

ERNEST *and* JOBELIN: Eh?

JOBELIN [*astounded*]: Hermance?

ERNEST [*also astounded*]: Mélanie?

JOBELIN [*reproachfully*]: Nephew!

ERNEST [*also reproachfully*]: Uncle!

BOTH: We have both been guilty. [*They embrace each other.*]

HERMANCE [*entering left*]: Good heavens! Why this sudden affection for each other?

JOBELIN [*quickly, to* HERMANCE]: Ah, Madame, the worst has happened. Krampach kept the money ... the cab-driver is furious ... he is going to write to your husband.

HERMANCE: Monsieur, I don't understand ... I don't know what you mean.

JOBELIN [*to himself*]: She's right! I thought I was speaking to Mélanie. [*Softly, to Ernest*] You tell her.

[*He pushes him to her.*]

ERNEST [*to* HERMANCE, *quickly*]: Krampach kept the money. The cab-driver has just written to your husband.

HERMANCE: We're lost! [*Filled with exaltation*] I can no longer see Marjavel again! The look in his eyes would kill me! Let us go! Let us fly! [*She moves back-stage.*]

ERNEST: Where?

HERMANCE: What's that matter? Switzerland. America.

JOBELIN: Perhaps Belgium ...

HERMANCE: It's too near.

ERNEST: But – a journey like that ...

HERMANCE: You hesitate! After dragging me down into the abyss!

ERNEST [*to himself*]: Oh, well, there's no getting out of it now! [*Moving back-stage, agitatedly*] Let us leave for America ... which one – North or South?

MARJAVEL [*entering left*]: Here I am! Oh! I'm perspiring!

HERMANCE: Him!

ERNEST *and* JOBELIN [*together*]: Too late!

MARJAVEL: I went to the Mayor's office. There was a most disagreeable man there.

HERMANCE [*softly, to* ERNEST]: He hasn't had the letter!

ERNEST [*softly, to* JOBELIN]: He hasn't had the letter!

JOBELIN [*softly, into the wings*]: He hasn't had the letter!

MARJAVEL: I said to him: 'Monsieur, I've come about the marriage of Monsieur Ernest Jobelin.' And he said to me: 'Are you the father or the mother of the young man?'

ERNEST [*with a forced laugh*]: Ha, ha! Very funny! The mother of the young man!

HERMANCE: Quite charming!

JOBELIN: It's as if it were in a play!

KRAMPACH [*entering with a letter in his hand*]: Monsieur, a letter for you.

HERMANCE, ERNEST and JOBELIN [*to themselves, terrified*]: The letter!

KRAMPACH: They're waiting for a reply.

HERMANCE [*softly*]: We're lost!

JOBELIN [*to himself*]: I don't feel well!

MARJAVEL [*after opening the letter*]: What strange handwriting. Where's my spectacles?

ERNEST [*quickly*]: Shall I read it?

MARJAVEL: No ... Krampach! [*He gives him the letter.*]

HERMANCE: But, my dear ...

MARJAVEL: I've no secrets from anybody! Anyhow, he'd better get used to doing it ... when I forget my spectacles ... go on!

KRAMPACH [*reading*]: 'You big booby ... if you do not send me three thousand francs at once ...'

MARJAVEL: What's he mean – booby?

KRAMPACH [*reading*]: 'I will tell your wife that you were out in my cab with one of those girls from ...'

[MARJAVEL *gives* KRAMPACH *a push and passes on.*]

HERMANCE: Eh?

JOBELIN: Ah!

MARJAVEL [*to himself*]: Good lord! My evening with Ginginette! And my wife has heard. I'm done for.

ERNEST [*softly*]: It seems we've all used the same cab.

HERMANCE [*to* MARJAVEL]: To deceive me! At your age! Good-bye ... Monsieur! [*She moves back-stage.*]

MARJAVEL: No, Hermance!

[*She moves forward again.*]

I will explain. [*Softly, to* KRAMACH] Eat the envelope!

[KRAMPACH *turns away, eats the letter and keeps the envelope.*]

[*Aloud*] This letter isn't for me. Think of it! Am I the sort of man to go out in a cab with ... one of those girls?

HERMANCE: Who is it for then?

MARJAVEL: Ah yes! Who? [*To himself*] I'll put everything on Ernest. [*Aloud, to* ERNEST] You miserable young man! [*He takes him by the arm and pulls him to him.*]

ERNEST: What?

MARJAVEL: This is how one learns to misconduct oneself, how one learns disorderly ways . . .

ERNEST: But it's not me! I protest!

MARJAVEL: Useless! I have proof! [*To* KRAMPACH] Give me the envelope.

KRAMPACH: I've eaten it.

MARJAVEL: Imbecile! Idiot! It had on it: 'To Monsieur Ernest Jobelin.'

HERMANCE: What?

ERNEST: Are you sure?

MARJAVEL [*taking the envelope from* KRAMPACH *and giving it to* ERNEST]: There, Monsieur, take back this letter which should never have entered this house.

ERNEST [*looking at it*]: This is the envelope.

MARJAVEL: What? Has he eaten the letter?

[*He shakes* KRAMPACH *violently* – KRAMPACH *not understanding what it is all about.*]

ERNEST [*reading the inscription*]: 'To Monsieur Marjavel.'

ALL: Eh?

MARJAVEL: It was for me? Oh, I see what it is . . . I was taking Aunt Isaure to the park . . . and somebody must have taken her for a . . . Well! Would you believe it!

HERMANCE: No, Monsieur, I don't! I shall have my revenge for this!

[LISBETH *enters with* BERTHE, *both carrying bunches of flowers.*]

BERTHE: Has the conference ended?

JOBELIN: Yes, everything's settled.

ERNEST: We were talking about the bridegroom's present to his bride.

MARJAVEL [*with regret*]: So Ernest is to get married. [*To* HERMANCE] We are losing a friend.

KRAMPACH: Ah, Monsieur, it will not be long before you find another.

MARJAVEL: May Heaven grant you are right!

CURTAIN

LET'S GET A DIVORCE!

by

VICTORIEN SARDOU

and

Émile de Najac

CHARACTERS

DES PRUNELLES, a wealthy landowner, forty to forty-five years of age.

ADHÉMAR DE GRATIGNAN, a government inspector of forests, twenty-five to thirty years of age.

CLAVIGNAC, forty to forty-five years of age.

BAFOURDIN

BASTIEN, Manservant.

JOSEPH, Head-Waiter.

CYPRIENNE, wife of Des Prunelles, twenty-five years of age.

MADAME DE BRIONNE, a young widow.

MADAME DE VALFONTAINE

MADEMOISELLE DE LUSIGNAN, a spinster.

JOSÉPHA, Maidservant.

A POLICE OFFICER

TWO POLICEMEN

TWO WAITERS

A CONCIERGE

A SHOP ASSISTANT

The action takes place at Rheims, in the year 1880.

ACT ONE

A very elegant little winter room, half drawing-room and half conservatory. All the right side looking on to the garden is glazed and decorated with climbing plants. Front right, a door leads into the garden. Back right is a window of ordinary glass with a venetian blind. This is raised at the beginning of the act, as are all the other venetian blinds along this side. Down left is the door to CYPRIENNE*'s room. Upstage of this is the mantelpiece and fireplace, and back left is the door leading into the dining-room. Back-stage left, through an archway, can be seen a very elegant hall, which leads, on the left, to the front door which cannot be seen, and on the right to* DES PRUNELLES*'s study. An ornate wooden staircase leads to the second floor. To the right of the entrance to the hall, which occupies the larger part of the back of the stage, is another door to* DES PRUNELLES*'s study, opening on to the winter room. Everywhere are pictures, portraits, vases, knick-knacks, Chinese lanterns etc. The furniture is varied and elegant. There are plants, flowers, palm-trees etc. Left centre is an oval table. Left of this is an armchair. A small chair between the table and the armchair. Behind the table, facing the audience, a large sofa. Right of the table another small chair and, a little further right, a pouf. Under the table is a stool. Front-stage right is an armchair. Behind the armchair, another small chair. In front of the window, a little table. Right of this table, between the window and the garden door, a work table. Another small chair between the entrance to the hall and the door to* DES PRUNELLES*'s study. On the table centre, pen, ink, blotting-paper, a bell, and books and brochures on divorce, some lying open and dog-eared. On the little table in front of the window, a coffee cup and a tray of liqueurs. On the work table, a sewing basket. On the mantelpiece, a clock and another coffee cup.*

JOSÉPHA *is leaning over the table, to the right of it, reading one of the books.* BASTIEN *enters from the hall followed by an assistant from a bookshop who is carrying some books and a note tied together with string.*

BASTIEN: Mademoiselle Josépha?

JOSÉPHA [*without moving*]: Well?

BASTIEN: The man from the bookshop has brought some more books for Madame.

JOSÉPHA: Put them on the table here.

BASTIEN [*taking the books and putting them on table centre, to the shop assistant*]: Thank you, that'll be all right.

JOSÉPHA: Wait. [*She takes the note from the books, opens it and reads*] *The Question of Divorce. Divorce. On Divorce. About Divorce. More about Divorce.* [*As she reads each title, she checks with the books.*] Yes, they're all here. [*She puts the note in her pocket.*]

BASTIEN [*to the shop assistant*]: All correct, thank you.

[*The shop assistant goes out.* BASTIEN *leans on the chair behind the armchair, gazing soulfully at* JOSÉPHA.]

JOSÉPHA: Have you nothing to do?

BASTIEN: Only worship you – from a distance.

JOSÉPHA: Don't you think you'd better get rid of these coffee cups? Madame's at home today, and it's gone three o'clock already.

BASTIEN [*moving back-stage*]: Why can't they leave their cups on the table? Where've they put them now?

JOSÉPHA [*sitting on the small couch and glancing through one of the books*]: Madame's is on the mantelpiece and Monsieur's is over on that little table.

BASTIEN [*crossing to the little table in front of the window*]: I see . . . they keep far enough apart from each other, don't they? [*He pours himself a small glass of liqueur.*]

JOSÉPHA [*still glancing through the book*]: If Monsieur catches you doing that . . .

BASTIEN [*pointing to the door back-stage*]: Don't worry. He's safe in there, in his little room, snoring his head off – or making his billiard balls and his napkin rings. I ask you! One of the richest landowners in Rheims! [*He drinks and crosses back to* JOSÉPHA.] You're the one who'd better look out – sticking your nose in Madame's books.

JOSÉPHA: Hah! She's safe in her room, like him!

BASTIEN: Does she snore too?

JOSÉPHA: Probably. She's bored enough.

BASTIEN: I can believe that all right – with a husband like him, always messing about with his locks and his clocks and his bells – what a life!

JOSÉPHA: It's the way all married couples end up.

BASTIEN [*coming nearer her*]: Oh, not us, Josépha! We wouldn't! If you'd marry me, there'd be no snoring, I promise you!

JOSÉPHA: Perhaps – for the first six months or so.

BASTIEN: A year, Josépha. I guarantee a year!

JOSÉPHA [*turning towards him*]: And after that?

BASTIEN: After?

JOSÉPHA: Yes.

BASTIEN [*moving forward, centre*]: Well, I mean to say . . . after?

JOSÉPHA [*getting up*]: There you are! That's what's wrong with marriage. It goes on too long. Everybody should marry for a year, eighteen months, two years at the most – and then everybody should swop round!

BASTIEN: That'd be the ideal arrangement. You can't expect that ever to happen.

JOSÉPHA: It's coming – and quicker than you think. As soon as we've got these divorce laws passed. Listen to this: [*Reading*] 'The thing that puts so many people off marriage is the impossibility of ever getting out of it once they're in it.'

BASTIEN: Oh, that's exaggerating it a bit!

JOSÉPHA: It's true!

BASTIEN: Who's the fellow who wrote that?

JOSÉPHA: A Monsieur Didon. [*She puts the book on the table.*] So don't talk to me of marriage until the divorce laws are through. I want to see a loophole for escape.

BASTIEN: All right, then! Let's not talk of marriage, Josépha. Let's talk of love – free love! You don't need any escape loophole from that! [*He tries to put his arm round her.*]

JOSÉPHA [*freeing herself*]: Stop that – or you'll get a slap on the face.

BASTIEN: But everybody's doing it nowadays!

JOSÉPHA: Ssh! Somebody's knocking on the window!

BASTIEN [*lowering his voice but not moving*]: Is it his cousin?

JOSÉPHA: Monsieur Adhémar? No, he wouldn't risk it at this

time of day. [*She turns to the window where the face of the concierge has appeared.*] Well! It's the concierge!

CONCIERGE [*outside*]: Monsieur Bastien!

BASTIEN [*opening the window*]: What are you doing there? Can't you use the door?

CONCIERGE [*putting his head in*]: It's locked, Monsieur Bastien.

BASTIEN: The door from the garden?

CONCIERGE: Yes.

BASTIEN [*going to the door right and trying to open it*]: He's right. It's locked.

JOSÉPHA: That's Monsieur, obviously.

BASTIEN [*softly*]: He must suspect his cousin comes in this way.

JOSÉPHA: Not so loud! [*Aloud to the concierge*] What is it you want then?

CONCIERGE [*passing the newspapers through the window*]: The Paris newspapers have just come.

[BASTIEN *hands the papers to* JOSÉPHA.]

JOSÉPHA: All right! Give me them! Madame's waiting for them. She's asked for them three times.

BASTIEN: So has Monsieur!

JOSÉPHA [*to the concierge*]: Thank you – you can go!

BASTIEN: Yes, go on – back to sleep again. [*He closes the window.*]

JOSÉPHA [*unfolding one of the newspapers*]: What can there be in these things that interests them so very much? [*She sits in armchair left.*]

BASTIEN: Some scandal ...

JOSÉPHA: Better keep an eye open!

BASTIEN [*kneeling on chair behind* JOSÉPHA *and leaning over her*]: Yes, have a look at the criminal cases – the second page ...

JOSÉPHA: No, the Stock Market first – the florin – up four per cent.

BASTIEN: What about the races – who won the two-thirty?

JOSÉPHA: What do I care? [*Looking at the first page*] Ah!

BASTIEN: What is it?

JOSÉPHA: Now I understand.

BASTIEN: What?

JOSÉPHA: Why Madame and Monsieur are so keen to see the newspapers. [*Reading*] 'If the Chamber discusses the report of the Commission on Divorce today, one of the most lively and interesting debates can be expected.'

BASTIEN: So that's it!

JOSÉPHA: Wait, listen! [BASTIEN *replaces the chair behind the armchair and comes forward left of* JOSÉPHA. *She reads*] 'According to all the forecasts, the vote ...'

DES PRUNELLES [*behind door back-stage*]: Bastien!

BASTIEN: Watch out! It's Monsieur! [*He moves upstage.*]

JOSÉPHA [*rising quickly and gathering up the newspapers*]: What a nuisance he is!

BASTIEN [*picking up the coffee cup from the mantelpiece*]: Hide them! Hide them! We'll read them later!

JOSÉPHA: Yes [*She hides the papers behind her.*]

[DES PRUNELLES *enters from his room.*]

DES PRUNELLES: Bastien!

BASTIEN: Monsieur?

DES PRUNELLES: Haven't the Paris papers come yet?

BASTIEN [*going to pick up the other cup, right*]: No, Monsieur.

DES PRUNELLES: It's half-past three. They should be here now.

BASTIEN: If Monsieur wishes, I'll go and ask the concierge.

DES PRUNELLES: Yes, hurry!

[BASTIEN *goes out back left carrying the tray with the cups.*]

[*To himself*]: What've they been up to in here, those two? [*To* JOSÉPHA, *brusquely*] What are you doing there, you?

JOSÉPHA [*in front of the mantelpiece, pretending to look busy with the clock*]: The clock has stopped, Monsieur, and I was looking to see ...

DES PRUNELLES: Don't touch it. That's my concern. You know very well I don't want anyone touching the clocks.

JOSÉPHA: It's the same with the bells. I don't know what's been the matter with them today.

DES PRUNELLES: Yes, yes, I know. They're not working. Don't touch them!

JOSÉPHA: Oh, Monsieur knows they're not working?

DES PRUNELLES: Yes, I'll fix them. Don't worry – I'll put them right.

[JOSÉPHA *goes out back left. A bell rings.*]

Here they come already! Visitors! For Madame, of course!

BASTIEN [*entering with a card on a salver*]: It is for you, Monsieur.

DES PRUNELLES [*taking the card*]: And the newspapers?

BASTIEN: Not come yet, Monsieur.

DES PRUNELLES [*looking at the card*]: Clavignac! Show him in.

[BASTIEN *goes to the door.* CLAVIGNAC *enters.* BASTIEN *goes.*]

It really is you, Clavignac! So you're back in Rheims?

CLAVIGNAC [*gaily, coming forward*]: Yes, it's me! And in Rheims!

DES PRUNELLES [*shaking hands*]: But everybody thinks you must be dead! Where the devil have you been?

CLAVIGNAC: In Spain!

DES PRUNELLES: Spain?

CLAVIGNAC: Having a change of air.

DES PRUNELLES: Lucky fellow! It's all right for you bachelors. Free to go where you please!

CLAVIGNAC [*taking the foot-stool from under the table and sitting on it*]: Not quite a bachelor – only separated.

DES PRUNELLES [*pulling the pouf a little to the left and sitting near* CLAVIGNAC]: It comes to the same thing.

CLAVIGNAC: Oh, no, it doesn't! My wife still finds ways to drive me crazy! How's yours, by the way? Well, I hope.

DES PRUNELLES: Oh, yes – thriving! But how does yours still drive you crazy?

CLAVIGNAC: I make her an allowance, don't I? Which is more then she deserves, considering the situation I surprised her in. That in itself proved she was well able to look after herself. Anyway, that was the verdict. It was no use arguing. So I pay up. But my wife finds the allowance far too small, and she's thought up a damned awkward way of trying to make me increase it. Wherever I settle down – doesn't matter whether it's a mountain resort, a country resort or a seaside resort – there she arrives accompanied by some idiotic gigolo – and then the scandal starts. Everybody looks at me with a smile, the local newspapers blazon forth her conquests, everybody remembers the law-suit. I'm driven crazy. I beg her to clear out. She replies: 'Oh, willingly – as long as someone pays for my hotel, my clothes, my transport etc.' Then the bill arrives – ten, twelve thousand francs. I pay. She disappears. She's played her ace – and won.

DES PRUNELLES: Then she followed you to Spain?

CLAVIGNAC: Ah! No! This time I played my ace! I let her know, in confidence, that I was going to spend the winter in Algeria. At this very moment she is arriving in Africa. That's my revenge!

DES PRUNELLES: Then you'll stay here?

CLAVIGNAC: For twenty-four hours.

DES PRUNELLES: No longer?

CLAVIGNAC: No longer! Just enough to collect my rents and take some papers to my lawyer.

DES PRUNELLES: You are reopening the case?

CLAVIGNAC: No. But the divorce law will be voted in and you'll appreciate I'll hasten to widen the abyss between Madame Clavignac and myself. Once divorced, she can produce as many aces as she likes. If she likes, I'll help her.

DES PRUNELLES: Then you think the divorce law will be brought in?

CLAVIGNAC: I certainly hope so!

DES PRUNELLES: If we only could be certain! You'll dine with me?

CLAVIGNAC: No – it's you who'll dine with me.

DES PRUNELLES: What?

CLAVIGNAC: This morning at lunch, Loisel and Tarentin and I decided we'd have a bachelor dinner tonight – like we used to. It's on me. We'll get some pretty girls in. They wouldn't frighten you off, would they?

DES PRUNELLES: What? Pretty girls? Me – at my age?

CLAVIGNAC: Bah! They'll rejuvenate you! I must go and look some of them up now. Seven-thirty this evening then! At Dagneau's – the Grand Vatel. Agreed?

DES PRUNELLES [*rising and moving left*]: It certainly isn't! No, I really can't dine with you.

CLAVIGNAC [*stopping, as he is about to leave*]: Come on, you must!

DES PRUNELLES: Absolutely no!

CLAVIGNAC: I could take this as an insult.

DES PRUNELLES: I can't, really!

CLAVIGNAC [*coming forward a little*]: Now, don't go too far... or I'll send my seconds and you'll have a duel on your hands!

DES PRUNELLES: Good! Just what I'm looking for.

CLAVIGNAC: What? A duel?

DES PRUNELLES: Almost. I can't go on like this.

CLAVIGNAC: You?

DES PRUNELLES: Me!

CLAVIGNAC [*lowering his voice*]: Because of your ...

DES PRUNELLES: Naturally!

CLAVIGNAC [*coming forward right*]: Well, well! Then let's be serious. Tell me everything. If anybody's in a position to advise you – it's certainly me!

DES PRUNELLES [*putting his hands on* CLAVIGNAC'*s shoulders and making him sit on the pouf*]: My dear old friend ... when we two got married, both of us did a ...

CLAVIGNAC: Damn silly thing – I know.

DES PRUNELLES [*sitting on the stool*]: Though you deserved what you got.

CLAVIGNAC: Thank you!

DES PRUNELLES: You married a flirt who'd started her little games even before she'd left school.

CLAVIGNAC: Yes, you knew – and you never warned me.

DES PRUNELLES: Now be fair. You never consulted me.

CLAVIGNAC: That's true.

DES PRUNELLES: While I married a modest, well-brought-up young girl. You know that better than anyone. You used to stay at their house. A little lively, perhaps ...

CLAVIGNAC: You can say that again. She used to go round boxing the maids' ears.

DES PRUNELLES: You never told me that!

CLAVIGNAC: Be fair. You never asked.

DES PRUNELLES: Well, anyway, after sowing all my wild oats, I thought I could look forward to a happy and peaceful married life.

CLAVIGNAC: And instead?

DES PRUNELLES: My dear old friend. Instead, I find myself embarked on a tempestuous, storm-swept sea.

CLAVIGNAC: Can you be less figurative? How? Why?

DES PRUNELLES: Does anyone ever know? It's usually called incompatibility of temperament. Madame wants to go out,

Monsieur wants to stay in. One's too hot when the other's shivering. One gets up when the other goes to bed. In fact, there's agreement only on one thing – the need to keep out of each other's way.

CLAVIGNAC: My case, exactly!

DES PRUNELLES: To crown it all, there arrives on the scene one of these fops that women go into ecstasies over. His cravat drenched in scent. Enough to make any woman drunk with her own silliness. And this confounded dandy is my own cousin . . .

CLAVIGNAC: Adhémar?

DES PRUNELLES: The one-and-only Adhémar. Nowadays he's the local chief government inspector for agriculture and fisheries. He sweeps in, booted up to here, jangling his spurs, cracking his whip. A fine specimen I look beside that comic-opera musketeer. Still, there are two reassuring signs, that give me a little hope.

CLAVIGNAC: Yes?

DES PRUNELLES: First, Madame des Prunelles is always on the defensive with me. The day she starts being charming I'll know the die has been cast.

CLAVIGNAC: I see what you mean.

DES PRUNELLES: And second, she's very preoccupied with divorce. Proof that she's still struggling. When she stops struggling, she'll stop thinking about divorce.

CLAVIGNAC: She's actually told you that?

DES PRUNELLES: No, but you've only to look at what she's reading. Legal books. [*He picks up the books.*] Look at them. Divorce, divorce, divorce – all of them. Underlined, annotated – even the pages dog-eared!

CLAVIGNAC: But, good heavens, man, defend yourself!

DES PRUNELLES: I would – to the last ditch – only I'm sick of it all. Oh, my friend, I'm so sick of it all! Catastrophe is hanging over me. I can sense it. And that's why I can't dine with you. One moment of forgetfulness and I'm done for.

CLAVIGNAC: Yes, if that's how things are, you'd better watch your step.

DES PRUNELLES: And also, today I plan to bring things to a head –

CLAVIGNAC: Today?

DES PRUNELLES [*leading him right*]: At any moment now! I have made it clear that I detest the sight of this creature. But since he's a relative, I tolerate his presence on Mondays, our 'at home' days – today, that is. At any other time, I would throw him out of the window. You can guess what was said to that. 'So, Monsieur, now you start insulting your own wife ...'

BOTH [*together*]: '... With your malicious imputations!'

DES PRUNELLES: '... It would serve you right ...'

BOTH [*together*]: '... If I justified them!'

DES PRUNELLES: I stood firm! Adhémar only appears now on our 'at home' days. But as soon as my back is turned, in he dashes by the garden door there. The cunning devil has actually rented an apartment right opposite my house! [*He moves back-stage and points right.*]

CLAVIGNAC [*following him*]: Well?

DES PRUNELLES: Well, as I have some mechanical ability, all last night I prepared a little trap for him for this afternoon. He'll lose his temper. I'll pull his nose for him. He will challenge me. We shall fight a duel.

CLAVIGNAC: He'll kill you!

DES PRUNELLES: I'll be at peace anyway.

CLAVIGNAC: How does this trap of yours work?

DES PRUNELLES: Oh, it's quite simple really. Think of a little coiled spring – Ssh! Here she is!

CLAVIGNAC: Your wife?

[CYPRIENNE *appears back-stage in the hall followed by* JOSÉPHA *to whom she gives an order. It is obvious from her gestures that she is in a bad mood.*]

DES PRUNELLES: Oh, my God!

CLAVIGNAC: What is it?

DES PRUNELLES: She's ... smiling, isn't she?

CLAVIGNAC: Quite the opposite, if you ask me.

DES PRUNELLES: Really?

CLAVIGNAC: Of course!

DES PRUNELLES [*his spirits reviving*]: Ah, my dear friend! So much the better! You reassure me!

[JOSÉPHA *goes out again and* CYPRIENNE *comes forward.*]

CLAVIGNAC [*bowing to* CYPRIENNE]: Dear Madame . . .

CYPRIENNE: Why Monsieur Clavignac . . . how kind of you . . .

CLAVIGNAC: As I was passing through Rheims, I simply had to call and pay my respects to you.

CYPRIENNE: I shan't ask you how Madame Clavignac is.

CLAVIGNAC: Excelling herself.

CYPRIENNE: Still separated?

CLAVIGNAC: Still separated.

CYPRIENNE: My congratulations – to both of you. [*She moves back-stage left.*]

DES PRUNELLES [*softly, to* CLAVIGNAC]: What did I tell you!

CLAVIGNAC [*softly, to* DES PRUNELLES]: Rather nasty, that!

DES PRUNELLES [*softly, to* CLAVIGNAC]: That's nothing! You wait a little!

[BAFOURDIN *enters back.*]

BASTIEN [*announcing him*]: Monsieur Bafourdin.

BAFOURDIN [*solemnly and sententiously*]: Dear Madame . . .

CYPRIENNE: Good afternoon, Monsieur Bafourdin. How are you?

BAFOURDIN: Overwhelmed by your kindness, dear lady. [*He moves right.*]

DES PRUNELLES [*shaking hands with him*]: My dear fellow! [*Introducing* CLAVIGNAC] My friend, Monsieur Clavignac. [*To* CLAVIGNAC] Monsieur Bafourdin, Registrar of Births, Deaths – and Marriages.

CLAVIGNAC: Charmed!

MADAME DE BRIONNE [*to* BASTIEN *at the door, as she enters*]: No need to announce me! I'm quite at home here!

CYPRIENNE [*shaking hands with her*]: How are you?

MADAME DE BRIONNE: Blooming, darling! [*They come forward left and she shakes hands with* DES PRUNELLES.] How do, neighbour! [*Passing in front of him to* BAFOURDIN] Hello there, Monsieur Bafourdin! [*Passing in front of* BAFOURDIN *to* CLAVIGNAC] Good heavens! You? So you've returned from the dead, have you?

[*During the following exchange between* MADAME DE BRIONNE *and* CLAVIGNAC, BAFOURDIN *goes and sits on the sofa.* DES PRUNELLES *puts the stools under the table, picks up the books and puts them on the little table near the window, and*

CYPRIENNE *puts the pamphlets on the mantelpiece. At the same time,* JOSÉPHA *enters left with tea on a tray. She puts the tray on the table, moves the armchair near the table and goes out.*]

CLAVIGNAC: Ah, to see you, where wouldn't one return from? Still the widow, are you?

MADAME DE BRIONNE: Just the same! And you?

CLAVIGNAC: Not yet.

MADAME DE BRIONNE [*laughing*]: A pity! We could have united our two lonely hearts!

CLAVIGNAC [*quickly*]: No need to be a widower for that!

MADAME DE BRIONNE [*laughing*]: No, no, it's a husband I'm after!

CYPRIENNE [*calling to her as she prepares the tea on the table*]: Estelle!

MADAME DE BRIONNE [*going to her*]: Darling!

CLAVIGNAC [*to* DES PRUNELLES]: Why has a lovely woman like her never remarried?

DES PRUNELLES: She would if she could. She's no money.

[ADHÉMAR *enters preceded by* BASTIEN.]

BASTIEN [*announcing*]: Monsieur Adhémar de Gratignan.

[CYPRIENNE, *by the table, gives a sudden start.*]

DES PRUNELLES [*softly to* CLAVIGNAC]: Here he comes – decked out to kill!

ADHÉMAR [*coming forward left to* CYPRIENNE, *shaking hands*]: My dear cousin, how have you been keeping [*pausing pointedly*] since last Monday?

CYPRIENNE [*nervously*]: Quite well, thank you.

DES PRUNELLES [*softly to* CLAVIGNAC]: Hypocrite! He sees her every day!

[ADHÉMAR *nods to him.* DES PRUNELLES *pretends not to see him.* CLAVIGNAC *moves back-stage to talk to* MADAME DE BRIONNE.]

BAFOURDIN [*standing with the cup of tea* CYPRIENNE *has given him*]: So you're leaving us, Monsieur de Gratignan?

ADHÉMAR [*to himself, annoyed*]: Now for it!

[CYPRIENNE, *pouring tea into a cup at the table turns to him quickly.* DES PRUNELLES, *moving back-stage to* CLAVIGNAC, *stops and listens.*]

CYPRIENNE: Leaving us! [*To* ADHÉMAR] You are going away?

ADHÉMAR [*quickly*]: No, no, of course not!

BAFOURDIN: I read in the newspaper this morning you had been appointed Deputy-Inspector for the Arachon Forests.

CYPRIENNE [*troubled and flustered by her husband's presence*]: And we knew nothing of it?

ADHÉMAR: Exactly! That's what I was about to tell you. I've been offered this position. But I've refused it.

DES PRUNELLES: A promotion?

ADHÉMAR: Only so I can stay in the bosom of my family. [*He crosses and puts his hat on the mantelpiece; then returns centre.*]

DES PRUNELLES [*softly, to* CLAVIGNAC]: That does it! It will have to be a duel!

MADAME DE BRIONNE [*back-stage, looking at a curio fixed to the wall*]: Monsieur des Prunelles?

DES PRUNELLES: Madame! [*He goes to her.*]

MADAME DE BRIONNE: Is it Chinese – this dragon?

DES PRUNELLES: Japanese!

[*He continues to talk to her back-stage right.* BAFOURDIN *sits again on the sofa. Profiting from them all moving away* CYPRIENNE *crosses to* ADHÉMAR *with a cup of tea.*]

CYPRIENNE [*softly, to* ADHÉMAR, *giving him the tea*]: You're doing this for me? Oh, my dear, you must not sacrifice yourself. I won't let you!

ADHÉMAR [*whispering, taking the tea*]: And leave you, Cyprienne? I'd rather die! [*He drinks.*]

CYPRIENNE [*whispering*]: I must speak to you – at once!

ADHÉMAR: In my apartment?

CYPRIENNE [*quickly*]: No, of course not! Later! I can't say now!

ADHÉMAR: Why not?

CYPRIENNE: No! It'll have to be here! I'll give you a signal!

ADHÉMAR: But . . .

CYPRIENNE: Ssh! They're looking at us! [*Aloud*] Monsieur de Clavignac, will you have some tea?

[CLAVIGNAC *and* DES PRUNELLES *move forward right.* MADAME DE BRIONNE *picks up a copy of* La Vie Parisienne *from the little table and moves back-stage glancing through it.*]

ADHÉMAR [*alone, front left, drinking his tea. To himself*]: Refuse the job? I'm not such a fool! Everything's settled. I just can't wait to get away.

BASTIEN [*at the door, announcing*]: Mademoiselle de Lusignan.

[MADEMOISELLE DE LUSIGNAN *enters.*]

CLAVIGNAC [*to* DES PRUNELLES]: Is she still on the shelf?

DES PRUNELLES: More and more – unfortunately!

CYPRIENNE [*going to meet* MADEMOISELLE DE LUSIGNAN]: And here's our neighbour. How nice to see you, my dear. [*She leads her to the chair near the table behind the sofa right and stays talking to* BAFOURDIN.]

MADEMOISELLE DE LUSIGNAN: Monsieur de Gratignan, isn't it?

ADHÉMAR: Er – pardon?

MADEMOISELLE DE LUSIGNAN [*moving in front of the table and speaking as she goes over to him*]: I thought it was! I often see you running along beneath my window. I call out good day to you but you never hear me. You run so quickly. [*Going to* DES PRUNELLES *and shaking hands with him*] I always say to myself: But, of course, he's going to see his cousin, Madame des Prunelles! [*She goes and sits in the wing chair, right of the table.*]

CLAVIGNAC [*softly, to* DES PRUNELLES]: I see what you mean!

CYPRIENNE [*quickly to* BAFOURDIN, *to change the conversation*]: Shan't we be seeing Madame Bafourdin?

BAFOURDIN: She has been obliged to keep to her room. A slight indisposition.

MADAME DE BRIONNE [*coming forward, holding* La Vie Parisienne *and sitting on the pouf after having moved it a little to the right with the help of* CLAVIGNAC]: I see they're voting on this famous Divorce Bill today.

ADHÉMAR: They certainly are!

DES PRUNELLES [*to* CLAVIGNAC]: Here it comes!

[*He moves and sits in armchair extreme right.* CLAVIGNAC *sits on chair near his armchair and between him and* MADAME DE BRIONNE.]

CYPRIENNE [*behind table right, serving tea to* MADEMOISELLE LUSIGNAN]: And it's about time too!

MADEMOISELLE DE LUSIGNAN: You think they'll pass it?

CYPRIENNE: If they've any sense they will.

BAFOURDIN: It appears to be the wish of the country!

CYPRIENNE: Oh, undoubtedly it is!

ADHÉMAR [*approaching the table*]: All the men are certainly for it.

CYPRIENNE *and* MADAME DE BRIONNE: And all the women!

CLAVIGNAC [*to* MADAME DE BRIONNE, *who is still looking at* La Vie Parisienne]: What about you? What good will it be to a widow?

MADAME DE BRIONNE [*laughing*]: Well, for one thing, it'll put more husbands on the market! I'd have more choice!

BASTIEN [*at the door, announcing*]: Madame de Valfontaine!

[MADAME DE VALFONTAINE *enters.* DES PRUNELLES *and* CLAVIGNAC *rise to bow to her and resume their seats.*]

CYPRIENNE [*going to her and leading her front left*]: And I'm quite sure Clarisse is for it as well!

MADAME DE VALFONTAINE [*shaking hands with her, waving her hand to* ADHÉMAR *and going in front of the table to shake hands with* MADAME DE BRIONNE]: For what?

CYPRIENNE: For the Divorce Bill! [*She pushes the armchair left, leaving a wide passage between it and the table.*]

MADAME DE VALFONTAINE: What! That terrible thing?

[*She shakes hands with* ADHÉMAR.]

ALL [*in surprise*]: Oh?

CLAVIGNAC [*to* DES PRUNELLES]: What's this?

DES PRUNELLES [*whispering*]: She gets on all right without it.

CLAVIGNAC [*whispering*]: You don't say!

CYPRIENNE [*offering her the armchair left*]: So your ladyship is against it?

MADAME DE VALFONTAINE [*sitting, while* CYPRIENNE *pours her tea*]: The whole idea is quite impossible. If people know they're married for ever, they resign themselves – they make concessions. But give them the hope of a divorce – and they'd do their best to break up their marriages! It would be the end of marriage! Completely!

MADEMOISELLE DE LUSIGNAN: All the better!

ALL: Oh, Mademoiselle!

[CYPRIENNE *brings tea to* MADAME DE VALFONTAINE *and* ADHÉMAR *tries to hold her hand behind the armchair.*]

MADEMOISELLE DE LUSIGNAN [*noticing this*]: We would be spared some of the horrors that marriage flaunts before our very eyes!

[ADHÉMAR *and* CYPRIENNE *separate quickly.* CYPRIENNE *moves back centre and leans on the back of the sofa, between* BAFOURDIN *and* MADEMOISELLE DE LUSIGNAN, *listening to what follows.*]

MADAME DE VALFONTAINE [*in a whisper, to* ADHÉMAR, *who looks away extreme left*]: He's too sharp for that!

BAFOURDIN [*rising from his chair*]: I beg your pardon, Madame, but in my opinion, divorce will encourage, not discourage, marriage, by offering a way out of it. [*He sits again.*]

CLAVIGNAC: Of course! Marriage is nothing but a cul-de-sac – a blind-alley – a dead-end. Divorce would provide an exit!

MADEMOISELLE DE LUSIGNAN: You're quite right. I agree absolutely!

BAFOURDIN [*sententiously*]: As would all thinking people!

MADEMOISELLE DE LUSIGNAN [*spitefully*]: Monsieur des Prunelles, in his corner there, is taking care to say nothing!

[*Everybody looks at* DES PRUNELLES.]

DES PRUNELLES: Oh, me! In principle I'm against divorce.

ALL: [*surprised*]: Oh?

DES PRUNELLES: But, in practice, I think it excellent.

CLAVIGNAC, ADHÉMAR, BAFOURDIN: Just like everyone!

ADHÉMAR: D'you know what I think is so good about divorce?

ALL: What?

ADHÉMAR: It will lessen the number of murders! As things are, unfortunate young men can't forget themselves with unhappy young wives without everybody shouting to the husbands: 'Kill them!' As things are, the poor husbands have no other way out. Why not give them divorce as the way out?

CLAVIGNAC: And then you'd have nothing more to fear!

ADHÉMAR: That's right! I'd have nothing . . . [*correcting himself*] the unfortunate young men would have nothing more to fear!

CLAVIGNAC: And the husband would have only to throw his wife into your arms to get his revenge.

[CYPRIENNE *goes towards* CLAVIGNAC. ADHÉMAR *moves away towards* MADAME DE VALFONTAINE.]

CYPRIENNE [*to* CLAVIGNAC]: Revenge? Did you say revenge? Revenge for what, may I ask?

DES PRUNELLES [*rising and speaking to* CYPRIENNE *over the head of the seated* CLAVIGNAC]: For the crime, Madame. For the crime this wife has committed!

CYPRIENNE: Crime?

DES PRUNELLES: Mistake, indiscretion – if that's how you'd rather think of it.

CYPRIENNE: Mistake? But with divorce, Monsieur, there won't be mistakes any longer. Divorce will rectify them.

CLAVIGNAC [*slipping out from between them and moving away*]: Of course, that's one way of looking at it . . .

DES PRUNELLES [*to* CYPRIENNE *as she moves away, moving after her*]: And the husband's honour, Madame?

CYPRIENNE [*to* DES PRUNELLES, *over the head of* MADAME DE BRIONNE]: Why, divorce restores his honour to him, Monsieur. Intact and as good as new! So what has he to complain about?

ADHÉMAR [*supporting her*]: A very good point!

[MADAME DE BRIONNE *gets up discreetly and moves away towards* CLAVIGNAC *back right.*]

CYPRIENNE [*taking up position centre-stage*]: Naturally, I understand that any decent woman, chained forever in marriage, has to stamp upon any passion she may feel rising in her heart . . . [*Addressing herself to* ADHÉMAR] 'No!' she has to say, 'I will not yield! For if we were discovered, it would mean scandal, dishonour, perhaps death itself!' . . . But with divorce . . . [*Gaily*] she would be able to say: [*addressing herself to* DES PRUNELLES] 'Well, Monsieur, I have deceived you. So let's get a divorce and that'll be the end of it.' Isn't that more honest – more frank – more straightforward? What more could anyone want?

DES PRUNELLES [*going to her*]: Exactly! No more scruples, no more hesitations! A fine morality that would be!

CYPRIENNE: Oh, now really, Monsieur, don't you see that the morality of divorce is precisely the freedom it gives to remedy all mistakes and indiscretions.

DES PRUNELLES [*exasperated*]: Which it encourages people to commit!

CLAVIGNAC *and* MADAME DE BRIONNE: Oh, come now, please! Calm yourselves! Calm down!

[*Everybody gets up.* MADAME DE BRIONNE, MADEMOISELLE DE LUSIGNAN *and* MADAME DE VALFONTAINE *move back-stage and take farewell of* CYPRIENNE *who goes with them to the door.* BAFOURDIN *goes back-stage to get his hat.* CLAVIGNAC, *right, tries to calm* DES PRUNELLES.]

ADHÉMAR [*to himself, coming forward centre*]: Perfect! If that's all that's stopping her, she's as good as mine! [*Aloud*] And to think – while we've been talking about it, this Divorce Bill may have already been voted in.

MADAME DE VALFONTAINE: Or out!

BAFOURDIN [*behind the sofa*]: Either way, we shan't know the results until late this evening.

ADHÉMAR: Oh, no. [*Looking at his watch*] We can know in less than an hour.

ALL: An hour?

ADHÉMAR [*going behind the table, he takes a piece of writing paper and begins writing*]: Yes. I have a journalist friend who has contacts. I'll send him a telegram to let us know as soon as the news is out. [*He picks up the paper on which he has written.*]

THE FOUR WOMEN: Oh, then hurry! Yes, run with it quickly!

ADHÉMAR: I'll go and send it at once. [*He picks up his cane and hat.*]

CYPRIENNE [*accompanying him to door, back*]: And let us know the result.

ADHÉMAR: Immediately! [*He goes out.*]

MADEMOISELLE DE LUSIGNAN [*crossing to* BAFOURDIN *who is preparing to leave*]: And is Madame Bafourdin against divorce, my dear Monsieur?

BAFOURDIN [*drily*]: Yes, Mademoiselle. And against remaining unmarried.

MADEMOISELLE DE LUSIGNAN [*to herself*]: Insolence!

MADAME DE VALFONTAINE [*to* CYPRIENNE]: Good-bye, my sweet.

CYPRIENNE: Good-bye.

BAFOURDIN [*taking his leave*]: Mesdames ... [*He goes out with* MADAME DE VALFONTAINE.]

MADEMOISELLE DE LUSIGNAN [*coming forward between table*

and sofa, to MADAME DE BRIONNE]: Are you coming, my dear?

MADAME DE BRIONNE: Not just yet, my dear.

MADEMOISELLE DE LUSIGNAN: Ah, you are too modest. You dread to think of the compliments I would pay you if you left before me.

MADAME DE BRIONNE [*laughing*]: No, it's the opposite I dread! [*She moves upstage above the sofa*] Would you care to accept a lift in my carriage?

MADEMOISELLE DE LUSIGNAN: With pleasure. [*To herself*] The silly fool!

MADAME DE BRIONNE [*going to* CYPRIENNE *who has moved back right*]: Hard luck, my dear. It's you she'll be running down to me.

CYPRIENNE: Let her.

MADAME DE BRIONNE [*laughing*]: She will, don't worry!

[*She nods to* DES PRUNELLES *and* CLAVIGNAC *and goes out with* MADEMOISELLE DE LUSIGNAN. JOSÉPHA *enters left with a tray on which she begins collecting the cups.*]

CYPRIENNE [*coming forward right*]: Will you stay to dinner, Monsieur Clavignac?

CLAVIGNAC: I regret it's impossible, dear Madame. I have to dine with some friends.

CYPRIENNE: Another time then.

[BASTIEN *enters from room back with* DES PRUNELLES'*s hat and overcoat.*]

Bastien, have the carriage brought round. I'm going out.

[*She passes in front of the table and goes to the mantelpiece to collect the books and brochures.*]

BASTIEN: Yes, Madame.

DES PRUNELLES [*his overcoat over his arm, to* CLAVIGNAC]: Will you come with me?

CLAVIGNAC: Where to?

DES PRUNELLES: My club.

CLAVIGNAC: Certainly.

CYPRIENNE: Well ... if I don't see you again ... have a good journey! [*She holds out her hand to* CLAVIGNAC.]

CLAVIGNAC: Thank you, Madame.

[CYPRIENNE *goes into her room.*]

DES PRUNELLES: [*passing in front of* CLAVIGNAC *and turning towards him as soon as* CYPRIENNE *has closed her door. Brusquely*] You see what she's up to?

CLAVIGNAC: No, not really.

DES PRUNELLES [*lowering his voice*]: She said she's going out. So I said I was. Because she's not going out. Adhémar's waiting across the road for her signal. [*He moves right.*] But I won't have gone out either – and when she gives her signal – he'll walk right into my little trap. [*He turns a switch, with a little click, on the garden door.*] Come into my room.

[*He moves back behind the sofa.* CLAVIGNAC *follows, picking up his hat.*]

CLAVIGNAC: And to think that probably every married couple . . .

DES PRUNELLES: Ssh! She'll be listening! [*Loudly*] Would you like a cigar?

CLAVIGNAC [*loudly*]: Yes, I'll have one for the street!

DES PRUNELLES [*loudly*]: Let's go, then!

CLAVIGNAC: Let us go!

[*Music. They move back-stage and pretend to go out left, but in the hall* DES PRUNELLES *stops* CLAVIGNAC, *pushes him right into his room and shuts the door.* CYPRIENNE *comes out of her room very cautiously, goes back-stage and having made sure they have gone, she crosses to the window without saying a word and pulls down the blind.*]

CYPRIENNE: The signal! [*She moves forward slowly front-stage.*] I've been puzzling over this problem long enough – how to respect my marriage vows – and how to forget them. And now I've solved it! It's been difficult but I've done it! I won't see Adhémar any more until the Divorce Bill is passed. That takes care of my marriage vows. And then . . . Here he comes!

ADHÉMAR [*to himself, entering stealthily by the garden door*]: The telegram's on its way! [*Aloud, seeing* CYPRIENNE] Are you alone?

CYPRIENNE: Alone! He's at his club. Quickly! Shut the door!

ADHÉMAR: Oh, Cyprienne!

[*He goes towards her, letting the door close itself behind him. Immediately an electric bell begins ringing and continues throughout the rest of the scene.* ADHÉMAR *stops, astonished*]

What the – ?

CYPRIENNE: Who is it? Who's ringing?

ADHÉMAR: How the devil do I know?

CYPRIENNE [*frightened*]: Why doesn't it stop?

ADHÉMAR: Perhaps it's the telegraph boy?

CYPRIENNE: Oh, make it stop! Make it stop!

ADHÉMAR [*bewildered*]: That's what I was going to say!

CYPRIENNE [*running to the door*]: It started when the door closed. It's the door, can't you see?

ADHÉMAR [*completely bewildered*]: The door?

CYPRIENNE: Oh! Oh! [*She moves back behind the sofa.*]

ADHÉMAR [*going to the garden door and trying to open it*]: Hell! It won't open!

CYPRIENNE: It's locked!

JOSÉPHA [*entering from* CYPRIENNE*'s room*]: Did you ring, Madame?

CYPRIENNE [*losing control of herself*]: It's not me! It's my husband!

[*Another bell begins ringing and adds to the confusion.*]

A trap! It's a trap! We're lost! Run! Run!

ADHÉMAR [*frantically, running past her*]: But where?

CYPRIENNE *and* JOSÉPHA [*pointing to the hall*]: That way!

ADHÉMAR [*running back again*]: Which way? Which way?

CYPRIENNE *and* JOSÉPHA: The hall! The hall!

[ADHÉMAR *dashes between the table and the armchair, followed by* CYPRIENNE. *Just as he is reaching the hall,* DES PRUNELLES *opens the door of his room which gives on to the hall, jumps in front of him and cuts off his escape.*]

CYPRIENNE: Too late!

[*Terrified,* ADHÉMAR *backs right centre.* DES PRUNELLES *advances on him menacingly.* ADHÉMAR *runs left stage.* DES PRUNELLES *goes to the garden door right, turns the switch and the bell stops ringing.*]

ADHÉMAR [*to himself*]: Caught!

DES PRUNELLES [*to* JOSÉPHA]: Leave us.

JOSÉPHA [*to herself*]: Hard luck, Madame! [*She goes out left into* CYPRIENNE*'s room.*]

DES PRUNELLES [*to* ADHÉMAR]: We will talk later. You were just about to leave, I think?

ADHÉMAR [*stunned*]: Yes, I think so ... yes, I think I was ... but ... which way?

DES PRUNELLES [*opening the garden door*]: This way.

ADHÉMAR [*hesitating*]: Without any music?

DES PRUNELLES: Without music.

ADHÉMAR [*bowing*]: Many thanks! [*He bolts out through the door.*]

DES PRUNELLES [*closing the door quickly*]: Until later!

CYPRIENNE [*to herself, behind armchair left*]: It's come! The crisis! This is it!

DES PRUNELLES [*moving the armchair from the table and motioning to his wife to sit in it*]: And now, if you don't mind, we two will have a little talk. Perhaps you are wondering how I found you were still seeing your cousin Adhémar after I had forbidden it?

CYPRIENNE [*seated*]: Not at all.

DES PRUNELLES: No? Well, I'll tell you all the same. [*Moving small chair in front of table and sitting*] Yesterday evening I was at the club. Adhémar came in. There was some laughter and some rather unpleasant jokes. The cause of this hilarity was a mere trifle – a woollen thread was hanging from the tail of his coat. Adhémar was about to remove the object in question when he noticed me. He immediately looked embarrassed, threw the bit of wool on to the floor, and said very loudly and with too much emphasis: 'It's easy to see I've been dining with my sister!' Then he slipped out quickly. I didn't say anything. I kept my eye on that piece of wool on the carpet. When nobody was looking, I picked it up. And here it is!

[CYPRIENNE *moves in her chair.*]

Yes, a mottled-pink colour, isn't it? [*He gets up and takes a skein of wool from the sewing basket on the small table near the window.*] When I got back here, I went straight to your basket and I found this skein of wool. [*He comes back to the table centre, with the skein in one hand and the bit of wool in the other.*] I compare. [*He holds them both out.*] And the similarity speaks so loudly that I need say no more.

CYPRIENNE [*coldly*]: And so, Monsieur?

DES PRUNELLES: So – since Adhémar has been here, have the goodness to tell me why you receive him behind my back? What excuse or justification have you for such a thing? I've not been a bad husband to you. I'm not brutal, uncouth, nor miserly, nor even unduly fussy. I've given you as easy and pleasant a life as I can. I never lose my temper. I've simple tastes. I lead a regular life – that was what I married you for. I'm not exactly handsome – but I think I possess a certain air of distinction. [*He sits again.*] I am not exactly passionate by nature, but now and then I do feel the tender emotion quite strongly – in fact, without flattering myself, I have the presumption to believe I make you as happy as any woman can be!

CYPRIENNE [*to herself, with a bitter little laugh*]: Ha, ha, ha!

DES PRUNELLES: I beg your pardon?

CYPRIENNE: I was waiting for that! It makes everything perfect! 'As happy as any woman can be!' But how do I know that, Monsieur? You say so! But how happy *can* a woman be? How can *I* find that out? When? Where? With whom?

DES PRUNELLES: But –

CYPRIENNE: When you tell your friends I'm all a woman should be – you are comparing me with others. You have standards of comparison. But where are my standards of comparison? – so that I can proclaim *you're* all a man should be?

DES PRUNELLES: I –

CYPRIENNE: No, it's outrageous – this smugness! Oh, you've certainly arranged things to suit yourselves, you men! It's perfect, the society you've created – perfect for yourselves! When you're young you swagger about – little lords of creation. Mama says to you: 'Have fun, my dear, it's proper at your age.' Papa says to you: 'Sow a few wild oats, lad, it's good for your health!' So you skip and caper from blonde to brunette to redhead. Then when you've had enough, when you're worn-out, exhausted and can't keep it up any longer – oh, then it's: 'If only I were married!' So they throw you into the arms of some poor trembling girl, completely naïve, always chaperoned by her mother, knowing nothing of life or of love, except what she tries to guess for herself. And you say to her as you hold her weakly in your exhausted arms: 'Aren't you lucky to have found an experienced lover like me? Nobody could make love to you better than I do!' And the poor girl, finding the embrace a little slack, sighs to herself: 'What? Is this all it is? And I'd thought . . . How strange! Ah, well!' The unsophisticated ones believe it, the indifferent ones resign themselves. [*She gets up.*]

But the woman, the real woman, like me, Monsieur, says to herself: 'Oh, no! There is better than this! It's not for this that people go mad, and poison and kill, it's not for this that Romeo risked his life. If this was all, the game wouldn't be worth the candle! There must be something else, something far, far better!' And this woman searches, questions, studies, inquires, and after thorough investigation she is in a position to say to you bluntly: [*she hits him on the shoulder*] 'You're a humbug! And I've been robbed!'

DES PRUNELLES [*getting up*]: Madame!

CYPRIENNE [*moving right*]: I've been robbed, Monsieur! In plain words, I've been robbed! What's more, that's what's supposed to happen. It's the same everywhere. Marriage – for you disabled old men, it's nothing but retirement on a pension – while for us it's the beginning of a battle, of a campaign! [*Sitting on the pouf*] When I was at school, what did I used to dream of? A marriage which reached the very heights of passion! A husband who was a knight-at-arms, and at the same time, my lover! I imagined you young, handsome, slim, elegant. Tender yet menacing! Submissive yet despotic! Sometimes kissing my feet in submission – at other times leaping on me like a tiger, and, with terrible embraces, bruising my quivering flesh! But at last there should come exquisite delight! Instead of that, nothing! Just nothing! Just a dreary solitude, a swamp, a pool of flat, stagnant water! Just the interminable tick-tock of the family cuckoo-clock, the monotonous bubbling of the daily stew! Never any spice, never any sauce! Never anything to tempt the appetite! And like somebody restricted to a diet of slops, I cry out to you: 'In the name of heaven, Monsieur, I'm young, I'm healthy, I beg you – some truffles, some champagne, some spices!' And your reply is: 'Oh, no! Some more slops, please, a little gruel – and some spinach!' [*She throws herself into the armchair extreme right.*]

DES PRUNELLES: I just don't know what you want me to do. I've done everything possible –

CYPRIENNE [*half-rising, then falling back with her face buried in the back of the armchair*]: Aaah! Mama!

DES PRUNELLES [*going to her*]: Do you really think – just to add a bit of spice to your life – I'm going to disguise myself as a Calabrian brigand and climb through your window?

CYPRIENNE: Oh, no, of course not! That's the sort of thing you did for your mistresses when you were young – and now you've had enough of that!

DES PRUNELLES: Me?

CYPRIENNE: What about that cupboard? The one Monsieur Bafourdin accidentally locked you in? In his wife's bedroom? You nearly suffocated!

DES PRUNELLES: How d'you know –

CYPRIENNE: And what about the pretty Mademoiselle Brignois – whom you used to visit disguised as a milliner?

DES PRUNELLES: But all that was long ago!

CYPRIENNE [*rising and moving left*]: What passion! What romance! What adventure! You had it all!

DES PRUNELLES [*modestly*]: Oh, good heavens, really ...!

CYPRIENNE: But me, Monsieur! What about me? When have I been able to experience things like that? Never! Except from what I'm told!

DES PRUNELLES: I'm glad to hear it!

CYPRIENNE: Thanks to this – this obsolete system – which represses us when we're young – oppresses us when we're married – and suppresses us when we're old!

DES PRUNELLES: Well, what is it you want it to do?

CYPRIENNE: What do I want, Monsieur? I want every young girl to have the same freedom as every young man. And when she's experienced something of life, I want her to be able to retire like you – on a pension – into marriage. And then – and only then – will you have a faithful, virtuous wife. Because she will no longer be burning to satisfy her unsatisfied curiosity!

DES PRUNELLES: Where the devil did you pick up such ideas?

CYPRIENNE: From thinking, Monsieur, and from reading. [*Going to the table left*] Read this latest book by –

DES PRUNELLES: God forbid! Do you really believe that any man would be mad enough to marry a woman like that?

CYPRIENNE [*behind the armchair, her hands on the back*]: There are plenty of women mad enough to marry men like that!

DES PRUNELLES [*in front of table*]: But damn it all – between a man and a woman – there's a devil of a difference.

CYPRIENNE: Yes! Marriage!

DES PRUNELLES: Oh, now look here . . .

CYPRIENNE: You look here! You're for things as they are! I'm for progress! We shall never agree – so let's get back to the point at issue!

DES PRUNELLES: Exactly! Adhémar!

CYPRIENNE: Yes, Adhémar!

DES PRUNELLES: What may your plans be in that direction?

CYPRIENNE: I was about to tell him he need hope for nothing – when you made your absurd appearance.

DES PRUNELLES: I am sorry.

CYPRIENNE: You wouldn't be a husband if you didn't do things you were sorry for.

DES PRUNELLES: Well, what happens next?

CYPRIENNE: Monsieur, I will be frank.

DES PRUNELLES: Oh, please – do!

CYPRIENNE: With most women, what you've just done would have meant the end of your marriage.

DES PRUNELLES: Now, wait a minute!

CYPRIENNE: But I am not like most women – unfortunately. Ever since I was a child, I've had thousands of false notions and absurd prejudices instilled into me. And I can't overcome them even now. Amongst these superstitions, I am weak enough to attach some importance to the vow of fidelity I made to you when we were married. Absurd or not, that vow was made. I intend to keep it.

DES PRUNELLES: That's something!

CYPRIENNE: No matter what it costs me.

DES PRUNELLES: Never mind that! Just keep it!

CYPRIENNE: But it's only fair to warn you that my fidelity is only of a temporary and transitory nature.

DES PRUNELLES: What?

CYPRIENNE: If this Divorce Bill is voted in – watch out!

DES PRUNELLES: Ah!

CYPRIENNE: Don't think I'm such a fool as not to profit by the means of escape that the law will offer me. Divorce will be a remedy for everything!

DES PRUNELLES: Yes, I know all that!

CYPRIENNE: So don't say you weren't warned!

DES PRUNELLES: That's as may be. In the meantime, Adhémar's out!

CYPRIENNE: Until the new dispensation, yes.

DES PRUNELLES: Until the new dispensation – or I'll cut his ears off.

CYPRIENNE: Agreed!

DES PRUNELLES: Done!

CYPRIENNE: Does that close the point at issue?

DES PRUNELLES: Completely.

CYPRIENNE: Then, if you don't mind, I will respectfully withdraw.

DES PRUNELLES [*moving back-stage right*]: Just as you please.

CYPRIENNE [*moving left*]: Nothing could please me more.

DES PRUNELLES [*at the door of his study, bowing*]: Madame!

CYPRIENNE [*at her door, bowing*]: Monsieur!

[*They each go into their rooms, slamming their doors behind them violently. As soon as they have gone,* ADHÉMAR *opens the garden door very gently. He then enters without closing the door for fear the bell begins ringing again. He stands half in the room, holding the door open with his hand as* JOSÉPHA *enters backstage and goes towards the door of her mistress's room.*]

ADHÉMAR [*calling to her in a whisper*]: Josépha!

JOSÉPHA [*starting*]: Oh!

ADHÉMAR [*still whispering*]: Be quiet!

JOSÉPHA [*whispering, frightened*]: But the bell! The door!

ADHÉMAR: It only rings when it's closed. I'll hold it. Where is your mistress?

JOSEPHA: In her room.

ADHÉMAR: Tell her to come!

JOSÉPHA: But –

ADHÉMAR: Quickly! It's urgent! Do as you're told!

JOSÉPHA: All right, all right! [*She goes into* CYPRIENNE*'s room left.*]

ADHÉMAR [*alone, keeping the door open with his hand or his foot*]: So, my crafty husband, I can play your little game with electric wires, as well as you. I've just sent another telegram to my friend Dumoulin and told him what answer I want him to send – as a practical joke on somebody. And what a joke it will be! [*He makes a gesture, the door slips from his grasp, but he grabs it again quickly.*] Dumoulin replied at once. Here it is. [*He pulls a telegram from his pocket.*] This will settle things once and for all. She won't be able to hide behind her scruples now. Now she'll be mine! [*He lets go of the door again and just catches it in time.*] Damn! This thing's a blasted nuisance!

[CYPRIENNE *appears in her doorway but stays there, frightened of being surprised by her husband.*]

CYPRIENNE: You?

ADHÉMAR [*holding the door*]: Me!

CYPRIENNE: Again?

ADHÉMAR: And forever!

CYPRIENNE: But the bell?

ADHÉMAR [*pointing to his foot which is stopping the door from closing*]: No! My foot!

CYPRIENNE [*pointing to the door back-right*]: My husband! Come back later!

ADHÉMAR: Never!

CYPRIENNE: What?

ADHÉMAR: It is you who will come to me!

CYPRIENNE: To you?

ADHÉMAR: What was it you said, my angel? Divorce will be a remedy for everything!

CYPRIENNE: Yes.

ADHÉMAR: When the bill is passed, no woman will hesitate about deceiving her husband?

CYPRIENNE: Yes! If only it could be true!

ADHÉMAR: It is.

CYPRIENNE: What?

ADHÉMAR: It's passed.

CYPRIENNE: The Divorce Bill?

ADHÉMAR: Now the law of the land.

CYPRIENNE: Oh!

ADHÉMAR: See for yourself. [*He holds out the telegram, and to shorten the distance, holds the door back with his cane, while stretching out his other arm full length.*]

CYPRIENNE [*frightened*]: The door!

ADHÉMAR: [*holding the door still, with his cane*]: No! I'm holding it with the cane! Quick! Read it!

CYPRIENNE [*advancing between table and sofa, she seizes the telegram and reads it*]: 'Bill passed. Enormous majority! Dumoulin.' Free!

[DES PRUNELLES'*s voice is heard. Music.*]

Go! Quickly! [*She moves back quickly to her door, leaving the telegram on the table.*]

ADHÉMAR [*back at garden door, about to go*]: Come to my apartment! I'll be waiting!

CYPRIENNE [*at her door, about to go*]: Now?

ADHÉMAR: At once!

CYPRIENNE: But ...

ADHÉMAR: Divorce!

CYPRIENNE: But –

ADHÉMAR: The remedy!

CYPRIENNE Well ...

ADHÉMAR: So you'll come!

CYPRIENNE: Yes! [*She runs into her room.*]

ADHÉMAR [*exultant, running out through garden door*]: Ah!

[*The door closes and the bell begins ringing again.*]

DES PRUNELLES [*opening his door violently and rushing into the room followed by* CLAVIGNAC]: That scoundrel! He was here!

CLAVIGNAC [*bewildered*]: What's the bell ringing for?

DES PRUNELLES [*stopping the bell. The music ceases*]: His funeral!

CLAVIGNAC: Henri!

DES PRUNELLES [*beside himself, coming forward*]: His life! I'll have his life for this!

CLAVIGNAC: Calm yourself!

DES PRUNELLES [*sitting right of the table and banging on the bell*]: Jump in your carriage and take that scoundrel my card! [*He writes quickly*] 'You contemptible villain! One of us is one too many! And that's you!'

CLAVIGNAC [*coming behind him, at the table*]: Take it easy!

DES PRUNELLES: 'That's you!' Where's the ink! I'm blind with rage! Ink! Ink! [*As he feels around for the inkwell, his pen pierces the telegram and so brings it to his notice.*] A telegram?

[JOSÉPHA *and* BASTIEN *enter.*]

[*He reads*] 'Dumoulin to Adhémar' [*He rises and moves right reading the telegram to himself. Then he looks at the garden door and begins to laugh sardonically.*] Ah, ha! The lying hypocrite! What a trick to play! [*He suddenly leaps round with a cry of dismay.*]

[*He runs at* JOSÉPHA *who is standing in front of the door of her mistress's room.*]

CLAVIGNAC *and* THE SERVANTS [*frightened*]: What is it?

DES PRUNELLES [*to* JOSÉPHA, *seizing her by the wrist and pointing anxiously to* CYPRIENNE'*s door*]: Madame? Is she – ?

JOSÉPHA [*terrified*]: Madame is dressing to go out!

DES PRUNELLES [*to himself*]: Thank heaven – just in time! She was going to him! [*To* JOSÉPHA] Get out of here, you!

[JOSÉPHA *runs out back quickly.* BASTIEN *makes to follow her.*]

You, stay where you are!

[BASTIEN *stops.* DES PRUNELLES *moves back left to the table and faces the audience.*]

CLAVIGNAC [*completely bewildered*]: He's having a fit!

DES PRUNELLES [*banging his forehead as if inspired, he tears up the letter and begins to write another, still standing*]: No! This will be better! 'My dear cousin, would you be so kind as to come over and have a little chat with me?' [*He folds the letter and puts it in the envelope already prepared.*] 'I have some very friendly propositions to put to you.'

CLAVIGNAC [*looking at him in blank dismay*]: He needs a cold shower!

DES PRUNELLES [*handing him the telegram*]: Here, read that. [*Holding out the letter to* BASTIEN] Bastien! Take this to Monsieur Adhémar! At once!

[BASTIEN *goes out.*]

CLAVIGNAC [*having read the telegram, seizing his hat*]: The Divorce Bill passed! I must run and tell my lawyer!

DES PRUNELLES: And the whole town!

CLAVIGNAC: Yes, everybody! Count on me! [*He runs on out back.*]

DES PRUNELLES [*coldly, lighting a cigarette, and throwing a look at* CYPRIENNE'*s door, left*]: Now, a cigarette – and then for a nice little game of cat-and-mouse!

[CURTAIN]

ACT TWO

The scene is the same. The flowers have been changed. The table centre is now perpendicular to the audience. To the left of the table, the sofa is now placed slantingly towards the audience. To the left of the sofa is a work-table and behind it, a small chair. Right of the centre table is the armchair which was on the left in the first act. Under the table is the stool. On the table are pen, ink, stamps and some brochures. The pouf is in front of the window. The rest is the same as Act One. The venetian blind is raised.

When the curtain rises JOSÉPHA *is putting* CYPRIENNE*'s coat on the chair behind the work-table. Then she moves to door left and stands in the threshold brushing* CYPRIENNE*'s hat.* BASTIEN *enters, back, with the newspapers on a tray.*

JOSÉPHA [*to* BASTIEN]: And about time, too! Why can't you get a move on?

BASTIEN: Yes, my sweet!

JOSÉPHA: Is the carriage ready?

BASTIEN: What carriage?

JOSÉPHA: For Madame!

BASTIEN: I've just been out on an errand for Monsieur, so how do I know? I'll ask about it as soon as I've seen Monsieur.

JOSÉPHA: No – quicker than that! [*She goes into* CYPRIENNE*'s room, left.*]

BASTIEN: Here he is!

[DES PRUNELLES *enters from his study.*]

BASTIEN [*behind the table*]: Here are Monsieur's newspapers. [*He puts them on the table.*]

DES PRUNELLES: You're back already? Have you been to Monsieur Adhémar's?

BASTIEN: Yes. I've just come back, Monsieur.

DES PRUNELLES: You saw him?

BASTIEN: Yes, Monsieur. I'd no sooner rung the bell than he

opened the door and shouted at me very excitedly: 'At last! It's you!' Perhaps I should add that when he saw it was me, he changed his tune.

DES PRUNELLES: You gave him my letter?

BASTIEN: Which he read twice over, Monsieur.

DES PRUNELLES: And did he give you a reply?

BASTIEN: No, Monsieur. He simply said, a little distantly: 'Tell Monsieur that I shall most certainly come.'

DES PRUNELLES: Good. You may go. [*He picks up the newspapers.*]

JOSÉPHA [*entering left, to* BASTIEN]: What about that carriage? Madame is getting impatient!

BASTIEN: All right! I'll go now.

DES PRUNELLES [*tranquilly, moving right*]: Don't bother. Tell Madame the carriage is not ready.

JOSÉPHA: What?

DES PRUNELLES: I have told the coachman not to harness the horses.

JOSÉPHA [*stupefied*]: What did you say, Monsieur?

DES PRUNELLES: The horses are not well.

JOSÉPHA: Not well?

DES PRUNELLES: That's right. [*To* BASTIEN] So what are you waiting for?

[BASTIEN *goes out, back.*]

JOSÉPHA [*trying to get away, left*]: Yes, of course! Thank you! excuse me! [*To herself*] Things are starting happening! I'd better make myself scarce!

DES PRUNELLES [*opening one of the newspapers*]: What did you say?

JOSÉPHA: Nothing, Monsieur! I was just saying 'Oh, those poor horses!' [*To herself*] Let's get out of here! [*She goes out, left.*]

DES PRUNELLES [*alone*]: So I was right. He was expecting her. That false telegram was simply to get her to make up her mind. So now I shall have the great pleasure of turning the tables on him. [*He sits in armchair right of table and begins reading a newspaper.*]

CYPRIENNE [*off-stage left, exasperatedly*]: Oh, Monsieur did, did he?

JOSÉPHA [*off-stage, left*]: Yes, Madame.

DES PRUNELLES [*to himself*]: Here it comes.

CYPRIENNE [*off-stage, left*]: Monsieur has actually . . .! [*She breaks off into a strident laugh and approaches the door.*] So! Oh, this is going to be very funny!

DES PRUNELLES [*pretending to laugh*]: Yes, here it comes – with a vengeance!

CYPRIENNE [*bursting in from her room, like a bullet, and throwing her hat on a chair in front of the sofa*]: Ah! So there you are, Monsieur! [*Sweeping round the sofa and armchair*] Was it you who forbad my coachman to harness my carriage?

DES PRUNELLES [*calmly, folding the newspaper and rising*]: It was, my dear.

CYPRIENNE: Under the pretext that my horses were ill?

DES PRUNELLES: As you say – under the pretext.

CYPRIENNE: Oh!

DES PRUNELLES: Excuse me a moment, my dear.

[*He puts the newspaper on the table, and goes calmly past the astounded* CYPRIENNE *to close the door left which she has left open. He returns to her, takes her hands and leads her to the sofa. Completely taken aback,* CYPRIENNE *hesitates to sit down. He insists gallantly.*]

There. [*He sits near her.*] This is how we'll chat together from now on – like old friends.

[*She lets him take her hands, in a state of complete stupefaction.*]

Hand in hand – thanks to this little piece of paper. [*He takes the telegram from his pocket and shows it her.*]

CYPRIENNE [*surprised*]: Oh!

DES PRUNELLES [*gaily*]: You've understood me?

CYPRIENNE [*with a cry of joy*]: Divorce?

DES PRUNELLES: Divorce – bless it!

CYPRIENNE [*uneasily*]: But just now, you were saying –

DES PRUNELLES: Just now, my dear child, I didn't dare believe it could happen. But now that it's been passed –

CYPRIENNE: You will consent?

DES PRUNELLES: Of course!

CYPRIENNE: And we'll get a divorce?

DES PRUNELLES: As soon as you please.

CYPRIENNE [*kissing him madly*]: Oh, you're wonderful! You're simply marvellous! Oh, how I love you! [*She stops.*] Are you serious? You mean it? You're not just leading me on for a joke? We'll get a divorce? You swear it?

DES PRUNELLES: You have my word!

CYPRIENNE: Oh, my darling! Oh, I'm so happy! But how?

DES PRUNELLES: That will be up to us, my dear. But we can decide all that later. At the moment, let's just sit and surrender ourselves to the joy of a separation so frank and forthright.

CYPRIENNE: And so friendly!

DES PRUNELLES: So tender!

CYPRIENNE: It's true! I've never felt I loved you so much! [*She takes his head between her hands and kisses him.*]

DES PRUNELLES [*kissing her in the same way*]: And it's all so simple! We don't get on together any more – so we part good friends. Instead of living a cat-and-dog life, forever quarrelling, forever making each other's life a misery . . .

CYPRIENNE [*laughing*]: Did you really think you made my life a misery?

DES PRUNELLES [*laughing also*]: I knew all your little tricks! Yes, we can laugh at it all now, can't we?

CYPRIENNE [*gaily*]: Yes, it seems all very funny now! Did you spy on me very much, you big bully? Did you? [*She pinches his chin.*]

DES PRUNELLES [*pinching her chin*]: Not enough!

CYPRIENNE [*pinching his chin*]: Is that so! And what about the electric bell?

DES PRUNELLES [*pinching her chin*]: Yes, my little bell found out quite enough, didn't it?

CYPRIENNE [*pinching his chin*]: The funniest part of it is – I actually heard you last night.

DES PRUNELLES [*pinching her chin*]: You didn't!

CYPRIENNE [*pinching his chin*]: Yes, I did! I said to myself what on earth's he up to in the conservatory?

DES PRUNELLES [*pinching her chin*]: But I was trying to be so quiet!

CYPRIENNE: I've good ears – and it gave me a nightmare.

DES PRUNELLES [*pinching her chin*]: Rubbish!

CYPRIENNE: It did! I dreamed about daggers and poison! I saw you sharpening your sword!

DES PRUNELLES [*laughing*]: No!

CYPRIENNE [*bursting out laughing*]: Wasn't I silly?

DES PRUNELLES: Well, if you want to know, there was something that stopped me sleeping as well.

CYPRIENNE: What?

DES PRUNELLES: How the devil Adhémar always knew when I'd be out.

CYPRIENNE [*laughing, then stopping*]: You won't be angry?

DES PRUNELLES: Of course not.

CYPRIENNE: Sure?

DES PRUNELLES: Of course! Why should I be now?

CYPRIENNE: Well – we had a signal.

DES PRUNELLES: Yes, but what? How? Where?

CYPRIENNE: Here.

DES PRUNELLES: Here?

CYPRIENNE: Yes! Go on, guess!

DES PRUNELLES [*pointing*]: From the window?

CYPRIENNE: Naturally.

DES PRUNELLES: A large piece of paper – and you wrote on it with charcoal? [*He makes gestures writing large letters.*]

CYPRIENNE [*laughing*]: Oh, that would take too long!

DES PRUNELLES: A candle, then? [*He makes gestures of raising and lowering a candle.*]

CYPRIENNE [*laughing*]: Oh, you'll never guess! I'd better tell you. The Venetian blind! [*She gets up, runs to the window right, and undoes the cord which holds the blind.*]

DES PRUNELLES: But how?

CYPRIENNE: Look! That means: he's here. [*She lowers it half-way.*] This means: he's going out. [*She lowers it all the way.*] He's gone out!

DES PRUNELLES: Charming! But dangerous! A servant could have –

CYPRIENNE [*interrupting him, coming back to the table*]: No, nobody touches that except Josépha and me.

DES PRUNELLES: Ah! Josépha is in it?

CYPRIENNE: Of course!

DES PRUNELLES: Good for her! I thought she was. And what about the handsome Adhémar? I say handsome to please you – between ourselves, and this is the only criticism I'll make – Adhémar isn't all that attractive, is he?

CYPRIENNE [*leaning over the back of the armchair*]: Oh, he's a nice boy!

DES PRUNELLES: Maybe – but you've got to admit, damn it, he's no Don Juan.

CYPRIENNE: What would I do with a Don Juan?

DES PRUNELLES: That's true.

CYPRIENNE [*moving behind armchair*]: Anyway, there's not much choice round here. One has to be content with what one can find. It gets so boring.

DES PRUNELLES: Still – you're really crazy over him?

CYPRIENNE: Crazy? Oh, no, there's no need to exaggerate.

DES PRUNELLES [*rising and going to her*]: Tell me about it a little. Now we've no longer anything to hide from each other.

CYPRIENNE: What good would that do?

DES PRUNELLES [*taking her hand*]: If we're going to get a divorce, it's best to get everything cleared up, so we know where we are, isn't it?

CYPRIENNE: Oh, yes – of course!

DES PRUNELLES: This morning, when you said you attached some importance to your vow of fidelity – you were just joking, were you?

CYPRIENNE: No, I wasn't!

DES PRUNELLES: Oh, come, we've agreed to speak plainly. You can't expect me to believe that?

CYPRIENNE: I do!

DES PRUNELLES: You mean you never –

CYPRIENNE: Never!

DES PRUNELLES: Not even – ?

CYPRIENNE [*sitting in armchair*]: On my word of honour!

DES PRUNELLES: In all the three months it's lasted?

CYPRIENNE: Four months!

DES PRUNELLES [*taking the stool from under the table*]: Four? I thought –

CYPRIENNE: Four!

DES PRUNELLES [*sitting on the stool in front of the table quite near her*]: For four whole months you've done nothing but – pick daisies together?

CYPRIENNE: Oh, my dear, if you only knew how difficult it's all been. Everybody watching you ... never a chance to be alone.

DES PRUNELLES: Good! But at least you had a little cuddle in the carriage with him?

CYPRIENNE: Never! And not for want of trying.

DES PRUNELLES: And you never went to his apartment?

CYPRIENNE: Absolutely never! Word of honour! I was going there now – after that telegram – for the first time. But I'd warned you about that.

DES PRUNELLES: But you must have met each other somewhere – besides here?

CYPRIENNE: Oh, yes, now and then – in courtyards, side streets, museums, art-galleries ...

DES PRUNELLES: And in all those places you did nothing but talk to each other?

CYPRIENNE: Nothing!

DES PRUNELLES: Not even the tiniest little kiss?

CYPRIENNE: Ah, yes!

DES PRUNELLES: Ah!

CYPRIENNE: But that's nothing serious! I thought you were talking about something – more serious!

DES PRUNELLES: Well?

CYPRIENNE [*laughing*]: Why d'you want to know all these things now?

DES PRUNELLES: It amuses me.

CYPRIENNE [*gaily, moving the armchair a little forward*]: All right, then, here you are! Kiss number one was four months ago. It was on my shoulder – while I was putting on my cloak at the Mayor's Ball ...

DES PRUNELLES: That's one, then.

CYPRIENNE: Number two was this summer ... [*She stops.*] You're sure this isn't annoying you?

DES PRUNELLES: Can't you see it isn't?

CYPRIENNE: Number two this summer was on my arm ... he even bit me!

DES PRUNELLES: That's two!

CYPRIENNE: And number three was a week ago, on my neck, while we were watching the goldfish.

DES PRUNELLES: And then?

CYPRIENNE: That's all!

DES PRUNELLES: Cyprienne!

CYPRIENNE: If there was anything else, I'd tell you – now.

DES PRUNELLES [*getting up*]: Well, what I'd most like to see would be . . .

CYPRIENNE: What?

DES PRUNELLES: Your correspondence.

CYPRIENNE: His letters? Would you? They're over there.

DES PRUNELLES: Where? I've looked everywhere. [*He moves left and puts one hand on the table as he waves the other round the room.*]

CYPRIENNE [*laughing*]: Ha, ha, ha!

DES PRUNELLES: Why d'you laugh?

CYPRIENNE: You've got your hand on them.

DES PRUNELLES [*pulling out the drawer of the work table*]: In here? A hidden compartment?

[CYPRIENNE *runs to the table, pushes a button and a secret drawer opens on the side facing the audience.*]

CYPRIENNE: There!

DES PRUNELLES: Well!

[CYPRIENNE *takes the drawer out and sits on the stool in front of the table.* DES PRUNELLES *moves behind the table and sits in the armchair right.*]

CYPRIENNE [*taking a packet of letters from the drawer*]: And all in date order!

DES PRUNELLES [*very anxiously*]: May I? Just the last one?

CYPRIENNE [*taking a letter from the packet and keeping the drawer on her knees*]: Here you are! The sixteenth of November 1880.

DES PRUNELLES [*taking the letter quickly*]: Yesterday! That's even better! [*Reading*] 'My dearest, it is one hundred and twenty-two days now, since first my love did I to you avow.' It's in verse!

CYPRIENNE: D'you think so?

DES PRUNELLES [*continuing to read*]: 'And I am now no further, than I was then!' [*He makes a movement expressing satisfaction.*] 'Cyprienne, take pity on my suffering and pain!'

CYPRIENNE: The poor boy!

DES PRUNELLES [*wiping his forehead and returning the letter*]: Phew!

CYPRIENNE [*putting the letter back in the packet and the packet into the drawer*]: You see – I have not deceived you.

DES PRUNELLES: No – and to tell the truth, I'm glad – despite the divorce. [*Rummaging in the drawer*] What are all these knick-knacks?

CYPRIENNE: Just souvenirs.

DES PRUNELLES: Flowers, ribbons ... a match? [*He picks up the match.*]

CYPRIENNE [*taking it out of his hand*]: Oh, that! That's a reminder of a fine fright you gave both of us a fortnight ago.

DES PRUNELLES: How?

CYPRIENNE: You came home unexpectedly one night. I was here with Adhémar. I heard you open the door – I'd hardly time to turn out the lamp. We stood like statues in the dark, terrified. You came in cursing the servants, groping your way to the mantelpiece. You found a box of matches. You struck one: it went out. You struck another: that went out. A third: it didn't even light. There were no more. You went out swearing. Adhémar slipped away – and I kept this match as a token of gratitude to the incompetence of the match industry! [*She throws the match back into the drawer.*]

DES PRUNELLES [*gaily*]: If I'd only known! [*Rummaging in the drawer and taking out a button*]: A button?

CYPRIENNE [*Quickly, putting the drawer on the table*]: The overcoat. Now this really is funny. You don't recognize it? [*She lifts his arm so that he is holding the button in front of his eyes.*]

DES PRUNELLES: No.

CYPRIENNE: You picked it up one day from the carpet and gave it to Josépha. You said: 'Here's a button off my overcoat. Sew it on again, will you?' [*She laughs.*] It was Adhémar's!

DES PRUNELLES [*laughing a little forcedly*]: Ha, ha, ha! Yes, very funny indeed! [*Putting the button back in the drawer and pulling out a vine leaf*] A vine leaf?

CYPRIENNE [*taking the leaf quickly*]: Oh, that! Yes, it's a vine leaf I found in my hair one day.

DES PRUNELLES: Oh?

CYPRIENNE [*rising*]: But it would take too long to tell.

DES PRUNELLES [*holding her back*]: No, it wouldn't!

CYPRIENNE: No, really, it's too . . . complicated.

DES PRUNELLES [*drawing her on to his knees*]: All the better! Tell me! Please!

CYPRIENNE: Really? Well . . . you remember we went to pick the grapes last Autumn – in our vineyard at Glissonière?

DES PRUNELLES: Yes?

CYPRIENNE: We were still getting along fine together – you'd only some slight suspicions about Adhémar. Well, he happened to be inspecting some trees near by, so I said to him the day before we left: 'Be in the old wine-press hut, down by the wood, at two o'clock tomorrow, and I'll meet you there.'

[DES PRUNELLES *moves and she makes as if to get up from his knees.*]

Am I heavy?

DES PRUNELLES [*holding her back*]: No, no! Go on!

CYPRIENNE: Well, at two o'clock next day, I set out. And so as to keep out of the sun as much as to avoid being seen, I went through the wood. Suddenly I saw you walking quickly through the trees. You can imagine how I felt when I saw you were heading straight for the wine-press hut! Adhémar was there! You would find him! Your suspicions would be confirmed! So to stop you, and to warn him, I shouted to you: 'Henri, where are you going?' – saying to myself: 'Adhémar will hear – he'll hide himself in some old wine cask.' You called back to me, without stopping: 'I'm going to the old wine-press hut to get a cask I need.' This was even worse! Suppose you found Adhémar inside your wine cask! You were nearly at the door. I shouted: 'Come here first!' You stopped and called: 'Why?' 'Hurry! Quick!' I called, 'I've been stung by some horrible insect!' And with a stroke of inspiration, I found a pin and pricked myself just above the garter. You came running. 'Let me see!' 'Here,' I said, 'but see if you can find the insect! Or it may bite me again!' You looked everywhere . . . very conscientiously!

DES PRUNELLES: And found nothing, naturally.

CYPRIENNE: Naturally. But it gave Adhémar time to get away.

DES PRUNELLES: During which time – if I remember correctly – I...

CYPRIENNE [*quickly covering his mouth with the vine leaf*]: Ssh!

DES PRUNELLES: Well? And this vine leaf?

CYPRIENNE: Yes – by right it's yours! [*She puts it in his button hole.*] Now you can't call that an infidelity, can you?

DES PRUNELLES [*gaily*]: It appears not! But I certainly had a narrow escape as well!

CYPRIENNE [*kissing him, laughing*]: I'll say you did!

[BASTIEN *and* ADHÉMAR *enter from the hall.*]

BASTIEN [*announcing*]: Monsieur de Gratignan!

[ADHÉMAR *and* BASTIEN *halt, stupefied, at the sight of* CYPRIENNE *in* DES PRUNELLES*'s arms.* BASTIEN *goes out quickly.*]

CYPRIENNE [*astonished*]: Adhémar?

DES PRUNELLES [*to* CYPRIENNE]: Yes, I wrote a note asking him to come over.

ADHÉMAR [*to himself, coming forward bewildered, left*]: So that I would see this?

DES PRUNELLES [*gaily*]: Come in, young man! Come along! You're not in the way!

ADHÉMAR: Huh!

[CYPRIENNE *gets up quickly.*]

DES PRUNELLES [*rising also and going towards* ADHÉMAR *gaily*]: Well, my young friend, so there's no way of damping this passion of yours, eh? It's the real thing – this great love of yours, what?

ADHÉMAR: Monsieur!

DES PRUNELLES: Cyprienne has told me all. [*Showing him the drawer*] The matches, the button, the vine leaf, the kisses on the neck, the shoulder, the arm. You're a fast worker! Yes, it seems you even bite, you young devil!

ADHÉMAR [*looking at* CYPRIENNE, *who is smiling*]: You know?

DES PRUNELLES [*also smiling, familiarly*]: To put it in a nutshell, you're determined to have her – and that's that, eh?

ADHÉMAR [*more astonished than ever*]: But...

DES PRUNELLES: Well, if that's how it is, take her, dear boy! [*Moving towards* CYPRIENNE] Take her! I yield her to you!

ADHÉMAR [*moving extreme left, completely bewildered*]: Uh?

DES PRUNELLES: Now say I'm not generous!

CYPRIENNE [*gaily*]: He doesn't understand!

DES PRUNELLES [*to* ADHÉMAR]: Divorce! The new law!

CYPRIENNE [*to* ADHÉMAR]: The bill has just been voted in!

ADHÉMAR [*forgetting himself*]: Rubbish!

CYPRIENNE [*surprised*]: But . . . your telegram?

DES PRUNELLES: Ah, I understand. In spite of the telegram, he can't believe it's true. That's it, isn't it? You can't believe your good luck?

ADHÉMAR: Oh, my God!

DES PRUNELLES: It was the same with me! I had to make sure. So I dashed over to the town hall. It's quite official.

ADHÉMAR: You're certain?

CYPRIENNE: Not a doubt about it!

ADHÉMAR [*to himself*]: Now what happens?

DES PRUNELLES: So I said to myself: 'Let's benefit from it! Let's all benefit at once!' And now we've had this very friendly little discussion, we are all agreed. What's done is done. It can't be helped. My dear boy, I give her to you.

ADHÉMAR [*going towards him, a little uneasy*]: Monsieur, this is really more than I had hoped for!

DES PRUNELLES: I believe you, my dear boy. A pretty wife – who will bring you four hundred thousand francs – all her own . . .

ADHÉMAR [*radiantly*]: Four hundred thousand . . .

DES PRUNELLES: Four hundred thousand! A wife and a fortune at one go! I call that good business when you haven't a penny yourself. You're in luck's way.

ADHÉMAR [*beaming with delight*]: No! Really? Four hundred thousand? [*To himself*] This puts a different complexion on it. [*He crosses and puts his hat on the mantelpiece and comes back to* DES PRUNELLES.] Ah, Monsieur! My benefactor!

[*He holds out his hand to* DES PRUNELLES. DES PRUNELLES *takes it and holds out his other hand to* CYPRIENNE. *With hands joined, they form a circle.*]

DES PRUNELLES: Yes, my friend, yes! But now, no more emotion. Let us be practical. [*To* ADHÉMAR] Sit down. We must discuss the divorce. We must go into ways and means. Thoroughly.

[*He sits on the sofa,* CYPRIENNE *on the stool right of the table.* ADHÉMAR *takes a chair from behind the sofa and sits left in front of the little table.*]

ADHÉMAR [*seated*]: That's it! Now let's think carefully.

CYPRIENNE [*seated, leaning with her elbows on the table*]: Yes, let's think!

DES PRUNELLES: I know a little about divorce – Cyprienne knows quite a bit though . . .

CYPRIENNE: Everything!

DES PRUNELLES: So we've no need for anybody else's advice. The new law is really only Section Four of the Civil Code slightly modified. It offers us several approaches. First, and simplest, is divorce by mutual consent. That's certainly our case – and we've filled the required conditions: two years of marriage.

CYPRIENNE: The trouble is – that takes too long!

ADHÉMAR: Too long?

CYPRIENNE [*authoritatively*]: Request for divorce to be renewed every three months, accompanied by renewed permission of father and mother if still living, signatures of four witnesses not less than fifty years of age, appearance before the President of the Tribunal together with all relevant official reports verbal and written, request for acceptance of plea by mutual consent, parental speech from the magistrate, friendly advice from the witnesses, recalcitrance of the parties concerned. Further verbal questioning, a court order, the court's decisions, verification, declaration of acceptance of plea by mutual consent, a further appearance before the Mayor and divorce is granted . . . too late! The parties concerned have gone mad – with rage!

ADHÉMAR: And how long does all that take?

DES PRUNELLES [*who has picked up the Civil Code from the table and opened it*]: Oh! Ten months!

ADHÉMAR [*jumping*]: Ten months!

DES PRUNELLES: That's if there's no setback.

CYPRIENNE: And that's not all!

ADHÉMAR: Eh?

CYPRIENNE: Article 297. [*To* DES PRUNELLES *who is searching through the Civil Code*] At the bottom of the page. 'In the case of divorce by mutual consent, neither of the parties concerned may contract a new marriage until three years after divorce has been granted.'

ADHÉMAR: Three years!

DES PRUNELLES [*passing him the book*]: Four, altogether!

CYPRIENNE: That settles it! Do you see me waiting four years with my arms folded, between one man who's no longer my husband and another who still isn't? Do you?

DES PRUNELLES: Not exactly!

CYPRIENNE: Never on your life!

DES PRUNELLES: Yes, that is rather impracticable. It looks as though we'll have to fall back on divorce on definite grounds.

ADHÉMAR [*who has been looking through the Civil Code, putting his finger suddenly on a page*]: Adultery! You surprise us both *in flagrante delicto*!

CYPRIENNE: Oh, yes, that would be perfect – then we'd never be able to marry!

ADHÉMAR [*frightened*]: Why not?

CYPRIENNE: Article 298. [*To* ADHÉMAR, *who is searching through the Civil Code*] At the top of the page! Turn over! 'If divorce is granted on grounds of adultery, the guilty party may not contract a marriage with his or her co-respondent.'

ADHÉMAR [*looking at the passage in the book*]: It can't be!

CYPRIENNE: For fear their marriage might succeed!

DES PRUNELLES: Besides, if I might be permitted to say, I am agreeing to a divorce so as not to be 'you-know-what'. Which is just what I would be, if I agreed to divorce on those grounds. You're asking too much!

ADHÉMAR: You're right!

DES PRUNELLES: Some other way then?

CYPRIENNE: There's not much left. We can't plead insanity, desertion, libel, slander, or immoral excesses.

ADHÉMAR [*who has again been looking through the Civil Code, putting his finger on another page*]: I've got it! Suppose we submit that Monsieur des Prunelles suffers from a certain lack of virility!

CYPRIENNE [*quickly*]: Oh, no! That's going too far!

DES PRUNELLES [*taking her hand*]: Thank you, my dear!

CYPRIENNE: No, all that's left is divorce on grounds of cruelty.

ADHÉMAR: Hitting each other?

DES PRUNELLES: That's easy enough. We'd only have to give each other a box on the ears.

CYPRIENNE: But it would only be the one I got that counted!

DES PRUNELLES: Of course!

CYPRIENNE: And in front of witnesses – in public! That would be fine, I must say!

DES PRUNELLES: Good heavens, it can all be arranged without any fuss. We'll have some friends in for dinner – we'll argue all the time and then over the dessert . . .

CYPRIENNE: No! No! It's horrible!

DES PRUNELLES: Pooh! There are plenty of women who wouldn't turn a hair.

CYPRIENNE [*getting up*]: Not in cold blood!

[ADHÉMAR *gets up and puts his chair back below the door.*]

DES PRUNELLES [*getting up*]: All right, then, mutual consent – four years!

CYPRIENNE [*crying out*]: Oh, no!

DES PRUNELLES: Then a slap!

ADHÉMAR [*going to* CYPRIENNE]: Darling, for my sake, please! Agree!

DES PRUNELLES: Just one little slap – the tiniest, weeniest possible!

CYPRIENNE: I suppose it's the only way.

DES PRUNELLES: Then you agree?

CYPRIENNE: I agree.

DES PRUNELLES: That's the spirit! That way, you'll only have to wait ten months.

CYPRIENNE: That's long enough as it is!

DES PRUNELLES [*passing between them*]: And there's something else I'd perhaps better mention. You'll admit I'm being most cooperative. And so you won't want to repay my – if I may term it – my unparalleled generosity with ingratitude.

ADHÉMAR: Oh, Monsieur!

CYPRIENNE: Darling!

DES PRUNELLES: Then I implore you to be patient during the next ten months. Until our divorce is granted, I beg you to respect my honour as much as – even better than – you have done up to now. If I were you, I would avoid all kisses as being dangerous and over-exciting. If you indulge in them now, how are you going to spend your evenings later on? And you, in particular, young man, should restrain yourself in your own interests. It's not every day you have such an unlooked-for stroke of good fortune. It's not every day that a young man with a salary of two thousand six hundred francs has the luck to marry an income of twenty thousand francs. Don't endanger such prospects. Ten months is a long time. Who can guarantee that your passion will not fade away? Who can guarantee that when the great moment comes one of you, the bride perhaps, may not cry out: 'Oh, good heavens, no! I've had enough! I don't want it any more!'

ADHÉMAR: Oh!

DES PRUNELLES: Your greatest danger is satiety. Don't ruin your dinner by too big a lunch.

ADHÉMAR: No, of course not, Monsieur!

DES PRUNELLES [*to* ADHÉMAR, *with guileless good-nature*]: I have it! D'you know what I would do, if I were in your place? This job at Arachon. I'd accept it at once and I'd leave tonight. Nobody would see me for some time!

ADHÉMAR: Really?

DES PRUNELLES: By far the wisest thing!

[ADHÉMAR *and* CYPRIENNE *look at each other pitifully.*]

Anyway, think it over. Consider it carefully. It's a piece of friendly advice I'm giving you! And it won't be the last, I hope. [*With emotion, putting* CYPRIENNE*'s arm through his*] When you are both one, you'll let me come and see you from time to time, won't you? You'll keep a little place between you for me, won't you, at your fire-side . . . at your table . . . on Sundays?

CYPRIENNE [*much moved*]: Of course, my dear!

ADHÉMAR [*also much moved*]: Yes, of course we will!

DES PRUNELLES: Good gracious me, I might even be of some use to you sometimes! The advice of experience. [*Patting* CYPRIENNE'*s hand*] I know all her little likes and dislikes so well. And then there's your business affairs! I will be able to advise you how to invest your little savings – if you're able to make any! Twenty-two thousand six hundred francs won't go very far.

[CYPRIENNE *reacts visibly to this observation.*]

Especially when one's used to spending sixty thousand on food alone like she is.

[CYPRIENNE *reacts again.*]

But with a little planning – some big reductions and economies on things like food – a small house – fewer dresses – getting rid of the carriage and the horses . . . dear me, what a lot of sacrifices you'll have to make! For you, my friend, it is a fortune; for her, it is a sacrifice. [*Taking* ADHÉMAR'*s arm without letting go of* CYPRIENNE'*s*] And I will be able to look at you both in your great happiness – for it is the greatest happiness to make sacrifices for the person one loves – and I will be able to say: 'They owe their happiness to me!' Dear me, it's foolish of me, but I really am deeply moved. [*To* CYPRIENNE, *taking her in his arms*] My dear . . . dear child. [*To* ADHÉMAR] You permit me?

ADHÉMAR: Please – I beg you.

DES PRUNELLES [*kissing* CYPRIENNE *on the forehead*]: One cannot end such a close intimacy as ours has been without a certain heart-break. [*To* CYPRIENNE, *arranging a curl on her forehead*] You will think of me sometimes, won't you?

CYPRIENNE [*troubled*]: Why are you so kind to me?

DES PRUNELLES: Yes. [*To* ADHÉMAR] You permit? . . . [*To* CYPRIENNE] Yes, you will think of me. [*He kisses her and turns her round towards* ADHÉMAR.] Thank you. [*Making* CYPRIENNE *stand beside* ADHÉMAR] And now you will want to be alone together. You will dine here, won't you, my dear successor?

ADHÉMAR: Oh, Monsieur!

DES PRUNELLES [*moving right*]: Please! Dine here . . . before you leave! It will please me so much! [*He holds out his hand.*]

ADHÉMAR [*moving to him, above table*]: Ah, Monsieur, how can I ever thank you?

DES PRUNELLES [*shaking his hand, with emotion*]: By making her happy. Until later then, dear children! Until later!

[*He opens the door of his study, turns to give* ADHÉMAR *a last shake of the hand, and goes out quickly.* ADHÉMAR *watches him go with admiration.*]

CYPRIENNE [*to herself, alone left in front of the table*]: Twenty thousand instead of sixty thousand. That's not going to be so good.

ADHÉMAR [*coming forward quickly to* CYPRIENNE, *on top of the world*]: Ah, Cyprienne! How happy we're going to be!

CYPRIENNE: Yes, indeed – you especially!

ADHÉMAR [*moving up and down and then extreme right, full of enthusiasm*]: Ah! To be able to love freely and openly! No more mystery! No more plotting! No more danger!

CYPRIENNE: You didn't like that? How funny! Those are just the things I enjoyed.

ADHÉMAR [*quickly, moving back a little and pointing to* DES PRUNELLES'*s door*]: Oh, I did, too! But I did used to feel a little uncomfortable deceiving such a good, kind man. While now we have security, peace!

CYPRIENNE: Oh, yes, peace. Yes, we've got peace all right.

ADHÉMAR [*moving forward towards* CYPRIENNE, *without looking at her*]: Do you think, Cyprienne, we shall be able to rise to the sacrifices he expects of us?

CYPRIENNE: Yes, of course.

ADHÉMAR [*still not looking at her*]: And we won't betray such great trust?

CYPRIENNE: No, of course not.

ADHÉMAR [*moving back towards* DES PRUNELLES'*s door*]: What a man! What generosity! What a heart! What a soul!

CYPRIENNE [*quietly*]: Yes, of course. It's I who am the heartless beast.

ADHÉMAR [*turning towards her*]: What?

CYPRIENNE: Well! If he has all the virtues, you must admit it's very wrong of me to desert him for my lover.

ADHÉMAR [*quickly*]: Never say that word again, Cyprienne. Your lover is no more. I am no longer your lover!

CYPRIENNE: No! Now you're my husband!

ADHÉMAR: Future husband! Your probationary husband! Who sees you as no more than his fiancée. And as such, honours and respects you.

CYPRIENNE: Yes, we're all agreed on that. You respect me. He respects me. I am a very respectable woman.

ADHÉMAR [*transported with his own thoughts*]: Ten months! After all, what's that?

CYPRIENNE: It's time forever lost.

ADHÉMAR [*not listening*]: Oh, I'll know how to wait all right!

CYPRIENNE: Thank you.

ADHÉMAR [*still not listening*]: I'll even leave first thing tomorrow – as he wishes. Just to prove how much I respect him.

CYPRIENNE [*quietly and ironically*]: Yes, I heard the word before. You have a great respect for us both.

ADHÉMAR [*surprised by her tone*]: You are a little on edge, Cyprienne?

CYPRIENNE: You think so?

ADHÉMAR: Yes, a little over excited. This sudden upheaval! [*Moving behind table and sofa to get his hat from the mantelpiece*] Calm yourself, my heart's delight! I'll just run over to my sister's. She's expecting me to dinner. I'll excuse myself and come right back.

CYPRIENNE: Yes, do that. And take care not to catch cold on the way.

ADHÉMAR [*behind the sofa*]: Oh, I've got my overcoat!

CYPRIENNE: Oh, that's all right then.

ADHÉMAR: And after dinner?

CYPRIENNE [*ironically*]: We shall play bézique.

ADHÉMAR [*passionately*]: If you want to!

CYPRIENNE: O rapture!

ADHÉMAR: I'll be back like a flash, my soul, my life, my treasure! [*To himself, as he goes out*] Four hundred thousand francs! Treasure is the word! [*Exit*]

CYPRIENNE [*alone, after a moment's reflection*]: Yes! It's true, all right! Now it's no longer forbidden – it hasn't at all the same taste!

[MADAME DE BRIONNE *comes running in and goes to* CYPRIENNE, *passing behind the table.* MADAME DE VAL-

FONTAINE *follows her.* CLAVIGNAC *enters after them and comes forward left.*]

MADAME DE BRIONNE [*quickly and gaily*]: Oh, my dear, is it really true?

MADAME DE VALFONTAINE: Has it been passed?

CYPRIENNE: What?

MADAME DE BRIONNE *and* MADAME DE VALFONTAINE: Divorce!

CYPRIENNE: Passed? Oh, yes.

MADAME DE BRIONNE: I've won! I've won!

CLAVIGNAC [*to* MADAME DE VALFONTAINE]: There! You see!

CYPRIENNE: What's the matter?

CLAVIGNAC [*to* CYPRIENNE]: I met these ladies as we were coming in. Madame de Valfontaine didn't want to believe it.

MADAME DE BRIONNE: We'd made a bet . . .

MADAME DE VALFONTAINE: And I still don't believe I've lost!

CYPRIENNE: Oh, now, really!

CLAVIGNAC: Where is the telegram?

MADAME DE BRIONNE: You have it?

CYPRIENNE: Monsieur has it. Wait.

[MADAME DE VALFONTAINE *has sat on the sofa,* MADAME DE BRIONNE *is standing left of her.* CLAVIGNAC *is extreme left.*]

[CYPRIENNE *knocks on the study door*] Henri!

DES PRUNELLES [*half opening the door, tenderly*]: Yes, my sweet?

CYPRIENNE [*affectionately*]: Can you spare one little moment, my pet?

DES PRUNELLES: But of course, my darling! I'll be with you in one second!

MADAME DE VALFONTAINE [*to* MADAME DE BRIONNE, *softly*]: Well! They're being very nice to each other.

CLAVIGNAC: There you are! Divorce gives hope!

[DES PRUNELLES *enters wearing dress suit and white tie. He takes* CYPRIENNE'*s hand affectionately in both of his and comes forward with her.*]

DES PRUNELLES: What is it, my dear child? [*Seeing the ladies, he turns to them, gallant and gay.*] Ah, Mesdames! A thousand pardons!

MADAME DE VALFONTAINE: Yes, we're back again!

DES PRUNELLES [*gallant, friendly, quite different from the first act*]: Splendid! It can never be too often! [*He shakes hands with* MADAME DE BRIONNE, *above the sofa.*]

CYPRIENNE: Darling, these ladies would so much like to contemplate the famous telegram.

DES PRUNELLES: Why, certainly! I carry it everywhere! [*He takes it from his wallet and passes it to* MADAME DE VALFONTAINE] There it is!

MADAME DE VALFONTAINE [*reading*]: 'Bill passed! Enormous majority!'

MADAME DE BRIONNE [*to* MADAME DE VALFONTAINE]: You've lost, my dear! It has been passed!

MADAME DE VALFONTAINE [*vexedly*]: It's been passed? But no! There's still the Senate!

ALL [*laughing*]: Oh!

MADAME DE BRIONNE: As if that mattered!

CYPRIENNE: What surprises me about it all, is that it's the married woman who is put out. And the widow is delighted!

MADAME DE VALFONTAINE: Everything worked so well as it was! What need was there for divorce?

CYPRIENNE [*to* MADAME DE BRIONNE]: Yes, but you, Estelle, why are you so pleased?

MADAME DE BRIONNE: First, because I've won my bet. Second, I always used to want to marry a widower as he'd have exhausted all his bad temper driving his first wife to the grave. But a divorced man would be even better. He must have been so exasperated by his first wife he'd not be able to find a fault with his second.

DES PRUNELLES [*laughing*]: Oh, very good! That's good! Very good! [*He kisses her hand.* CYPRIENNE *looks at him with astonishment.*]

MADAME DE BRIONNE [*taking the telegram from* MADAME DE VALFONTAINE]: May I? [*To* DES PRUNELLES] May I, darling?

CYPRIENNE [*to herself*]: Darling? Well!

MADAME DE BRIONNE: About twenty people followed us here – they're all waiting at the door. I promised to show them the telegram – if there was one.

DES PRUNELLES [*opening the door right*]: Show it, dear lady. Show it! We mustn't be selfish!

MADAME DE BRIONNE [*turning to him*]: They're all married too.

CLAVIGNAC: Yes, we must give them hope, as well, then.

[MADAME DE BRIONNE *goes out by garden door right.* MADAME DE VALFONTAINE *and* CYPRIENNE *stand on the threshold watching.* DES PRUNELLES *goes over to* CLAVIGNAC *and pulls him down left.*]

DES PRUNELLES [*softly, to* CLAVIGNAC]: Many thanks!

CLAVIGNAC [*softly*]: What for?

DES PRUNELLES [*softly*]: For spreading the rumour.

[*Shouts of satisfaction are heard outside*]

CLAVIGNAC [*softly*]: You mean – the telegram?

DES PRUNELLES: Adhémar played a trick on me. He sent it. It's false!

CLAVIGNAC [*exclaiming loudly*]: What?

DES PRUNELLES: Quiet, you fool!

CLAVIGNAC: You devil! You actually gave me hope – by making out you believed it yourself!

DES PRUNELLES: That's my little trick!

CLAVIGNAC: Couldn't you have taken me into your confidence?

DES PRUNELLES: Would you have spread the rumour so quickly then?

CLAVIGNAC: You deserve to be ... what on earth good d'you think it will do?

DES PRUNELLES: It'll bring my wife back to me, that's all.

CLAVIGNAC: Ha! And Adhémar?

DES PRUNELLES: Him? I've spiked his guns for him already! All I've to do now is make them both look fools.

CLAVIGNAC: How?

DES PRUNELLES: I get a divorce! And they get married!

CLAVIGNAC: And that brings your wife back to you?

DES PRUNELLES: Exactly!

CLAVIGNAC: This is beyond me.

DES PRUNELLES: Don't you see, you idiot, now that he'll be the husband ...

CLAVIGNAC: You'll be the lover!

DES PRUNELLES [*seeing the women returning*]: Ssh!

MADAME DE BRIONNE [*entering with* CYPRIENNE *and* MADAME DE VALFONTAINE]: They went mad with joy! In raptures! Here, you dear man, here is your talisman! [*She gives* DES PRUNELLES *back the telegram.*]

DES PRUNELLES [*kissing her hand*]: And may it bring every happiness to you!

MADAME DE BRIONNE [*flirtatiously*]: D'you know, I think it will! [*To* CYPRIENNE] Good-bye, darling. [*She goes out back, into the hall.*]

CYPRIENNE: See you tomorrow! [*Leading* MADAME DE VALFONTAINE *towards the hall*] Come, cheer up, my dear!

MADAME DE VALFONTAINE: Never! The days of secret meetings are over!

[MADAME DE VALFONTAINE *and* MADAME DE BRIONNE *go out accompanied by* CYPRIENNE.]

CLAVIGNAC [*aside, to* DES PRUNELLES]: So now you can dine with me?

DES PRUNELLES: Not with you. Near you, perhaps.

CLAVIGNAC: How?

DES PRUNELLES [*seeing his wife returning*]: Ssh! Go now! And not a word!

CLAVIGNAC [*to* CYPRIENNE, *bowing*]: Madame!

[CYPRIENNE *bows without speaking.* CLAVIGNAC *goes out. At the same time,* BASTIEN *enters from* DES PRUNELLES*'s study, puts* DES PRUNELLES*'s overcoat and hat on the pouf and goes out again.*]

DES PRUNELLES [*putting on his hat and coat while* CYPRIENNE *moves forward left*]: And now, dear child, I also will say good night.

CYPRIENNE [*startled*]: Good night? But – aren't you dining here?

DES PRUNELLES: Oh, no!

CYPRIENNE: You invited Adhémar, didn't you?

DES PRUNELLES: To dine with you! Not me!

CYPRIENNE: Oh! I'd thought ... It would be so nice. An engagement party. And just the three of us.

DES PRUNELLES [*adjusting his overcoat round his shoulders*]: It'll be even nicer with just the two of you. I'd only get in the dear boy's way.

CYPRIENNE [*still down left*]: No, no, it would be just the opposite. You'd make him feel more at ease. Now that he's got to marry me, he's gone all stiff . . . frozen up.

DES PRUNELLES [*crossing to her, behind the sofa*]: Well, to be quite frank with you, I'm not at all sorry to be able to feel free to get out and stretch my arms a little.

CYPRIENNE: Now my whole evening's spoilt. Please stay!

DES PRUNELLES [*moving away*]: Really, I can't. Good night. [*He holds out his hand above the table.*]

CYPRIENNE [*going to the table, taking his hand and holding it*]: But where are you dining?

DES PRUNELLES [*trying to get away*]: At Dagneau's, the Grand Vatel.

CYPRIENNE [*still holding his hand*]: Alone?

DES PRUNELLES: Probably. [*He frees his hand.*]

CYPRIENNE: You're not sure?

DES PRUNELLES: I must go!

CYPRIENNE: Somebody's waiting for you there?

DES PRUNELLES: No . . . but maybe I'll come across some friend . . .

CYPRIENNE: A woman?

DES PRUNELLES [*laughing*]: Oh, come now!

CYPRIENNE: Admit it! You're dining with some woman!

DES PRUNELLES [*laughing*]: I assure you I'm not!

CYPRIENNE: Henri, don't lie.

DES PRUNELLES [*still laughing*]: But I'm not lying!

CYPRIENNE: You are! It's not fair. I told you everything. So you tell me everything! Who is it? Please! Tell me who it is!

DES PRUNELLES [*still laughing*]: But how can I if I don't know myself?

CYPRIENNE [*going to him and ruffling his tie*]: Did you get all dressed up like this just to dine alone?

DES PRUNELLES: Of course!

CYPRIENNE: You never did so for me!

DES PRUNELLES: Oh, now, really!

CYPRIENNE [*half-annoyed and half-coaxing*]: Oh, isn't this all a little unnecessary now? All this air of mystery? I mean why? [*She takes him by the arm coaxingly.*] What's it matter now – when we're both no more than just good friends?

DES PRUNELLES: Exactly.

CYPRIENNE: Well, then?

DES PRUNELLES: Well, then – why does it matter so much to you?

CYPRIENNE: Just so that I know! It annoys me not to know!

DES PRUNELLES [*laughing*]: Then I'll repeat – there isn't any one.

CYPRIENNE [*letting go of his arm*]: You can't say it without laughing.

DES PRUNELLES: I'm laughing ... because it's so absurd, this outburst of posthumous jealousy!

CYPRIENNE: It is not jealousy! It's curiosity. And that's quite natural, see? Every woman ...

DES PRUNELLES: I still can't tell you ...

CYPRIENNE [*quickly*]: Ah! You can't! There, you see?

DES PRUNELLES: Because ...

CYPRIENNE: You're frightened of compromising her?

DES PRUNELLES: No, because ...

CYPRIENNE [*without listening*]: Do I know her?

DES PRUNELLES: No more than I do.

CYPRIENNE [*quickly*]: But just as well, eh? It's one of my friends?

DES PRUNELLES: If you ...

CYPRIENNE: Let's bet it's one of my friends!

DES PRUNELLES: Oh!

CYPRIENNE: That's always how it is! I bet that if I ... [*Suddenly*] Madame de Brionne!

DES PRUNELLES: Estelle?

CYPRIENNE: Estelle! That proves it!

DES PRUNELLES: But, no!

CYPRIENNE: You said: 'Estelle'! You betrayed yourself!

DES PRUNELLES: But I call her 'Estelle' like you do!

CYPRIENNE: No, I don't call her like that. I say: 'Estelle' – quite short – like that! But you said: 'Est . . .e . . .lle.' You linger on her name! It goes on for an hour!

DES PRUNELLES: But ...

CYPRIENNE: Besides, I guessed as much, see?

DES PRUNELLES: Ah!

CYPRIENNE: She's always barging in here and I never could

stand her – the stuck-up snob with her affected airs and graces – the sly, cunning, jealous, little trollop!

DES PRUNELLES: Oh!

CYPRIENNE [*leaning on the table*]: Oh, naturally you defend her! Made-up from head to toe! Hair, eyebrows, eyelashes – nothing's her own! All paint, polish and varnish! And that silly smile of hers! I wonder what she sticks that on with!

DES PRUNELLES: Oh!

CYPRIENNE: Besides, she gave herself away all right ... when she told us she was hoping for divorce so as she could get hold of someone's husband! And to think she was here, under my very nose, pleased as punch – almost dancing for joy! And you kissing away at her hands! It was indecent!

DES PRUNELLES: If you'd let me ...

CYPRIENNE: So she's your conquest! That one! Well, I don't congratulate you!

DES PRUNELLES: You know, my sweet, this is all not in very good taste, is it? I don't pull your Adhémar to pieces, do I?

CYPRIENNE [*moving back left*]: Estelle! I ask you! Estelle! And you're even fool enough to marry her!

DES PRUNELLES: May I point out that ...

CYPRIENNE [*her hands on the back of the sofa*]: Are you going to marry her?

DES PRUNELLES: I don't say that!

CYPRIENNE: Then you are! [*With a cry of horror*] You're going to marry that strumpet who deceived her first husband, who'll deceive you like she did him, and who'll deceive her third, when you're dead, poisoned by all that paint and varnish she's got all over her! [*She is now behind the table.*]

DES PRUNELLES: You're going too far! [*He sits on the sofa, putting on his gloves.*]

CYPRIENNE [*coming front-stage right*]: And that cat will take my place here! She'll install herself in my house. [*She moves back and bangs on the armchair.*] Use my furniture! My horses! My carriages! [*Going to* DES PRUNELLES *in front of the table*] If I'd known this ... rather than let you do this I'd never have agreed to divorce you!

DES PRUNELLES: And Adhémar?

CYPRIENNE [*falling into the armchair right of the table*]: Oh, Adhémar! ... To be left for that painted doll! No! Really! It's too much!

DES PRUNELLES [*standing*]: I am not leaving you. We are leaving each other.

CYPRIENNE [*rising and coming forward*]: Anyone else, and I wouldn't have minded! But that one! Oh!

DES PRUNELLES [*behind her*]: All right. Be happy. It's not her.

CYPRIENNE [*turning quickly and seizing the lapels of his coat so as to look him straight in the face*]: It's someone else, then?

DES PRUNELLES: I ...

CYPRIENNE: Who?

DES PRUNELLES: You said you wouldn't have minded ...

CYPRIENNE: Never mind what I said! Tell me all the same – who?

DES PRUNELLES: But ...

CYPRIENNE: Young? ... Pretty? ...

DES PRUNELLES: But since you ...

CYPRIENNE: Prettier than me?

DES PRUNELLES: What should that matter to you?

CYPRIENNE [*determinedly but almost in tears*]: But it does!

DES PRUNELLES: Bah!

CYPRIENNE: It does matter to me ... that you should go off like this ... so soon ... to gad about with someone else. It's absurd, I know ... but I can't help it! It infuriates me!

DES PRUNELLES [*laughing*]: But ...

CYPRIENNE: And you're too happy! You look too happy! I've never seen you so happy as this!

DES PRUNELLES [*taking her hand as if to say good-bye, both by the armchair*]: But I've every reason to, my darling. My independence, your contentment, our mutual good luck. I'm happy to see you happy ... for, after all, you are happy, aren't you?

CYPRIENNE [*kneeling on the armchair, without conviction*]: Yes.

DES PRUNELLES: Well, then?

CYPRIENNE [*almost in tears*]: Except for one thing!

DES PRUNELLES: What?

CYPRIENNE [*falling into his arms across the armchair and bursting into tears*]: You're not sorry enough to leave me!

DES PRUNELLES: Ah!

CYPRIENNE [*as before*]: No, it's not very nice of you! You're just throwing me aside like a piece of old junk. As if you were saying: 'Good riddance!' It's humiliating! I don't want to be . . . cast off like this!

DES PRUNELLES [*holding her to him and patting her shoulder*]: You're not happy, then, about our separation?

CYPRIENNE: Yes, but that doesn't stop me having regrets. I do have some regrets, but you haven't, not one! After all, we have had some good times together.

DES PRUNELLES: A few.

CYPRIENNE [*still in tears in his arms*]: A lot! You see, it's you who's forgotten them! It's only me who remembers them still!

DES PRUNELLES [*kissing the curls on her forehead*]: That's not true.

CYPRIENNE: Have dinner with me then just once more. After all, this is a special day for both of us. You can have dinner tomorrow with this other one.

DES PRUNELLES [*still holding her*]: But there is no other one!

CYPRIENNE [*in tears still in his arms*]: Oh!

DES PRUNELLES [*patting her shoulder still*]: Would you like me to prove it?

CYPRIENNE [*as above*]: How?

DES PRUNELLES [*as above*]: Come and dine with me.

CYPRIENNE [*joyfully, lifting her head*]: At Dagneau's? In the Grand Vatel?

DES PRUNELLES: Just the two of us.

CYPRIENNE: Alone?

DES PRUNELLES: Tête-à-tête.

CYPRIENNE: Oh, yes!

DES PRUNELLES: I'll give you a meal you'll never forget!

CYPRIENNE: And you'll make me tipsy?

DES PRUNELLES: If you wish!

CYPRIENNE [*laughing and jumping for joy, she goes left to get her hat and coat*]: Oh, what a wonderful idea! Just like this – without any arranging – on the spur of the moment! Oh, it's marvellous!

DES PRUNELLES: It is, isn't it?

CYPRIENNE [*taking her hat which is on a chair behind the sofa and picking up her coat*]: Oh, I'm going to enjoy this! Really, I am! Oh, I could kiss you! [*She kisses* DES PRUNELLES *who has come forward right.*] And now I'll be certain you're not dining with this other one! [*She puts her coat on the armchair extreme right and ties the ribbons on her hat.*]

DES PRUNELLES [*quickly, pretending surprise*]: You mean you're coming?

CYPRIENNE: Of course!

DES PRUNELLES: I was only fooling!

CYPRIENNE: All the worse for you! I'm taking you at your word! So that's that!

DES PRUNELLES: But what about Adhémar, poor chap?

CYPRIENNE: Oh, Adhémar! Won't I be dining with Adhémar every night of my life?

DES PRUNELLES: But suppose he's annoyed?

CYPRIENNE: Then he'll be annoyed!

DES PRUNELLES: He'll make a scene!

CYPRIENNE: He'd better not! [*With dignity*] Besides, how can I dine tête-à-tête with him, here, without you? How would that look – to the servants?

DES PRUNELLES: What they'll see – in future.

CYPRIENNE: How can one know that? No, either all three of us, or just you and I.

DES PRUNELLES: That's better still.

CYPRIENNE [*taking his arm and holding herself close to him while putting on her gloves*]: Oh, this really is an inspired idea! It's like having a wedding dinner all over again. Only in reverse!

DES PRUNELLES: Our last tête-à-tête!

CYPRIENNE: Let's go! He'll be coming back! [*She rings the bell.*]

DES PRUNELLES [*going to pick up his hat and coat back right and looking into the hall*]: Here he is!

CYPRIENNE: Adhémar?

DES PRUNELLES: Coming through the courtyard.

[JOSÉPHA *enters down left.*]

CYPRIENNE [*to* JOSÉPHA]: Josépha!

JOSÉPHA: Yes, Madame?

CYPRIENNE [*quickly*]: There's Monsieur coming back! No! I mean Adhémar!

DES PRUNELLES: Yes, yes! That's it exactly! Monsieur!

CYPRIENNE [*very agitated*]: Tell him I've had to go out!

DES PRUNELLES [*opening the garden door*]: Alone!

CYPRIENNE: Alone! Alone!

JOSÉPHA [*surprised*]: Ah?

CYPRIENNE [*moving right to* DES PRUNELLES]: Someone came for me ... make any excuse ... you've always been able to. Tell him to excuse me ... he can dine here, if he wants to.

JOSÉPHA [*stupefied*]: Yes, Madame.

DES PRUNELLES: Here he is!

CYPRIENNE [*pushing him in front of her*]: Quick then! He'll catch us! [*They go out door right.*]

JOSÉPHA [*looking after them, completely bewildered*]: Uh? Are they back together again, then?

[ADHÉMAR *enters from the hall in dress suit, white tie, white gloves, and carrying a bouquet of white roses. He looks like a married man.* BASTIEN *appears in the doorway back left, wearing a waiter's clothes.*]

JOSÉPHA [*quickly*]: Monsieur is not at home!

ADHÉMAR [*radiant, moving right*]: That's all right with me! Where's Madame?

JOSÉPHA: Madame asks you to excuse her, Monsieur. She's just gone out.

ADHÉMAR: Gone out?

JOSÉPHA: Yes, Monsieur ... Her aunt is very ill.

ADHÉMAR [*staggered*]: Already! [*Throwing his bouquet on the table.*] Her aunt? ... We'll soon see about that! I'll go there! To her aunt's! [*He goes out quickly.*]

BASTIEN: Dinner is served, madame!

[*He offers his arm to* JOSÉPHA *who picks up the bouquet from the table and both enter the dining-room, back left, aping their master and mistress. This very quick exit should be played while the curtain is closing.*]

ACT THREE

A small private room of a very elegant restaurant. Back-stage, swinging doors give on to an ante-room at the back of which can be seen a service table. The corners back-stage, either side of the swinging doors, are raked. Down-stage left is a door to a dressing-room. Upstage from this door is a piano with a stool. Back-stage from this, in the raked wall, is a small window. Between the window and the swinging doors is a small service table on which are plates, forks, spoons, knives and a cruet stand. Down-stage right is a mantelpiece over a fireplace on which are a clock, two candelabra, a decanter and two finger-bowls. Upstage of this is a folding screen with seven sections, folded so that it is half open. Back-stage from this, in the raked wall, is a door. Centre-stage is a round table set for two. Left of the table is a chair. Stage-left is a small sofa for two people, with cushions. Right, above the mantelpiece, an armchair. There is an unlighted chandelier. Two candles only are burning on the candelabra on the mantelpiece. There is a chair in front of the window.

As the curtain rises, the head-waiter, JOSEPH, *opens the swinging doors, back, for* DES PRUNELLES *who enters with* CYPRIENNE *on his arm. He is followed by two waiters, one of whom carries a rod with a burning wick to light the chandelier.*

JOSEPH: This little room will suit Madame perfectly!

DES PRUNELLES: Yes.

CYPRIENNE: It's not very warm in here.

JOSEPH: Oh, when they've lighted the fire and the gas, madame!

[*One waiter lights the fire, the other gets ready to light the chandelier.*]

DES PRUNELLES: No, no, don't light the chandelier. Just the candles.

JOSEPH [*to the first waiter*]: The candles!

[*The first waiter lights the candelabra. The second prepares the service at the table, rear.*]

[*To* DES PRUNELLES] It's at least two years since we saw Monsieur. [*He helps* DES PRUNELLES *take off his overcoat.*]

DES PRUNELLES: Isn't this room number eight?

JOSEPH: Monsieur recognizes it?

DES PRUNELLES: Yes ... it's been done up a bit, though.

JOSEPH: And also, for the convenience of our guests, we have added this little ante-room, and this dressing-room where Madame may remove her hat and coat.

CYPRIENNE: Yes, when I'm a little warmer. [*She goes to the fireplace and warms her feet.* JOSEPH *puts* DES PRUNELLES'*s hat and overcoat in the dressing-room.*]

DES PRUNELLES [*taking off his gloves*]: You are expecting Monsieur Clavignac this evening, aren't you?

JOSEPH [*returning*]: Yes, Monsieur. In number eleven. A party of six. Monsieur is not expecting anybody? Just for two?

DES PRUNELLES: Yes.

JOSEPH: Would Madame like to have the table nearer the fire?

CYPRIENNE: Yes, and open the screen. There's a little draught that way.

JOSEPH: Yes, Madame.

[*During the following, the waiters move the table in front of the fireplace, open the screen perpendicular to the wall, carry the chair near the table, turn the armchair to the other side of the table and continue working at the service table.*]

JOSEPH [*handing the menu to* DES PRUNELLES]: Monsieur will try some oysters? Marennes? Ostende?

DES PRUNELLES [*to* CYPRIENNE, *as he sits on the chair*]: Would you like some oysters, my dear?

CYPRIENNE [*still warming her feet, seated on the arm of the armchair*]: I don't care for them.

DES PRUNELLES [*seated in the chair, consulting the menu on the table*]: Nor I.

JOSEPH [*pulling a notebook and a pencil from his pocket, ready to write*]: Shell-fish soup, Crécy, Saint-Germain?

CYPRIENNE: Shell-fish soup.

JOSEPH [*as he writes*]: Fish: turbot, salmon?

DES PRUNELLES: After shell-fish soup?

[*The two waiters go out.*]

JOSEPH: It is usual.

CYPRIENNE: I prefer lobster.

DES PRUNELLES: Yes, no fish. You can give us some Bordeaux lobster to finish with.

JOSEPH: Very well, Monsieur. For an entrée, may I suggest a fish pie?

DES PRUNELLES: No! Lamb chops! Well-done!

JOSEPH [*writing*]: Well-done! . . .

DES PRUNELLES: Next.

JOSEPH: Some nice fowl? Quail? Our quail is excellent.

DES PRUNELLES: No, truffled partridge.

JOSEPH [*writing*]: Truffled! . . .

DES PRUNELLES: And Russian salad . . . a real one.

JOSEPH: Our salad is recommended.

DES PRUNELLES: Then the lobster! [*He puts the menu on the table.*]

JOSEPH: And for dessert! A little ice-cream?

DES PRUNELLES: No, no! No ice-cream. Unless Madame . . .?

CYPRIENNE: No. Some fruit, that's all. Grapes.

DES PRUNELLES: Is that clear?

JOSEPH: I understand, Monsieur. A delicate choice, if I may say so. But distinguished. Very distinguished, monsieur. Some coffee, of course.

DES PRUNELLES: No. Madame and I do not take it in the evening.

JOSEPH: Would Monsieur care to select his wine?

DES PRUNELLES: As usual . . . iced champagne.

JOSEPH: Moët? Cliquot?

DES PRUNELLES: No, Roederer. And your Chambertin, if you still have any?

JOSEPH: 'Sixty-eight?

DES PRUNELLES: Yes.

JOSEPH: There will be some for Monsieur.

DES PRUNELLES: Hurry it, a little.

JOSEPH: Yes, Monsieur. [*To the waiters who have just entered back*] Come! Quickly!

[JOSEPH *and the waiters go out.*]

DES PRUNELLES: Well? Are you warmer now?

CYPRIENNE [*taking off her hat and coat and putting them on the armchair*]: A little. You seem to be well known here.

DES PRUNELLES: I used to be.

CYPRIENNE: And you're going to be again?

DES PRUNELLES: Probably.

CYPRIENNE: So it's here Monsieur sowed his wild oats?

DES PRUNELLES: Not so many as you think.

CYPRIENNE: I'm certain those waiters take me for one of your loose women.

DES PRUNELLES: Good heavens, no! They probably think you're my mistress. How wrong they are!

CYPRIENNE: So now I'm compromised?

DES PRUNELLES: A little!

JOSEPH [*entering back with a card on a tray*]: Monsieur, there is a person outside who says he has been informed that Monsieur is here. He asks if Monsieur will see him?

[JOSEPH *passes the card to* DES PRUNELLES. *A waiter enters carrying the soup which he places on the service table and goes out.*]

DES PRUNELLES [*to* CYPRIENNE, *having read the card*]: Adhémar!

CYPRIENNE: Ah!

DES PRUNELLES [*to* JOSEPH]: A moment, please!

[JOSEPH *moves discreetly upstage and remains by the swing doors one of which stays open.*]

[*To* CYPRIENNE, *softly*] Shall I invite him in?

CYPRIENNE [*quickly*]: Oh, no!

DES PRUNELLES: But . . .

CYPRIENNE: No, no! I don't want it!

DES PRUNELLES: It's very difficult. After having invited him to dine at home.

CYPRIENNE [*tearing up the card*]: Then let him go and dine there! What's he want coming here for? Can't he let us get divorced in peace? [*She throws the pieces in the fire.*]

DES PRUNELLES [*getting up*]: Well, as he doesn't know you're here, I'll send him away. Stay in there a moment. [*He points to the dressing-room.*]

CYPRIENNE [*taking her hat and coat from the armchair and crossing left*]: All right! But be quick – I'm hungry! [*She goes into the dressing-room.*]

DES PRUNELLES [*to* JOSEPH]: Show him in.

JOSEPH [*opening the door back and speaking off-stage*]: If Monsieur would . . .

ADHÉMAR [*entering*]: Ah! I can come in then?

DES PRUNELLES: Yes, yes! Come in!

[JOSEPH *goes out.*]

ADHÉMAR [*soaking wet and carrying an umbrella*]: I beg your pardon, Monsieur. I hope I am not intruding? [*He puts his hat on the sofa left.*]

DES PRUNELLES: Good lord, no! I'm waiting for someone.

[*Letting him move right and offering him his chair*]

Come over, do! But how did you find me?

ADHÉMAR [*putting his umbrella against the back of the chair*]: Your club told me you were supposed to be dining here with Monsieur de Clavignac.

DES PRUNELLES: Ah, yes! Well, what is the trouble?

ADHÉMAR [*sitting on the chair*]: Yes, you are indeed looking at a very troubled man! It was agreed, wasn't it, that we were to dine together?

DES PRUNELLES: Not with me! You and Cyprienne.

ADHÉMAR: Precisely, I and Cyprienne – I beg your pardon, your wife and . . . that is to say . . . my . . . well, our wife.

DES PRUNELLES: Yes.

ADHÉMAR: I arrive! No one there! They told me you'd just gone out.

DES PRUNELLES: Really?

ADHÉMAR: And Cyprienne too!

DES PRUNELLES: She had gone out?

ADHÉMAR: After you had.

DES PRUNELLES: But where did she go?

ADHÉMAR [*looking at him, piteously*]: To her sick aunt's.

DES PRUNELLES: Ah!

ADHÉMAR [*quickly*]: Then you knew nothing about it?

DES PRUNELLES: No.

ADHÉMAR: I believe you! I've just come from her aunt's. She was bursting with health. And not a sign of Cyprienne.

DES PRUNELLES: Pardon. You mean her aunt . . .?

ADHÉMAR: Guérin, the widow Guérin, Boulevard du Temple.

DES PRUNELLES: Oh, no, she wouldn't be the one at all!

ADHÉMAR: No?

DES PRUNELLES: No, no! It would be Aunt Nicole, the asthmatic one, eighty-three years old, rue de Paris, number ninety-two.

ADHÉMAR: Oh, hang it! That's miles away! And in this weather!

DES PRUNELLES [*crossing to the window*]: Is it raining?

ADHÉMAR [*getting his hat from the sofa*]: Sleeting and not a cab to be found.

DES PRUNELLES: The devil it is!

[*He comes forward again.* CYPRIENNE *opens the dressing-room door and listens.*]

ADHÉMAR: If only I could be sure! Tell me, between ourselves – this aunt of hers – what d'you think about it?

DES PRUNELLES: Me?

ADHÉMAR: Yes.

DES PRUNELLES: Well – I don't really know.

ADHÉMAR: Seems a bit of a tall one, don't you think?

DES PRUNELLES: Look, my opinion's not much use now, is it? I mean, all this isn't my concern any longer.

ADHÉMAR: Yes, but as my predecessor, you could give me a tip or two, couldn't you? Has she ever tried this aunt of hers on with you?

DES PRUNELLES: Not much. Why?

ADHÉMAR: So I'd know if this was one of her usual tricks.

CYPRIENNE [*to herself, behind the door*]: Oh!

DES PRUNELLES: You don't believe it?

ADHÉMAR: Oh, it's just that I know how spiteful she is, that woman. I've seen her put you through it.

DES PRUNELLES: Ah! Yes.

ADHÉMAR: She certainly had you where she wanted you.

DES PRUNELLES: She got away with it with me. What about you?

ADHÉMAR: It won't work with me, I can tell you that.

DES PRUNELLES: That's the spirit!

ADHÉMAR: No, I shan't be such a simpleton as you were. [*Putting on his hat, with authority*] She'll have to toe the line, with me!

DES PRUNELLES [*with a wink to* CYPRIENNE]: Ah, good lad!

ADHÉMAR: Who did you say . . . this aunt?

DES PRUNELLES: Nicole, ninety-two, rue de Paris.

ADHÉMAR [*sitting on the sofa*]: Hell! [*To himself, turning up the ends of his trousers*] If it wasn't for that four hundred thousand! [*Aloud, getting up*] Well, I'll be off. Many thanks. And have a good time! [*He moves back-stage.*]

DES PRUNELLES: Thank you. [*Calling him back and picking up his umbrella*] Your umbrella!

ADHÉMAR [*returning*]: Oh, yes, of course! Thank you!

[*They make as if to shake hands both holding the umbrella.*]

DES PRUNELLES: The best of luck!

[ADHÉMAR *goes out.* DES PRUNELLES *closes the door and goes behind the sofa towards the dressing-room door.*]

I'd put paid to that fellow for good – if he wasn't playing my game for me so well!

CYPRIENNE [*appearing in the doorway left, whispering*]: Has he gone?

DES PRUNELLES [*making as if to call* ADHÉMAR *back*]: You've changed your mind? You want him back?

CYPRIENNE [*still whispering*]: No, no! Good heavens, no!

DES PRUNELLES [*coming forward*]: Poor boy! He's dashing off on a fool's errand.

CYPRIENNE: Let him! Did you ever hear anything like it! He's actually got the nerve to suspect me already!

DES PRUNELLES: It's a bad sign.

CYPRIENNE: My tricks! That woman! What way's that to talk? And spiteful, am I? Put you through it, did I?

DES PRUNELLES: No, no, of course you're not. Of course you didn't.

CYPRIENNE: And the way he said it! [*Imitating him*] 'It won't work with me! She'll have to toe the line with me!' I'd like to see anybody make me toe the line!

DES PRUNELLES [*encouraging her*]: So would I!

CYPRIENNE [*moving right*]: Oh, it's too much! That Adhémar is a complete fool!

[JOSEPH *and the two waiters enter back.* JOSEPH *carries a plate of fruit which he places on the table back-stage. He begins serving the soup.*]

DES PRUNELLES: Calm yourself! [*To the waiters*] You may serve us now. [*To* CYPRIENNE] Calm down, and have something to eat.

[*They sit at the table,* DES PRUNELLES *on the chair and* CYPRIENNE *on the armchair. The two waiters serve them with soup and then go out back with* JOSEPH *leaving the door open.* JOSEPH *can be seen in the ante-room*]

CYPRIENNE: The soup will be cold – thanks to him!

DES PRUNELLES [*taking his soup*]: My darling . . . you'll have to get rid of this notion that the lover and the husband can ever be found combined in the same person. He's only playing his role, now, poor boy. A little clumsily, I'll admit.

CYPRIENNE: Bad-tempered . . . grumbling . . .

DES PRUNELLES [*interrupting her*]: But that's not his fault. All that's part and parcel of being a husband. Why was I grumbling, only this morning? And why am I in such a good temper this evening? Because this morning I was the husband, and this evening I'm not. It's his turn now to grumble – he's simply defending himself!

CYPRIENNE: But he threatens to be more bad tempered than you!

DES PRUNELLES: Naturally! He's younger. He's lived less!

[JOSEPH *and the two waiters re-enter.* JOSEPH *carries a bottle of champagne in a bucket, which he places to the right of* DES PRUNELLES. *The first waiter carries the tray of lamb chops which he puts in the middle of the table. The second waiter removes the soup plates.*]

DES PRUNELLES [*continuing talking, while the above action takes place, in such a way that waiters will not understand*]: But it would be in bad taste for me to cast aspersions on the man to whom I've yielded the continuance of my affairs. He seems to me, on the contrary, to be a man of superior intelligence, with all that's necessary to make the enterprise prosper. He'll certainly not be able to avoid the inconveniences of his new situation.

[JOSEPH *and the waiters go out.* DES PRUNELLES *puts the bucket with the champagne on his left between* CYPRIENNE *and himself.*]

To sum up, and mark this well, all husbands conform to one single type: the husband. And all lovers to one other type: the lover! The husband has all the faults; the lover has all the virtues. Everyone's agreed on that. Actually, the husband has only one fault, being a husband. And the lover has only one virtue, being a lover.

[CYPRIENNE *pours herself some champagne.*]

This is so true that the same man can at the same time be the most annoying husband to his own wife and the most agreeable lover to someone else's wife. The difference is therefore not in the individual but in the function.

[*He pours himself a drink.* JOSEPH *enters carrying a bottle of wine cradled in a basket.*]

CYPRIENNE: Then one should not get married?

DES PRUNELLES: Oh, there are also a lot of disadvantages if one doesn't. [*He drinks.*]

CYPRIENNE: Such as what?

DES PRUNELLES: Oh, good heavens! [*To* JOSEPH *who is about to pour him a glass*] I'll help myself. And try to see we are not disturbed.

[JOSEPH *goes out and shuts the door.*]

Oh, good heavens, you've got to be reasonable! Happiness isn't found by going to extremes! A sense of proportion – the happy mean – that's happiness.

CYPRIENNE: Real happiness?

DES PRUNELLES: Yes. But it requires a little give and take on both sides.

[JOSEPH *and the two waiters re-enter back.* JOSEPH *holds a plate in one hand and the partridge in the other. He goes to* DES PRUNELLES*'s right. The first waiter, with a plate, goes to between* DES PRUNELLES *and* CYPRIENNE. *The second waiter carries a salad bowl which he puts on the service table.*]

DES PRUNELLES: For instance, in Switzerland, they had a very ingenious custom once. I don't know whether it still exists. [*To* JOSEPH] Put it there. I will carve it.

[DES PRUNELLES *and* CYPRIENNE *pass their plates to the first waiter who gives to* CYPRIENNE *the plate he has in his hand, while* JOSEPH *does the same with* DES PRUNELLES. JOSEPH *puts the partridge on the table and removes the lamb chops. The two waiters go out and* JOSEPH *goes to the service table to prepare the salad.* DES PRUNELLES *carves the partridge.*]

DES PRUNELLES: When two people wanted to get a divorce, they were shut up in one room for a week, with one table, one plate, one chair and one bed! And their food was passed in through the fanlight over the door!

CYPRIENNE [*laughing*]: Ah!

JOSEPH [*coming forward to* DES PRUNELLES *and showing him a little pot*]: Monsieur will take some red pepper?

DES PRUNELLES: Yes, yes!

[JOSEPH *returns to the service table.*]

At the end of the week there's a knock at the door: 'Knock! Knock!' [*He knocks on the table with his knife.*]

JOSEPH [*coming forward quickly*]: Monsieur?

DES PRUNELLES: No, not you. [*Going on*] 'Eh, you in there? How are you doing? What about that divorce?'

CYPRIENNE: Complete silence! They'd eaten each other!

DES PRUNELLES: Not at all! Three out of five no longer wanted a divorce!

[JOSEPH *brings the salad to the table and starts to go out.* DES PRUNELLES *calls him back.*]

One moment! [*He tastes the salad.*] Good! All right!

[JOSEPH *goes out back*]

CYPRIENNE [*laughing*]: Then you think they should shut us up?

DES PRUNELLES [*serving her*]: Oh, I'm not speaking about us. We're reasonable people. We know what we're doing. That goes without saying!

CYPRIENNE [*gaily*]: It wouldn't be too bad – shut up in here!

DES PRUNELLES: Home from home! This salad is very good!

CYPRIENNE: Yes – but too much pepper.

DES PRUNELLES: Your glass. [*He pours them both some of the Chambertin*] Of course, during that week, we could at least get to know each other.

CYPRIENNE [*laughing*]: Get to know each other?

DES PRUNELLES: Yes.

CYPRIENNE [*laughing still more*]: Oh, you are silly! Why, we've been married two years!

DES PRUNELLES: And twenty-two days! The twenty-sixth of October. [*They raise their glasses and drink.*]

CYPRIENNE: And we don't know each other?

DES PRUNELLES: Not at all.

CYPRIENNE: Now really!

DES PRUNELLES [*serving her*]: You admit you've never seen me in such a good temper?

CYPRIENNE: That's true.

DES PRUNELLES: You see – you don't know me. And how can you? In two years, we've only been really together for two weeks!

CYPRIENNE [*shrieking with laughter*]: Oh, now, stop it!

DES PRUNELLES: I'll prove it to you if you like. [*He rings the bell.*] Shall we bet on it? [*To* JOSEPH *who enters*] Oh, waiter, have you a pencil?

JOSEPH: Yes, Monsieur.

DES PRUNELLES: Give it me. All right, you may go now.

[JOSEPH *goes out.* DES PRUNELLES *pushes back the plates and glasses to clear a space on the table. He moves the table nearer still to the fireplace.* CYPRIENNE *helps him and puts the bucket of champagne on her left. Then* DES PRUNELLES *picks up the menu and draws his chair closer to* CYPRIENNE*'s armchair.*]

DES PRUNELLES [*writing numbers on the back of the menu*]: All right, first of all two years and twenty-two days of marriage, that is to say seven hundred and thirty plus twenty-two. Total seven hundred and fifty-two days. Which gives us in hours ... I'll be fair with you – I'll count twelve hours to a day.

CYPRIENNE: That all?

DES PRUNELLES: It's only fair. I never see you in the morning – before midday for lunch. We part company at night, don't we? So on average we live together from about midday to about midnight – twelve hours only.

CYPRIENNE: You're right!

DES PRUNELLES: So, seven hundred and fifty-two multiplied by twelve makes ... [*Writing numbers and adding them up quickly under his breath*] Two, four, five, fourteen ... nine thousand and twenty-four hours of marriage.

CYPRIENNE [*bursting with laughter*]: And we haven't had time to get to know each other – in nine thousand hours? [*She gets up with her glass in her hand, and warms her feet.*]

DES PRUNELLES: Oh, but wait! How many of those twelve hours are we alone together every day?

CYPRIENNE: Five or six?

DES PRUNELLES: Never on your life! Meals can't be counted – the servants are always there. We'll call it one hour – and I'm being generous.

CYPRIENNE: All right! One hour a day!

DES PRUNELLES [*drinking from time to time and becoming more animated*]: Now, let's deduct all the days we have visitors or when we go out to the theatre, to people's houses etc. You'll agree to a deduction of at least half for all that?

CYPRIENNE: More like three quarters!

DES PRUNELLES: Then that leaves us with, on average, a quarter of an hour a day. That means that out of nine thousand and twenty-four hours of marriage, we've had one hundred and eighty-eight hours alone together!

CYPRIENNE [*surprised*]: Oh!

DES PRUNELLES: There are the figures! A hundred and eighty-eight! And a good third of those have been spent nagging at each other. And another third not speaking to each other . . .

CYPRIENNE [*leaning on his shoulder*]: Oh, but they're part of being alone together . . .

DES PRUNELLES: I'm allowing that! Divide by twelve: fifteen and a fraction. So, the conclusion: out of two years of marriage, we've spent two weeks and four hours alone together. I was out by four hours.

CYPRIENNE [*bursting out laughing*]: Oh, no, it's not possible!

DES PRUNELLES: There are the figures!

CYPRIENNE: Ha, ha, ha!

DES PRUNELLES: It amuses you?

CYPRIENNE [*beginning to be a little gay*]: No! I'm laughing . . . laughing because . . . Ha, ha, ha! . . .

DES PRUNELLES: Why?

CYPRIENNE [*sitting on his knees*]: I just wondered something! . . . Ha, ha, ha! . . . Yes, how I'd like to know . . . Ha, ha, ha! . . .

DES PRUNELLES: Know what?

CYPRIENNE: How many of those hours . . .

DES PRUNELLES: Well?

CYPRIENNE: How many of them were spent ... [*she smothers the word by laughing in his shoulder*] ... love-making?

DES PRUNELLES: Oh, that's very easy!

[JOSEPH *enters with a plate of lobster. Seeing* CYPRIENNE *on* DES PRUNELLES'*s knees, he advances discreetly, puts the plate down right of* DES PRUNELLES *and steals out. Hearing him, they both turn away. Then* DES PRUNELLES *goes back to his accounts.*] We can state without exaggeration, can't we, that love had its good three hours a week?

CYPRIENNE [*exclaiming*]: Oh!

DES PRUNELLES: Or more even!

CYPRIENNE: Oh, no, it didn't!

DES PRUNELLES: Oh, yes, it did! Because the first few times ...

CYPRIENNE [*laughing*]: Yes, but what about the last few times?

DES PRUNELLES: Exactly, they balance out! Three hours, you agree?

CYPRIENNE [*still on his knees, kissing him*]: Stop boasting! All right! Put down three hours!

DES PRUNELLES [*adding up*]: So ... two years and twenty-two days ... [*Muttering the numbers quickly*] Fifty-one, two, three, one hundred and seven weeks at three hours per week, total, three hundred and twenty-one hours!

CYPRIENNE: Of making love?

DES PRUNELLES: Of making love!

CYPRIENNE [*drinking and laughing*]: As much as that! I don't believe it!

DES PRUNELLES: There's the figures! Now three hundred and twenty-one divided by twelve gives twenty-six and a fraction. From which we get the result that out of fifteen days alone together, I devoted twenty-six and a fraction to love-making!

CYPRIENNE [*laughing*]: And a fraction!

DES PRUNELLES: Twenty-six out of fifteen! See how unfair you are!

CYPRIENNE [*bursting with laughter*]: Ha, ha, ha! [*Kissing him*] You big brute, you! You are funny!

[*A sound of voices is heard at the door back. The waiters are heard struggling to prevent* ADHÉMAR *from entering.*]

THE WAITERS [*off-stage*]: No, Monsieur! You can't go in!

ADHÉMAR [*off-stage*]: I am! I'm going in, I tell you!

[*The altercation continues.*]

CYPRIENNE [*jumping up*]: Again! That man's becoming a nuisance!

DES PRUNELLES [*getting up*]: Hide yourself! [*He folds the screen round* CYPRIENNE *and pushes the table still nearer the fireplace.*]

CYPRIENNE: Throw him out for good this time! Get it finished with!

[*She sits in the armchair hidden by the screen. The door opens violently and* ADHÉMAR *rushes into the room, pushing aside the waiters. He is soaking wet, his umbrella dripping, and his hair and moustache in a pitiful state. During this scene,* CYPRIENNE, *comfortably seated by the table in view of the audience but hidden from* ADHÉMAR, *eats some lobster then washes her fingers in the finger bowl.*]

DES PRUNELLES [*napkin in hand*]: Well, well, what's all this about?

ADHÉMAR [*forcing his voice hoarsely*]: Monsieur ... I lack words ...

DES PRUNELLES: Yes, you sound bad!

ADHÉMAR: ... to describe your conduct! I have just been to Aunt Nicole's.

DES PRUNELLES: Oh, yes. How is she?

ADHÉMAR: She isn't!

DES PRUNELLES: Ah? You mean?

ADHÉMAR: She died three months ago!

DES PRUNELLES: Really? I didn't know. She was a very distant aunt.

[*He makes a sign to* JOSEPH *and the two waiters and they go out.*]

ADHÉMAR [*opening his umbrella and putting it to dry, left*]: Three miles, there and back! Not a cab anywhere! And no sign of Cyprienne. I dashed back to your house to see if she had returned. All I found was Bastien and Josépha eating your dinner and putting back your Pommard. Ha! Your Pommard's going to look a bit sick. They were both tight and that Josépha had the nerve to call after me: 'You still running after Madame? Didn't you know you'd been jilted?'

DES PRUNELLES: Oh!

ADHÉMAR: 'Jilted'! A blinding light hit me! I rushed over here. I questioned the woman at the bottom of the stairs, the one that opens the oysters. She knows me well. 'Did you see Monsieur Des Prunelles come in?' I said. 'Yes, monsieur.' 'With a lady?' 'Yes.' 'Describe her.' 'Small, plump, like a quail!' [*He gives a savage shout*] Aaah!

[DES PRUNELLES *takes a step back.*]

'Jilted'! – Yes! I've been tricked! You're dining here! Both of you! It's not fair – you gave her to me! You've broken your agreement!

DES PRUNELLES [*stammering a little*]: My dear successor! Now . . . don't be hasty! . . . How can she be here? I mean – where?

ADHÉMAR: Behind that screen!

[CYPRIENNE *gives a little laugh.*]

DES PRUNELLES: She'd be in your arms by now!

ADHÉMAR: Who knows? These women – they're all unpredictable! Perhaps she's getting a thrill now out of deceiving me with you?

CYPRIENNE [*giving a little involuntary cry of protest*]: Oh!

ADHÉMAR: There, what did I say! She's here! [*He hurls himself towards the screen.*]

DES PRUNELLES [*catching him by the sleeve and whirling him round*]: Pardon me! It's a friend of mine!

ADHÉMAR: Then let me see her!

DES PRUNELLES: That's not done!

ADHÉMAR: Make her say something, then!

DES PRUNELLES: Nor that! But . . . and this is very obliging of me . . .

ADHÉMAR: What?

DES PRUNELLES: Cyprienne's charming little foot. You must certainly know that well?

ADHÉMAR: Of course!

DES PRUNELLES: Well, if Madame will consent to show you her foot – that ought to convince you. [*Going to screen*] If you agree, Madame, will you tap on your plate?

[CYPRIENNE *gives two little taps on her plate with her knife.*]

ADHÉMAR: Ah.

DES PRUNELLES: Don't move! Are you ready, Madame?

[ADHÉMAR, *on the left, bends down to see better.* DES PRUNELLES, *also, leans forward next to the screen.* CYPRIENNE, *on the other side of the screen, is seated in the armchair.*]

Would you be so kind as to slide your shoe gently along the screen so that we can see the end of it?

[CYPRIENNE *does so very slowly, and gradually the point of her shoe appears from behind the screen.*]

That's it! Thank you! That's enough! [*To* ADHÉMAR] Well? Is that it?

ADHÉMAR [*with a gesture of despair*]: No.

DES PRUNELLES and CYPRIENNE [*together*]: Ah!

[CYPRIENNE *pulls her foot back quickly, giving a kick in the air in* ADHÉMAR*'s direction.*]

ADHÉMAR [*standing upright*]: Madame ... I am a little confused ... a thousand pardons! [*Nodding towards the screen, as he shakes* DES PRUNELLES*'s hand*] My compliments, Monsieur.

DES PRUNELLES: Thank you.

ADHÉMAR [*picking up his umbrella and closing it*]: Where *is* that wretched woman, then?

DES PRUNELLES: Well, that's your affair. You'd better go on searching.

ADHÉMAR: I must get something to eat first. I'm dying of hunger! [*He goes towards door back.*]

DES PRUNELLES [*accompanying him*]: You'd better take care. You sound as though you're getting a bad cold.

ADHÉMAR [*beginning to sneeze*]: Yes, I feel awful, just awful! [*He sneezes.*] What a situation to be in! Since she's been mine, she's been less mine than when she wasn't mine!

DES PRUNELLES: It's often like that. I'd have some lime-tea, if I were you.

ADHÉMAR [*at door back*]: Lime-tea?

DES PRUNELLES: Yes, boiling hot.

ADHÉMAR: Thank you.

[*He sneezes and goes out.* DES PRUNELLES *closes the door after him.*]

DES PRUNELLES: Bless you!

CYPRIENNE [*pulling back the screen, bursting with laughter*]:

What an idiot! Oh, what an idiot! He didn't even know my foot!

DES PRUNELLES [*gaily, going to her*]: It goes to show how mistaken you can be. [*Touching her foot*] Why, it was the first thing I noticed about you!

CYPRIENNE: But after four months! No, it's too much!

DES PRUNELLES [*laughing*]: That's how it is!

CYPRIENNE [*moving left, laughing, and sitting on the sofa, pleasantly tipsy*]: But he's an idiot! He is! An idiot! A complete idiot! [*Hitting the cushion*] How can anyone be such an idiot!

DES PRUNELLES: Don't ask me!

CYPRIENNE: Really! What fun would there be in deceiving an idiot like that?

DES PRUNELLES [*going to her*]: Oh ... one day!

CYPRIENNE: One day? But now?

DES PRUNELLES: Why now?

CYPRIENNE: Oh, just supposing! He wouldn't be worth it!

DES PRUNELLES: Even if our roles were really reversed? And I – was running after you?

CYPRIENNE: Yes ... What did you say? ... Oh ... Do you think so?

DES PRUNELLES [*sitting near her on the sofa*]: Do *you* think so? If he were the husband and I the lover?

CYPRIENNE: Ooh! La! la!

BOTH [*with a passionate movement towards each other*]: Oh!

DES PRUNELLES [*putting his arm around her*]: Irresistibly drawn to each other!

CYPRIENNE [*hugging him*]: Like this?

DES PRUNELLES [*letting her go*]: Instead of the apathy that separates us!

CYPRIENNE: Apathy! You can't be so easily tired, if you can keep it up for twenty-six days!

DES PRUNELLES: I was meaning you.

CYPRIENNE: Me? I'm only tired of Adhémar! [*She gets up and goes left to the piano where she sits playing and singing.*]

Was it worth all the torment
Just to make a change in government?...

DES PRUNELLES [*kneeling on the right end of the sofa*]: Take care. He may be outside – with his lime-tea.

CYPRIENNE: And his umbrella! [*Bursting out laughing*] Ha, ha, ha! Oh, no, that would be too much!

DES PRUNELLES [*sitting on the sofa*]: What would? What are you laughing at now?

CYPRIENNE [*without looking at him*]: Nothing! Just a completely mad idea! I could never tell you! [*She plays a sentimental waltz.*]

DES PRUNELLES [*after she has played a few bars, without looking at her*]: And besides, it wouldn't be fair.

CYPRIENNE: No, it wouldn't be fair!

DES PRUNELLES: Because you aren't mine any more.

CYPRIENNE [*attracted by the idea, but still playing*]: That's true.

DES PRUNELLES: Yes, it's forbidden to us.

CYPRIENNE [*playing only with one hand*]: Forbidden?

DES PRUNELLES: Illegal!

CYPRIENNE [*quickly*]: Illegal? [*She stops playing.*]

DES PRUNELLES: Yes. A crime.

CYPRIENNE [*turning quickly on the piano stool to face* DES PRUNELLES *but separated from him by the sofa*]: A crime? ... You think so? Really?

DES PRUNELLES: Cyprienne, don't look at me with those eyes of yours! [*He turns away on the sofa, looking front.*]

CYPRIENNE: Oh! I'm warm! And your lobster has given me a thirst! [*She goes to the service table, back, sees the bunch of grapes, picks them up, and eating one, moves back to behind* DES PRUNELLES *on the sofa.*] Ah, that's better! So you think it would be a crime?

DES PRUNELLES: Good lord, yes!

CYPRIENNE [*putting a grape in his mouth*]: Have one, darling. It would be wicked, wouldn't it? You really think it would?

DES PRUNELLES [*leaning his head on the back of the sofa*]: Oh, Cyprienne!

CYPRIENNE [*leaning over him looking into his eyes and putting another grape in his mouth*]: Another one ... my lover!

DES PRUNELLES: To deceive him! No!

CYPRIENNE [*as above*]: Yes ... Now another one, my beloved.

[*After putting another grape in his mouth, she dangles the bunch of grapes over his face.*]

CYPRIENNE: Don't they remind you of something? These grapes?

DES PRUNELLES: Yes ... Adam and Eve.

CYPRIENNE [*moving right of the sofa*]: Beast! You're thinking of that vine leaf!

DES PRUNELLES: Oh, that! Yes, that was really good.

CYPRIENNE: This would be even better! [*As she puts her arm round his neck there is a noise of voices off-stage, back.*]

DES PRUNELLES [*feeding her a grape, then her him*]: What's that?

ADHÉMAR [*outside*]: You're in there, Madame! I know your voice! But I'll be revenged! I will have vengeance! Yes, revenge! Revenge!

DES PRUNELLES: Revenge?

WAITERS [*off-stage*]: Get him out of here! Take him away!

ADHÉMAR: But she's my wife!

VOICES [*off-stage*]: Send for the police! [*The voices fade away.*]

DES PRUNELLES: They've gone!

[*There is a knock at the door.*]

CYPRIENNE: Someone's knocking!

DES PRUNELLES [*getting up*]: Who is it?

JOSEPH [*outside*]: Monsieur!

CYPRIENNE: It's the waiter!

DES PRUNELLES: The waiter? [*He goes to the door.*]

JOSEPH [*knocking again*]: Open quickly, Monsieur!

DES PRUNELLES [*half-opening the door to* JOSEPH *who can be half seen*]: What is it?

JOSEPH: A policeman has taken him to the police station over the road, but the police will probably be back. Would Madame care to disguise herself in my clothes?

[CYPRIENNE *gestures refusal and runs to the window.*]

DES PRUNELLES: No. [*He pushes the waiter out.*]

JOSEPH: That's how it's done in Paris, Monsieur!

DES PRUNELLES: No, no! Thank you! [*He shuts the door, locks it, and pours himself a glass of champagne at the table.*]

CYPRIENNE [*climbing on a chair to look out of the window and laughing loudly*]: It's true! A sergeant's pulling him across the street! He's soaking wet! He does look funny! And ugly!

DES PRUNELLES: [*crossing to* CYPRIENNE, *his glass in his hand*] Is that so?

CYPRIENNE: Yes . . . I've never seen him . . . like that. [*She stumbles and falls into* DES PRUNELLES'*s arms.*]

DES PRUNELLES: Look out! The champagne's all over me!

CYPRIENNE: Oh, my poor darling! Wait! [*She tries to wipe him with her handkerchief.*] Don't move!

DES PRUNELLES: I'd better put it in front of the fire. [*She helps him take off his coat, of which one sleeve remains inside out.*]

CYPRIENNE [*taking the coat*]: Give it me! [*She spreads it over the armchair in front of the fireplace.*] Phew! This fire! It's stifling in here! [*She unfastens the top of her dress.*]

DES PRUNELLES: Revenge for what? What did he mean? A duel?

CYPRIENNE: A duel! I forbid you to fight him, d'you hear?

DES PRUNELLES: But . . .

CYPRIENNE [*throwing herself in his arms*]: I don't want you to fight! He would kill you!

DES PRUNELLES: Bah!

CYPRIENNE: And just for him? For that man? That man? Is it possible? Oh, I've been blind! I've been mad! [*Falling on the sofa*] Oh, I'm to blame for it all! [*She turns quickly to* DES PRUNELLES, *who is standing near her looking at the door back, seizes his arms and pulls him on to his knees before her.*] Get on your knees, you miserable thing! And beg my pardon!

DES PRUNELLES: Eh?

CYPRIENNE: For having thrown me into that creature's arms! For wanting me to have him as a husband!

DES PRUNELLES [*on his knees, bewildered*]: But . . .

CYPRIENNE: I hate him, d'you hear? He's ridiculous . . . stupid . . . ugly, your Adhémar! He's horrible, do you hear me? It's only you I love! Tell me you still love me! Tell me! Tell me! Quickly!

DES PRUNELLES: I . . .

CYPRIENNE: And that you're sorry for having deserted me like this! And that you'll never leave me again! Never! Never! Never!

DES PRUNELLES: Never. I . . .

CYPRIENNE: That's enough! You are sorry! I'll forget everything! I forgive you! Come to my arms! I adore you!

[*Three loud knocks are heard at the door, then a voice.*]

A VOICE: Open! In the name of the law!

DES PRUNELLES [*to* CYPRIENNE]: The police!

CYPRIENNE [*frightened*]: Why?

DES PRUNELLES [*getting up*]: How do I know? Outrage to morals ... scandal in a public place.

CYPRIENNE: Ah!

POLICE OFFICER [*off-stage*]: You refuse to open?

CYPRIENNE [*noticing the disorder of her dress*]: Don't open ... now I'm ready ... Here, your coat! [*She goes to the fireplace and throws him his coat.*]

POLICE OFFICER [*off-stage*]: Open! Or I'll have the door broken down!

[CYPRIENNE *folds the screen round her*]

DES PRUNELLES: All right! All right!

[*He unlocks the door. A* POLICE OFFICER *enters followed by two* POLICEMEN *who place themselves back right.* JOSEPH *and the waiters follow and stand back left.* ADHÉMAR, *with his umbrella, passes behind them and comes between the piano and the sofa. Several onlookers can be seen through the doorway.*]

DES PRUNELLES [*completely bewildered, trying to put his coat on*]: Please excuse me, officer, but ...

POLICE OFFICER [*pointing to the disordered dinner table*]: Monsieur, you have a woman here with you! Don't deny it!

DES PRUNELLES: Yes, officer. My wife.

POLICE OFFICER: Your wife! This needs looking into! [*Pointing to* ADHÉMAR, *left*] This gentleman has been creating a disturbance, claiming that you are here with his wife!

DES PRUNELLES: Adhémar! [*He bursts out laughing.*]

[*Everybody looks at* ADHÉMAR *with pity.*]

ADHÉMAR [*to himself*]: I've deceived the police ... that could mean two weeks' prison ... but it's worth it to break up their little orgy!

DES PRUNELLES: Oh, that's good! That's very good! [*Speaking to* CYPRIENNE *behind the screen*] Did you hear that? Adhémar, your husband! [CYPRIENNE*'s hands can be seen raised above* *the screen in protestation.*] There, you see, officer. She's throwing a fit at the idea! Look at her!

POLICE OFFICER: Indecent, Monsieur! Like your dress! Put your sleeve the right way!

DES PRUNELLES: Let's get everything the right way, officer. *I* am her husband.

POLICE OFFICER: This attitude will get you nowhere, monsieur.

DES PRUNELLES: Oh, to hell with him then!

POLICE OFFICER: And no swearing! Have some respect for the law!

DES PRUNELLES: But . . .

POLICE OFFICER: Silence! [DES PRUNELLES, *intimidated, finishes putting on his coat the right way and moves extreme right. The* POLICE OFFICER *continues to* ADHÉMAR, *with tactful considerateness*] Monsieur, I am going to question your wife. Perhaps it would be better for you to wait outside. This screen . . . [ADHÉMAR *wipes his eyes with his handkerchief, then blows his nose dolorously.*] . . . the state she's probably in . . .

ADHÉMAR [*in a hoarse voice which is taken for emotion*]: No, Monsieur. I will be strong. Thank you.

[*The* POLICE OFFICER, *after making a gesture of consent turns to the screen and taps on it with his cane.*]

POLICE OFFICER: Madame!

CYPRIENNE [*behind the screen*]: Monsieur?

POLICE OFFICER: Are you presentable?

CYPRIENNE: Always, Monsieur. [*She comes out, her hair disordered, her dress buttoned up crooked.*]

[*There is a general movement of consternation.*]

ADHÉMAR: Ah! You wretched woman! [*He falls on to the sofa.* JOSEPH *holds the vinegar cruet under his nose. The waiters fold the screen against the wall.*]

DES PRUNELLES: No, this is too much! If a man and his wife can't . . .

POLICE OFFICER [*going to him*]: Silence, you!

DES PRUNELLES [*intimidated by the police*]: Suppression of the right to be heard! That's what it is! [*He falls into the chair in front of the table.*]

POLICE OFFICER [*to* CYPRIENNE]: Madame, you realize that

you have been surprised here with this gentleman, under conditions which leave no doubt that your relations with him are...

CYPRIENNE [*interrupting him*]: Exactly what they should be, Monsieur!

ALL [*in revulsion*]: Oh!

POLICE OFFICER [*to* ADHÉMAR, *speaking to him behind the back of* CYPRIENNE *who is in between them*]: Courage, Monsieur! [*Then speaking to him in front of* CYPRIENNE] All will be well! [*To* CYPRIENNE] So, you confess?

CYPRIENNE [*pointing to* DES PRUNELLES]: Behold, my husband!

POLICE OFFICER [*sarcastically*]: So you're taking the same attitude, are you? You want to be funny, as well? All right, then! If this person is your husband... [*pointing to* ADHÉMAR] ... who's he?

CYPRIENNE: Him? He's an idiot!

ADHÉMAR [*giving the vinegar back to* JOSEPH *and standing*]: Oh, Cyprienne!

CYPRIENNE: Don't come near me, you! Or I'll scratch your eyes out!

POLICE OFFICER: And you say he's not your husband?

CYPRIENNE: There's my husband! There! He's the one I love! [*She tries to run towards* DES PRUNELLES.]

POLICE OFFICER [*placing himself in front of her and forcing her left*]: Don't make things worse for yourself, Madame!

DES PRUNELLES [*rising, exasperated*]: Officer, you must be blind! Everybody will tell you she's my wife! Wait! There are some friends of mine in Room Eleven...

[*The* POLICE OFFICER *turns to* JOSEPH.]

JOSEPH: They've gone.

DES PRUNELLES: Damn! What luck!

POLICE OFFICER [*to one of the* POLICEMEN]: Clear a passage out there for Madame. We shall all go to the station to make the necessary charges.

JOSEPH: There's a crowd out in the street as well.

CYPRIENNE [*weeping*]: Oh! In front of everybody!

DES PRUNELLES: Like common criminals!

[*He and* CYPRIENNE *rush towards each other and fall into each others arms centre stage.*]

POLICE OFFICER [*losing control of himself*]: Separate them! They've gone mad!

[*The two* POLICEMEN *seize* DES PRUNELLES. *The* POLICE OFFICER *tries to prise* CYPRIENNE *loose from him.*]

CYPRIENNE [*clinging tight to* DES PRUNELLES]: No! With him! Till death us do part!

DES PRUNELLES: Yes! And I with her!

[*They are separated.*]

CYPRIENNE [*furiously*]: Killers! Murderers! Assassins! [*She falls on to the sofa.*]

DES PRUNELLES [*back-right*]: This is ridiculous! There's no other word for it! We're almost just next door to the notary who married us! I'm getting him! [*He dashes out through the open door, back.*]

POLICE OFFICER: Stop him!

One of the POLICEMEN, JOSEPH and THE WAITERS [*rushing out after him, shouting*]: Stop him! Stop him!

CYPRIENNE: Henri! Wait for me! [*She tries to run after him.*]

POLICE OFFICER [*barring the door*]: No, Madame, no!

[*The other* POLICEMAN *has opened the dressing-room door.*]

You get in there!

ADHÉMAR [*pleadingly*]: Cyprienne!

CYPRIENNE [*crossing in front of the* OFFICER]: Don't you come near me!

ADHÉMAR: Oh, Cyprienne! Forgive! Forget!

CYPRIENNE: Take that, you . . . monster! [*She slaps his face and goes into the dressing-room.*]

ADHÉMAR [*spinning round and falling on the sofa*]: Oh!

POLICE OFFICER [*as the* POLICEMAN *locks the door*]: That will be added to the charges, Monsieur! Come! Let us find the other one!

[*He runs out back, followed by the* POLICEMAN *and* ADHÉMAR, *holding his cheek.* DES PRUNELLES *re-enters by the other door back right, closely followed by* JOSEPH, *the second* POLICEMAN *and the two waiters.*]

DES PRUNELLES: Caught! Trapped! [*They surround him.*] I give up. I surrender.

JOSEPH: Lock him up! [*He pushes the sofa to one side and goes to the dressing-room door.*]

WAITERS: Yes, lock him up!

DES PRUNELLES [*crossing in front of the waiters*]: Don't touch me!

JOSEPH: Here! In the dressing-room! [*He unlocks the door.*]

DES PRUNELLES: All right, I'm going! Keep your hands off me! [*He goes into the dressing-room where* CYPRIENNE *is.*]

JOSEPH [*turning the key*]: There! That'll calm him down. Where's the woman?

ALL [*looking around*]: She's disappeared!

JOSEPH: Gone! After her!

[*They all rush towards the swing doors back centre. The* POLICE OFFICER, ADHÉMAR *and the first* POLICEMAN *re-enter by the other door back right.*]

POLICE OFFICER, ADHÉMAR *and* FIRST POLICEMAN: The man? Where's the man?

JOSEPH, WAITERS *and* SECOND POLICEMAN: The woman? Where's the woman?

POLICE OFFICER: We've got the woman!

JOSEPH: And the man!

POLICE OFFICER: The woman's in there! [*He points to the dressing-room.*]

JOSEPH: The man's in there! [*He points to the dressing-room.*]

POLICE OFFICER [*correcting him*]: No, she is!

JOSEPH [*correcting him*]: No, he is!

POLICE OFFICER: Both of them!

ALL [*turning to look at the door*]: Together!

ADHÉMAR [*forgetting himself*]: With his wife?

ALL [*turning quickly towards him*]: His wife?

ADHÉMAR [*terrified*]: Caught! Let me out! [*He rushes out back right.*]

POLICE OFFICER: Stop him! Stop the scoundrel!

[*The* POLICEMEN *and waiters dash out after* ADHÉMAR. *The* POLICE OFFICER *remains alone.*]

In there with his wife? Well, I suppose it's my job to encourage that sort of thing! [*Going to the dressing-room door and unlocking it*] A thousand pardons, Monsieur! Everything's all right, Monsieur. Quite all right. You've done well, Monsieur. Married – and yet still in love!

[DES PRUNELLES *half opens the door; his hand appears; the* POLICE OFFICER *shakes it.*]

I congratulate you, Monsieur! Continue! Keep it up!

[DES PRUNELLES *comes out with his wife who has put on her hat and coat.*]

DES PRUNELLES: Allow me to present Madame Des Prunelles.

POLICE OFFICER: Ah, Madame! Ah, Monsieur! A thousand pardons!

[*All the others return back centre, pushing in* ADHÉMAR.]

ALL: Here he is! We've got him!

POLICE OFFICER: As for this gentleman – who thinks he can make fools of the police . . .

CYPRIENNE: Oh, no, please, Officer! Have pity on him! Let him off!

DES PRUNELLES: Yes, after all, he's saved our marriage.

POLICE OFFICER: Well, if it will please you – and since it's I who should be asking favours of you. [*To the* POLICEMEN] Let him go.

ADHÉMAR [*to himself*]: I was counting on that.

[*Music.*]

DES PRUNELLES [*going to* ADHÉMAR, *softly*]: No more from you – or I'll have you put away for misusing the telegraph service. [*He shows him the telegram.*]

ADHÉMAR [*softly*]: You knew all the time?

DES PRUNELLES: What d'you think! Good heavens, lad, you never had a chance!

ADHÉMAR: Maybe I hadn't . . . but there'll be another time . . . with someone else!

DES PRUNELLES: Make sure it's someone else. [*To* CYPRIENNE] What's he keep holding his cheek for?

CYPRIENNE [*laughing, as she crosses in front of the* POLICE OFFICER]: Oh, that was me! [*She makes a gesture of slapping somebody.*]

DES PRUNELLES: What? You slapped his face? [*Severely, making her stand in front of* ADHÉMAR] Make it better!

[ADHÉMAR *removes his hand from his cheek and looks at her enticingly.* CYPRIENNE *looks at* ADHÉMAR*'s cheek and kisses her husband's. She then takes* DES PRUNELLES*'s arm and bows prettily to the* POLICE OFFICER.]

ALL [*bowing to the* POLICE OFFICER]: Monsieur!

POLICE OFFICER [*bowing to* DES PRUNELLES]: May you have continued success, Monsieur, in your noble work! Keep it up, Monsieur, keep it up!

[ADHÉMAR *has fallen on to the chair.* JOSEPH *is bathing his cheek with a napkin soaked in a glass of water. The curtain falls as* DES PRUNELLES *and his wife are going out, briskly and gaily, in between the* POLICEMAN *and the waiters, who bow to them respectfully.*]

CURTAIN

GET OUT OF MY HAIR!

by

Georges Feydeau

CHARACTERS

BOUZIN
THE GENERAL
BOIS-D'ENGHIEN
LANTERY
DE CHENNEVIETTE
DE FONTANET
ANTONIO
JEAN
FIRMIN
THE CONCIERGE
A GENTLEMAN

ÉMILE
LUCETTE
MADAME DUVERGER
VIVIANE
MARCELINE
NINI
FRÄULEIN BETT
A LADY
WEDDING GUESTS
A FLORIST
TWO POLICEMEN

ACT ONE

A drawing-room in the house of LUCETTE GAUTIER. *Elegantly furnished. The room has the corner cut off on the left side, and has a right-angle on the right side. On the left upstage a door gives into Lucette's bedroom. Back-stage, facing the audience, are two doors. One, almost centre stage, leads to the dining-room. This door opens away from the audience so that they can see into the room. The door back right opens into the hall where a hatstand can be seen. In the dining-room can be seen a sideboard laden with food. On the left, in the diagonal corner, is a fireplace with a mirror and decorations. Up-stage right is another door.* [*All these doors are double-doors.*] *Down-stage right, against the wall, a piano and a stool. Down-stage left, a console table and vase. On the right, near the piano, but far enough away to allow passage, a sofa almost at right angles to the audience, and with its back to the piano. Right of the sofa, a small table; at the other end of the sofa, a light chair. Left stage, not far from the console table, and facing the audience, a rectangular table with a chair right, left, and behind it. In front of the fireplace, a pouf. Left of the fire-place, and against the wall, a chair. Between the two doors back-stage, a small chiffonier. Knick-knacks here and there, vases on the mantelpiece, pictures on the walls, on the table left, a folded copy of* Figaro.

[*At the rise of the curtain,* MARCELINE *is standing by the fireplace, leaning on it with her right arm and drumming with her fingers as if fed-up with waiting. At the same time, back-stage,* FIRMIN *has finished laying the table in the dining-room and is looking at his watch as if saying to himself: 'What a time to have a meal!'*]

MARCELINE [*going to the sofa and sitting*]: Firmin! If you don't bring in something to eat, I'll faint!

FIRMIN [*coming forward to her*]: But, Mademoiselle, I can't serve while Madame is still in her bedroom.

MARCELINE [*sulkily*]: Oh, that sister of mine's the limit! Only yesterday I was congratulating her ... I actually said to her: 'Poor Lucette, even if your lover has left you – even if it's made you so miserable – at least you're getting to bed at a decent hour and we're able to have breakfast before midday!' It looks as though I spoke too soon!

FIRMIN: Madame has perhaps found a successor to Monsieur de Bois-d'Enghien?

MARCELINE: Her? Oh, no! Not her! She's incapable of such a thing! She takes after my father. She's a woman of principle! Anyway, if she had [*changing her tone*] I'd have known about it two days ago at least.

FIRMIN [*persuaded by this argument*]: Yes, perhaps you're right...

MARCELINE [*rising*]: But even if she had, that would be no reason for staying in bed till a quarter past twelve. Oh, I know love is supposed to make you forget time. [*Giggling*] Of course, not that I know about such things ...

FIRMIN: No?

MARCELINE: No.

FIRMIN: Ah, you should!

MARCELINE [*with a sigh*]: How can I? I'm only the sister of a celebrity! Who wants to marry the sister of a famous night-club singer? Anyway, I should have thought – even if a girl's crazy over a man – surely – by midday! I mean – why even farmyard animals – they're up and about by four in the morning, aren't they? [*She sits again on the sofa.*]

FIRMIN: Quite so!

[LUCETTE *enters with a rush, left.* FIRMIN *moves back-stage.*]

LUCETTE [*as she enters from her bedroom*]: Marceline! ...

MARCELINE [*seated, throwing wide her arms*]: So you're here at last!

LUCETTE: An aspirin! Quick! An aspirin!

MARCELINE [*rising*]: An aspirin? Why – are you ill?

LUCETTE [*radiantly*]: Me? I've never felt better! No, it's for him! He's a bad headache! [*She sits right, by the table.*]

MARCELINE: Him? Who?

LUCETTE [*radiantly*]: Fernand! He's come back!

MARCELINE: Monsieur de Bois-d'Enghien? No!

LUCETTE: Yes!

MARCELINE [*calling to* FIRMIN *as she moves upstage to the chiffonier and opens a drawer in it*]: Firmin! Monsieur de Bois-d'Enghien is back!

FIRMIN [*wiping a plate, as he comes forward to Lucette*]: Monsieur de Bois-d'Enghien! Good heavens! I mean . . . Madame must be pleased?

LUCETTE: Oh, yes, I'm pleased all right. You read my thoughts.

[FIRMIN *returns back-stage.*]

[*To* MARCELINE *who comes forward with a small box of aspirins*] Just imagine what I felt when he walked in here again last night. [*Taking the aspirin* MARCELINE *gives her*] Thank you. [*Changing her tone*] And just imagine – for the last fortnight I've been thinking the most terrible things about him – and all the time the poor boy's been having the most ghastly fainting spells! [*She moves forward, left.*]

MARCELINE: No? . . . Oh, how awful! [*She moves right a little.*]

LUCETTE [*moving between small table and console table*]: Yes, I can't talk about it! It's too terrible – just suppose he'd never come back! He's so divinely handsome! [*To* FIRMIN, *who is busy in the dining-room*] He is, isn't he, Firmin?

FIRMIN [*who has not been listening, coming forward a little*]: What was that, Madame?

LUCETTE: I said Monsieur de Bois-d'Enghien is so divinely handsome, isn't he?

FIRMIN [*without conviction*]: Quite so, Madame.

LUCETTE [*effusively*]: Oh, how I adore him!

BOIS-D'ENGHIEN'S VOICE: Lucette!

LUCETTE: There! He's calling to me! [*To* MARCELINE] You remember his voice?

MARCELINE: How couldn't I?

LUCETTE [*going to bedroom door, left*]: Here I am, my sweet!

MARCELINE [*going to her*]: Is one permitted to see him?

LUCETTE: Yes, of course! [*Speaking off-stage, into bedroom*] Darling, it's only Marceline! She just wants to say welcome back again.

BOIS-D'ENGHIEN'S VOICE: Oh, hello, Marceline.

MARCELINE: Good morning, Monsieur Fernand!

FIRMIN [*behind* MARCELINE]: Are you feeling better, Monsieur Fernand?

BOIS-D'ENGHIEN: Is that you, Firmin? Not so bad, thank you. Just a little headache.

MARCELINE *and* FIRMIN: Oh, what a shame! That's too bad!

LUCETTE [*going into bedroom*]: Now come along and get ready, darling. Because we're all going to have lunch. [*She disappears into the bedroom as the bell rings.*]

MARCELINE: Now who can that be?

FIRMIN [*going out by door back right*]: I'll go and see.

MARCELINE: Lunch! What happened to breakfast? They're trying to starve me to death!

FIRMIN [*entering back right, to* MARCELINE]: It's Monsieur de Chenneviette! [*To* DE CHENNEVIETTE, *who has followed him in*] Has Monsieur come to lunch?

DE CHENNEVIETTE: Yes, Firmin, I have!

FIRMIN [*to himself, sarcastically*]: Naturally!

DE CHENNEVIETTE [*without going to her*]: Morning, Marceline.

MARCELINE [*grumpily*]: Morning.

FIRMIN: Has Monsieur heard the news? He's back again!

DE CHENNEVIETTE: Who?

MARCELINE: Monsieur de Bois-d'Enghien!

DE CHENNEVIETTE: No!

FIRMIN: Last night! It's true!

DE CHENNEVIETTE: All right. I'm killing myself laughing.

FIRMIN: My sentiments exactly, Monsieur. I'll tell Madame you're here.

DE CHENNEVIETTE: What a lot! Always swopping and changing!

FIRMIN [*knocking at* LUCETTE'*s door while* MARCELINE *makes conversation with* DE CHENNEVIETTE]: Madame!

LUCETTE'S VOICE: What is it?

FIRMIN: Monsieur is here, Madame.

LUCETTE'S VOICE: Monsieur who?

FIRMIN [*continuing, as if announcing somebody*]: Monsieur the father of Madame's child.

LUCETTE'S VOICE: Oh, good! Tell him I'm coming!

FIRMIN [*to* DE CHENNEVIETTE *without coming forward*]: Madame is coming.

DE CHENNEVIETTE: Thank you, Firmin. [*To* MARCELINE, *as* FIRMIN *returns to dining-room*] He really *is* back – picking up from where he left off?

MARCELINE: Well? [*She glances significantly towards* LUCETTE*'s bedroom door.*] What's it look like?

DE CHENNEVIETTE [*sitting on sofa*]: Poor Lucette! When's she going to stop falling for these fellows? Oh, Bois d'Enghien's all right. I don't deny it. Charming fellow, but how's it going to end? I mean to say, he hasn't a penny to his name. Not a sou!

MARCELINE: Ah! But you should hear Lucette! [*Confidentially*] It seems that those without a penny to their name are the best – when it comes to making love.

DE CHENNEVIETTE [*cynically*]: You don't say!

MARCELINE [*quickly*]: Not that I'd know. A young girl like me. [*She sits right by the table.*]

DE CHENNEVIETTE [*mockingly*]: Really? I'd never have guessed it! [*Remembering something*] By the way, what happend to that flashy fellow? The South American?

MARCELINE: Who? General Irrigua? It looks as if he's been put in cold storage.

DE CHENNEVIETTE [*rising*]: There you are! That's what I mean! She comes across a chap like him! Rolling in money – and dotty over her! A general, as well! Oh, I know they're all generals where he comes from – but all the same...

MARCELINE [*getting up, agreeing with him*]: Yes – and quite a gentleman, too! Only the day before yesterday – at the club where Lucette was singing – when he found out I was her sister, he got himself introduced to me – and gave me a huge box of chocolates!

DE CHENNEVIETTE: And only yesterday she'd definitely finished with Bois d' Enghien. She'd definitely agreed to meet this South American fellow. And now what? Bois d'Enghien comes back – and we're all back where we were again.

MARCELINE: That's what it looks like.

DE CHENNEVIETTE: It's ridiculous! Still – it's her lookout. [*He moves right as the bell rings.*]

MARCELINE: Oh, now who is it?

[FIRMIN *enters back right followed by* NINI GALANT.]

FIRMIN: In here, please, Mademoiselle.

MARCELINE *and* DE CHENNEVIETTE: Nini Galant!

NINI [*back-stage*]: Yes, it's me! How's everybody? [*She puts her handbag by the sofa near the chair and moves down-stage.*]

MARCELINE and DE CHENNEVIETTE: Not too bad!

FIRMIN: And has Mademoiselle heard the news?

NINI: No? What?

ALL: He's back!

NINI: Who?

ALL: Monsieur de Bois-d'Enghien!

NINI: No! I don't believe it!

[LUCETTE *comes out of her bedroom and, after shaking hands with* NINI *and* DE CHENNEVIETTE, *finds herself placed between them.* FIRMIN *returns back-stage.*]

LUCETTE: Nini, darling! How nice to see you! [*To* DE CHENNEVIETTE] Hello, Pierre! Well, have you both heard the news?

NINI: Yes, they've just told me! Your Fernand is back!

LUCETTE: Yes! Isn't it too, too marvellous!

NINI: I'm so terribly, terribly happy for you, darling! Is he ... in there?

LUCETTE: Of course! Wait! I'll call him! [*Going to door, left, and calling*] Fernand, it's Nini ... What? ... Now don't be such a silly! Come out as you are! Everybody knows you! [*To the others*] Here he is!

[*Everybody gets in a line, as though lining a processional route, for the entrance of* BOIS-D'ENGHIEN. *He appears enveloped in a large, striped dressing gown, tied round the waist with a cord. He holds in his hand a brush with which he has been brushing his hair. He moves above the table to centre-stage in between* FIRMIN *and* LUCETTE.]

ALL: Hip! Hip! Hip! Hurray!

BOIS-D'ENGHIEN [*bowing*]: Mesdames ... Messieurs ...

[*Everybody moves forward. The following lines should be spoken very quickly, one on top of the other, until* 'I wasn't coming back!']

NINI: Lo and behold! The prodigal lover himself!

BOIS-D'ENGHIEN: What? Oh, yes, well, I ...

MARCELINE: Naughty boy! Playing hard to get!

BOIS-D'ENGHIEN [*protesting*]: Oh I say! Really!

DE CHENNEVIETTE: Good to see you again, old chap.

BOIS-D'ENGHIEN: Er ... yes ... thanks.

FIRMIN: Perhaps I may be permitted to say that Monsieur's absence would, if continued, have turned Madame's hair grey?

BOIS-D'ENGHIEN [*shaking hands with everybody*]: Oh, I say ... really ... I mean ...

ALL: Anyway, he's back again! Yes, he's back! That's the important thing!

BOIS-D'ENGHIEN [*with a forced smile*]: Oh yes, he's back all right. [*To himself, as he moves left pushing the brush distractedly through his hair*] Just to tell her I wasn't coming back! [*He sits by the table.*]

[FIRMIN *goes out.* MARCELINE *has moved upstage.* LUCETTE *has sat on the sofa next to, and to the right of,* NINI. DE CHENNEVIETTE *is standing behind the sofa.*]

LUCETTE [*to* NINI] You'll stay for lunch, darling, won't you?

NINI: Oh, my dear, that's what I popped in to tell you. I can't!

LUCETTE: You can't?

MARCELINE [*in a hurry to eat*]: Then I'd better go and tell Firmin.

LUCETTE: Tell him to serve the eggs.

MARCELINE: Eggs! Yes, of course! Eggs! [*She goes out back.*]

LUCETTE: Why can't you stay?

NINI: Because ... well, as a matter of fact, I've some wonderful news as well. Wedding-bells, darling!

LUCETTE *and* DE CHENNEVIETTE: You!

BOIS-D'ENGHIEN [*to himself*]: So I'm not the only one!

NINI: Yes, me! I'm getting married, darling! And with all the frills!

LUCETTE: Darling! Congratulations!

DE CHENNEVIETTE [*moving centre above sofa*]: Who's the – lucky fellow?

NINI: My lover, of course!

DE CHENNEVIETTE [*sarcastically*]: Your lover? And he's marrying you? What's he after?

NINI: What d'you mean – 'what's he after'? I don't call that funny!

LUCETTE: Which lover, darling?

NINI: Well, I haven't all that many ... serious ones of course. There's always only been one of *them*, darling!

LUCETTE: Only one, dear?

NINI: Yes, dear. Only one. The Duc de la Courtille! I'm going to be the Duchesse de la Courtille!

LUCETTE: No!

DE CHENNEVIETTE: I say! Good for you!

LUCETTE: Darling! I'm terribly, terribly happy for you!

[*During the preceding dialogue,* BOIS-D'ENGHIEN *has been glancing through the newspaper* Figaro *on the table near him. Now he suddenly jumps up, muttering to himself.*]

BOIS-D'ENGHIEN [*to himself*]: Oh, my God! The announcement of my marriage! In *Figaro*! [*He crumples the newspaper up into a ball and hides it inside his dressing-gown.*]

LUCETTE [*who, like the others, has seen this bit of by-play, runs over to him*]: What is it? What's wrong?

BOIS-D'ENGHIEN: Nothing! Nothing! Just nerves!

LUCETTE: Oh, my poor Fernand! You're not ill again, are you?

BOIS-D'ENGHIEN: No, no, really, I'm fine!

[*To himself, as* LUCETTE, *reassured, returns to* NINI *explaining,* sotto-voce, *to her that* BOIS-D'ENGHIEN has *been ill*]

Heavens! She mustn't read that before I've prepared her for it!

DE CHENNEVIETTE: That reminds me, did you see that good bit – about you – in *Figaro* this morning?

LUCETTE: No?

DE CHENNEVIETTE: I brought it with me, in case you hadn't! Just a moment . . . [*He takes a copy of* Figaro *from his pocket and opens it.*]

BOIS-D'ENGHIEN: [*to himself*] Hell!

DE CHENNEVIETTE: There you are.

BOIS-D'ENGHIEN [*throwing himself at* DE CHENNEVIETTE *and snatching the newspaper out of his hand*]: No! Not now! Not now! [*He pushes it, like the other copy, inside his dressing-gown.*]

ALL: What's the matter?

BOIS-D'ENGHIEN: We . . . we're just going to have lunch! This isn't the time to read newspapers!

DE CHENNEVIETTE: What's the matter with him?

MARCELINE [*appearing back, from dining-room*]: It's ready! Come on, everybody!

BOIS-D'ENGHIEN: There you are, you see! It's ready!

DE CHENNEVIETTE: There's something wrong with him, all right!

[*A bell rings.*]

BOIS-D'ENGHIEN [*going to door of bedroom, left*]: Wait while I finish dressing. [*To himself, as he goes out*] I'll leave tackling this problem till after lunch! [*He goes out, carrying his hairbrush.*]

FIRMIN [*entering from the hall*]: Monsieur de Fontanet is here, Madame.

LUCETTE: Him! Oh heavens, yes! I'd forgotten! You'll have to lay an extra place... and show him in! [*She rises and goes left.*]

NINI [*going to her*]: What? You're having de Fontanet to lunch? [*Laughing*] Well, I pity you!

LUCETTE: Why?

NINI [*laughing, good naturedly*]: My dear! His breath! It's enough to knock you over!

LUCETTE [*laughing also*]: Oh, that! What if his breath does smell? He's good company – and he means well. He wouldn't hurt a fly!

DE CHENNEVIETTE [*right, also laughing*]: That depends how far away the fly is when he's speaking to it!

NINI [*laughing*]: How right you are!

LUCETTE [*going to door to meet* DE FONTANET]: Stop being naughty, both of you!

[*During this preceding dialogue,* DE FONTANET *can be seen through the hall doorway, taking off his coat, helped by* FIRMIN.]

DE FONTANET [*entering*]: Ah! dear celebrity! I come to kiss your hand!

LUCETTE [*indicating* NINI]: Nini was only just speaking of you!

DE FONTANET [*bowing, flattered*]: How very nice of her! [*To* LUCETTE] Well, I'm here, as you see! You really shouldn't have invited me! I always take people at their word!

LUCETTE: But I was counting on you coming!

[NINI *sits left of the table and chats with* MARCELINE *who is standing beside her.*]

DE FONTANET [*to* LUCETTE, *as he shakes hands with* DE CHENNEVIETTE]: Well, my dear, I hope you've been pleased with that marvellous article in *Figaro*?

LUCETTE: I don't know. Just imagine, I've not even seen it yet.

DE FONTANET [*pulling a copy of* Figaro *from his pocket*]: You haven't! Well, isn't that lucky. I thought of bringing it along!

LUCETTE: Oh, do let's see!

DE FONTANET [*opening out the newspaper*]: There!

BOIS-D'ENGHIEN [*entering left*]: Right! I'm ready! [*Seeing the newspaper*] My God, another of them! [*He hurls himself between* LUCETTE *and* DE FONTANET *and snatches the paper from him.*] Give me that! Give me that!

ALL: What, again!

DE FONTANET [*bewildered*]: Good gracious!

BOIS-D'ENGHIEN: No, this is not the time to read newspapers! It's lunch-time! We're going to have lunch! [*He rolls the paper into a ball.*]

LUCETTE: Now, don't be tiresome, darling. There's an article about me in it!

BOIS-D'ENGHIEN [*pushing the paper into his pocket*]: All right, I'll keep it for you! I'll keep it! [*To himself*] Has everybody got this damn paper!

DE FONTANET [*a little provoked*]: But look here, Monsieur!

BOIS-D'ENGHIEN [*challengingly*]: Well, Monsieur?

LUCETTE [*quickly*]: Gentlemen, please! Monsieur de Fontanet, may I introduce you to my ... friend, Monsieur de Bois-d'Enghien. [*She pauses significantly on the word 'friend'.*]

DE FONTANET [*disconcerted, bowing*]: Enchanted, Monsieur.

BOIS-D'ENGHIEN: I also, Monsieur! [*They shake hands.*]

DE FONTANET: I am not in a position to congratulate you. I am only one of Madame Gautier's platonic admirers. Nevertheless, I may say that her charm equals her talent and ... [*Noticing that* BOIS-D'ENGHIEN *has started sniffing the air*] What's the matter?

BOIS-D'ENGHIEN [*ingenuously*]: Nothing really! Don't you think there's rather a strange smell in here?

[DE CHENNEVIETTE, LUCETTE, MARCELINE *and* NINI *try to stop themselves from laughing*]

DE FONTANET [*sniffing*]: In here? No ... but you can't go by my sense of smell. I seem to have a very poor one. People often say that to me, but I can never smell anything. [*He sits on the sofa and begins chatting with* DE CHENNEVIETTE *who is standing behind it.*]

LUCETTE [*in a low voice, quickly, to* BOIS-D'ENGHIEN]: Be quiet! Can't you see it's him!

BOIS-D'ENGHIEN: Him? Oh, you mean . . .? [*Goes to* DE FONTANET *and says foolishly*] I say, I'm awfully sorry! I didn't know.

DE FONTANET: Know what?

BOIS-D'ENGHIEN: Oh . . . er . . . nothing! Nothing! [*Coming forward, to himself*] Phew! It's enough to knock you over!

FIRMIN [*entering back, from dining-room*]: Lunch is served, Madame.

LUCETTE: Good! Come along, everyone!

MARCELINE [*hurrying to be first*]: And about time too!

[*She goes into the dining-room.* BOIS-D'ENGHIEN *looks at her with a laugh as she passes him.*]

NINI: And I must be going, darling!

LUCETTE [*going with her to hall door*]: You really won't stay?

NINI [*picking up her bag from against sofa*]: No, no, really . . .

LUCETTE [*while* NINI *shakes hands with* DE FONTANET *and* DE CHENNEVIETTE]: I won't insist, then! I hope you'll still drop in now and then, when you're Duchesse de la Courtille.

NINI [*naïvely*]: Of course I will, dear. It will be so nice to still have some ordinary friends.

LUCETTE [*curtseying*]: Your grace, how kind of you! [*The others laugh.*]

NINI [*realizing what she has said, but laughing with them*]: Oh, you know that's not what I meant!

MARCELINE [*reappearing at dining-room door, with her mouth full*]: Well? Aren't you coming?

LUCETTE: Yes, all right! [*To* NINI, *at hall door*] Good-bye, darling!

NINI: Bye bye, darling! [*She goes out.*]

DE CHENNEVIETTE [*seated on piano stool*]: So! There goes the Duchesse de la Courtille!

LUCETTE: Ha! That won't make her any more of a lady!

DE FONTANET: How true!

LUCETTE: Well, let's go and eat! [BOIS-D'ENGHIEN *enters the dining-room and she says to* FONTANET *who makes way for her*] Please, after you.

DE FONTANET: Thank you, Madame. [*He goes in.*]

LUCETTE [*to* DE CHENNEVIETTE *who has moved, lost in thought, to above sofa*]: What about you? Aren't you coming?

DE CHENNEVIETTE [*as if embarrassed*]: Yes . . . only . . . I'd like a word with you first.

LUCETTE [*coming forward*]: What is it?

DE CHENNEVIETTE [*more embarrassed*]: It's about the child . . . his allowance is due you know and I . . .

LUCETTE [*straightforwardly*]: All right. I'll let you have it after lunch.

DE CHENNEVIETTE [*with a forced laugh*]: I hate asking you, but things aren't too good at the moment . . .

LUCETTE: I know. [*She turns to go and then comes back.*] But this time, don't spend it all on the horses, will you?

DE CHENNEVIETTE [*petulantly*]: You're always throwing that up at me! I told you it seemed a marvellous tip!

LUCETTE: Yes, they're all marvellous – your tips.

DE CHENNEVIETTE: But this one was. The owner himself told me in confidence, 'My horse is the favourite. But don't bet on him. My jockey's going to hold him back.'

LUCETTE: And so?

DE CHENNEVIETTE: Well, I told you. The jockey didn't. And the horse won. [*With the most complete conviction*] So how can you blame me? It wasn't my fault, was it, if the jockey was a crook?

FIRMIN [*entering from the dining-room*]: Mademoiselle Marceline wishes me to ask Madame and Monsieur to come into lunch.

LUCETTE [*impatiently*]: Oh, for heaven's sake, she's always wanting to eat!

[FIRMIN *goes back into dining-room*]

Can't she eat without us? [*The bell rings. To* DE CHENNEVIETTE] Come on, before whoever that is stops us!

[*They enter the dining-room where they are greeted with an 'Ah!' of satisfaction. They close the door behind them.* FIRMIN *enters from the hall, followed by* MADAME DUVERGER.]

FIRMIN: I'm afraid Madame has just gone into lunch with her guests.

MADAME DUVERGER [*put out*]: Oh what a nuisance! But I really must see her. It's about something which must be arranged at once.

FIRMIN: Well, Madame, I can only try. Who shall I say it is?

MADAME DUVERGER: Oh, Madame Gautier doesn't know me... just say it's a lady who would like her to come and sing at a party she's giving.

FIRMIN: Very well, Madame. [*He offers her the chair right of the table, and goes towards dining-room door. The bell rings. He turns about and goes towards the hall door.*] One moment, please.

[*He goes out through hall door.* MADAME DUVERGER *sits, looks round her a little, then, to pass the time, opens a copy of* Figaro *which she is carrying, unfolding it slightly as if she does not intend reading it for long.*]

MADAME DUVERGER [*after a moment*]: Ah, there it is! The marriage of my daughter to Monsieur Bois-d'Enghien! They've got it in, all right!

[*She continues reading* sotto voce *nodding her head with satisfaction.* BOUZIN *enters through hall door, followed by* FIRMIN.]

BOUZIN [*to* FIRMIN]: Well, you can ask if she'll see me, can't you? Bouzin's my name. Don't forget – Bouzin.

FIRMIN: Very well, Monsieur.

BOUZIN: It's about my song.

FIRMIN: Yes Monsieur. If you will take a seat, Monsieur. This lady is already waiting to see Madame.

BOUZIN: I see. Thank you. [*He bows to* MADAME DUVERGER *who raises her eyes and acknowledges him with a nod. A bell with a different ring to the previous ones sounds.*]

FIRMIN [*aside*]: Now the kitchen! What can *they* want? I'll never be able to see about these two!

[*He goes out by door back right.* MADAME DUVERGER *continues reading.* BOUZIN, *after putting his umbrella in the corner by the piano, sits down on the chair beside the sofa. There is a moment of silence while he glances round the room. His glance stops on the paper* MADAME DUVERGER *is reading. He stretches his neck to see better and then gets up and goes to her.*]

BOUZIN: Yes, it is... it's *Figaro* you are reading, isn't it?

MADAME DUVERGER [*raising her head*]: I beg your pardon?

BOUZIN [*friendly*]: I said... it's *Figaro* you're reading, isn't it?

MADAME DUVERGER [*astonished*]: Yes, Monsieur. [*She goes on reading.*]

BOUZIN: Yes, it's an excellent paper.

MADAME DUVERGER [*looking up slightly*]: Really? [*She continues reading.*]

BOUZIN [*trying again*]: Rather! As a matter of fact, there's a very interesting bit of news on page four. Perhaps you've seen it?

MADAME DUVERGER [*a little contemptuously*]: No, Monsieur, I haven't.

BOUZIN: You haven't? Oh, you really mustn't miss it! Allow me! [*He takes the newspaper and unfolds it before the astonished gaze of* MADAME DUVERGER.] There you are! In the theatre column. It's really quite interesting ... look ... [*He reads*] 'Every evening, at the Alcazar, the successful song-hit by Mademoiselle Maya "He makes me go all googie-woogie!" ' [*He gives the paper back to her with an air of great satisfaction.*] There! See for yourself!

MADAME DUVERGER [*taking the newspaper*]: Monsieur, what makes you think it is of the slightest interest to me that Mademoiselle whatever-her-name-is feels herself going all googie-woogie?

BOUZIN: What?

MADAME DUVERGER: Or is it supposed to be a humorous song?

BOUZIN: Certainly not!

MADAME DUVERGER [*doubtfully*]: You're quite sure?

BOUZIN [*simply*]: Oh, absolutely! It's one of mine, you see. I wrote it.

MADAME DUVERGER: Really? I beg your pardon, Monsieur. I did not know you were a composer.

BOUZIN: Oh, it's just a hobby of mine, really. I'm a notary's clerk by profession.

[FIRMIN *enters back right, carrying a magnificent bouquet of flowers.*]

BOUZIN *and* MADAME DUVERGER [*to* FIRMIN]: Well?

FIRMIN [*behind the sofa*]: I've not been able to see Madame yet. They rang from the kitchen for me to bring these flowers up.

MADAME DUVERGER: Oh? [*She takes up her paper again.*]

BOUZIN [*pointing to the bouquet*]: I say, they're a bit of all right! D'you get many like that?

FIRMIN [*simply*]: We receive very many, Monsieur.

BOUZIN: Must have plenty of money, eh? The chap who sent that?

FIRMIN [*indifferently*]: I do not know, Monsieur. There is no card with it. It is from an anonymous admirer. [*He puts the bouquet on the piano.*]

BOUZIN: Anonymous? No, really? D'you mean there are people daft enough to do that?

MADAME DUVERGER [*to* FIRMIN]: Will you kindly tell Madame I am here?

FIRMIN [*going towards dining-room*]: Certainly, Madame.

BOUZIN [*running to him*]: You haven't forgotten my name?

FIRMIN: No, Monsieur Boosey.

BOUZIN: Bouzin!

FIRMIN: Of course, 'Bouzin'.

BOUZIN [*putting his hat on the chair near the sofa*]: Wait, I'll give you my card. [*He looks for one.*]

FIRMIN: There's no need, Monsieur. Your name is Bouzin and you've written a song for Madame.

BOUZIN: That's it! [*He follows* FIRMIN *to the door of the dining-room, back right.*] But perhaps you'd better take my card.

[FIRMIN *takes no notice and goes into dining-room.* BOUZIN *returns to the sofa, putting his card back in his wallet.*]

He's sure to get my name wrong! [*He has a look at the bouquet.*] Some bouquet, that, all the same!

[*He is about to replace his wallet in his pocket when an idea comes to him. He makes sure that* MADAME DUVERGER *is not looking, then takes out his card and pushes it among the flowers.*]

BOUZIN [*to himself*]: After all, since it's anonymous, somebody might as well benefit by it. [*He puts the wallet back in his pocket. There is a moment's silence. Suddenly he begins to laugh, which makes* MADAME DUVERGER *raise her head.*]

BOUZIN: Sorry. I laugh when I think about this song of mine.

[*There is another silence.* MADAME DUVERGER *goes on reading.* BOUZIN *suddenly laughs again.*]

BOUZIN: I expect you're wondering what it's about?

MADAME DUVERGER: Me? Not in the least, Monsieur! [*She makes a show of going on reading.*]

BOUZIN [*going towards her*]: Oh! I don't mind if you are! It's quite natural. Well, it's a song I've written specially for Lucette Gautier. Everyone kept saying to me: 'Why don't you write a song for Lucette Gautier?' Well, naturally, she'd be only too pleased to sing something of mine – so I've done one!

[MADAME DUVERGER *pretends to go on reading.*]

Listen, here's the chorus. It'll give you an idea.

[*He sings and* MADAME DUVERGER, *in despair, folds her paper and puts it on the table.*]

She's my gal, oh, yes, she is!
She's the gal I like to kiss.
Each guy has his special dish
And she's mine, oh, boy, she is!

MADAME DUVERGER [*trying to sound approving*]: Ah-hah!

BOUZIN [*seeking a compliment*]: Well?

MADAME DUVERGER [*not knowing what to say*]: Oh yes! Quite!

BOUZIN: It's good, isn't it? [*A moment's silence.*] Of course, it's not exactly for children.

MADAME DUVERGER: No?

BOUZIN: But young girls – well if they don't understand it they don't learn much – and if they do understand it – well, they don't have much to learn, eh!

MADAME DUVERGER: Obviously!

BOUZIN [*abruptly, after considering her for a moment*]: Excuse me being personal, Madame, but your face seems familiar. Wasn't it you who used to sing 'The flag of France, that's me!' at the Eldorado?

MADAME DUVERGER [*stifling a laugh as she rises*]: No, Monsieur, no! I am not a singer. I am the Baroness Duverger . . .

BOUZIN: Oh? Then it couldn't have been you. No.

[*He moves upstage as* FIRMIN *comes in from the dining-room with a folded piece of paper in his hand.* BOUZIN *crosses anxiously to him.*]

BOUZIN [*to* FIRMIN]: Did you tell her I was here . . . about my song?

FIRMIN: Yes, Monsieur.

BOUZIN: What did she say?

FIRMIN: She said it was stupid and told me to give it you back.

BOUZIN [*curtly, changing his expression*]: Eh?

FIRMIN [*handing him back the song*]: There you are, Monsieur.

BOUZIN [*annoyed*]: Oh I see! Just because it's a bit different from the usual trash she sings!

FIRMIN [*friendly*]: Take a hint from me, young fellow.

[BOUZIN *picks up his hat from the sofa.*]

Next time, before you write anything for Madame, come and have a word with me!

BOUZIN [*disdainfully*]: With you?

FIRMIN: Yes, you see I'm used to seeing the sort of songs people write for her, and I know what's wanted.

BOUZIN [*contemptuously*]: Thanks for nothing! I never collaborate with anyone. [*Moving towards door*] I'll take my song to Yvette Guilbert. She's got talent. She'll appreciate it.

FIRMIN: As you wish, Monsieur.

BOUZIN [*grumbling sulkily*]: Stupid, is it? Ha! A lot she knows! [*He points to the bouquet*] And to think it was I who . . . [*He picks up the bouquet as if to carry it away with him, goes as far as the door and then thinks better of it.*] No! [*He puts the bouquet back on the piano and then says to* FIRMIN *as he goes out*] Good day to you!

FIRMIN: Good day, Monsieur.

MADAME DUVERGER: What about me? Have you . . .

FIRMIN: Yes, Madame. But it's just as I expected. Madame has guests and she cannot discuss business matters at the moment.

MADAME DUVERGER [*put out*]: Oh, what a nuisance!

FIRMIN: Perhaps Madame could call later?

MADAME DUVERGER: Well, if I must, I must. It's for my daughter's engagement party, this very evening. Will you tell Madame I'll call again in an hour?

FIRMIN: Yes, Madame.

[*As she moves back-stage*]

This way, Madame.

[MADAME DUVERGER *goes out, followed by* FIRMIN *who shuts the door behind him. At the same time* DE CHENNEVIETTE *opens the dining-room door a little and pokes his head in.*]

DE CHENNEVIETTE [*opening the door wide*]: All clear! We can come in! [*He enters followed by* LUCETTE, MARCELINE, BOIS-D'ENGHIEN *and* DE FONTANET.]

ALL [*as they enter*]: Thank goodness for that!

[*They each carry a cup of coffee.* DE CHENNEVIETTE *goes to the fireplace.* DE FONTANET *comes down left of the table.*]

LUCETTE [*to* BOIS-D'ENGHIEN, *downstage right*]: What's the matter, darling? You don't look very happy.

BOIS-D'ENGHIEN: Me? Oh, I'm all right! [*To himself*] How the devil do I tell her! [*He goes to the sofa and sits.*]

LUCETTE [*going behind the sofa and putting her arms round his neck just as he is going to swallow a mouthful of coffee*]: You love me?

BOIS-D'ENGHIEN: I adore you! [*To himself*] She'll never believe me!

[LUCETTE *moves round the sofa and throws herself on her knees beside him to his right.*]

DE FONTANET [*seated left of the table, noticing the bouquet*]: I say, what a magnificent bouquet!

ALL: Bouquet? Where?

DE FONTANET [*pointing to it*]: There! On the piano!

ALL [*looking towards it*]: It's beautiful!

LUCETTE: Now who on earth could have sent that?

DE CHENNEVIETTE [*picking up the bouquet and carrying it centre stage*]: Yes, there's a card. [*Reading*] 'Camille Bouzin.' Well, well, well!

LUCETTE [*taking the bouquet from him*]: What? Bouzin? It's from Bouzin? Oh, the poor boy! To think I gave him his song back as though it were . . .

DE CHENNEVIETTE [*finishing for her*]: Stupid, I think was the word.

LUCETTE: Yes. [*To* DE FONTANET] That was his song I showed you all at lunch.

DE FONTANET [*recalling it*]: Oh, yes, of course!

LUCETTE [*going towards the fireplace with the bouquet*]: But really, it's true. Oh why did his song have to be so stupid! If only something could be done with it. [*She smells the flowers.*] Oh, aren't they lovely! [*Suddenly*] Oh, look! What's this? It's a jewel-case! [*She pulls it out of the bouquet and puts the latter in one of the vases on the mantelpiece.*]

ALL: A jewel-box!

LUCETTE [*moving forward right of table*]: Yes! [*Opening it*] Oh, no! This is too much! Just look at it! A ring set with rubies and diamonds! [*She puts the ring on her finger.*]

DE CHENNEVIETTE [*moving behind table*]: This Bouzin has sent you that?

BOIS-D'ENGHIEN: He must have plenty of money!

LUCETTE: You'd never think so to look at him! The way he dresses! You feel like giving him a couple of sous.

DE CHENNEVIETTE: Well, he's rich all right if he can give presents like that!

DE FONTANET: I'd go further: I'd say he's rich and in love!

LUCETTE [*laughing*]: You think so?

BOIS-D'ENGHIEN [*who has moved right, to himself*]: Now that's an idea! If I could pass this Bouzin on to Lucette – that would let me out, all right!

[*During this aside of* BOIS-D'ENGHIEN'*s*, DE FONTANET *has moved back to the fireplace.*]

LUCETTE: But that song of his! Surely something can be done with it. Couldn't we see what a collaborator could do with it?

BOIS-D'ENGHIEN [*sitting on the sofa*]: Yes, it probably just needs a little tinkering with.

DE FONTANET [*coming forward, pulling under him the pouf on which he is sitting*]: I've got it! Listen! Why couldn't it be made into a satirical song? You know, give it a bit of a political twist!

LUCETTE [*sitting right of table*]: He's right.

DE CHENNEVIETTE [*sitting left of table*]: But how?

LUCETTE [*to* DE CHENNEVIETTE]: Wait –

DE FONTANET: It's simple: All you've to do is put the names of some politicians: 'So-and-so makes me go all googie-woogie!'

ALL [*laughing approvingly*]: That's it! Not bad! What a good idea!

DE FONTANET [*with the importance that success brings*]: Yes – it could even be a deputy – who makes her go all googie-woogie! A certain deputy, of course!

BOIS-D'ENGHIEN: That would get them!

LUCETTE: It's a wonderful idea! I'll suggest it to him. [*She gets up.*]

DE FONTANET [*rising and pushing back the pouf which* LUCETTE *restores to its place by the fireplace*]: Oh I'm full of ideas! The trouble is putting them into operation!

BOIS-D'ENGHIEN [*rising*]: Most people have that trouble!

DE FONTANET: I did try to make up a song once ... bit of nonsense really [*speaking into* BOIS-D'ENGHIEN*'s face*] I remember – I called it 'For You!'

BOIS-D'ENGHIEN [*drawing back quickly, then pretending to smile at* FONTANET, *withdraws right, saying to himself*]: Phew! Why does he have to come so close!

LUCETTE [*to* DE FONTANET]: And did you manage to finish it?

DE FONTANET [*very modestly*]: I made the top notes too long ... I ran out of breath!

BOIS-D'ENGHIEN [*with conviction*]: Marvellous!

[*They all burst out laughing.*]

DE FONTANET [*not understanding, but laughing with them*]: What's there to laugh at? Did I say something funny?

LUCETTE [*laughing and pointing to* BOIS-D'ENGHIEN *sitting on the sofa*]: No, no ... it's Fernand ... he can't be serious!

DE FONTANET [*looking at* BOIS-D'ENGHIEN *who is still convulsed with laughter*]: Oh, he's like that, is he? But what could I have said? I don't understand.

LUCETTE [*speaking in between laughing*]: But I told you – it's just him! Don't worry! It's not worth it! [*Still laughing but trying to change the subject*] Let's be serious! What shall we talk about? Are you coming to hear me this evening?

DE FONTANET: No, not tonight. I'm going to a party.

LUCETTE [*still laughing a little*]: I don't know why I asked you that. I'm not singing this evening. I'm having a night off.

DE FONTANET: That makes it all right then. I'm going to one of my old friends, the Baroness Duverger.

BOIS-D'ENGHIEN [*who was still laughing, now suddenly stops and jumps to his feet with a startled expression.*] [*To himself*]: Good Lord! My future mother-in-law!

DE FONTANET: She's giving a party for her daugher – who's marrying a Monsieur – what was it? They told me his name.

BOIS-D'ENGHIEN: Oh my God!

DE FONTANET [*searching his memory*]: Monsieur ... Monsieur ...

BOIS-D'ENGHIEN [*comingbetween* LUCETTE *and* DE FONTANET]: Don't bother! What's it to us what his name is!

DE FONTANET: Yes, that's it! It's a name something like yours!

BOIS-D'ENGHIEN: It's not! It can't be! There aren't any!

LUCETTE: What are you getting so excited about?

BOIS-D'ENGHIEN: I'm not getting excited! It's just that it's like these people who say to you: 'Give me a moment – it's a name beginning with Q...'

DE FONTANET [*loudly*]: It's coming! It's on the tip of my tongue!

BOIS-D'ENGHIEN: Duval!

DE FONTANET: No!

BOIS-D'ENGHIEN: What's it matter to us, the names of these people? We'll never meet them!'

[*The bell rings.*]

DE CHENNEVIETTE: He's right, you know.

BOIS-D'ENGHIEN: Of course I am! So stop trying to remember it!

LUCETTE [*to* FIRMIN, *who enters and is looking for something behind the furniture*]: What is it, Firmin?

FIRMIN [*with a jocular disdain*]: Oh, nothing, Madame. It's only that man ... Bouzin. He says he left his umbrella.

ALL: Bouzin!

LUCETTE [*moving upstage, in front of* FIRMIN]: But show him in!

FIRMIN [*astonished*]: Oh?

[BOIS-D'ENGHIEN *moves slightly back-stage.* DE FONTANET *moves left.*]

LUCETTE [*going to the hall door*]: Do come in, Monsieur Bouzin! [*Introducing him*] Monsieur Bouzin – my friends!

BOIS-D'ENGHIEN
DE FONTANET
DE CHENNEVIETTE } [*making him welcome*]: Ah, Monsieur Bouzin!

[FIRMIN *goes out.*]

BOUZIN [*very taken aback by this reception, he bows embarrassedly*]: I'm awfully sorry – it's just that I think I forgot...

LUCETTE [*with solicitude*]: Do please sit down, Monsieur Bouzin! [*She brings him the chair that was behind the table.*]

ALL [*showing great concern*]: Yes, please do sit down, Monsieur Bouzin.

[*Each of them brings him a chair:* BOIS-D'ENGHIEN *the chair from behind the sofa which he places next to the chair brought by* LUCETTE; DE FONTANET *the chair from right of the table; and* DE CHENNEVIETTE *the chair from left of the table; so that there is a row of chairs behind* BOUZIN.]

BOUZIN [*sitting, first, half on one chair and half on another, then on that brought by* LUCETTE]: But . . . really . . . I . . .

LUCETTE [*sitting beside him on his right,* DE FONTANET *to the right of* LUCETTE *and* BOIS-D'ENGHIEN *to the left of* BOUZIN; DE CHENNEVIETTE *in the corner of the table*]: Now I shall scold you. What do you mean by running off with your song like that?

BOUZIN [*bitterly*]: Well, I like that! After sending your servant to tell me you thought it stupid!

LUCETTE [*protesting*]: Stupid? Your song? Oh, he misunderstood me!

ALL: He misunderstood! He got it all wrong!

BOUZIN [*his face brightening*]: Really? I did wonder whether . . .

LUCETTE: But first, I must thank you for your marvellous bouquet!

BOUZIN [*embarrassed*]: What? Oh . . . me . . . oh, it was nothing really.

LUCETTE: Nothing? I think it was very very charming of you!

ALL: Perfectly charming!

LUCETTE [*thrusting forward her hand, showing the ring*]: And my ring? You see the ring?

BOUZIN [*not understanding*]: Your ring? Oh . . . yes!

ALL: It's magnificent!

LUCETTE [*coquettishly*]: I've got it on, you see!

BOUZIN [*more confused*]: Yes . . . you have . . . [*To himself*] What's her ring to do with me?

LUCETTE: It's the ruby which takes my breath away!

BOUZIN: The ruby? Oh . . . that's what it is, is it? [*A small pause.*] Yes, just think what that must have cost.

[*They all look at each other in astonishment, not knowing what to say.*]

LUCETTE [*a little taken aback*]: Why yes . . . I certainly appreciate that.

BOUZIN: Yes, it may not look it, but a ring like that's worth more than seven thousand francs.

DE CHENNEVIETTE [*moving to behind table*]: Seven thousand!

LUCETTE [*to* DE CHENNEVIETTE]: Certainly! Yes, it cost at least that much!

[DE CHENNEVIETTE *moves behind the sofa.*]

BOUZIN: You could keep a whole family for a couple of years on that. Still, I expect it'll be a good investment...

[*General stupefaction.*]

BOIS-D'ENGHIEN [*aside to* DE CHENNEVIETTE, *looking at* BOUZIN *with disgust*]: Caddish remark to make, what?

DE CHENNEVIETTE [*aside to* BOIS-D'ENGHIEN]: Absolutely disgusting!

[*He moves back-stage.* BOIS-D'ENGHIEN *gets up and replaces his chair beside the sofa.*]

LUCETTE [*still wanting to be pleasant*]: Anyway, that proves how generous the person was who gave it to me.

BOUZIN: It certainly does! [*To himself*] Proves what an idiot he is! [*Aloud*] But to get back to my song...

LUCETTE: Of course! Your song!

DE FONTANET [*rising and replacing his chair by the table*]: Well, star of my life, I see you've work to do, so I'll leave you.

LUCETTE [*rising*]: You're going! Wait, I'll see you out. [*She replaces her chair behind the table.*]

DE FONTANET: No, please!

LUCETTE [*accompanying him out through hall door*]: Of course I will! [*To* DE CHENNEVIETTE] You come along too, and I'll let you have you-know-what: for the child. You can send it off to him right away.

DE CHENNEVIETTE: Oh, good!

[BOUZIN, *without getting up, has followed all this movement by pivoting his chair little by little until he ends up with his back to the audience.*]

LUCETTE: You will excuse me, won't you, Monsieur Bouzin? I'll be with you in a moment.

[*They all go out except* BOIS-D'ENGHIEN *and* BOUZIN. BOIS-D'ENGHIEN *watches them go and begins pacing up and down.*]

BOIS-D'ENGHIEN [*stopping in front of* BOUZIN *just as he has risen and is about to replace his chair to the left of the table*]: D'you want to know what I think? I think you're in love with Lucette!

BOUZIN: Me!

BOIS-D'ENGHIEN: Yes, yes! Oh, don't try to pretend you're not – of course you're in love with her! But don't be so timid about it! Be bold! Go ahead and take her!

BOUZIN: What!

BOIS-D'ENGHIEN: Are you man or mouse? Lucette is yours!

BOUZIN: Mine! But, I say, really . . .

BOIS-D'ENGHIEN [*quickly*]: Ssh! Here she is! Not a word today! Attack tomorrow! [*He moves right whistling, with his hands in his pockets, trying to appear unconcerned.*]

BOUZIN [*to himself*]: What the devil's he up to?

[LUCETTE *returns by hall door.*]

LUCETTE [*to* BOUZIN]: I'm so sorry I had to leave you.

BOUZIN [*who has moved back above table*]: That's all right! [*To himself*] Of course I'm not in love with her!

LUCETTE [*sitting right of the table*]: Now we can chat away in peace.

BOUZIN [*sitting at the table, facing audience*]: That's right.

LUCETTE: Now where were we! Of course, your song! Yes, it's charming! There's no other word for it! Absolutely charming!

BOUZIN: It's nice of you to say so. [*To himself, as he bends to put his hat under the table*] And that fool thought she said it was stupid!

LUCETTE: Yes, completely charming . . . yet, all the same . . . how shall I put it, . . . don't you think perhaps it lacks that . . . little something?

BOUZIN [*protesting*]: What something?

LUCETTE: Yes, I can see you don't mind my speaking frankly. It's absolutely charming – but . . . is that enough?

BOUZIN [*completely bewildered*]: Enough?

LUCETTE [*to* BOIS-D'ENGHIEN, *who is discreetly keeping his distance, leaning against the mantelpiece*]: I'm right, aren't I?

BOIS-D'ENGHIEN: Oh yes, absolutely! [*Comes forward and sits left of table.*] And what's more – if you don't mind my giving my opinion – I'm not too happy about its form.

LUCETTE: Yes, I quite agree with you – but I don't think that's quite so important.

BOIS-D'ENGHIEN: And then again – it needs a bit more punch.

LUCETTE: Ah, now there you're right. Yes, it gives one the feeling that it was written by somebody frightfully clever . . . somebody frightfully clever . . .

BOIS-D'ENGHIEN: . . . who'd got somebody else to write it for him!

LUCETTE: Exactly!

BOUZIN [*nodding his head*]: How odd! [*There is a short silence.*] Apart from that, you think it's good?

BOIS-D'ENGHIEN *and* LUCETTE: Oh, very good!

LUCETTE: Very, very good indeed! [*Changing her tone*] So this is what we thought . . . Have you the song with you?

BOUZIN: Oh dear – I left it at home!

LUCETTE: What a pity!

BOUZIN: But that's all right! I live quite near. I'll run and get it!

LUCETTE [*rising*]: Good! If you're sure you don't mind. It would mean we could start work on it.

BOUZIN: Of course! I compose very quickly, you know!

BOIS-D'ENGHIEN: Really?

BOUZIN: Oh, yes! I can throw you off a song just like that!

BOIS-D'ENGHIEN [*getting up*]: Extraordinary! [*To himself*] He's as stupid as his song.

BOUZIN [*going towards hall door*]: I'll be back in no time!

LUCETTE [*pointing to his umbrella as she follows him*]: Your umbrella!

BOUZIN: Oh, yes, of course! Thank you!

[*He takes his umbrella from behind the piano and goes out accompanied by* LUCETTE.]

BOIS-D'ENGHIEN [*alone, moving right*]: Now I've prepared the ground there, with this Bouzin creature, I must get it over with. I've got to sign the marriage contract this evening, so I must finish with Lucette.

LUCETTE [*calling back offstage, as she enters*]: Good! That will be fine! Don't be long, will you?

BOIS-D'ENGHIEN [*to himself, sitting on sofa*]: But how the devil am I to begin?

LUCETTE [*coming behind sofa and putting her arms round his neck*]: You love me?

BOIS-D'ENGHIEN: Madly!

LUCETTE: Darling!

[*She moves round the sofa and sits beside him on his left.*]

BOIS-D'ENGHIEN [*to himself*]: That's no good!

LUCETTE [*seated on his left*]: Oh I was so happy to see you. I could hardly believe my eyes! It was really very naughty of you, though! If you knew how miserable I was. I thought you'd finished with me for good!

BOIS-D'ENGHIEN [*protesting hypocritically*]: 'Finished' with you!

LUCETTE [*passionately*]: And now I have you again! Tell me that I've really got you back again!

BOIS-D'ENGHIEN [*obliging unwillingly*]: You've got me back again!

LUCETTE [*looking into his eyes*]: And it'll never be finished between us!

BOIS-D'ENGHIEN [*obliging again*]: Never!

LUCETTE [*seizing his head passionately and holding it to her breast*]: Oh, yum – yum – yum – yum!

BOIS-D'ENGHIEN: Oh, my Lulu!

[LUCETTE *lays her head, making a pillow of her two arms, on* BOIS-D'ENGHIEN*'s hip, so that he finds himself stretched on her knees, sideways and awkwardly.*]

BOIS-D'ENGHIEN [*to himself*]: Hell! I started off wrong ...

LUCETTE [*in the same position, languorously*]: Oh, how comfy I am!

BOIS-D'ENGHIEN [*to himself*]: Well, I'm not!

LUCETTE [*as above*]: I could stay like this for twenty years! Couldn't you?

BOIS-D'ENGHIEN: Twenty years would be rather long!

LUCETTE: I would keep on saying 'Yum – yum – yum – yum!' and you would keep on answering 'My Lulu!' And so the years would roll by!

BOIS-D'ENGHIEN [*to himself*]: What fun!

LUCETTE [*sitting up, and so allowing* BOIS-D'ENGHIEN *to do the same*]: But, alas, that cannot be! [*She rises, walks round the sofa, then again with passion*] You *do* love me?

BOIS-D'ENGHIEN: Oh, I adore you!

LUCETTE: Ah! Darling! Come on, then!

[*She moves upstage.*]

BOIS-D'ENGHIEN [*to himself*]: Damn and blast! It's all gone wrong!

LUCETTE [*back centre, with a look full of meaning*]: Then ... aren't you coming ... to help me dress?

BOIS-D'ENGHIEN [*like a sulky child*]: No! Not yet!

LUCETTE [*coming forward*]: What's the matter?

BOIS-D'ENGHIEN [*as above*]: Nothing!

LUCETTE: There is! You look, miserable!

BOIS-D'ENGHIEN [*getting up and steeling himself*]: Well, if you want to know, there is! This can't go on!

LUCETTE: What can't?

BOIS-D'ENGHIEN: Us! [*To himself*] That's done it! [*Aloud*] It would have had to happen sooner or later. I'd rather get it over with now. Lucette, we'll have to finish with each other!

LUCETTE [*choking*]: What?

BOIS-D'ENGHIEN: There's nothing else for it! We can't go on!

LUCETTE [*with sudden understanding*]: Well, I'll be ...! You're getting married!

BOIS-D'ENGHIEN [*hypocritically*]: Me? Good heavens, no! What would I want to get married for?

LUCETTE: Then, why? Why?

BOIS-D'ENGHIEN: Well ... my position being what it is ... I'm just not able to ... well, give you what you deserve ...

LUCETTE: Is that all? [*Bursting out laughing and falling against him with her hands against his shoulders*] Oh, what a goose you are!

BOIS-D'ENGHIEN: Eh?

LUCETTE [*tenderly, putting her arms round him*]: Don't you think I'm happy – just the way things are?

BOIS-D'ENGHIEN: Yes ... but ... there's my dignity!

LUCETTE: Oh leave your dignity to look after itself! What's that matter so long as you know I love you? [*Moving left a little, passionately*] Oh, yes! Yes! I love you!

BOIS-D'ENGHIEN [*to himself*]: Oh, this is ridiculous!

LUCETTE: Oh! I can't bear to think of it! [*Going back to him and holding him as if she were going to lose him*] Tell me you'll never get married! Never!

BOIS-D'ENGHIEN: Me? Oh, no, of course not!

LUCETTE [*with gratitude*]: Thank you! [*Breaking away*] Still, if you ever did, I know only too well what I'd do.

BOIS-D'ENGHIEN [*uneasily*]: What?

LUCETTE: Oh, it would be soon over. Just one bullet through the head!

BOIS-D'ENGHIEN [*his eyes popping out of their sockets*]: Whose head?

LUCETTE: Mine, of course!

BOIS-D'ENGHIEN: [*reassured*]: Oh! Well!

LUCETTE [*going to the table, nervously playing with the copy of* Figaro *left there by Madame Duverger*]: Oh, no, I wouldn't be afraid to end it all, if I ever found out, if I read about it in the newspaper . . . [*She holds up the paper in her hand.*]

BOIS-D'ENGHIEN [*to himself, terrified, but not moving*]: Blast! That damn paper again!

LUCETTE: But I'm being silly! It will never happen, so why should I talk like this! [*She throws the copy of* Figaro *on the table and moves left.*]

BOIS-D'ENGHIEN [*pouncing on the paper and pushing it inside his coat, to himself*]: It sprouts everywhere, this damn thing!

[LUCETTE *turns at the noise and* BOIS-D'ENGHIEN *laughs foolishly to cover himself*].

LUCETTE [*coming to him and throwing herself passionately in his arms*]: You love me?

BOIS-D'ENGHIEN: I adore you!

LUCETTE: Darling! [*She moves back-stage.*]

BOIS-D'ENGHIEN [*to himself*]: Now I'll never be able to tell her! Not after that! Never! [*He goes right and drops dejectedly on to the sofa.* DE CHENNEVIETTE *enters from the hall, sealing an envelope.*]

DE CHENNEVIETTE [*to* LUCETTE]: There! The letter's ready. Have you a stamp?

LUCETTE [*going towards her room*]: Yes, in here . . . wait!

DE CHENNEVIETTE: Here's the money for it.

LUCETTE [*good humouredly*]: Now, do I need that?

DE CHENNEVIETTE: [*annoyed*]: Well I'm sure I don't! There's no reason I should accept little things like that from you, is there?

LUCETTE: Oh, well, just as you please . . . [*She takes the money and goes into her bedroom.*]

DE CHENNEVIETTE [*to* BOIS-D'ENGHIEN]: It's funny, but women just don't seem to understand these little things!

BOIS-D'ENGHIEN [*preoccupied*]: Yes . . . yes!

DE CHENNEVIETTE: What's the matter? You look fed-up.

BOIS-D'ENGHIEN: Fed-up? That's putting it mildly. I'm sunk! Done for!

DE CHENNEVIETTE: Good heavens! What's wrong?

BOIS-D'ENGHIEN [*getting up and going to him*]: But, of course! You're the one who can help me! It's something I don't know how to tell Lucette. But I can tell you! After all, you're her husband – or almost! It's absolutely necessary for her and me to finish with each other!

DE CHENNEVIETTE [*thunderstruck*]: What was that you said?

BOIS-D'ENGHIEN: It's true, old chap! I'm getting married!

DE CHENNEVIETTE: You!

BOIS-D'ENGHIEN: Me! And the marriage contract is to be signed this evening!

DE CHENNEVIETTE: Good Lord!

BOIS-D'ENGHIEN [*taking him by the arm and in his most persuasive tone*]: It will be the best thing for her, in the end, don't you see?

DE CHENNEVIETTE: Maybe. It's certainly true there's a – marvellous opportunity – waiting for her at this very moment, if she wanted to take it.

[*The bell rings.*]

BOIS-D'ENGHIEN: Then, for heaven's sake, tell her! Speak to her seriously. She'll listen to you.

DE CHENNEVIETTE [*doubtfully*]: Oh, no, not her!

[FIRMIN *enters back through hall door*]

FIRMIN [*announcing*]: General Irrigua!

DE CHENNEVIETTE: Him! Bring him in! [*Quickly as* FIRMIN *turns to go*] No! When we've gone! [*To* BOIS-D'ENGHIEN] Quick! Let's go this way!

BOIS-D'ENGHIEN: Why?

DE CHENNEVIETTE: Because – we'll be in the way! We're not needed!

BOIS-D'ENGHIEN: What? You mean ...

DE CHENNEVIETTE: Exactly! It's the marvellous opportunity – himself!

BOIS-D'ENGHIEN: Good Lord! Let's get out of here then!

[*They slip off furtively, back, into dining-room, like two accomplices.*]

MARCELINE [*entering right as* FIRMIN *is about to show in the* GENERAL]: Who was that that rang, Firmin?

FIRMIN: General Irrigua, Mademoiselle.

MARCELINE: The General! Quick, then! Show him in, and go and warn my sister!

[*She goes forward between piano and sofa.*]

FIRMIN: If Monsieur would be good enough to enter ...

THE GENERAL: Bueno! I enter!

[*He comes in, followed by* ANTONIO *carrying two bouquets, one enormous and the other quite small. He holds the latter behind his back.*]

MARCELINE [*dropping a curtsey*]: General!

THE GENERAL [*recognizing her*]: Ah! The seester! Am your servant, Mam'selle. [*He calls* FIRMIN] Hombre! [FIRMIN *does not respond, so he raises his voice*] You – servant – futman!

FIRMIN [*coming forward again*]: Oh! It's me ...?

THE GENERAL: Of course it ees you! It ees not me! [*To himself*] Qué bruta este hombre! [*Aloud*] Go tell your meestress, I ees here!

FIRMIN: Yes, Monsieur. [*To himself as he goes towards the door of* LUCETTE*'s bedroom*] Risen from the ranks, this fellow! [*Aloud, as* LUCETTE *comes out of her bedroom*] Here is Madame. [*He goes out back.*]

THE GENERAL [*to* LUCETTE, *who halts in astonishment on seeing the General*]: Madame! Thees day ees mowst beautiful of my life!

LUCETTE [*with a questioning look*]: Monsieur?

MARCELINE [*introducing him*]: This is General Irrigua.

THE GENERAL [*bowing*]: Heemself!

LUCETTE: Oh, General, I beg your pardon. [*She acknowledges* ANTONIO, *back-stage*] Monsieur ...

THE GENERAL [*moving forward a little*]: He ees nothing ... my interpreter!

LUCETTE: I'm delighted to meet you, General.

THE GENERAL: Ees me who ees the delighted! [*To* ANTONIO] Antonio ... the bouquets ...

[ANTONIO *presents the large bouquet to* LUCETTE, *without letting the little one be seen.*]

Permit, please, some leetle flowers – that I geeve to you.

LUCETTE [*taking the bouquet*]: Oh, General!

THE GENERAL [*taking the tiny bouquet from* ANTONIO *and presenting it to* MARCELINE]: And so! I theenk also of the seester!

MARCELINE [*taking the bouquet*]: For me? Oh, really, General!

THE GENERAL [*to* MARCELINE]: It ees more leetle – but more easy to carry! [*To* ANTONIO] Antonio, go wait in hall for my command!

ANTONIO: Bueno.

[*He goes out.*]

LUCETTE: But how nice of you! I simply adore flowers!

THE GENERAL [*gallantly*]: Ah, I weesh to be a flower!

MARCELINE [*to* THE GENERAL, *simpering and smelling her flowers*]: Oh, I adore them, too!

THE GENERAL [*over his shoulder*]: Si, but I say that just for Madame.

LUCETTE [*opening the bouquet*]: Oh, just look, Marceline! Aren't they lovely!

THE GENERAL: They are your subjects! That I put at your feet.

LUCETTE [*laughing*]: My subjects?

THE GENERAL: Bueno! Roses ... at the feet of the queen of the roses!

LUCETTE *and* MARCELINE [*laughing forcedly*]: Aah!

THE GENERAL [*pleased with himself*]: I say clever thing, ha?

LUCETTE: You are very gallant, General!

THE GENERAL: I am doing always what ees possible.

MARCELINE [*aside to* LUCETTE]: Rather hard to understand, isn't he?

LUCETTE [*to* MARCELINE]: Leave us, Marceline.

MARCELINE: Me?

THE GENERAL [*with a lordly gesture*]: Leave us ... seester! ...

MARCELINE: Well!

THE GENERAL [*very polite, but in a tone which admits of no refusal*]: Out! ... pleese! ... Mam'selle! [*He moves back-stage waiting for her to go.*]

MARCELINE: All right! I'm going ... [*To herself*] What manners!

[*She goes out right.* LUCETTE *meanwhile has been putting the roses in the vase on the console table.* THE GENERAL *has moved behind sofa.*]

THE GENERAL [*explosively, as* LUCETTE *returns right of table*]: Ees dream come true! You! Me! Here! Together! Alone!

LUCETTE [*sitting right of table*]: Do sit down, won't you, General?

THE GENERAL [*passionately*]: I am not able!

LUCETTE [*astonished*]: You can't sit down?

THE GENERAL [*still passionately*]: I am not able! I full with passion! Ah! When your letter come to me – your letter which grant to me such great favour – permission to veeseet you ... Ah! Caramba! Caramba! [*Unable to express his feelings*] What I feel ... I ees not able to say!

LUCETTE: Why, what is it? You look quite upset!

THE GENERAL: That ees what I am! For why? Ees simple! I luf you! We are alone! [*Becoming venturesome*] Loucette!

LUCETTE [*quickly, rising and going left of the table*]: Take care, General, you're advancing on dangerous territory!

THE GENERAL [*moving forward right a little*]: I have not fear of danger! In my country I was Meeneester of War!

LUCETTE [*moving behind table*]: You!

THE GENERAL [*bowing*]: Heemself!

LUCETTE: Why, General! This is an honour! Minister of War!

THE GENERAL [*correcting her*]: Ess! ... Ess!

LUCETTE [*not understanding*]: Ess? Ess ... What?

THE GENERAL: Ess-meeneester! I am not eet no more.

LUCETTE [*consolingly*]: Ah, well! What are you now, then?

THE GENERAL: I! – condemned to death!

LUCETTE [*recoiling*]: You?

THE GENERAL [*with a reassuring gesture*]: It ees nothing ... only becose I come to France to buy for my government two battle-sheeps, three cruiser and five torpedo-boats.

LUCETTE [*not understanding*]: Well?

THE GENERAL: Bueno! I have lost them! At gambling-table!

LUCETTE: You lost them – gambling? [*Reproachfully*] Oh, General, how could you!

THE GENERAL [*naïvely*]: Ees that I have no luck! Always same theeng! So I lose much money!

LUCETTE [*sitting right of table*]: Oh, that's bad, that is, General.

THE GENERAL [*unconcernedly*]: Tees, so-so – but nothing for me. Ees much left steell! For you.

LUCETTE: For me?

THE GENERAL [*in lordly fashion*]: All of eet!

LUCETTE: But . . . why?

THE GENERAL: So I be able to luf you! Si! I lorve you, Loucette! My heart – it ees too small to contain all the lorve I have for you! Your charm, your beauty – they have – they have – [*changing his tone*] Excuse! – one moment, pleese! [*He moves back-stage.*]

LUCETTE [*to herself*]: Now what's he up to?

THE GENERAL [*opening the hall door and calling*]: Antonio!

ANTONIO [*coming to the door*]: Cheneral?

THE GENERAL: Como se dice 'subjugar'?

ANTONIO: 'Subjugate.'

THE GENERAL [*indicating that he can go back into the hall*]: Bueno! Gracias, Antonio!

ANTONIO: Bueno!

[*He goes out.*]

THE GENERAL [*to* LUCETTE, *taking up again his passionate voice*]: You have 'subjugate' me! So, everything that ees mine ees also yours! My life, my money, even the last dollar – and also even the meesery that my lorve for you makes in me!

LUCETTE [*shaking her head doubtfully*]: Misery? It's obvious you don't know what that is!

THE GENERAL [*coming forward right*]: Excuse! I do know! I am not always reech! Before I am general een army, I have not money . . . [*approaching her.*]

LUCETTE [*as he comes near*]: Won't you sit down, General?

THE GENERAL: I am not able! In front of you I seet only on my knees. [*He kneels before her.*] You ees a goddess to kneel in front . . . a saint to worsheep . . .

LUCETTE: Oh, now, really, General!

THE GENERAL [*conversationally*]: Where ees your bedroom?

LUCETTE [*gasping*]: What?

THE GENERAL: [*passionately*]: I say: where ees your bedroom?

LUCETTE: Oh, General, what a question!

THE GENERAL: It ees lorve which speak weeth my mouth! Becose bedroom of beautiful woman you lorve ees like . . . ees like . . . [*he gets up*] Excuse! . . . one moment, please!

LUCETTE [*to herself, mockingly*]: Here we go again!

THE GENERAL [*at hall-door*]: Antonio!

ANTONIO [*coming to the door*]: Cheneral?

THE GENERAL: Como se dice 'tabernaculo'?

ANTONIO: 'Tabernacle.'

THE GENERAL: Bueno! Gracias, Antonio!

ANTONIO: Bueno! [*He goes out.*]

[*Without saying a word, the* GENERAL *goes back to* LUCETTE *and kneels in a matter-of-fact way before her, as he was previously.*]

THE GENERAL [*exclaiming passionately*]: Ees like 'tabernacle' ... where to worsheep goddess! [*He takes her left hand in his.*]

LUCETTE [*placing her right hand, which wears the ring, on his*]: General! Your outrageous flattery would pardon you almost anything!

THE GENERAL [*who is looking at the ring on her finger*]: Si! That ees so. [*Rising*] Excuse please – eef I say that I theenk that I see on your feenger a reeng?

LUCETTE [*getting up, in a matter-of-fact voice*]: A ring? Oh, that? Oh ... yes.

THE GENERAL: It ees preetty, you theenk?

LUCETTE [*casually, moving forward left a little*]: Oh, it's nothing – just a knick-knack!

THE GENERAL [*shaking his head*]: A kneeck-knack? What ees a kneeck-knack?

LUCETTE: Oh you know – a bagatelle!

THE GENERAL [*shaking his head again*]: A barcatil ... Si ... si! [*Changing his tone*] Excuse! One moment, please! [*Going to hall door and calling*] Antonio!

ANTONIO [*appearing again*]: Cheneral?

THE GENERAL: Cose significa 'a barcatil' en espagnol?

LUCETTE [*without moving in her seat*]: No, I was telling the General something was just a bagatelle.

ANTONIO [*understanding*]: Ah! 'A bagatelle'. [*Translating to the* GENERAL] La Senora dice a usted que es ... poca cosa.

THE GENERAL: Ah! Si! Si! A barcatil ... si ... si ... [*To* ANTONIO, *waving him out*] Bueno! Bueno! Bueno! Gracias, Antonio!

ANTONIO: Bueno! [*He goes out.*]

THE GENERAL [*coming forward, to* LUCETTE]: A barcatil, si, si!

LUCETTE: It has a sentimental value for me. That's all. It reminds me of someone.

THE GENERAL [*much moved*]: Ah! So? That is good, Loucette!

LUCETTE: Yes, it was my mother's.

THE GENERAL [*stupefied*]: What ees eet you say?

LUCETTE [*surprised*]: I beg your pardon?

THE GENERAL [*bewildered*]: Thees reeng . . . it ees from me, thees reeng! I send you eet thees morning weeth flowers!

LUCETTE: You?

THE GENERAL: Si! Si!

LUCETTE [*crossing right*]: Then . . . but . . . you? . . . him? . . . you?

THE GENERAL [*coming forward*]: Bueno! I tell you!

LUCETTE [*to herself*]: Oh, this is too much! . . . That Bouzin had the cheek to . . . The nerve of it! And that song of his! We'll see about that, all right!

THE GENERAL [*seeing her agitation*]: What ees wrong?

LUCETTE: Oh nothing! Nothing!

THE GENERAL [*gallantly but with a touch of sarcasm*]: Bueno, thees reeng ees not then the reeng of the mother?

LUCETTE: The ring? Oh, no, of course not! I thought you were talking about another ring . . . not this one. Oh no! But I didn't realize it was you I had to thank for it.

THE GENERAL [*modestly*]: Eet ees nothing! [*Moving right and with a lordly gesture*] Eet ees a 'barcatil'! [*Coming back to her*] Permit, please, to accept bracelet that goes weeth it.

[*He offers her another jewel-box that he has taken from his pocket.*]

LUCETTE [*taking the jewel-box*]: Oh, General, you are spoiling me! What have I done to deserve this?

THE GENERAL [*very simply*]: I lorve you! That ees all!

LUCETTE: You love me? [*With a sigh*] Oh, General, why has it to be like that?

THE GENERAL [*with unanswerable logic*]: Becose eet has!

LUCETTE: No, no! Don't say that!

THE GENERAL [*calmly decisive*]: I say eet!

LUCETTE [*holding out to him the jewel-box that he has just given her*]: Then, General, take back these presents. I haven't the right to accept them.

THE GENERAL [*pushing back the jewel-box and gasping*]: Why? Why?

LUCETTE: Because I cannot love you.

THE GENERAL [*jumping*]: What you say?

LUCETTE [*turning her head*]: I love another.

[*Without any pretence at hiding what she is doing, she puts the jewel-box in her pocket.*]

THE GENERAL: Another! You! . . . a man?

LUCETTE: Naturally.

THE GENERAL [*moving right*]: Caramba! Who ees thees man? So I see heem! So I know heem!

LUCETTE: Calm yourself, General.

THE GENERAL [*with despair*]: Si! Si! It ees told me that you have a man – a preety man.

LUCETTE: Oh, yes – very pretty!

THE GENERAL: But I not believe eet...becorse I receive your letter . . . And now he exeest! He exeest! Who ees thees man?

LUCETTE: General, please . . .

THE GENERAL [*with a roar of rage*]: Oh!

LUCETTE [*putting her hands gently on his shoulders*]: I would like you to know, that if my heart were free, it would be yours or nobody's.

THE GENERAL [*trying to contain his despair*]: Oh, Loucette, you make me have pain een the heart.

LUCETTE: But you do see, don't you, I can't love anybody else – while I love him?

THE GENERAL [*struggling a little with himself, then with resignation*]: Bueno! How long then, weell you lorve heem?

LUCETTE: How long? Why, I'll love him as long as he lives, of course.

THE GENERAL [*decisively*]: Bueno! Now I see what eet ees I must do!

LUCETTE: What?

THE GENERAL [*still decisively*]: Nothing! But I see!

LUCETTE [*to herself, moving to table*]: Oh, good heavens! Now he's frightening me!

[*There is a knock at the door of the dining-room.*]

LUCETTE: Who is it? Come in.

BOIS-D'ENGHIEN [*opening the door slightly, disguising his voice*]: Someone is asking if Mademoiselle Gautier can come for a moment.

LUCETTE [*recognizing his voice*]: Oh – oh, yes! Of course! I'll come right away! [*To herself*] The silly ass!

[*The* GENERAL *has moved noiselessly behind the sofa and roughly pulls open the door which* BOIS-D'ENGHIEN *is holding on the other side.*]

THE GENERAL [*violently*]: What ees it you want?

[BOIS-D'ENGHIEN, *forcibly pulled into the room through his hand still holding the door knob, stands pathetically bowing, trying to be pleasant.*]

BOIS-D'ENGHIEN: How are you, Monsieur?

LUCETTE [*to herself*]: Oh, my God! [*Quickly, introducing* BOIS-D'ENGHIEN] This is Monsieur Bois-d'Enghien, General. An old friend of mine.

THE GENERAL [*suspiciously*]: Ah?

BOIS-D'ENGHIEN: Yes, an old friend. That's right. Just an old friend. Nothing more.

[*The bell rings.*]

THE GENERAL [*distrustful*]: Old friend? That ees all?

LUCETTE: Why, of course, that's all, General.

BOIS-D'ENGHIEN: Oh yes ... even less!

THE GENERAL: Bueno ... eef old friend ... [*He shakes his hand and moves down-stage.*]

FIRMIN: [*entering from the dining-room, to* LUCETTE]: Madame?

LUCETTE: What is it?

FIRMIN: It's that lady, Madame, who was here earlier. The one who wants Madame to sing at her party this evening. I've put her in the dining-room.

LUCETTE: All right, I'll come.

[FIRMIN *goes out by the hall door leaving it open.*]

Please excuse me a moment, General, will you?

THE GENERAL [*bowing*]: Please!

[LUCETTE *moves back-stage; the* GENERAL *moves extreme right.*]

BOIS-D'ENGHIEN [*aside, quickly to* LUCETTE]: I say, I'll have to be going!

LUCETTE: Oh, wait a little. I won't be a minute. Keep the General company.

BOIS-D'ENGHIEN: All right – but be quick, won't you?

LUCETTE: Yes! [*She goes into the dining-room.*]

[THE GENERAL *and* BOIS-D'ENGHIEN *exchange smiles and little laughs for a few moments like people who haven't much to say to each other.*]

THE GENERAL [*breaking the silence*]: Mam'selle Gautier ... much energy! ... much life ... No?

BOIS-D'ENGHIEN: Yes, as you say, General – 'much energy'.

THE GENERAL [*going towards* BOIS-D'ENGHIEN]: So ... you at same night-cloob with Loucette, eh?

BOIS-D'ENGHIEN: Well, I'm ...

THE GENERAL: Bueno – you old friend – so I ask eef you at same night-cloob?

BOIS-D'ENGHIEN: Oh yes ... yes! Exactly!

THE GENERAL [*uncompromisingly*]: You ees tenor seenger!

BOIS-D'ENGHIEN: Tenor? Oh yes ... yes! You're quite right! [*To himself*] Where the devil is she?

THE GENERAL: I tell by the head.

BOIS-D'ENGHIEN: Oh really? You're a phrenologist? [*Singing softly*]

'When evening shadows fall
Then sings the nightingale
[*He coughs*]
Do-ray-me – Hum! Hum!'

THE GENERAL [*to himself, making a face*]: *He* seeng in night-cloob!

BOIS-D'ENGHIEN [*coughing*]: Hum! Hum! A bit of catarrh about, isn't there?

THE GENERAL [*beckoning him to come near*]: Tell me, Monsieur Bodégué ...

BOIS-D'ENGHIEN [*correcting him*]: Excuse me, it's 'Bois-d'Enghien'.

THE GENERAL: Bueno! What I say, 'Bodégué'.

BOIS-D'ENGHIEN [*giving up*]: All right! Yes!

THE GENERAL [*confidentially, taking his arm in his*]: You ... good friend of Mam'selle Gautier?

BOIS-D'ENGHIEN [*cagey*]: Well ... I suppose so ... well, yes!

THE GENERAL: You able tell me then . . . about her lover.

BOIS-D'ENGHIEN: Eh?

THE GENERAL [*taking his arm away*]: Si, I know . . . she tell me.

BOIS-D'ENGHIEN: She did? Oh, then, there's no need . . . [*To himself*] And me making a fool of myself for nothing!

THE GENERAL: Si – a preetty man.

BOIS-D'ENGHIEN [*smiling embarrassedly*]: Well, I don't know about that . . .

THE GENERAL: But I not see preetty man here.

BOIS-D'ENGHIEN [*to himself*]: Thanks very much!

THE GENERAL: Bueno! So who ees thees man? You know heem, eh?

BOIS-D'ENGHIEN [*to himself*]: After all, why not? Since he knows so much. [*Aloud*] You really want me to tell you?

THE GENERAL: I beg you! Please!

BOIS-D'ENGHIEN [*fatuously*]: Well, it's . . . [*laughing*] You really do want to know?

THE GENERAL [*laughing also*]: Si! . . . [*Seriously*] Becose I weel keell heem!

BOIS-D'ENGHIEN [*swallowing what he was about to say, and moving right, to himself*]: Kill me! [*Laughing to disguise his feelings*] Ha, haha! Oh, that's a good one, that is!

[*The* GENERAL *laughs also, out of politeness.*]

[*Both of them are now right stage. Whilst this has been going on, through the open hall door* MADAME DUVERGER *and* LUCETTE *can be seen in the hall, unnoticed by the two men.*]

LUCETTE [*in the hall, addressing* MADAME DUVERGER *once she is out of sight*]: Of course, Madame, that's settled then. I'll see you this evening.

[*The outside door, invisible to the audience, can be heard closing.*]

THE GENERAL [*stopping laughing and coming back to his obsession*]: Bueno! So you tell me hees name?

BOIS-D'ENGHIEN [*seeing* LUCETTE *in the hall*]: Ssh! Yes! But not now! Wait a moment!

THE GENERAL: Ah! bueno! bueno! [*He moves right.*]

BOIS-D'ENGHIEN [*to himself*]: My God, he wants to kill me!

LUCETTE [*entering with some cards in her hand and going towards the bedroom*]: Well, that's that! I've to sing at a party this evening.

[*To the* GENERAL] Excuse me, General, just another moment!

THE GENERAL [*bowing*]: Please!

LUCETTE [*about to enter her bedroom, she returns to* BOIS-D'ENGHIEN]: D'you want to come along? I've some invitations.

BOIS-D'ENGHIEN: No, not tonight. I'm afraid I can't. [*To himself*] I've something else to do tonight!

LUCETTE: What about you, General?

THE GENERAL: Oh! Si! Weeth pleasure! [*He comes forward.*]

LUCETTE: Be early, then! Oh, wait! Here's an invitation. [*She gives him a card.*]

THE GENERAL: Muchas gracias! [*He puts the card in his pocket.*]

LUCETTE: I won't be a moment. [*She goes into her bedroom.*]

BOIS-D'ENGHIEN [*to himself, slightly left of table*]: To think I was just going to tell him ...

THE GENERAL [*moving forward towards* BOIS-D'ENGHIEN]: Bueno! Now! What ees her name?

BOIS-D'ENGHIEN: Her? Whose?

THE GENERAL: Thees man.

BOIS-D'ENGHIEN: Man?

THE GENERAL: Thees preety man.

BOIS-D'ENGHIEN [*playing nervously with the jewel-box on the table – which had contained the ring*]: Oh ... yes! ... well ... [*Looking at the jewel-box and suddenly exclaiming*] Bouzin! That's his name! Bouzin!

THE GENERAL: Boussin? Bueno! Boussin ees a dead man! [*He moves right. The bell rings.*]

BOIS-D'ENGHIEN [*to himself, shuddering*]: Ugh! That was a narrow escape! He makes me shiver!

[FIRMIN *enters at hall door.*]

FIRMIN: [*announcing*]: Monsieur Bouzin!

THE GENERAL: Boussin!!

BOIS-D'ENGHIEN: Oh my God!

[FIRMIN *goes out as* BOUZIN *enters. Very pleased with himself, he puts his umbrella against the chair near the sofa.*]

BOUZIN: Well, here I am! I've brought the song! [*He looks round.*] Oh, isn't Mademoiselle Gautier here?

BOIS-D'ENGHIEN [*seeing the* GENERAL *advancing on* BOUZIN *and rushing between them*]: What? No! Yes ... she's ...

[*During the following,* BOIS-D'ENGHIEN, *out of his wits with fright, not knowing what to do or what to say, keeps trying to put himself between the* GENERAL *and* BOUZIN, *while* BOUZIN, *on the contrary, does all he can to go towards the* GENERAL.]

THE GENERAL [*to* BOUZIN]: Pardon! Monsieur Boussin?

BOUZIN [*very friendly*]: Yes, Monsieur, that's me!

BOIS-D'ENGHIEN: That's right! Yes, he's Bouzin! He's Bouzin!

THE GENERAL: Enchanted to meet weeth you!

BOUZIN: I am enchanted also, Monsieur ... but ...

THE GENERAL: Geeve me your card!

BOUZIN: My card! Why certainly. With pleasure ... [*He looks for a card in his pocket, pushing* BOIS-D'ENGHIEN *aside in order to go to the* GENERAL.]

BOIS-D'ENGHIEN [*resigned*]: Now for it!

THE GENERAL: Here ees mine!

[*He hands* BOUZIN *his card.* BOUZIN *gives him his.*]

BOUZIN [*reading*]: General Irrigua ...

THE GENERAL [*bowing*]: Heemself!

BOUZIN [*bowing*]: General!

THE GENERAL: And, now, please ... we meet tomorrow ... een the morning?

BOUZIN [*puzzled*]: Tomorrow? But why?

THE GENERAL [*becoming more and more explosive*]: Becose I want eet! Becose I want your head! [*Seizing him by the collar*] Becose I want to keell you!

BOUZIN: Good heavens! What did he say?

BOIS-D'ENGHIEN [*pleadingly*]: Please! General!

THE GENERAL [*shaking* BOUZIN]: Becose I do not like eet for you to get een my way. Eef something ees obstacle to me – I remove eet!

[*He pulls* BOUZIN *round by the collar so that he is on his left.*]

BOUZIN: For heaven's sake, let me go! Let me go!

BOIS-D'ENGHIEN [*trying to separate them*]: General! Calm yourself!

THE GENERAL [*pushing him away with his right hand while continuing to shake* BOUZIN *with his left*]: Leave me, Bodégué! [*To* BOUZIN, *shaking him*] You not preetty at all, you hear? Not preetty at all!

BOUZIN: Help! Help!

[*General tumult and shouting.*]

LUCETTE [*running in*]: What is it? What's happening?

BOUZIN [*whom the* GENERAL *has let go with a push on* LUCETTE*'s entrance, regaining his balance*]: Oh, Madame! It's this gentleman!

LUCETTE [*to* BOUZIN]: Bouzin! You here! Get out!

[*The* GENERAL *comes right of* LUCETTE.]

BOUZIN: But . . . but why? I've brought the song.

LUCETTE: And take your song with you! A lot of stupid nonsense!

BOIS-D'ENGHIEN: Stupid!

THE GENERAL [*with conviction, without even knowing what it is all about*]: Si! It ees stoopeed! Your song ees stoopeed!

LUCETTE [*pointing to the door*]: Outside! Go on! Out!

BOUZIN: Me?

BOIS-D'ENGHIEN: You've been told to get out – so – out!

THE GENERAL: Out, Boussin! Get you out!

ALL [*pushing to door*]: Out! Get out!

BOUZIN [*panic stricken*]: They're all mad! Mad! [*He goes out.*]

[*All the preceding should be played very quickly, in order not to slow down the end of the act.*]

LUCETTE [*moving forward near* BOIS-D'ENGHIEN]: The nerve of the man! Who does he think he is!

THE GENERAL [*coming forward also*]: Ah, Loucette! For me you do thees!

LUCETTE: Do what?

THE GENERAL: You poot thees man out for me!

LUCETTE: Oh, that! Well, he certainly won't come back now, if that's all you want.

THE GENERAL [*kissing her hand*]: Thank you! Thank you!

[*During the preceding* BOUZIN *has tip-toed back to get his umbrella. In his nervousness he knocks over the chair against which he had left the umbrella.*]

ALL [*turning and seeing* BOUZIN]: Him again!

BOUZIN [*choking with fright*]: I forgot it! My umbrella! I forgot it!

ALL: Get out! Out, Bouzin, out! Get out!

[*He dashes out as they all move towards him.*]

CURTAIN

ACT TWO

MADAME DUVERGER'*s bedroom: a large, square, rich, elegant room, opening at the back by means of a wide, four-panelled folding door on to the drawing-room.* [*The two extreme panels are fixed or moveable, at will.*] *There is a door on the left, upstage, and another door on the right down-stage. Back-stage left is the canopy of a four-poster bed. The bed has been removed for the occasion and its place taken by an armchair. At the back, facing the audience and left of the large entrance, is a large stylish wardrobe – empty. Right of the large entrance back-stage, almost completely hidden by a six-panelled screen whose last panel is fixed to the side of the set, is a lady's dressing-table. In front of the screen is a square table with a chair behind it. There are two chairs against the wall on either side of the door right. Left centre is a chaise-longue placed almost vertically to the audience with its head back-stage and slightly raised. Almost at the foot of the chaise-longue is a small pedestal table on which there is an electric bell button. Left of the canopy is an occasional chair. Underneath the canopy is an electric light with a tulip-shaped shade which would ordinarily be used for reading in bed. There is a lighted chandelier in the middle of the room. Through the open doors, back-stage, a fireplace can be seen in the drawing-room, facing the audience. Everybody is in evening dress throughout this act.*

VIVIANE [*standing right of the sofa, to* FRÄULEIN BETT, *who is on her knees beside her arranging her dress*]: Bist du fertig, Fräulein?

FRÄULEIN BETT: Augenblick mal! Sticknadel, bitte!

VIVIANE [*giving her a pin*]: Again? I think you must want my fiancé to stick them in his fingers.

FRÄULEIN BETT: [*half-laughing, half-shocked*]: Oh, Fräulein Viviane! Böses Kind!

[*They both laugh.*]

MADAME DUVERGER [*entering back from the drawing-room*]: Well, Viviane, are you ready?

VIVIANE: When Fräulein Bett has finished sticking pins in me. I don't know why she wants to stop my fiancé from touching me. Perhaps she's afraid he might go too far!

MADAME DUVERGER [*flabbergasted*]: Viviane! What a thing to say!

VIVIANE [*naïvely*]: I don't see anything wrong in it!

MADAME DUVERGER [*to herself*]: What an innocent little thing she is!

VIVIANE [*changing her tone*]: Oh, Mama, I think you should tell Miss Bett that it's not very nice of her to refuse to come to my party.

MADAME DUVERGER: What? Doesn't she want to stay and help?

VIVIANE: No! And I did want her to meet my fiancé!

MADAME DUVERGER [*to* FRÄULEIN BETT, *who has just stood up, in a tone of friendly reproach*]: Oh, but of course you must stay for our party, Fräulein.

FRÄULEIN BETT [*smiling*]: Wie bitte?

MADAME DUVERGER [*trying to make her understand*]: No ... I said, 'Fräulein, you must stay for our party.' [*Seeing the Fräulein smile without understanding, she tries to put on a German accent*] Sie most vor our party vith us stay! ... Party! ... Dance! Dance! ... [*She makes a few dancing steps while* FRÄULEIN BETT *looks at her smiling but puzzled. Then to the audience*] She's not understood a word! I can't make it any simpler than that!

FRÄULEIN BETT [*still smiling*]: Was bedeutet das?

MADAME DUVERGER [*to* VIVIANE]: Oh, you explain to her! I give up!

VIVIANE [*to* FRÄULEIN BETT, *in German*]: Meine Mutter sagt: 'Möchten Sie zur Abendgesellschaft bleiben?'

FRÄULEIN BETT [*to* MADAME DUVERGER, *very rapidly*]: Es tut mir wirklich sehr leid: meine Mutter ist krank und ich muss den Abend bei ihr verbringen.

MADAME DUVERGER [*who has listened to this torrent of words with a serio-comic expression, nodding her head as if she understood*]: Yes, yes, yes – but it's not worth saying all that to me. I can't make out a word of it! [*To* VIVIANE, *laughing*] What did she say?

VIVIANE: She says she's very sorry, but she's got to spend the evening with her sick mother.

MADAME DUVERGER [*with interest*]: Ah yes, yes. Ja! Ja! Mutter sick! Ill! Not well!

FRÄULEIN BETT [*sadly*]: Oh, ja. Ich bin sehr besorgt um sie.

MADAME DUVERGER [*who has not understood a word*]: Yes, yes, ja, ja!

VIVIANE [*to* FRÄULEIN BETT, *who has stood back looking at the dress*]: Bist du fertig?

FRÄULEIN BETT [*to* VIVIANE]: Ja, es ist fertig.

VIVIANE [*moving centre*]: It's not at all bad! Danke schön!

FRÄULEIN BETT: Also, wenn du mich nicht mehr brauchst, könntest du deine Mutter fragen, ob ich gehen kann?

MADAME DUVERGER: What did she say?

VIVIANE: She wants to know if she may go.

MADAME DUVERGER: If she wants to. Only, tell her to be here early tomorrow. Because I won't be able to take you to your singing lesson – with Monsieur Capoul – and I'd like her to go with you instead.

VIVIANE: All right. [*To* FRÄULEIN BETT] Ja, Sie dürfen gehen. Aber Mama möchte, dass Sie morgen früh kommen, um mich in die Singstunde bein Monsieur Capoul zu bringen.

FRÄULEIN BETT [*to Madame Duverger*]: Oh, ja. Mit Vergnügen. Auf Wiedersehen.

VIVIANE [*sitting at end of chaise-longue*]: Auf Wiedersehen.

FRÄULEIN BETT [*going towards door*]: Auf Wiedersehen, Madame.

MADAME DUVERGER [*moving to door with her*]: Owf veederzane. Owf weederzane. [*To herself, coming forward again*] It's like talking to the wall! But I'm beginning to pick up a few words myself!

MADAME DUVERGER [*goes towards* VIVIANE, *looks at her tenderly, kisses her, then sits beside her on the chaise-longue*]: Well, my dear, the great day has arrived!

VIVIANE [*indifferently*]: Oh, yes . . .

MADAME DUVERGER [*putting her arm round* VIVIANE*'s waist*]: And you're happy to be the wife of Monsieur Bois-d'Enghien?

VIVIANE: Oh, it's all the same to me.

MADAME DUVERGER [*taken aback*]: What *do* you mean – all the same to you?

VIVIANE [*firmly*]: Well, after all, he's only becoming my husband!

MADAME DUVERGER: I should have thought that was enough! Ah! Perhaps you ... why d'you think people get married?

VIVIANE: Because everybody does! You leave your nursemaid for a governess, and then you leave your governess for a husband.

MADAME DUVERGER [*astonished*]: Oh!

VIVIANE: Like having a lady's maid – only he's a man, of course.

MADAME DUVERGER: But ... there's more to it than that! You will become a mother as well! What about that?

VIVIANE: Oh, yes, that would be nice! ... But what's a husband got to do with that?

MADAME DUVERGER: What *do* you mean ... 'what's he got to do with that'?

VIVIANE [*being firmly logical*]: Well, I mean to say, there are lots of unmarried girls, aren't there, who have children, and there are lots of married women who don't. So where does the husband come into it?

MADAME DUVERGER [*trying to reply but finding no words, she gets up and moves right, to herself*]: Oh this is too much! [*Aloud to* VIVIANE] All right. What is it you don't like about Monsieur Bois-d'Enghien?

VIVIANE [*moving behind chaise-longue*]: Oh for a husband he's all right. In any marriage where there are two men, the husband's always the ugliest!

MADAME DUVERGER [*moving forward*]: Two men! But that's not essential, is it? Why not look for a husband who is your ideal man? Then you wouldn't have to try to make up the difference elsewhere.

VIVIANE [*going to her*]: But that's just it! My ideal man is exactly the man I could never marry ...

MADAME DUVERGER: Why on earth not?

VIVIANE: Because you'd never let me! I would want a man who – was a sort of celebrity ...

MADAME DUVERGER: Well, I can understand that. An artist or a poet, for instance ...

VIVIANE: No ... a real rotter of a Don Juan.

MADAME DUVERGER [*jumping*]: *What* did you say?

VIVIANE: A man like Monsieur de Frenel, for instance.

[*Reaction from* MADAME DUVERGER.]

There are plenty like him. You know, the man we met last summer at Trouville! Now, he would have suited me down to the ground.

MADAME DUVERGER: But this is terrible! That man is an absolute scoundrel! His reputation's . . .

VIVIANE [*emphasizing the word*]: Scandalous! Oh yes, mama! That's what makes a man attractive!

MADAME DUVERGER: Oh!

VIVIANE: He's probably lost count of all his mistresses!

MADAME DUVERGER [*scandalized*]: 'Mistresses'! Viviane! Where *did* you learn that word?

VIVIANE [*very naturally*]: From reading history, mama. [*Reciting*] Henry IV, Louis XIV, Louis XV, 1715–1774.

MADAME DUVERGER: Oh, those kings!

VIVIANE: It seems three of his mistresses even died for him.

MADAME DUVERGER: For Louis XV?

VIVIANE: No, no! For Monsieur de Frenel! Two shot themselves and the third starved herself. [*Changing her tone*] That's why every woman in Trouville was running after him!

MADAME DUVERGER [*stopping her moving left*]: But you! You! That doesn't explain what you found so attractive in him!

VIVIANE: Of course it does! It was when I saw all the other women wanted him! Why does one want anything? Because others want it. It's like supply and demand. Well, with Monsieur de Frenel . . .

MADAME DUVERGER: There was a big demand?

VIVIANE: Exactly! So I said to myself: 'That's the sort of husband I'd like!' There'd be a prestige in having a husband like that. Like having a sort of Legion of Honour decoration. It makes you proud for two reasons – first for the distinction it brings you – and then because it infuriates all the other women!

MADAME DUVERGER: But that's just vanity! That's not love!

VIVIANE: Pardon me, but that's just what love is! Love is when you can say: 'You'd like to have had that man, wouldn't you? Well, it's I who've got him, and you haven't!' [*She makes a little curtsey.*] That's all that love is!

MADAME DUVERGER [*coming forward a little*]: I just can't understand you!

VIVIANE [*coming behind her, putting her arms round her and her head on her shoulder*]: Don't worry, mama. You're still a little too young ...

MADAME DUVERGER [*laughing*]: Perhaps you're right! [*She kisses her.*]

VIVIANE: That's really all I have against Monsieur Bois-d'Enghien. He's very nice ... but ... well, he's never done anything – scandalous! Why, he's never even had one woman kill herself for him!

MADAME DUVERGER: And that will stop him making you happy?

VIVIANE [*leaving her mother and moving left*]: Oh, I suppose he'll do that. [*Coming back to her*] But if he doesn't, there's always divorce, isn't there? [*She moves left.*]

MADAME DUVERGER [*to the audience*]: It seems to me she's ready for marriage, all right!

[ÉMILE *enters by drawing-room door, followed by* BOIS-D'ENGHIEN.]

ÉMILE: Monsieur de Bois-d'Enghien, Madame.

MADAME DUVERGER: It's him! Show him in!

BOIS-D'ENGHIEN [*entering, gaily and eagerly, carrying a bouquet*]: Good evening, mother! Good evening, wife-to-be!

MADAME DUVERGER: Good evening, son-in-law!

VIVIANE [*smiling at him and taking the flowers*]: More flowers!

BOIS-D'ENGHIEN: For you – never too many!

[VIVIANE *puts the flowers on the side-table.*]

MADAME DUVERGER: Aren't you going to kiss her? It is allowed today, you know.

BOIS-D'ENGHIEN: And every day! From now on!

[*He kisses her and pricks his finger on one of the pins in her dress.*]

Oh!

VIVIANE [*mockingly*]: Take care! There are pins all over me.

BOIS-D'ENGHIEN [*sucking his fingers*]: If you hadn't told me, I'd never have known.

VIVIANE: That will teach you not to put your hands ...

BOIS-D'ENGHIEN: All right! Once more, then, with no hands!

VIVIANE: Ooh! Greedy!

[*He kisses her, keeping his hands behind him.*]

MADAME DUVERGER [*jocularly*]: What about me? Hands too! I've no pins!

BOIS-D'ENGHIEN: Here goes!

MADAME DUVERGER: And now, some good news for you. The church is booked up on the day we'd planned, so we'll have to have the wedding two days earlier.

BOIS-D'ENGHIEN [*delighted*]: Good! That suits me fine! [*To* VIVIANE] Darling, I am so very happy!

MADAME DUVERGER [*to* BOIS-D'ENGHIEN*'s back*]: You'll make her happy as well, won't you?

BOIS-D'ENGHIEN [*turning*]: Who?

MADAME DUVERGER: Well! My daughter, of course! Who d'you think?

BOIS-D'ENGHIEN: Oh, yes, yes, absolutely!

VIVIANE: And anyway, as I was saying to mama, there is always divorce, isn't there?

BOIS-D'ENGHIEN [*taken aback*]: What? You're already thinking of ...

VIVIANE: Oh, it's just that I think it must be rather fun – being divorced, you know.

BOIS-D'ENGHIEN: Oh?

VIVIANE: Yes, much better than being a widow.

BOIS-D'ENGHIEN: Well, if you put it like that – so do I!

MADAME DUVERGER [*a little back-stage, to* BOIS D'ENGHIEN, *taking his left hand in her left hand, and putting her other hand on his shoulder*]: Anyway, you'll never have troubles or difficulties with Fernand here, thank goodness! He's a steady, serious young man.

VIVIANE [*with a sigh*]: Yes, so he is!

BOIS-D'ENGHIEN: Oh, I say!

MADAME DUVERGER [*letting go his hand*]: No doubt, like most young men, he's had his little peccadillos.

BOIS-D'ENGHIEN [*quickly*]: Never!

MADAME DUVERGER [*softly, to* BOIS D'ENGHIEN, *with delight*]: What? Not even one tiny little one?

BOIS-D'ENGHIEN: Me? Well ... of course I've often seen young fellows running after girls, but that sort of thing never really interested me. I mean to say, what's the point of it all?

VIVIANE [*to herself, pityingly*]: Oh, dear, oh dear!

BOIS-D'ENGHIEN: No, there's only been one woman I loved.

VIVIANE *and* MADAME DUVERGER [*approaching him together, the first as if saying 'It's not possible!' the other as if saying 'I knew it!'*]: Ah!

BOIS-D'ENGHIEN: Yes, that was my mother!

[VIVIANE, *who had approached him hopefully, moves back to her former position, disillusioned.*]

MADAME DUVERGER [*touched*]: Oh, how nice!

BOIS-D'ENGHIEN: I've always said to myself: I am going to keep myself unspoiled for her who will one day be my wife.

MADAME DUVERGER [*shaking his hand and turning to her daughter*]: There you are, you see! I told you! You don't know – you just don't know how to appreciate the man you're marrying!

BOIS-D'ENGHIEN: I don't want anybody to be able to say of me, like they say of so many, that I brought to my wife the dregs of my life as a bachelor.

VIVIANE: Dregs? What dregs?

BOIS-D'ENGHIEN [*nonplussed*]: Eh? I don't know! It's just an expression. Everybody uses it. It's a sort of generalization – a figure of speech!

MADAME DUVERGER: Yes! That's right!

BOIS-D'ENGHIEN [*to* VIVIANE]: Well! So – by marrying me, you could almost say to yourself that morally it's as if you were marrying ... Joan of Arc.

VIVIANE [*looking at him*]: Joan of Arc?

BOIS-D'ENGHIEN: Sex apart, of course!

VIVIANE: Why Joan of Arc? Did you save France?

BOIS-D'ENGHIEN: No! I haven't had that opportunity! But I'm ending my bachelor life with a heart as pure ... as Joan of Arc's at the end of her life of heroism!

MADAME DUVERGER: Oh Fernand! You're a husband in a million!

VIVIANE: Even I would never have believed this of him!

BOIS-D'ENGHIEN [*to himself, moving right*]: This isn't playing the game – but it's making me look good!

[ÉMILE *enters back by drawing-room door.*]

EMILE: One of the guests is here already, Madame!

MADAME DUVERGER: Oh, dear! Who is it?

EMILE: Monsieur de Fontanet.

BOIS-D'ENGHIEN [*to himself, giving an involuntary start*]: Fontanet! The fellow this morning! Hell!

MADAME DUVERGER: What is it? Do you know him?

BOIS-D'ENGHIEN [*quickly*]: Me? No, not at all!

MADAME DUVERGER: Oh, I thought ... [*To* ÉMILE] Ask Monsieur to come and join us here.

[ÉMILE *goes out.*]

BOIS-D'ENGHIEN: What, here? In your bedroom?

MADAME DUVERGER: Why not? I don't stand on ceremony with Fontanet.

BOIS-D'ENGHIEN [*to himself*]: Good heavens! How can I warn him? So he doesn't put his foot in it!

ÉMILE [*showing* DE FONTANET *in*]: This way, Monsieur.

[ÉMILE *goes out again.*]

DE FONTANET: Good evening, Baroness! Good evening!

BOIS-D'ENGHIEN [*rushing forward and putting himself between* DE FONTANET *and* MADAME DUVERGER]: Well, well, this is a surprise! How is everything with you?

[*He pulls* DE FONTANET *front-stage.*]

DE FONTANET [*astonished by this welcome*]: Good Lord! You here! ...

BOIS-D'ENGHIEN: Yes, it's me!

MADAME DUVERGER [*bewildered*]: But I thought ...

BOIS-D'ENGHIEN [*rapidly to* DE FONTANET, *lowering his voice*]: Don't drop any bricks! Keep your mouth shut! [*Aloud*] Well, well! My dear Fontanet!

MADAME DUVERGER: You do know him then?

BOIS-D'ENGHIEN: I'll say I know him!

MADAME DUVERGER: But you just told me ...

BOIS-D'ENGHIEN: I'd no idea you meant him! But of course I know him! My dear Fontanet! [*He shakes him by the hand.*]

DE FONTANET: Why, it was only today we had lunch together!

BOIS-D'ENGHIEN [*foreseeing trouble*]: Today? Oh yes, we did ... a little ... I wasn't very hungry really ...

MADAME DUVERGER: Oh? Where did you lunch?

BOIS-D'ENGHIEN [*making signs to* DE FONTANET]: Oh . . . you know . . . what's that place called . . .

DE FONTANET: It was with our dear celebrity!

BOIS-D'ENGHIEN: The idiot.

MADAME DUVERGER: Celebrity?

VIVIANE: What celebrity?

BOIS-D'ENGHIEN [*quickly*]: It's a restaurant! The Celebrity Restaurant!

DE FONTANET [*to himself*]: What's he talking about?

BOIS-D'ENGHIEN [*to* MADAME DUVERGER *and* VIVIANE, *forcing a laugh*]: What, you don't know the Celebrity Restaurant?

MADAME DUVERGER *and* VIVIANE: No!

BOIS-D'ENGHIEN [*laughing very loudly to extricate himself*]: Well, fancy that, Fontanet, they don't know the Celebrity Restaurant!

DU FONTANET [*laughing with him*]: Ha, ha, ha! [*Changing his tone*] Neither do I!

BOIS-D'ENGHIEN [*unable to prevent a grimace*]: Oh! [*Trying another laugh but without conviction*] What, you neither! [*Pointing to him*] Ha, ha, ha! He goes to a restaurant and doesn't even know it's name! [*Advancing on him and pushing him towards wings*] Dear old Fontanet! Doesn't even know the Celebrity Restaurant! [*Aside to him, softly*] Shut up, will you? Just shut up!

MADAME DUVERGER [*who has been laughing gaily with them*]: And how *do* you get to this restaurant?

BOIS-D'ENGHIEN [*foolishly*]: Get to it?

MADAME DUVERGER: Yes.

BOIS-D'ENGHIEN: Oh . . . yes! 'How do I get to . . . the Celebrity Restaurant?' [*To* DE FONTANET] She says how do you get to it.

MADAME DUVERGER: Well, how?

BOIS-D'ENGHIEN: I heard you! [*To himself*] Who the hell mentioned this blasted restaurant!

VIVIANE: Well?

BOIS-D'ENGHIEN [*completely confused*]: Well . . . let's see . . . . . . it's quite a distance!

MADAME DUVERGER [*gaily*]: That doesn't matter!

BOIS-D'ENGHIEN: Oh, good! Well ... suppose you're in front of the Opéra ... you know where the Opéra is?

MADAME DUVERGER: Yes, yes, of course!

BOIS-D'ENGHIEN: Well you've the Opéra in front of you, and Avenue behind you. You've got that? Good! [*He makes a quick about-turn and everybody follows suit.*] You do a quick about-turn! [*Suddenly speaking calmly*] So that you've got the Opéra behind you, and the Avenue opposite you ...

MADAME DUVERGER: Excuse me ... wouldn't it have been simpler to begin like that?

BOIS-D'ENGHIEN: That's true – but that's not how we got there.

MADAME DUVERGER [*as* BOIS-D'ENGHIEN *is about to continue*]: Anyway, it doesn't really matter how you got to it ... I just asked ...

BOIS-D'ENGHIEN: Oh, well, it doesn't matter then, does it? [*To himself*] Thank goodness for that!

DE FONTANET [*to himself, watching* BOIS-D'ENGHIEN]: What's the matter with him?

MADAME DUVERGER [*to* DE FONTANET]: The point is – since you know each other – I don't need to introduce you to my daughter's fiancé.

DE FONTANET: Your daughter's fiancé? Who's that?

MADAME DUVERGER: Why – him – Monsieur Bois-d'Enghien, of course!

DE FONTANET: What? You mean, he is ... [*To himself*] Lucette's lover ... so that's it! Him and his Celebrity Restaurant! [*Aloud*] Well, well, didn't I say to you this morning her fiancé had a name something like yours?

BOIS-D'ENGHIEN [*to himself*]: The damn' fool!

[*At the end of his tether,* BOIS-D'ENGHIEN *stamps forcibly with his heel on* DE FONTANET*'s foot.*]

DE FONTANET [*howling with pain*]: Ow! Ow! Oh – ow!

ALL: What is it? What's the matter?

BOIS-D'ENGHIEN [*making more noise than all of them*]: What is it? Is something the matter with you? Yes, there's something the matter with him! ... What's the matter with you? Tell us!

DE FONTANET [*who has gone hopping over to the sofa and sat down*]: Oh, my foot! Oh, my foot!

BOIS-D'ENGHIEN [*to himself*]: That's made him change the subject! [*He moves back-stage.*]

DE FONTANET [*furiously*]: It was you! With your heel!

BOIS-D'ENGHIEN: Me? How?

DE FONTANET: Ow! Right on my corn!

BOIS-D'ENGHIEN: You have corns? He has corns! Ugly-looking things, aren't they?

DE FONTANET: I don't care if they're ugly – when you step on them, they hurt!

VIVIANE [*on the other side of the sofa*]: Oh, dear, does it still hurt, Monsieur de Fontanet?

DE FONTANET [*getting up and moving right with difficulty*]: Thank you, it's a little better, Mademoiselle, thank you.

BOIS-D'ENGHIEN: Of course it is! That won't prevent you witnessing us sign the contract when Monsieur Lantery gets here.

DE FONTANET [*rubbing his foot which he has still not put on the ground*]: Monsieur Lantery? Is he your lawyer?

MADAME DUVERGER: Yes. A very good lawyer!

BOIS-D'ENGHIEN: Yes, isn't he?

DE FONTANET: He's only got one fault, poor chap. His breath! Should do something about it.

ALL [*trying to stop themselves laughing*]: Oh?

DE FONTANET: What? You haven't noticed it? Hoo! [*He blows thus into* BOIS-D'ENGHIEN*'s face.*] It's unbearable! [*He moves right.*]

BOIS-D'ENGHIEN [*to himself*]: The pot calling the kettle black! [ÉMILE *enters carrying a tray with a visitor's card on it.*]

ÉMILE [*going to* MADAME DUVERGER]: Madame, a lady is here with two other persons. She says Madame is expecting her. Here is her card.

MADAME DUVERGER: Oh, yes, of course! I'll come now.

[ÉMILE *goes out again.*]

BOIS-D'ENGHIEN: What is it?

MADAME DUVERGER: Ah! It's a surprise I've arranged for my guests!

DE FONTANET: Really?

BOIS-D'ENGHIEN: But you can tell us, can't you?

MADAME DUVERGER: No, no! You'll see! You'll see! It's a surprise! You'll like it! Come along, Viviane!

VIVIANE: Yes, mama.

[MADAME DUVERGER *and* VIVIANE *go out back.*]

BOIS-D'ENGHIEN [*who has accompanied* MADAME *back-stage, comes forward quickly to* DE FONTANET]: You're a fine one, you are! Couldn't you see what a fix you were putting me in?

DE FONTANET: I did – after you trod on my foot. But, my dear fellow, how was I to know you were her fiancé! What about Lucette Gautier?

BOIS-D'ENGHIEN: Oh, Lucette? Oh that's all been finished – a couple of weeks now!

DE FONTANET: But I saw you there – only this morning!

BOIS-D'ENGHIEN: What's that prove? This morning ... I was just passing by ... and called in for old time's sake. [*He moves left.*]

DE FONTANET: Oh?

BOIS-D'ENGHIEN [*coming back to him quickly*]: If you see Lucette Gautier, not a word about my marriage! She'll know all too soon about that!

DE FONTANET: Oh, of course! Of course!

[*Sound of voices off-stage.*]

DE FONTANET: Ah, here's the Baroness coming back!

BOIS-D'ENGHIEN [*indifferently*]: With her surprise, I suppose.

DE FONTANET: Let's have a quick look!

[BOIS-D'ENGHIEN *remains down-stage;* DE FONTANET *goes back and looks through drawing-room door.*]

Good heavens, it's her! What are you doing here? [*He disappears into drawing-room.*]

BOIS-D'ENGHIEN [*overtaken also with curiosity*]: Who does he mean – 'her' – 'you'? [*He goes to drawing-room door, looks through, and gives a jump.*] Oh my God! ... Lucette Gautier! [*He rushes to door left but cannot open it.*] Damn! It's locked! [*Panic-stricken, he looks round, not knowing where to go.*] Lucette here! But how? ... Why? ... [*He is crossing stage to door right when he sees the others approaching from the drawing-room and has time only to throw himself into the wardrobe back-stage.*] Heaven have mercy on me! [*He closes the wardrobe doors on himself.*]

[DE FONTANET, MADAME DUVERGER, VIVIANE, LUCETTE, MARCELINE, DE CHENNEVIETTE *appear in the drawing-room back-stage and can be seen through the open doors.*]

DE FONTANET: Well, this certainly is a surprise! A big surprise!

MADAME DUVERGER: It is, isn't it? [*To* LUCETTE] This way, Mademoiselle . . . in here . . .

DE FONTANET [*to himself*]: Good heavens! He's in there! [*Aloud, barring the door to prevent them entering*] No! No! Not in here! Not in here!

ALL [*astonished*]: Why not?

DE FONTANET: Because . . . because . . . [*He throws a quick glance round the room and cannot see* BOIS-D'ENGHIEN. *To himself*] Where's he gone? [*Aloud*] Well – of course, if you really want to . . .

ALL: Well, really!

DE FONTANET [*to himself*]: He must have got away, thank heaven!

[*Everyone enters from the drawing-room.* VIVIANE *and* DE FONTANET *move behind the chaise-longue;* LUCETTE *and* MADAME DUVERGER *come centre;* MARCELINE *and* DE CHENNEVIETTE *are near the table right.*]

MADAME DUVERGER [*to* LUCETTE]: I hope this room will be all right for you, Mademoiselle?

LUCETTE: Why, of course, Madame! It will be perfect!

MADAME DUVERGER [*to* MARCELINE, *who is carrying a huge costume box*]: You, girl, you can put that over there!

MARCELINE [*to herself*]: Huh! Who's she think she is! [*She puts the box on the table back-stage.*]

LUCETTE [*introducing* DE CHENNEVIETTE, *who is holding a leather bag containing her make-up*]: May I present Monsieur de Chenneviette. I took the liberty of bringing him along. He is a very old friend – and something of a relation of mine – and so he acts as my manager for private occasions like this.

MADAME DUVERGER: Delighted, Monsieur.

[DE CHENNEVIETTE *bows.*]

MARCELINE [*to herself*]: I'm never introduced!

MADAME DUVERGER [*to* LUCETTE]: Well, Mademoiselle, you

will find all you need here. It's my bedroom. I've had it specially arranged for the occasion.

LUCETTE: I'm so sorry to give you so much trouble!

MADAME DUVERGER: Not at all! I had to make sure we had a dressing-room worthy of a star like yourself.

LUCETTE: How nice of you! [*Noticing the armchair placed under the canopy of the bed*] What on earth's that? It's a throne!

ALL: A throne!

LUCETTE: Oh, really now, that is going too far!

MADAME DUVERGER: A throne? Where? Oh, that! That's not a throne! It's the canopy of my bed! I had the bed taken out and that chair put in its place.

LUCETTE [*a little put-out*]: Oh, of course, that's just what I ...

MARCELINE [*to herself*]: As if she couldn't see it's not a throne!

MADAME DUVERGER [*going round pointing things out, followed by* DE CHENNEVIETTE *in his role as manager*]: You should find all the necessary toilet articles behind this screen. [*Approaching the wardrobe as if to open it*] And here is a wardrobe where you can hang your dresses. It is empty. [*She leaves the wardrobe and moves left to the chaise-longue.*]

LUCETTE: Perfect!

[DE CHENNEVIETTE *stays behind the chaise-longue.*]

MADAME DUVERGER: If you need anybody you've only to press the button on this table – it is an electric bell. But, of course, this door ... [*She goes to the door left.*] Now who could have locked it? [*To* VIVIANE, *who has moved near the cupboard talking to* DE FONTANET] Darling, go round and open it, will you? The key must be on the other side.

VIVIANE: Yes, mama. [*She goes out back through drawing-room.*]

MADAME DUVERGER: This door leads to the servants' quarters. Your maid could go down herself quicker this way if you need anything.

MARCELINE [*annoyed*]: Maid? What maid?

MADAME DUVERGER: But aren't you ...?

MARCELINE [*huffily*]: Certainly not! I am Mademoiselle Gautier's sister!

MADAME DUVERGER: Oh I do beg your pardon, Mademoiselle, I really do!

MARCELINE [*sullenly*]: Oh, that's all right! [*To herself*] She's even got to have maidservants now! [*She goes to the table and begins to open the costume box.*]

VIVIANE [*entering left*]: There you are! It's open now! [*She goes left of the chaise-longue and picks up her bouquet from the pedestal table.*]

MADAME DUVERGER [*to* LUCETTE]: Perhaps you would like to come into the drawing-room Mademoiselle to see that everything is as you would wish it ... the piano ... the platform ...

LUCETTE: Oh that? Oh, my manager looks after all that! [*To* DE CHENNEVIETTE] Chenneviette darling, over to you!

DE CHENNEVIETTE: Oh, all right ... [*He gives her the handbag; then to* MADAME DUVERGER] If Madame could kindly show me the way.

MADAME DUVERGER [*moving back-stage*]: We'll all go with you. Are you coming, Fontanet?

DE FONTANET [*who is in the drawing-room with his back to the fireplace*]: I am at your disposal, Madame.

LUCETTE [*opening her handbag on the pedestal table*]: In the meantime – with my sister's help – I'll start getting my things ready.

MADAME DUVERGER [*about to go out, back*]: Of course. Come along, Viviane! But what's become of your fiancé?

VIVIANE: I don't know, mama. He's probably gone out for a breath of fresh air. [*She goes out back with her mother, carrying her bouquet.*]

MARCELINE [*who has opened her costume box on the table back-stage and put the lid upright against the back of the chair beside the table*]: It's nice to be taken for your maid!

LUCETTE: How was she to know you were my sister? You don't resemble me in looks!

MARCELINE: No, but you like seeing me humiliated!

LUCETTE: Look, will you stop grumbling, and unpack my costumes. They'll all be crushed in that box. And hang them in the wardrobe.

MARCELINE [*unpacking*]: Oh, you! You'll be the cause if I really let myself go one day!

LUCETTE: And just what d'you mean by that, for heaven's sake?

MARCELINE [*moving centre with one of the costumes over her arm*]: I'll get a lover!

LUCETTE: You!

MARCELINE: You don't know me! [*She crumples the costume nervously without realizing what she is doing.*]

LUCETTE [*laughing*]: Oh, la, la! A lover! You! [*Changing her tone*] Look what you're doing there! Can't you even carry a costume? [*Moving right while* MARCELINE *is at the wardrobe*] No, I'll say you're not a maid! Because if you were, nobody would keep you for long!

MARCELINE [*at the wardrobe*]: You mean *I* wouldn't put up with *you* for long! [*Pulling in vain at the wardrobe door*] What's the matter with this wardrobe! It won't open!

LUCETTE [*behind the table, about to put the lid back on the box*]: Perhaps it's locked. Turn the key.

MARCELINE: That's what I'm doing. It won't work.

LUCETTE: What d'you mean, it won't work? [*Going to the wardrobe*] Can't you even open a wardrobe? Here, get out of the way! [*She pushes her aside and tries to open the door.*] It does seem to be stuck! On the inside! You pull as well! Come on! One! Two, Three! Now!

[*The door opens and* BOIS-D'ENGHIEN *almost falls out on top of them.*]

LUCETTE, MARCELINE [*uttering a shrill scream*]: Oh!

[*They recoil with fright, not daring to look.*]

LUCETTE: A man!

MARCELINE: A burglar!

BOIS-D'ENGHIEN [*who has regained his equilibrium in the wardrobe, very calmly*]: Oh, it's you, is it?

LUCETTE: Fernand!

MARCELINE: Bois-d'Enghien!

LUCETTE [*half in anger, half in fright*]: What the devil are you doing in there?

BOIS-D'ENGHIEN [*coming out of the wardrobe*]: Well, you see ... I was ...... er ... I was ... waiting for you!

LUCETTE: In the wardrobe!

BOIS-D'ENGHIEN: Yes, of course ... in the ... in the wardrobe

...... you know how it is sometimes ... one feels the need to get away from everybody ... Well, how are things going?

LUCETTE: Don't you ever give me a fright like that again! You must be going out of your mind!

MARCELINE: Yes, only an idiot would do a thing like that!

BOIS-D'ENGHIEN [*forcing a laugh to hide his embarrassment*]: Ha, ha! Did I really frighten you? Ha, ha, ha! My little joke really did succeed then?

LUCETTE: You call that a joke?

BOIS-D'ENGHIEN [*still laughing forcedly*]: Yes, I said to myself: 'She'll open the wardrobe and she'll find me inside.' A jolly good joke, that!

LUCETTE: Oh yes, very funny!

MARCELINE: Stupid, I'd say!

BOIS-D'ENGHIEN: Thank you! [*To himself, coming forward left*] My God! I hope the others don't barge in!

[DE CHENNEVIETTE *enters from the drawing-room.*]

DE CHENNEVIETTE: Everything's ready in there! [*Seeing* BOIS-D'ENGHIEN] Good Lord! Bois-d'Enghien!

BOIS-D'ENGHIEN: Chenneviette!

DE CHENNEVIETTE: You? You here?

BOIS-D'ENGHIEN [*trying to look unconcerned*]: Good heavens, yes, of course I'm here.

LUCETTE: But you won't guess where I found him! In the wardrobe!

DE CHENNEVIETTE: In the wardrobe?

BOIS-D'ENGHIEN [*laughing loudly but without conviction*]: Yes, jolly funny, don't you think?

DE CHENNEVIETTE [*to himself*]: Good heavens, he's gone mad!

MARCELINE [*who, during the preceding, has been hanging the dress in the wardrobe, now picks up the box*]: I'll take this out this way.

LUCETTE: Yes, yes!

MARCELINE [*going out left, grumbling*]: Yes, by the servants' door!

[*She goes.*]

LUCETTE [*to* BOIS-D'ENGHIEN]: But ... then you must know Madame Duverger?

BOIS-D'ENGHIEN [*with confidence he doesn't feel*]: Oh, yes, of course! Why, I've known Madame Duverger since she was a child!

ALL: Eh?

BOIS-D'ENGHIEN [*correcting himself*]: I mean – Madame Duverger's known me since I was a child!

LUCETTE: Oh? That's funny ...

BOIS-D'ENGHIEN [*moving left, laughing loudly*]: Yes, it is funny, isn't it? Very funny!

LUCETTE [*looking at him in astonishment, as* DE CHENNEVIETTE *does also*]: What's he laughing all the time for?

BOIS-D'ENGHIEN [*becoming suddenly serious, he swoops on* LUCETTE, *while* DE CHENNEVIETTE *moves down left*]: And now, you'll do me a favour and not sing in this house, eh?

LUCETTE [*astonished*]: *Not* sing here? But – why not?

BOIS-D'ENGHIEN: Why? She asks why! Because ... because because ... there are draughts here!

LUCETTE: Draughts? Where?

BOIS-D'ENGHIEN [*no longer knowing what he is saying*]: Everywhere! All round where you'll be singing!

LUCETTE: Draughts? On the platform? [*Brusquely*] I'll see about that! Where's the Baroness? [*She moves back-stage towards the dressing-room door.*]

BOIS-D'ENGHIEN [*seizing her with his right hand and pulling her back again*]: That would be telling tales: she'd know it was me who told you!

LUCETTE: Of course she won't! I won't even mention your name!

[MADAME DUVERGER *appears in the drawing-room.*]

There she is now. I'll go and have it out with her.

BOIS-D'ENGHIEN [*to himself, rushing left*]: Heavens, my mother-in-law!

LUCETTE: Wait! Where are you going?

BOIS-D'ENGHIEN [*at the door left*]: You haven't seen me! You haven't seen me! [*He disappears, left.*]

LUCETTE: What on earth's the matter with him!

DE CHENNEVIETTE [*to himself, having watched this scene with absolute bewilderment*]: I'd like to know what this is all about!

[MADAME DUVERGER *enters from the drawing-room.*]

MADAME DUVERGER: Has my son-in-law gone through here?

LUCETTE: Ah, Madame, I was hoping to have a word with you.

[*They both move forward, centre.*]

It seems there are draughts in your drawing-room.

MADAME DUVERGER [*with a sudden start*]: In my drawing-room?

LUCETTE [*polite but adamant*]: Yes, Madame, that is what I have been told, and I must inform you that I am unable to sing with a draught on my shoulders.

MADAME DUVERGER [*turning from* LUCETTE *to* DE CHENNEVIETTE *in her bewilderment*]: But, Madame, I don't know what you mean! A draught in my drawing-room! But that's nonsense! See for yourself, Monsieur! Oh, really – in my drawing-room, Madame? A draught! There isn't the slightest! Come and see for yourselves!

LUCETTE: Very well! Let us go and see. Because you understand, for me to sing under such conditions . . .

MADAME DUVERGER: Come, please! I beg you! [*Going out together*] A draught! In my drawing-room! Oh, no!

[*They both go into the drawing-room speaking these last lines together.*]

DE CHENNEVIETTE [*moving left*]: But there isn't any! There isn't any draught in there!

BOIS-D'ENGHIEN [*shooting through door right like a cannonball*]: Phew! You're alone.

DE CHENNEVIETTE: Now what's going on? You go out that way – and now you . . .

BOIS-D'ENGHIEN: Yes, yes, I had to go out that way. [*He points to the door left.*] And then I . . . [*He indicates by a gesture that he has gone upstairs and come down on the right.*]

DE CHENNEVIETTE: Look, what's the matter? Just what's going on round here?

BOIS-D'ENGHIEN: I'll tell you what's going on! I'm sitting on a volcano that's going to erupt any moment! That's all! Lucette's here and my marriage contract is going to be signed any moment.

DE CHENNEVIETTE [*with a start*]: Your marriage contract?

BOIS-D'ENGHIEN [*hopelessly*]: Yes, yes.

DE CHENNEVIETTE [*slapping himself on the thigh*]: Hell's bells! [*This movement leaves him standing with his back half-turned to* BOIS-D'ENGHIEN.]

BOIS-D'ENGHIEN: Yes! [*Causing him to pivot round in a circle by pushing him on the right shoulder and pulling him on the left shoulder*] And all hell's bells will be ringing if you don't help me get Lucette out of here!

DE CHENNEVIETTE: But how? How?

BOIS-D'ENGHIEN: I don't know! But it's got to be done!

DE CHENNEVIETTE [*making a half-turn as before*]: Well, I'll try ...

BOIS-D'ENGHIEN [*causing him to pivot in a circle as before*]: Where is she now? Where is she?

DE CHENNEVIETTE [*furious at being pushed about in this way, and freeing himself*]: With the Baroness, in the drawing-room, trying to find that draught of yours. [*He moves back-stage again.*]

BOIS-D'ENGHIEN: Oh, good lord! That means the balloon's going up any moment!

[*Voices off-stage*]

DE CHENNEVIETTE [*quickly, to* BOIS-D'ENGHIEN]: Look out! They're coming back!

BOIS-D'ENGHIEN: Oh!

[*He rushes to door right to avoid them and bumps into* VIVIANE *as she enters.*]

VIVIANE
BOIS-D'ENGHIEN } [*together*]: Oh!

[*They stand rubbing their bruised shoulders, where each has been carried by the force of their collision.*]

BOIS-D'ENGHIEN [*to himself*]: Blast it all! [*Aloud, pretending to laugh*] Well, well! So there you are!

VIVIANE: I like that! Where've you been? I've been looking for you for half-an-hour!

BOIS-D'ENGHIEN: So have I! So have I! [*Trying to pull her out*] Let's go and look together, now! Let's go and look together!

VIVIANE [*holding him back*]: Look for what? We've found each other, haven't we?

BOIS-D'ENGHIEN: You're right! [*To himself*] I don't know what I'm saying now!

VIVIANE [*to herself*]: He's a bigger idiot than I thought!

DE CHENNEVIETTE [*to himself, moving forward extreme left*]: Now he's babbling, poor chap! Babbling!

[MADAME DUVERGER*'s voice is heard off-stage.*]

DE CHENNEVIETTE
BOIS-D'ENGHIEN: } It's them!

[BOIS-D'ENGHIEN *sidles stealthily towards door right to escape without being seen.*]

MADAME DUVERGER [*entering back from drawing-room*]: So you see I was quite right, Mademoiselle.

LUCETTE: Indeed you were!

MADAME DUVERGER [*as* BOIS-D'ENGHIEN *is about to disappear right*]: Ah, Bois-d'Enghien! There you are, at last!

BOIS-D'ENGHIEN [*pivoting on his heels, prepared to die fighting*]: Yes . . . I was just coming.

MADAME DUVERGER [*to* LUCETTE, *to introduce* BOIS-D'ENGHIEN *to her*]: Mademoiselle . . .

BOIS-D'ENGHIEN [*to himself*]: Now for it!

MADAME DUVERGER [*to* LUCETTE, *who is already nodding her head to show that she knows him*]: Allow me to introduce . . .

[DE CHENNEVIETTE *rushes between* LUCETTE *and* MADAME DUVERGER, *pushes the latter aside, and seizing* LUCETTE *by the hand, pulls her back-stage.*]

DE CHENNEVIETTE: No, don't bother! She knows him! She knows him!

ALL: Eh? What is it? What's wrong?

[*General confusion.*]

DE CHENNEVIETTE [*pulling* LUCETTE]: Come with me! Come with me!

LUCETTE [*struggling*]: Where? Where?

DE CHENNEVIETTE [*still pulling her towards drawing-room door*]: To find that draught! I know where it is! I know where it is!

LUCETTE [*disappearing through the door, pulled forcibly by* DE CHENNEVIETTE]: No! No! Stop! Let me go!

BOIS-D'ENGHIEN [*who alone has not moved upstage, to himself joyfully*]: Saved, thank heaven!

MADAME DUVERGER [*upstage with* VIVIANE]: What *is* the matter? Why's he pulling her away like that?

BOIS-D'ENGHIEN: Why? [*He strides purposefully to the two women and taking each by the hand strides purposefully forward again so that they have to follow as best they can.*] Because . . . because you were going to make a terrible mistake!

MADAME DUVERGER: A mistake! Me?

VIVIANE: But how?

BOIS-D'ENGHIEN: You were going to introduce me ... you were going to say: 'Monsieur de Bois-d'Enghien, my future son-in-law' or 'My daughter's fiancé' or something like that, weren't you?

MADAME DUVERGER: Well, naturally.

BOIS-D'ENGHIEN [*adopting a tone of profound mystery*]: That is just what you must never do! It was that gentleman who warned me. That's why he pulled her away. The words 'fiancé' and 'son-in-law' must never be uttered in front of Lucette Gautier!

MADAME DUVERGER: Why not?

BOIS-D'ENGHIEN: Ah! Well ... because it seems ... it was that gentleman who warned me ... it seems she had an unhappy love affair once.

VIVIANE [*with interest*]: Really?

BOIS-D'ENGHIEN [*adopting a mournful tone*]: A fine young man whom she adored and was just about to marry. Unfortunately he had a human weakness. [*With a sigh*] One day ... he succumbed.

MADAME DUVERGER: Good heavens! What to?

BOIS-D'ENGHIEN [*changing his tone*]: To a very rich old lady who took him off to America ...

MADAME DUVERGER
VIVIANE: } Oh!

BOIS-D'ENGHIEN [*adopting a dramatic tone*]: The marriage was off! Lucette Gautier never recovered! One has only to utter those words – 'son-in-law' or 'fiancé' – in front of her ... it was that gentleman who warned me ... and the result will be fainting-fits, hysterics – complete nervous breakdown!

MADAME DUVERGER: Oh, that's terrible! You did right to tell me!

VIVIANE: It's like out of a novel! It's beautiful! A real love story!

BOIS-D'ENGHIEN: Well – that's how it is ... and if that gentleman hadn't warned me ...

MADAME DUVERGER [*as* BOIS-D'ENGHIEN *moves upstage to be on the look-out for* LUCETTE]: Oh, I *am* very glad to know about it!

VIVIANE: Yes, indeed! So am I!

[LUCETTE *can be seen in the drawing-room arguing with* DE FONTANET *and* DE CHENNEVIETTE.]

BOIS-D'ENGHIEN [*to himself, as he sees them*]: It's them! [*He comes forward like a bomb, seizes* MADAME DUVERGER *and* VIVIANE *by the hand and pulls them right.*] Come quick! With me!

MADAME DUVERGER *and* VIVIANE [*bewildered*]: What? Why? What's the matter?

BOIS-D'ENGHIEN [*pushing them through the door right,* VIVIANE *first and* MADAME DUVERGER *next*]: I've something more to tell you! To show you! It's upstairs! Upstairs! Come on! Quickly! [*Despite their protests, he pushes them out right and follows them.*]

LUCETTE [*entering through the drawing-room door, to* DE CHENNEVIETTE *who precedes her*]: Well, I still say – you're a fool!

DE CHENNEVIETTE [*to himself, moving forward left to the chaise-longue*]: It's that fool, Bois-d'Enghien, who made me act like one!

DE FONTANET: I'm not intruding, am I?

LUCETTE [*sitting on the chaise-longue, powdering her face and looking in her mirror*]: No, no, not at all.

DE FONTANET [*coming forward right*]: I'm bored stiff! Everybody's gone off and left me on my own – as if I had the plague or something!

LUCETTE: Poor Fontanet!

DE FONTANET: It's true! I'm fed up!

ÉMILE [*appears at the drawing-room door, announcing*]: General Irrigua!

DE FONTANET: Who's he?

LUCETTE: Him? Oh, of course!

DE CHENNEVIETTE: Have they invited that fellow?

LUCETTE [*without getting up*]: I asked him. [*To* THE GENERAL *who enters back*] Come along in, General!

THE GENERAL [*entering hastily and going to* LUCETTE, *with a bouquet in his hand*]: I ees late! Please to forgeeve me! Time weeth you, eet ees lost forever! Please forgeeve!

LUCETTE: But of course you're not late, General. There is nothing to forgive!

DE CHENNEVIETTE: How d'you do, General!

THE GENERAL [*giving him a friendly nod*]: How do! [*He nods similarly to* DE FONTANET, *who bows.*] Buenos dias! [*To* LUCETTE, *offering her the bouquet of wild flowers*] Permeet, please . . . a leetle geeft . . .

LUCETTE [*without taking them*]: Oh, wild flowers! What an original idea!

THE GENERAL [*gallantly*]: When I theenk of the flowers of the field, I theenk of stars, of seengeeng – of you who are the seengeeng star!

ALL [*with mock admiration*]: Charming! Charming!

THE GENERAL [*with deprecatory self-satisfaction*]: It ees nothing! I am weetty!

DE FONTANET [*flatteringly*]: True Parisian wit, General!

THE GENERAL [*offering again to* LUCETTE *the bouquet which is tied with a string of pearls*]: But if the flowers ees poor, the streeng ees good!

LUCETTE [*rising and taking the flowers and removing the necklace*]: A string of pearls! Oh, really, General!

THE GENERAL [*in a lordly manner*]: It ees nothing. A barcatil!

DE FONTANET [*to* THE GENERAL]: May I?

[*He passes in front of* THE GENERAL *and goes to admire the pearls with the others.*]

ALL: Why, they're beautiful! Charming! Lovely!

DE CHENNEVIETTE: Absolutely splendid!

LUCETTE [*as* DE CHENNEVIETTE *fastens the pearls round her neck*]: Oh, I'm so happy! You've no idea how happy I am!

DE FONTANET : Chosen with perfect taste, if I may say so!

[THE GENERAL *bows modestly.*]

LUCETTE [*introducing* DE FONTANET, *without leaving* DE CHENNEVIETTE *who is fastening the string of pearls*]: General, Monsieur Ignace de Fontanet.

THE GENERAL [*holding out his hand*]: Eet ees pleasure!

DE FONTANET: Enchanted, General! And accept my compliments. You have the grand manner, General. You do things in style. And if I may say so you . . .

THE GENERAL [*sniffing the air around him*]: Please – eet ees nothing!

DE FONTANET [*going on speaking full in* THE GENERAL'*s face, so that* THE GENERAL *is forced to retreat*]: If I may say so it is a fine thing to be a millionaire and a gentleman. There are so many millionaires who are not gentlemen, and so many gentlemen who are not millionaires!

THE GENERAL [*still retreating and still followed by* DE FONTANET]: Si! Si! [*Taking a little box from his waistcoat and offering it to* DE FONTANET] Take a pastille!

DE FONTANET: What? What for?

THE GENERAL: I take the pastille when I have smoked the ceegar.

DE FONTANET [*bowing and speaking straight into* THE GENERAL'*s nose*]: No use to me, General. I don't smoke.

THE GENERAL [*quickly, holding his opera hat to his face, apparently as a gesture of regret, but really to shield himself from the smell*]: I am sorry! [*Holding out the box again*] Take one all the same!

DE FONTANET: Just to please you then.

THE GENERAL: You make me very much pleased!

[THE GENERAL *moves left pursued by* DE FONTANET *who continues to speak to him. He defends himself as well as he can by holding his opera hat as a barrier between them.*]

THE GENERAL [*to* DE FONTANET *as he sees* MADAME DUVERGER *entering right*]: Excuse, please!

MADAME DUVERGER [*entering right*]: Really! I simply can't understand it! He makes us climb three staircases to the attic. And then he says: 'Have you noticed you haven't a lightning conductor on this house!'

THE GENERAL [*nodding to her*]: Madame!

LUCETTE: Oh, Madame, may I introduce a good friend of mine, General Irrigua?

THE GENERAL [*bowing*]: Heemself!

LUCETTE: Who was happy to accept one of your invitation cards.

THE GENERAL [*producing the card*]: I have the teecket!

MADAME DUVERGER [*smiling*]: Quite unnecessary, General ... This is just a family affair, you know.

THE GENERAL [*very graciously, as if he were saying the politest thing in the world*]: It ees no matter – I come for Mademoiselle Gautier.

MADAME DUVERGER [*taken aback*]: Oh? Really? [*To herself, as* THE GENERAL *goes to speak to* LUCETTE] Well, he certainly doesn't mince words!

VIVIANE [*entering right, pulling* BOIS-D'ENGHIEN *in with her*]: Come on in! What's the matter with you this evening?

BOIS-D'ENGHIEN: Nothing! Nothing's the matter! [*To himself*] The General! Oh; that makes everything just perfect!

THE GENERAL [*turning and recognizing* BOIS-D'ENGHIEN]: Ah! Eet ees Bodégué! You come to seeng somethееng for us, eh?

ALL: What? Sing something?

THE GENERAL: Bueno! Becose he ees tenor seenger!

ALL: No?

VIVIANE: What? You? A tenor singer?

BOIS-D'ENGHIEN: Oh, *you* know! Just a little! A very little!

VIVIANE: But I didn't know! We'll be able to sing together! Duets!

BOIS-D'ENGHIEN [*aside, to the audience*]: Oh, that'll be marvellous!

[ÉMILE *enters through drawing-room door followed by* LANTERY]

ÉMILE [*announcing*]: Monsieur Lantery! [*He goes out again.*]

MADAME DUVERGER [*going to meet the notary*]: Ah, the notary! How d'you do, Monsieur Lantery!

LANTERY [*coming forward to the right a little with* MADAME DUVERGER]: Good evening, Baroness. Ladies . . . Gentlemen . . .

[THE GENERAL, *after having moved upstage, comes forward to talk to* DE CHENNEVIETTE *left of the chaise-longue.*]

MADAME DUVERGER: Now you're here we can begin right away. You have the contract?

LANTERY: No, but one of my clerks is bringing it. Ah, here he is now!

[BOUZIN *appears at drawing-room door speaking to* ÉMILE.]

MADAME DUVERGER: Good!

BOIS-D'ENGHIEN [*to himself*]: Bouzin! That's done it! [*Aside, crossing to* LUCETTE] Look! It's Bouzin!

LUCETTE [*aside to* BOIS-D'ENGHIEN]: Bouzin? Oh! If the General sees *him*!

[*She distracts* THE GENERAL'*s attention by talking to him with her back to the audience, so preventing him from turning and seeing* BOUZIN.]

MADAME DUVERGER [*following* LANTERY *who has gone back-stage to* BOUZIN]: Will everybody come in here? We're going to hear the contract read.

DE FONTANET, VIVIANE, BOIS-D'ENGHIEN: } Of course! Certainly!

[*They go into the drawing-room except* BOIS-D'ENGHIEN *who moves right.*]

MADAME DUVERGER [*from drawing-room*]: Monsieur de Chenneviette?

DE CHENNEVIETTE [*who is talking to* THE GENERAL]: It is an honour, Madame! [*To* THE GENERAL] You will excuse me, General?

THE GENERAL: Eet ees pleasure, Cheviotte!

[*He continues talking to* LUCETTE. DE CHENNEVIETTE *goes into drawing-room.*]

MADAME DUVERGER [*to* BOUZIN, *in the drawing-room*]: Why! It's the gentleman I met this morning!

BOUZIN [*recognizing her*]: Ah! Madame! Baroness! I'd no idea this was ... I mean how nice to meet again!

MADAME DUVERGER: Er – yes – isn't it?

[BOUZIN, LANTERY, VIVIANE, FONTANET *and* CHENNEVIETTE *disappear off-stage.* MADAME DUVERGER *remains at drawing-room door speaking to* LUCETTE]: Won't you join us, Madame?

BOIS-D'ENGHIEN [*with a start*]: What?

LUCETTE: Please excuse me, Madame. I must start getting ready. [*She goes to the wardrobe to get a dress which* MARCELINE *has hung there previously.*]

MADAME DUVERGER: As you wish, Madame.

BOIS-D'ENGHIEN [*giving a sigh of relief*]: Ouf!

MADAME DUVERGER [*to* THE GENERAL]: And you, General?

THE GENERAL [*bowing*]: Thank you – but I stay weeth Mademoiselle Gautier! [*He goes extreme left.*]

MADAME DUVERGER [*to herself*]: Naturally! [*Aloud*] Come along, Bois-d'Enghien! [*She disappears off-stage.*]

BOIS-D'ENGHIEN [*with assumed fervour*]: Coming! Coming!

LUCETTE [*moving forward by chaise-longue, undoing laces on dress she is holding*]: You're not going in there, are you?

BOIS-D'ENGHIEN [*suddenly rooted to the spot*]: Well ... don't you think ? ...

LUCETTE: What's their silly contract to do with you?

BOIS-D'ENGHIEN [*assuming an air of indifference*]: Oh! ...

LUCETTE: Well? No concern of yours, is it?

BOIS-D'ENGHIEN [*with exaggerated indifference*]: Of mine? Hah!

THE GENERAL [*presenting an unanswerable argument*]: Ees eet that I go? No! So why you go?

BOIS-D'ENGHIEN: You? – Well, yes, of course! [*Aside to the audience*] It's not *his* marriage contract!

LUCETTE [*going towards the wardrobe*]: If you really want to, you could slip in just before they finish ...

BOIS-D'ENGHIEN [*grasping at this straw*]: Yes – why not?

LUCETTE [*stopping on her way to the wardrobe*]: With me! [*She continues to the wardrobe and hangs up the dress again.*]

BOIS-D'ENGHIEN [*to himself*]: That finishes it!

ALL [*off-stage*]: Bois-d'Enghien! Bois-d'Enghien!

BOIS-D'ENGHIEN [*to himself*]: Now *they've* started! [*Aloud, anxiously*] Coming! Coming!

LUCETTE [*coming forward to chaise-longue*]: But what do they want you for?

BOIS-D'ENGHIEN [*pretending to laugh*]: I don't know! That's what I was wondering!

[*Everybody, except* LANTERY, *reappears in the drawing-room.*]

MADAME DUVERGER [*at drawing-room door*]: Come along, Bois-d'Enghien! What's keeping you? [*She enters, followed by* BOUZIN, *who goes, by bureaucratic habit, behind table right.*] Monsieur, here, is waiting to read the contract.

THE GENERAL [*giving a jump as he sees* BOUZIN]: Boussin!

BOUZIN: It's that General! Let me out of here!

[THE GENERAL *chases him backwards and forwards round the table amid general confusion.*]

THE GENERAL [*chasing* BOUZIN]: Boussin! Here! Boussin! Eet ees always Boussin! Wait, Boussin! While I keel you, Boussin! [BOUZIN *saves himself by knocking over a chair right and* THE

GENERAL *falls over it.* BOUZIN *then dashes out through door right.*]

MADAME DUVERGER [*amid the general confusion*] What's the matter? Where are they going?

LUCETTE: It's all right! Don't worry, Madame! Chenneviette, stop them, will you!

DE CHENNEVIETTE: I'll try!

[*During the preceding quick dialogue,* THE GENERAL *has picked himself up and stepped over the chair. He gets to the door right but is stopped by* BOIS-D'ENGHIEN *who, running after him, grabs him by his coat-tails.* THE GENERAL *breaks away and dashes out right after* BOUZIN. DE CHENNEVIETTE *pushes* BOIS-D'ENGHIEN *aside and dashes out after him. All the others, meanwhile, enter from the drawing-room, where suddenly the pursuit is seen to continue. First* BOUZIN *is seen to dash past the open drawing-room door followed, successively, by* THE GENERAL *and by* DE CHENNEVIETTE.]

MADAME DUVERGER [*to* LUCETTE]: Really, this is too much! Who is that man? And why is he chasing Monsieur Bouzin?

LUCETTE: Please, you must excuse him, Madame! You see . . .

MADAME DUVERGER: All I see is the most disgraceful behaviour in my house! [*The two women go on speaking at the same time:* LUCETTE *to excuse* THE GENERAL, *and* MADAME DUVERGER *to express her annoyance. At last* MADAME DUVERGER *becomes authoritative.*] That's enough! The contract has not been read yet! Bois-d'Enghien, give my daughter your arm, and come at once! [*She moves back-stage.*]

LUCETTE [*with sudden suspicion*]: But . . . why Bois-d'Enghien?

MADAME DUVERGER [*under the stress of the moment, without thinking*]: Why? Why? Because he's her fiancé, that's why!

LUCETTE: Her fiancé? Him! [*She shrieks and faints.*]

ALL: What's happened? What's the matter?

MARCELINE [*who has caught* LUCETTE *in her arms as she fainted*]: Oh, good heavens! She's fainted! Lucette!

[*Everybody – except* MADAME DUVERGER *and* VIVIANE *who remain rooted where they are – surround* LUCETTE *and lay her on the chaise-longue.*]

BOIS-D'ENGHIEN [*going back to* MADAME DUVERGER, *making the most of it*]: There! Now see what you've done! You said that word 'fiancé'!

MADAME DUVERGER: Me?

VIVIANE [*also turning on her mother*]: Yes! Yes, you did!

BOIS-D'ENGHIEN: And after being warned not to! [*He returns to* LUCETTE.]

VIVIANE: Yes, you were told never to mention the word 'fiancé'!

[MADAME DUVERGER *shrugs her shoulders as if everything is getting too much for her.*]

THE GENERAL [*dashing in up-left, closely followed by* DE CHENNEVIETTE]: So! He ees feeneeshed! That Boussin! I have keecked him out!

DE CHENNEVIETTE [*to himself, wiping his forehead*]: My God! What an evening!

THE GENERAL [*seeing* LUCETTE *on the chaise-longue*]: Caramba! Loucette! [*He goes to her.*] Loucette! What ees eet?

BOIS-D'ENGHIEN [*leaving* LUCETTE *and clapping his hands*]: Quick, somebody! Get some vinegar! Some salts!

MARCELINE: I'll go!

[*She runs out left while* BOIS-D'ENGHIEN, MADAME DUVERGER *and* VIVIANE *look frantically for smelling salts on the dressing-table.*]

THE GENERAL [*rubbing* LUCETTE'*s hand while* DE CHENNEVIETTE *on the other side rubs the other hand*]: Mam'selle Gautier! Come back to me! Come back to me!

DE FONTANET [*bending over* LUCETTE'*s face from behind the chaise-longue, naïvely*]: What she needs is some fresh air . . .

BOIS-D'ENGHIEN [*coming back with a bottle of smelling salts*]: Then you get away from there!

DE CHENNEVIETTE *and* THE GENERAL: Yes, get away from her, all of you!

BOIS-D'ENGHIEN [*quickly, moving centre*]: That's right! Let's all move away from her! [*To* MADAME DUVERGER *and* VIVIANE *who are a little upstage*] We can leave these gentlemen with her – while we finish signing the contract in there!

ALL: Yes, that's best!

THE GENRAL [*very loudly, just as* BOIS-D'ENGHIEN *is about to go into the drawing-room with the two women*]: A key! Queeck! Who has a key?

BOIS-D'ENGHIEN [*frantically pulling a key from his pocket, running to* THE GENERAL *and back again*]: A key? . . . Here! . . . Why?

THE GENERAL: Gracias! [*He tries to put the key down the back of* LUCETTE'*s dress.*]

BOIS-D'ENGHIEN [*running back to get the key*]: Are you mad? That's the key of my apartment! Her nose isn't bleeding!

THE GENERAL [*succeeding in putting the key down her back*]: I see eef thees do same. Maybe.

MADAME DUVERGER [*impatiently to* BOIS-D'ENGHIEN]: Well? Are you coming with us?

BOIS-D'ENGHIEN [*jumping back and forwards not knowing which way to go*]: Oh, all right! All right! [*To himself*] I'll sign and get back here!

[*They all go out except* DE FONTANET, THE GENERAL, DE CHENNEVIETTE *and of course* LUCETTE. *The drawing-room door is closed. The two centre panels, only, open again at the end of the act.*]

THE GENERAL: Queeck! Water! Veenegar. Breeng sometheeng!

DE FONTANET [*going back to dressing-table*]: Wait! I'll look here!

DE CHENNEVIETTE: My God! What an evening!

THE GENERAL: Dios Mios! Mam'selle Gautier! Come back to me! Come back to me, Mam'selle Gautier!

DE FONTANET [*returning with a napkin soaked in water*]: Here! Try this! It's soaking wet!

THE GENERAL: Gracias! [*dabbing* LUCETTE'*s forehead with it, and pleading*] Come back to me, Gautier! Gautier, come back to me!

DE FONTANET [*who has taken up his previous position, behind the chaise-longue*]: Do you think a little air – if I blew in her face . . .

DE CHENNEVIETTE / THE GENERAL [*pushing him away, together*]: No!

DE FONTANET [*moving centre*]: Poor girl! I knew she'd go to pieces when she heard about Bois d'Enghien's marriage!

DE CHENNEVIETTE [*to himself, with a start*]: That's done it!

THE GENERAL [*looking at* DE FONTANET *but still dabbing at* LUCETTE'*s forehead*]: The tenor seenger? What has hees marriage to do weeth Lucette?

DE FONTANET: That's a good one! After all, he's her lover, you know!

THE GENERAL [*jumping up, throwing the napkin without realizing it on* LUCETTE'*s face*]: What you say?

DE CHENNEVIETTE [*to himself*]: The imbecile! [*Seeing the napkin on* LUCETTE'*s face*] Oh! [*He pulls it off and begins dabbing her forehead with it.*]

THE GENERAL [*seizing* FONTANET *by the throat and shaking him*]: What ees eet you say? Bodégué? Bodégué ees her lover?

DE FONTANET [*speaking straight into* THE GENERAL'*s face*]: Yes, of course! What's the matter with you?

THE GENERAL [*recoiling from* DE FONTANET, *but continuing to shake him*]: Bodégué ees her lover?

DE FONTANET [*half-strangled*]: Let me go! What's come over you? Stop it!

BOIS-D'ENGHIEN [*entering back quickly, opening the two centre panels of the drawing-room door only*]: Well, is she better?

[THE GENERAL *pushes* DE FONTANET *away violently so that he almost falls, then hurls himself at* BOIS-D'ENGHIEN, *seizing him by the throat*]

THE GENERAL: Ees you lover of Mam'selle Gautier?

BOIS-D'ENGHIEN [*suffocating*]: What? What is it?

THE GENERAL [*shaking him*]: Ees you who ees lover?

DE FONTANET [*to himself*]: I must have put my foot in it! [*He hastily escapes into the drawing-room.*]

BOIS-D'ENGHIEN: What's the matter with you! Let me go!

DE CHENNEVIETTE [*trying to calm them without leaving* LUCETTE]: Please! General! That's enough!

THE GENERAL [*hurling* BOIS-D'ENGHIEN *away from him*]: So! You theenk you Don Juan, eh?

BOIS-D'ENGHIEN: Me?

THE GENERAL: You! So I keell you! [*He returns to* LUCETTE *to slap and rub her hands.*]

BOIS-D'ENGHIEN [*furiously*]: So you're going to kill me! And why? Why, may I ask?

THE GENERAL [*coming back to him, shouting loudly*]: Becose I love her and becose I do not permeet you to be in my way!

BOIS-D'ENGHIEN [*shouting even louder*]: How the devil can I be in your way when I'm getting married? When all I want is for you to take your Lucette off my hands?

THE GENERAL [*suddenly becoming calm*]: Ees eet so? You ees no more een love weeth Loucette?

BOIS-D'ENGHIEN [*still shouting, and articulating each syllable*]: I've just told you I'm getting married!

THE GENERAL: Ah! Bodégué! You ees my friend! [*He shakes* BOIS-D'ENGHIEN *by both hands.*]

DE CHENNEVIETTE: She's opening her eyes!

BOIS-D'ENGHIEN: Leave me with her! I'll make one last attempt!

THE GENERAL [*going out*]: Bueno! I leave you! [*To* LUCETTE, *as he goes*] Come back to heem, Gautier! Gautier! come back to heem!

[THE GENERAL *and* DE CHENNEVIETTE *go out back into drawing-room and* BOIS-D'ENGHIEN *closes the door after them.*]

LUCETTE [*coming to herself*]: What happened? What happened?

BOIS-D'ENGHIEN [*falling on his knees beside her*]: Lucette!

LUCETTE [*plaintively, putting her hands gently on his shoulders*]: Is that you, darling?

BOIS-D'ENGHIEN: Lucette, forgive me! It's all my fault! Forgive me!

[*At these words,* LUCETTE'*s face changes as she gradually remembers what happened.*]

LUCETTE [*suddenly, pushing him away so that he almost falls backwards*]: You! Don't speak to me! You beast! [*She rises and moves right.*]

BOIS-D'ENGHIEN [*following her on his hands and knees, pleadingly*]: Lulu, darling! Lulu!

LUCETTE [*choking with emotion*]: So, it's true! This marriage-contract! It's yours!

BOIS-D'ENGHIEN [*getting up and speaking as if admitting guilt*]: All right, yes! It *is* mine!

LUCETTE: It's his – he admits it! Why, you – you wretch!

BOIS-D'ENGHIEN [*pleadingly*]: Lucette!

LUCETTE [*warding him off with a gesture and a bitter smile*]: Very well! There is only one thing left for me! [*She makes a dramatic gesture as if saying 'There is no alternative' and moves left.*]

BOIS-D'ENGHIEN [*uneasily*]: What?

LUCETTE [*opening her handbag and feeling around in it*]: Don't you remember the promise I made you?

BOIS-D'ENGHIEN [*to himself*]: What promise?

LUCETTE [*choking back her sobs*]: Don't worry – I shall keep it! [*She pulls a revolver from her handbag, sobbing.*] Good-bye! And be happy!

BOIS-D'ENGHIEN [*rushing at her to disarm her, and holding her arms to her sides*]: Lucette! For heaven's sake! Are you mad?

LUCETTE [*struggling*]: Let me go! Let me go!

BOIS-D'ENGHIEN [*trying to take the revolver and at the same time to calm her*]: Lucette! Please! You can't! Not in someone else's house!

LUCETTE [*laughing bitterly*]: What do I care!

BOIS-D'ENGHIEN [*still holding her, but losing control of himself*]: For heaven's sake just listen to me, will you? If you kill yourself how can I explain everything to you!

LUCETTE [*breaking away from him*]: All right! Explain!

BOIS-D'ENGHIEN [*quickly*]: Give me that gun first!

LUCETTE [*avoiding him*]: No! You explain first!

BOIS-D'ENGHIEN [*in despair*]: Oh, I give up!

VOICE OF MADAME DUVERGER [*off-stage*]: Bois-d'Enghien! Bois-d'Enghien!

BOIS-D'ENGHIEN [*to himself, exasperated*]: All right! All right! [*Moving back-stage*] Oh, I give up! I give up! [*Aloud, opening door-back and half-disappearing*] Well, what is it?

LUCETTE [*tiring of her histrionics*]: Oh! I'm hot! [*She pulls the trigger of the revolver, so releasing a fan with which she fans herself nervously.*]

BOIS-D'ENGHIEN [*speaking into the wings, bad-temperedly*]: Yes, yes! Right away! [*He closes the door.*] What are they in such a hurry for?

LUCETTE [*to herself*]: You're not married yet, my friend! Just you wait! [*She shuts the fan, puts the revolver back into her bag and moves upstage above the pedestal table, to the left of the chaise-longue, on which she kneels.*]

BOIS-D'ENGHIEN [*going to her pleadingly*]: Please, Lucette!

Have courage! Try to be brave! Think of all the happy times we've had together. For the sake of our love, be generous!

LUCETTE [*raising her arms and flinging herself full length on the chaise-longue on her stomach*]: Our love! What love? [*She sobs, her face hidden in her arms which are crossed across the raised back of the chaise-longue.*]

BOIS-D'ENGHIEN [*crouching behind the chaise-longue so that he is face to face with* LUCETTE *when she raises her head*]: How can you say that!

LUCETTE [*raising her head, sobbing*]: How can *you* go and get married then?

BOIS-D'ENGHIEN: What does that matter? I can get married and still love you, can't I?

LUCETTE [*kneeling on the chaise-longue, in a hesitant little voice, as if half-convinced*]: You can?

BOIS-D'ENGHIEN [*with feigned conviction*]: Of course I can! [*He rises and moves round the chaise-longue.*]

LUCETTE [*aside, to the audience*]: Oh, what a twister!

BOIS-D'ENGHIEN [*to himself*]: Once I'm married I'll soon get rid of her. [*Aloud, sitting on right side of the chaise-longue*] My little Lulu!

LUCETTE [*on her knees on left side of chaise-longue*]: Ah, my youm-youm! You do love me?

BOIS-D'ENGHIEN: I adore you!

LUCETTE: Darling! [*She moves herself round, still on her knees, and her right hand touches against the bouquet on the pedestal table. To herself*] Ah! That's an idea! [*She carries on playing her role and puts her arms around his neck.*] Then we can go on as we've always done?

BOIS-D'ENGHIEN [*playing his role*]: Why not?

LUCETTE [*with feigned joy*]: Oh, darling! And to think I was just saying to myself ... you'll never guess what I was telling myself! That our love was finished! Think of that!

BOIS-D'ENGHIEN: You were? Silly little Lulu!

LUCETTE [*pointing to the bouquet, with her left arm still round his neck*]: Oh, look! These wild flowers! Don't they remind you of something?

BOIS-D'ENGHIEN [*sentimentally*]: Ah, yes! They remind me of the country.

LUCETTE [*with a sigh, raising herself to her knees and with her arms in the air as if evoking the memories, while* BOIS-D'ENGHIEN, *his right arm around her waist, listens with his head bent*]: Ah, yes! The country! Remember when we were students, darling, and we used to wander in the meadows!

BOIS-D'ENGHIEN: Ah, happy days!

LUCETTE [*turning, putting her face up to his and taking his chin in her hand*]: They *were* happy, weren't they, darling?

BOIS-D'ENGHIEN [*playing his role*]: Blissful, my darling!

LUCETTE: We used to lie under the trees and I used to tickle you with blades of grass and push some down your neck!

[*Profiting from* BOIS-D'ENGHIEN'*s position, his head bent listening to her, she pushes a flower down his neck.*]

BOIS-D'ENGHIEN [*struggling*]: Ow! What are you doing!

LUCETTE [*pushing the flower and thorns further down*]: Right down ... down ... [*emphasizing each word with a wink to the audience as if to say 'Just wait!'*] ... down ...

BOIS-D'ENGHIEN [*jumping up, trying to pull the flower out again*]: What a damn fool thing to do! I can't get at it!

LUCETTE [*still kneeling on the chaise-longue, in an ingenuous little voice*]: Really! Does it bother you, dear?

BOIS-D'ENGHIEN: The damn thing's got thorns on it!

LUCETTE [*with feigned compassion*]: Oh, darling! [*Changing her tone*] Well, get it out, then!

BOIS-D'ENGHIEN [*making desperate efforts to reach the flower*]: What d'you think I'm trying to do! It's right inside my vest, next to my skin!

LUCETTE [*in the most natural tone*]: Well, take your clothes off, then!

BOIS-D'ENGHIEN [*furiously*]: Are you mad? Take my clothes off? Here? With my fiancée in the next room!

LUCETTE [*rising and moving round the chaise-longue*]: What are you frightened of? We can lock the doors. [*She locks all the doors and then comes forward again.*] There! If anyone comes they'll think I'm getting dressed, and you've gone!

BOIS-D'ENGHIEN: No, no, I won't.

LUCETTE [*lyrically*]: I see you no longer love me!

BOIS-D'ENGHIEN: But I do! I do!

LUCETTE: Then why d'you mind getting undressed in front of me?

BOIS-D'ENGHIEN [*still struggling to get at the flower*]: Oh, this is terrible! [*Jerking his elbows to make the flower drop further down*] Ow! The damn thing, sticking in me!

LUCETTE: Then don't be so obstinate! Go behind that screen and get it out!

BOIS-D'ENGHIEN [*moving back-stage*]: I suppose I'll have to! I can't go on like this! You're sure they're locked?

LUCETTE: Yes, yes! [BOIS-D'ENGHIEN *goes behind the screen pulling it round him, while* LUCETTE *whispers triumphantly in an aside to the audience*] Got him! [*Then she goes round unlocking all the doors. Aloud*] While you're doing that, darling, I'll get dressed for my performance. [*She gets her costume from the wardrobe and comes back to the chaise-longue.*]

BOIS-D'ENGHIEN [*behind the screen*]: This is ridiculous! At a time like this! And all through you!

LUCETTE [*taking off her skirt*]: Why? What's wrong in taking out a thorn that happens to be sticking in you?

BOIS-D'ENGHIEN: Happens to be sticking in me! You jolly well did it on purpose! [*He throws his shirt so that it appears hanging over the screen.*] There! I've got it!

LUCETTE [*by the chaise-longue – with mock passion*] You've got it? Oh – please – give it to me!

BOIS-D'ENGHIEN: Why?

LUCETTE: To keep! Because it has been close to your heart!

BOIS-D'ENGHIEN [*half appearing from behind screen in trousers and woollen vest, the flower in his hand*]: Well, it wasn't! It was down the bottom of my back! [*He turns as if to go back behind the screen.*]

LUCETTE: Give it me all the same!

BOIS-D'ENGHIEN [*taking it to her*]: Oh, here you are! [*He tries to return to the screen but* LUCETTE *has grasped his hand tightly and pulls him to her.*]

LUCETTE: Oh, you great, big, handsome thing, you!

BOIS-D'ENGHIEN [*fatuously*]: Well ...?

LUCETTE [*with feigned admiration*]: Oh you look wonderful like that.

BOISE-D'ENGHIEN: Please, Lucette! Suppose someone came in! You're sure the doors are locked?

LUCETTE: Yes, yes! [*Holding him close to her*] Oh to feel you near me. [*Stroking his chest with her right hand, while still holding him with her left*] All mine ... in woollen vest and all!

BOIS-D'ENGHIEN: Oh, now, really!

LUCETTE: And when I think – when I think that all this is going to be taken from me ... Oh no! Never! I won't let them! [*She grasps him crazily round the neck so that he falls on to the sofa while she falls beside him in such a way, that he finds himself unable to get up, paralysed by her grip.*] Oh Fernand, my Fernand! I love you! I love you! I love you! [*She raises her voice to a scream.*]

BOIS-D'ENGHIEN [*scared stiff*]: Be quiet, for heaven's sake! You'll have them all in here!

LUCETTE [*screaming*]: What do I care! Let them come! Let them see how I love you! Oh, my Fernand, I love you. I love you ... [*She presses the electric bell button which rings loud and long.*]

BOIS-D'ENGHIEN [*losing his head, getting to his knees with his neck still encircled tightly by* LUCETTE*'s other arm*]: Oh my God! Now it's the telephone! Where's the telephone?

[LUCETTE *continues shouting and screaming.*]

VOICES OUTSIDE: What's the matter? Open the door!

BOIS-D'ENGHIEN: You can't come in! [*To* LUCETTE] Will you stop that now, for heaven's sake!

[*The door of the drawing-room back-stage opens and all the others appear in the doorway.* MARCELINE *is on the left.* LUCETTE *is still on the chaise-longue.* BOIS-D'ENGHIEN *rises and stands right of the chaise-longue.* DE CHENNEVIETTE *and* DE FONTANET *come forward behind the chaise-longue.* MADAME DUVERGER *and* VIVIANE *move right.*]

ALL: Oh!

BOIS-D'ENGHIEN [*rising*]: You can't come in! I told you you can't come in!

MADAME DUVERGER [*hiding her daughter's face against her bosom*]: He's nothing on! Only his vest!

LUCETTE [*as if coming out of a dream*]: Never! Never have I been made love to like that!

BOIS-D'ENGHIEN: What's she talking about?

ALL: Scandalous! Disgraceful!

MADAME DUVERGER: And in my house! Get out, Monsieur! The engagement is broken! Get out!

BOIS-D'ENGHIEN: But, Madame . . .!

THE GENERAL [*who has just entered from the drawing-room and advances on* BOIS-D'ENGHIEN]: Tomorrow! In the morning! I keell you!

BOIS-D'ENGHIEN [*in hysterical despair*]: Oh, I give up! This is too much! They've all gone mad! Mad! Ha! ha! ha! Ha! ha! ha! [*He continues laughing hysterically as the curtain falls.*]

CURTAIN

ACT THREE

The set is divided into two parts. The right side which occupies three quarters of the set represents the second floor landing of a new house. Back-stage, a very elegant staircase rises from right to left. Facing the audience, by the staircase, is a bench. Down right there is a door with an electric bell leading into BOIS-D'ENGHIEN'*s apartment. To the right of this door, there is a curved seat upholstered like the bench. Down-stage left, in the partition dividing the stage in two, and opposite the door right is another door leading direct into* BOIS-D'ENGHIEN'*s dressing-room. This door opens inwards. It is this room which occupies the left side of the set. Right centre in it is a window opening inwards. Back left, facing the audience, is a door opening on to a corridor. Right of this door is a large washstand with the usual accessories, brushes, combs, sponges, glass and tooth-brushes, towels, etc. Down left is a chair with articles of gentleman's clothing on it. Upstage from this is an armchair. Between the armchair and the window is a hook with a lady's dressing gown hanging from it; and beneath it, on the floor, a pair of lady's slippers. Near the washstand is a coat rack with three arms. The two doors on the landing are furnished with locks and keys and open inwards.*

As the curtain raises, JEAN *is standing in the dressing-room near the armchair. He is holding one of* BOIS-D'ENGHIEN'*s shoes in his hand and polishing it with a flannel.*

JEAN [*rubbing the shoe vigorously*]: He's the absolute limit, that's what he is! Goes out last night to sign his marriage contract and now it's ten o'clock next morning and he's not back yet! It's scandalous, that's what it is! [*He puts down the shoe, picks up the other and begins polishing it equally vigorously.*] Not that I'm setting myself up as better than anyone else, but when you get engaged you should go to bed in your own house. [*He blows on the shoe to make it shine.*] Or at least do what I did ... go to bed with your future wife and not somebody else. [*During this soliloquy, the florist has come up the stairs with a basket of flowers on his head. He stops on the landing, looks at the door on the right and then at the door on the left, and then rings at the door right.*] Now who's that? It can't be Monsieur; he has his key. [*Pointing to the door which opens on to the corridor*] Hah! If you think I'm going all the way round just to open the other door! [*He opens the door on to the landing and calls*] Who is it? What d'you want?

FLORIST [*coming to him from the other side of the landing*]: Beg pardon – I'm looking for the Brugnot wedding.

JEAN [*testily*]: The Brugnot wedding! It's upstairs! The third floor!

FLORIST: The concierge told me it was the second.

JEAN: Well, it's the second above the first floor, isn't it?

FLORIST: Yes, I suppose so. – Sorry to trouble you.

[JEAN *shuts the door bad-temperedly. The florist continues up the staircase.*]

JEAN: It's too much! That's the sixth one today looking for the Brugnot wedding. I'll put a notice outside soon.

[BOIS-D'ENGHIEN *appears on the landing, looking tired and dishevelled. Under his overcoat, his evening clothes are in disarray: shirt rumpled, tie askew.*]

BOIS-D'ENGHIEN: My God, what a night!

[*He rings the bell right, long and loud.*]

JEAN: There! Another one for the Brugnot wedding! [*Opening the door from the dressing-room on to the landing and shouting abruptly*] It's not here! It's upstairs!

BOIS-D'ENGHIEN: Eh?

JEAN [*recognizing* BOIS-D'ENGHIEN]: Monsieur! It's you, Monsieur!

BOIS-D'ENGHIEN [*grumpily, entering*]: Of course it's me! Who d'you think it was!

JEAN: Oh, Monsieur, ten o'clock in the morning! Is this any time to be coming home – after your engagement party?

BOIS-D'ENGHIEN [*angrily*]: Oh, shut up!

JEAN: Yes, Monsieur!

BOIS-D'ENGHIEN [*giving* JEAN *his overcoat and hat*]: No – perhaps we'd better have it out – since it's because of you I had to spend last night in an hotel!

JEAN: Because of me?

BOIS-D'ENGHIEN: Certainly! If you'd been here when I got back last night . . . but, oh, no! I could have stood there ringing the bell forever!

JEAN: But, Monsieur, didn't you have your key?

BOIS-D'ENGHIEN: Yes, I *had* it all right. Only it disappeared down somebody's back!

JEAN [*going to the coat rack to hang up the hat and coat*]: Really, Monsieur! If you will leave your key in such places!

BOIS-D'ENGHIEN [*taking off his coat, waistcoat, tie, collar*]: Oh, stop talking rubbish! Why weren't you here? Where were you?

JEAN: You know quite well, Monsieur! I was with my wife. Monsieur has always allowed me one night a week . . . to pay my respects to Madame Jean.

BOIS-D'ENGHIEN: Your Madame Jean's getting a nuisance!

JEAN [*annoyed*]: A nuisance? . . . For you, you mean, Monsieur?

BOIS-D'ENGHIEN: Of course – for me!

JEAN: Because I hope Monsieur realizes that for Madame Jean I have the . . .

BOIS-D'ENGHIEN [*furiously*]: Will you shut up about your Madame Jean! It's me I'm talking about!

JEAN [*sarcastically*]: So I see, Monsieur.

BOIS-D'ENGHIEN [*still furiously*]: May I ask what Madame Jean's got that makes her so attractive?

JEAN: I hope Monsieur does not wish me to supply details. In brief, Monsieur, since neither you, nor anybody else, can give me the sound of little pattering feet, I have to do the best I can to obtain them myself.

BOIS-D'ENGHIEN: All right, all right, I should have known better than ask! I want to think what to do – not stand here talking about your marital problems. As if I've not got enough of my own! First of all, my key . . .

JEAN [*without waiting for him to finish*]: You want me to go and get it, Monsieur?

BOIS-D'ENGHIEN [*stopping him*]: No! No! Wait! It can stay where it is! Go and find a locksmith to put a new lock on so the old keys will be no good.

JEAN: Right, I'll go at once. [*He moves to go out by door back.*]

BOIS-D'ENGHIEN [*pointing to the door on to the landing*]: No, go that way – it will be quicker.

JEAN: Very well, Monsieur. You will find everything ready for you to change your clothes, Monsieur.

BOIS-D'ENGHIEN: Good, good! Be quick!

[JEAN *leaves by the door on to the landing without closing it behind him.*]

BOIS-D'ENGHIEN [*sitting on the armchair and taking off his trousers*]: Well, I won't forget last night in a hurry! Lucette must be feeling damn pleased with herself! Breaking up my marriage, getting me kicked out of the house! Oh, yes, she must be feeling very pleased. But if she thinks she's going to get away with it, she'd better think again! [*He goes to the washstand and turns on the tap to fill the bowl.*] And then to top it all, that hotel! No, she'll find I won't forget last night in a hurry!

[*He plunges his face in the bowl and washes himself; a lady and gentleman appear on the landing. The gentleman is about to go higher.*]

THE LADY [*pointing to the door, left open by* JEAN]: No, my dear, this must be it.

THE GENTLEMAN: Do you think so?

THE LADY: Of course! They've left the door open for the guests to walk in. That's always done.

THE GENTLEMAN: Ah? I expect you're right. [*He walks boldly into* BOIS-D'ENGHIEN*'s dressing-room, followed by his wife.*] That's funny! You're sure this is it?

BOIS-D'ENGHIEN [*back-stage, face dripping, sponge in hand*]: Who the devil are you?

THE LADY }
GENTLEMAN: } Oh!

[THE LADY *moves extreme left.*]

THE GENTLEMAN: I beg your pardon!

THE LADY: He's got no clothes on!

BOIS-D'ENGHIEN: What are you doing in here?

THE GENTLEMAN: Isn't this the Brugnot wedding?

BOIS-D'ENGHIEN: You can see damn well it isn't, can't you? It's upstairs! Walking in like that when I'm getting dressed!

THE LADY: When one is in that state one should shut one's door.

BOIS-D'ENGHIEN: I didn't ask you to come in, did I? What do you think this is – Liberty Hall? Get out! Go on – get out! [*He slams the door after them as they go out quickly.*]

THE GENTLEMAN [*on the landing*]: Ignorant lout!

BOIS-D'ENGHIEN: Did you ever see anything like it! Cheek! [*He wipes his face.*]

THE GENTLEMAN [*following his wife upstairs*]: You see? I knew quite well it was upstairs!

THE LADY: Now, now, dear! Anyone can make a mistake, you know.

[*They disappear off-stage.*]

BOIS-D'ENGHIEN: That's all I needed – that idiot Jean to go and forget to shut the door!

[BOUZIN *comes up the stairs and goes to the door right.*]

BOUZIN: Bois-d'Enghien ... second floor! This is it! [*He rings the bell right.*]

BOIS-D'ENGHIEN [*who has poured some water into the glass to brush his teeth*]: Oh, no! Somebody else now! And of course that idiot Jean isn't here! Well, they'll just have to wait!

BOUZIN: Oh dear! It looks as though nobody's in! [*He rings again.*]

BOIS-D'ENGHIEN: That's right! Ring again! I'll come when I'm ready!

BOUZIN [*impatiently*]: All right! I'll make sure! [*He rings for a long time.*]

BOIS-D'ENGHIEN [*opening the door a little and poking his head out only*]: Who is it?

BOUZIN [*crossing the landing to him*]: Ah! Monsieur Bois-d'Enghien! It's me!

BOIS-D'ENGHIEN: You! What d'you want? You can't come in now! [*He tries to shut the door.*]

BOUZIN [*holding the door open*]: I won't keep you a moment, Monsieur. Monsieur Lantery sent me ...

BOIS-D'ENGHIEN [*still trying to shut the door*]: No, not now! I'm getting dressed!

BOUZIN [*still keeping it open*]: Oh, that's all right, Monsieur.

BOIS-D'ENGHIEN: Oh, all right, then! What is it you want?

[BOUZIN *enters the dressing-room.* BOIS-D'ENGHIEN *shuts the door.*]

BOUZIN: It's quite simple. Monsieur Lantery has asked me to give you this copy of your marriage contract, that's all. [*He takes the folded document from his pocket.*]

BOIS-D'ENGHIEN: My marriage contract! That's a joke, that is! You can tear it up, that's what you can do!

BOUZIN: But . . .?

BOIS-D'ENGHIEN: Don't you know? Haven't you heard? It's finished, my marriage! Over! Done with! [*He starts brushing his teeth with one hand, and takes the contract from* BOUZIN *with the other.*] Here's what I do with your contract! [*Leaving the toothbrush in his mouth, he tears the contract in two.*]

BOUZIN: Oh, dear! And I was supposed to give you our bill as well.

BOIS-D'ENGHIEN [*with a bitter laugh, while* BOUZIN *picks up the pieces of the contract*]: The bill! That's an even better joke still! You're excelling yourself! If they think I'm going to pay for a broken marriage contract, they can damn well think again!

BOUZIN: But, really, you know . . .

[*During the preceding,* THE GENERAL, *obviously very angry, races up the staircase and rings the bell right.*]

BOIS-D'ENGHIEN: Now who the devil is it this time?

BOUZIN: I'm awfully sorry, but . . .

BOIS-D'ENGHIEN: Yes, yes, I know, the bill! Don't bother me now! Wait, do me a favour, please, will you? See who it is?

BOUZIN: Certainly! [*He makes as if to go to the door on to the landing.*]

BOIS-D'ENGHIEN [*stopping him and pointing to the door back leading to the corridor*]: No, this way! Go along the corridor and turn right. Just say I'm sorry but I can't see anybody.

BOUZIN: Yes, of course.

[*He goes out the door back as* THE GENERAL *rings again.*]

BOIS-D'ENGHIEN: Ringing the bell like that at this hour of the morning!

THE GENERAL [*furiously*]: Caramba! Me van hacer esperar toda la vida? [*He rings the bell continuously.*]

BOIS-D'ENGHIEN [*laughing*]: They're getting impatient!

VOICE OF BOUZIN [*off-stage, right*]: All right, all right!

THE GENERAL [*moving back to middle of landing*]: Bueno! Eeet ees time too!

[BOUZIN *opens the door right.*]

Monsieur Bodégué?

BOUZIN [*recognizing* THE GENERAL *after having taken two steps out on to the landing*]: Heavens! It's that maniac!

[*He does a rapid about-turn, rushes back into the apartment, slamming the door in* THE GENERAL'*s face.*]

THE GENERAL [*furiously*]: Boussin! Open the door, Boussin! Open eet, Boussin! [*He rings the bell and bangs furiously on the door.*]

BOIS-D'ENGHIEN [*at the noise made by* THE GENERAL, *opening the door left on to the landing and poking his head out*]: Who the devil's making all that row! Oh – it's you, General?

THE GENERAL [*turning and rushing into the dressing-room, pushing* BOIS-D'ENGHIEN *aside*]: Eet ees you! Bueno! I feex you later! Boussin ees here?

BOIS-D'ENGHIEN: Well, yes – why?

THE GENERAL: Do not ask seelly question! [*He moves extreme left.*]

BOUZIN [*appearing, panic-stricken, at the door back*]: Monsieur, it's the Gen ... [*seeing* THE GENERAL] Oh, my God, it's him *again*! [*He slams the door and disappears.*]

THE GENERAL: Wait, Boussin! Wait, Boussin!

BOIS-D'ENGHIEN [*trying to hold him back*]: I say, now, look here ...

THE GENERAL: Leave me! I feex you later!

[*He pushes* BOIS-D'ENGHIEN *aside and dashes out back in pursuit of* BOUZIN.]

BOIS-D'ENGHIEN: Of course, they had to come here to murder each other! [*He opens the door on to the landing to see what is happening.*]

BOUZIN [*appearing through door right which he slams behind him, passing in front of* BOIS-D'ENGHIEN *without stopping, and rushing up the stairs*]: Don't tell him.

BOIS-D'ENGHIEN [*laughing*]: No, I won't! No!

[BOUZIN *collides with* THE FLORIST *who is hurrying down the stairs.*]

FLORIST: Look where you're going!

[*They disentangle themselves,* THE FLORIST *coming on down,* BOUZIN *continuing up the stairs.*]

THE GENERAL [*bursting out through door right*]: Where ees he? Boussin! Where ees he?

BOIS-D'ENGHIEN [*his head poking out of door left*]: He went downstairs! Down!

THE GENERAL [*leaning over the banisters*]: Bueno! I see heem! [*He rushes madly down the stairs.*] Wait, Boussin! Wait, Boussin! [*He disappears.*]

BOIS-D'ENGHIEN: Have a good run! You'll be lucky if you catch him!

BOUZIN [*coming cautiously down the stairs*]: Has he gone?

BOIS-D'ENGHIEN [*in doorway, left, laughing*]: I'll say! He's just gone running down after you!

BOUZIN [*entering the dressing-room and collapsing into the armchair*]: Oh, my God, that was terrible!

BOIS-D'ENGHIEN [*closing the door*]: Really? I thought it was very funny!

BOUZIN: The man's mad! He's a maniac! Why is he always after me? What have I done to him? What's he got against me? Do *you* know?

BOIS-D'ENGHIEN [*pretending to be serious*]: But didn't you know? He's found out that you are Lucette Gautier's lover.

BOUZIN [*getting up, protesting vigorously*]: Me? But that's not true! You must tell him! You must tell him it's not true! There's never been anything between me and Mademoiselle Gautier! Never! [*Mistaking* BOIS-D'ENGHIEN*'s smile for disbelief*] I give you my word of honour!

BOIS-D'ENGHIEN [*pretending disbelief*]: Never?

BOUZIN [*emphatically*]: Never! Of course I don't know how Mademoiselle Gautier feels towards me ... she's never said anything ... but as far as I'm concerned, well ... and if Mademoiselle Gautier's been making up things ... well, I hate to say it ... she's just flattering herself! [*Pleadingly*] I beg you to help me. It can't go on like this. It'll be the end of me!

BOIS-D'ENGHIEN: All right. I'll speak to him.

[LUCETTE *comes up the stairs on to the landing.*]

LUCETTE [*stopping to gain her breath, then ringing bell right*]: Oh, dear, I don't know how to go about this!

BOIS-D'ENGHIEN: Another one! [BOUZIN's *face expresses horror.*] See who it is now, will you?

BOUZIN [*getting behind the armchair*]: Me? No! No! I'm not opening it! I'm not opening it!

BOIS-D'ENGHIEN: Oh, now, look here ...

BOUZIN: Oh, no! It could be the General back again!

[LUCETTE *rings again.*]

BOIS-D'ENGHIEN [*indicating his state of dress*]: But look – you can't expect me to go to the door like this!

LUCETTE: He must guess it's me. That's why he's not answering. But how silly of me! I've got that key that was down my back. [*She takes the key from her pocket and crosses to the other door.*]

BOIS-D'ENGHIEN [*trying to persuade* BOUZIN]: Oh, go on, Bouzin, please!

BOUZIN [*refusing to move*]: No! No! No! No!

[LUCETTE *puts the key in the lock of the door left.*]

BOIS-D'ENGHIEN [*hearing the noise of the key in the lock*]: What's that? [*The door opens.*] Who's there?

LUCETTE [*entering, coldly resolute*]: It's me!

BOUZIN: Lucette Gautier!

BOIS-D'ENGHIEN [*moving extreme left*]: And just what d'you think you're doing here?

LUCETTE: Oh, just called to see you.

BOIS-D'ENGHIEN: You've got a nerve, you have!

LUCETTE [*very clearly*]: I must speak to you.

BOUZIN [*back centre*]: To me?

LUCETTE [*disdainfully*]: To you! Hah! [*To* BOIS-D'ENGHIEN] To you! [*To* BOUZIN] Leave us, Monsieur Bouzin!

BOIS-D'ENGHIEN [*haughtily*]: That's not necessary! Anything you have to say to me can be said in public!

LUCETTE [*authoritatively, emphasizing each syllable*]: I must speak to you. [*To* BOUZIN] Leave us, Monsieur Bouzin.

BOIS-D'ENGHIEN [*with disdainful condescension*]: All right, Bouzin, wait in the next room a moment, will you? I'll call as soon as ... Madame has finished.

BOUZIN [*moving towards door back, then pausing before going out*]: You don't think she could have followed me here, do you? [*He goes out.*]

BOIS-D'ENGHIEN [*containing his anger*]: And now, what is it? What d'you want?

LUCETTE: I come to . . . to . . . [*intimidated by* BOIS-D'ENGHIEN'*s hard gaze*] to bring you back your key.

BOIS-D'ENGHIEN: Very well. Put it down there. [*She puts the key in the washstand.*] I suppose you've nothing else to say to me?

LUCETTE: Yes! I have! [*Throwing her arms round his neck*] I love you!

BOIS-D'ENGHIEN [*releasing himself*]: Oh, no! No more of that, Madame! Those little games are over!

LUCETTE: Oh!

BOIS-D'ENGHIEN: I've been fooled long enough! You think that's all you need do, isn't it? You break up my marriage, make me look ridiculous and then all you need do is come back and say 'I love you' and I'll forget about it all!

LUCETTE [*bitterly*]: You forget easily!

BOIS-D'ENGHIEN: Well, you're wrong, see? You love me, do you? Well, I couldn't care less! To hell with your love! I'm fed-up with your love! *And* I'll prove it! [*He opens the door.*] The door is open! Use it!

LUCETTE [*righteously indignant*]: You're turning me out? Me? Me?

BOIS-D'ENGHIEN: No hysterics! Out! That's all! Out!

LUCETTE: So that's the way you want it, is it? All right! You don't need to tell me twice!

[*She goes out.* BOIS-D'ENGHIEN *is shutting the door but she comes rushing back in again.*]

LUCETTE: But I warn you! If you let me cross the threshold of that door you'll never see me again!

BOIS-D'ENGHIEN: That's a bargain!

LUCETTE: Good! [*She does the same again, goes out and comes rushing back again just as he is shutting the door.*] Think it over well!

BOIS-D'ENGHIEN [*to himself*]: Will you get-out-of-my-hair!

LUCETTE: If you let me cross . . .

BOIS-D'ENGHIEN: Yes, yes, I heard you!

LUCETTE: Very well, then! [*She goes out and* BOIS-D'ENGHIEN *closes the door sharply on her. She turns intending to come back again as before.*] But you know ... [*Finding the door closed*] Fernand! Open the door! D'you hear me?

BOIS-D'ENGHIEN [*in his room*]: No!

LUCETTE [*from the other side of the door*]: Fernand, think well what you're doing! This is forever, you know!

BOIS-D'ENGHIEN: Oh yes, indeed! Forever and ever!

LUCETTE [*collapsing on to the bench*]: You heartless beast!

BOIS-D'ENGHIEN [*who has gone to the coat rack, taken down the dressing-gown, rolled it into a ball, and now opening the door, throws it at her feet*]: And there! Your dressing-gown! [*He shuts the door quickly and runs to pick up her slippers.*]

LUCETTE [*indignantly*]: Oh!

BOIS-D'ENGHIEN [*opening the door again*]: Your slippers! [*He shuts the door again.*]

LUCETTE: Oh! [*The other side of the door*] So, it's like that, is it? All right! You can blame yourself then for what I'm going to do! Yes, it'll be you who drove me to it!

BOIS-D'ENGHIEN: To what?

LUCETTE [*pulling out of her pocket the revolver she used in Act Two*]: I still have my gun, remember! I'm going to kill myself!

BOIS-D'ENGHIEN [*dashing out, leaving the door wide open*]: Kill yourself? Here! [*Throwing himself on her*] Give me that!

LUCETTE [*struggling*]: Never! Never!

BOIS-D'ENGHIEN [*trying to wrest the revolver from her*]: Give it me, d'you hear? [*Holding her arm, trying to reach the revolver*] Let go! Let it go!

LUCETTE [*still struggling*]: You let me go!

BOIS-D'ENGHIEN: Give it to me!

LUCETTE: No!

BOIS-D'ENGHIEN: Yes! [*He seizes the revolver by the barrel.* LUCETTE *pulls the other way with the result that the fan comes out and he is left holding it. He stares at the fan.*] What the devil!

LUCETTE: Oh!

BOIS-D'ENGHIEN: It's a fan!

LUCETTE [*furiously, dancing with rage*]: Oh! You ... you beast!

BOIS-D'ENGHIEN [*laughing sarcastically*]: Ha, ha! Look what she's going to kill herself with!

LUCETTE [*still dancing with fury*]: You beast, you beast, you beast!

BOIS-D'ENGHIEN: Ha! Ha! Ha! That's what she was going to kill herself with! Always play-acting, aren't you?

LUCETTE [*completely overcome with rage*]: You'll never see me again! [*She rushes away down the staircase.*]

BOIS-D'ENGHIEN: It'll be a pleasure! [*He puts the fan on the bench and picks up the dressing-gown and slippers.*] You've forgotten your dressing-gown! [*He throws it down over the banisters.*] And your slippers! [*He throws them after it.*]

VOICE OF LUCETTE: Oh!

BOIS-D'ENGHIEN [*picking up the fan from the bench*]: Ha! And to think I was fool enough to be taken in! And with a fan! [*He puts the fan back in the revolver and puts it on the chair right.*] Well anyway, I'll get some peace now. [*He is extreme right and turns to go back into his dressing-room. As he does so a gust of wind blows open the window of the dressing-room and the door shuts itself violently. He tries to reach it in time but is too late and bangs his nose on the door.*] Damn! Now I'm shut out! [*Calling and knocking on the door*] Jean! Open the door! Oh, blast it! He's out, of course! And I've gone and left the key on the washstand. [*Not knowing what to do*] But I can't stay out here on the landing dressed like this! What the devil am I to do? [*He calls over the banisters down the stairs.*] Concierge! Concierge!

BOUZIN [*having knocked at the door at the back of the dressing-room puts his head timidly into the room*]: You haven't forgotten me, have you, Monsieur de Bois-d'Enghien? ... ... There's nobody here! Where's he gone? [*Seeing the window open, he shuts it.*]

BOIS-D'ENGHIEN [*flopping on to the bench by the stairs*]: Oh, good heavens – there's that wedding upstairs as well!

BOUZIN: Well, I'll just have to come back later, that's all. [*He makes towards the door opening on to the landing.*]

BOIS-D'ENGHIEN: Of course! If I ring, Bouzin will hear me! [*He goes to door right and rings continuously.*]

BOUZIN [*who has his hand on the door knob, stands petrified*]: My God! It must be the General again! And I'm all alone! [*He rushes back through the door on to the corridor.*]

BOIS-D'ENGHIEN [*continuing to ring*]: Why the devil doesn't he come! Of course – he's heard it but he doesn't dare open! Oh, that's fine, that is! [*He goes and leans over the banister.*] Concierge! Concierge! [*Sharply*] Oh my God, somebody's coming up! [*He dashes up the staircase to next floor, disappears for a moment, then reappears absolutely panic-stricken.*] The wedding-guests! They're all coming down! I'm caught! Surrounded!

[*He crouches down in the doorway right trying to make himself as small as possible. The wedding guests come down the stairs all speaking at the same time: We'll have to hurry! But we've plenty of time! We've to be there by eleven o'clock! etc. etc.*]

ALL [*seeing* BOIS-D'ENGHIEN]: Oh!

BOIS-D'ENGHIEN [*trying to put on a bold front*]: Congratulations! My best wishes!

ALL [*raising their hands in horror*]: Shocking! It's a scandal!

THE BRIDE'S FATHER: He's in his underclothes!

THE BRIDEGROOM: Somebody should make a complaint!

THE BRIDE'S MOTHER: The concierge should be told!

BOIS-D'ENGHIEN [*making a semi-circle he edges round to the left side of the landing*]: Ladies ... gentlemen ...

ALL: Go away! Hide yourself! Put something on! Shocking!

[*They all continue down the stiars, scandalized, passing* THE GENERAL *on his way up.*]

BOIS-D'ENGHIEN [*in despair*] Oh, this is terrible! [*Seeing* THE GENERAL] Oh, no! Not him again!

THE GENERAL [*astonished to find* BOIS-D'ENGHIEN *in a state of undress on the landing*]: Bodégué! Why you no trousers?

BOIS-D'ENGHIEN [*to himself, exasperated*]: Now he's starting!

THE GENERAL: Why you wear no trousers?

BOIS-D'ENGHIEN [*furiously*]: Why? Why? Because I can't get in! The door slammed in my face!

THE GENERAL [*laughing*]: Ha! ha! ha! Ees funny, no?

BOIS-D'ENGHIEN [*laughing sarcastically*]: Ha! Ha! No, it isn't!

THE GENERAL [*wiping his forehead*]: Thees Boussin! I have run after heem!

BOIS-D'ENGHIEN [*fed-up*]: And didn't catch him! So what?

THE GENERAL: I catch heem, si! I keeck heem in pants! But he ees not Boussin! When he turn round he ees another!

BOIS-D'ENGHIEN: Ha!

THE GENERAL: But when I catch heem – thees Boussin – I weell . . .

BOIS-D'ENGHIEN [*interrupting him*]: Keell heem! All right! But what's that to do with me?

THE GENERAL: Eet ees not that I come speak about . . .

BOIS-D'ENGHIEN: I've something else to do beside standing about talking, so . . .

THE GENERAL: What ees eet you have to do?

BOIS-D'ENGHIEN: Look, I've just told you! I'm locked out!

THE GENERAL: Ees no matter! Ees 'barcatil'! We talk out here.

BOIS-D'ENGHIEN: But, good heavens, man . . . [*Leaning over the banister and seeing someone coming up*] Now here's someone else! [*He runs up the stairs and disappears.*]

THE GENERAL: Where he go? Where he go? [*Going up three steps and calling*] Bodégué! Bodégué!

BOIS-D'ENGHIEN [*from the floor above*]: Not now! Later! Later!

THE GENERAL: Ees mad!

[*A gentleman comes up the stairs, nods to* THE GENERAL *as he passes, and continues up the stairs to the next floor.* THE GENERAL *nods to him.*]

Buenos dias! [*Calling*] Bodégué! Why you go upstairs? Bodégué! Come down, Bodégué!

BOIS-D'ENGHIEN [*reappearing, coming down the stairs*]: Oh, it is too much! People are coming up and down all the time!

THE GENERAL [*descending to landing*]: What ees matter that you run like rabbit?

BOIS-D'ENGHIEN [*back on landing*]: You can't pick a lock, can you?

THE GENERAL [*not understanding*]: Peeckalot?

BOIS-D'ENGHIEN [*shrugging his shoulders*]: Oh, never mind! What d'you want here, anyway?

THE GENERAL: I come to do what I have said to you yesterday! I come to keell you!

BOIS-D'ENGHIEN [*furiously*]: What, again? Oh, go to blazes!

THE GENERAL [*with panache*]: I wait for your commands, Bodégué!

BOIS-D'ENGHIEN: You do, eh? Well go and find me some trousers!

THE GENERAL [*jumping with fury*]: Trousers? Me? [*Changing his tone*] Bodégué, please, do not be septic!

BOIS-D'ENGHIEN [*not understanding*]: Be what?

THE GENERAL: I say, do not be septic.

BOIS-D'ENGHIEN [*understanding*]: Oh, you mean sceptic! You should pronounce the 'c', like a 'k'. S-k-e-p-t-i-c: Sceptic!

THE GENERAL: Ees no deefference! Septic, sceptic! Eet ees all same!

BOIS-D'ENGHIEN: Oh, all right! Let's get this over with! You want to kill me?

THE GENERAL: No!

BOIS-D'ENGHIEN: What d'you mean – no?

THE GENERAL: Si, that ees what I come for. But now I no more want to keell you!

BOIS-D'ENGHIEN: Oh? Good! So much the better!

THE GENERAL [*with a sigh of resignation*]: No, becose I have just see Lucette Gautier, downstairs.

BOIS-D'ENGHEIN: Oh?

THE GENERAL: She say to me a theeng – eet upset me – but eet geeve me no choice. She say to me: 'I do not be yours, only eef Bodégué be mine steell!'

BOIS-D'ENGHIEN [*recoiling*]: What?

THE GENERAL: Eet ees so! Eet ees a great blow to me! Above all, when I theenk of the sandal of yesterday.

BOIS-D'ENGHIEN: The sandal? What d'you mean – sandal?

THE GENERAL: The sandal you make with Loucette at the house of Madame Duverger.

BOIS-D'ENGHIEN: Oh, you mean 'the scandal'! You should pronounce the 'c'. Like a 'k' 's-k-a-n-d-a-l': 'Scandal!'

THE GENERAL: Bodégué! Ees eet that you try to make fool of me? I tell you just now 'septeec'. You tell me 'skepteec'! Now I say 'sandal'. You say 'skandal'. [*Threateningly*] Bodégué!

BOIS-D'ENGHIEN [*taking the same tone*]: General?

THE GENERAL: You be careful, Bodégué!

BOIS-D'ENGHIEN: What for?

THE GENERAL [*calming down suddenly*]: Bueno! I tell you now you make eet up with Loucette.

BOIS-D'ENGHIEN: Me? [*Leaning towards* THE GENERAL'*s ear as if to make a confidence, then shouting loudly*]: Never on your life!

THE GENERAL: No? ... Then I re-keell you!

BOIS-D'ENGHIEN [*moving forward left*]: All right, go ahead! Re-kill me! [*Coming back to him*] Why the devil can't you make up your mind? Just now it was because I was Lucette's lover. Now it's because I'm not! Just what is it you do want?

THE GENERAL: What ees eet I want? Bodégué, you ees a fool!

BOIS-D'ENGHIEN: Now look here ...

THE GENERAL: What I want ees Loucette.

BOIS-D'ENGHIEN: Then she's yours. And I'll tell you how.

THE GENERAL: You weell tell me how! Ah, Bodégué, you ees my friend!

BOIS-D'ENGHIEN: You will go and tell her that you have seen me and that I absolutely refuse to make it up with her.

THE GENERAL: Why?

BOIS-D'ENGHIEN: There you go again! Why? Because of certain defects she has.

THE GENERAL: What you say?

BOIS-D'ENGHIEN [*in* THE GENERAL'*s ear*]: Certain defects that only somebody intimately acquainted with her could know about.

THE GENERAL [*at the top of his voice*]: Defects? Lucette? She has defects?

BOIS-D'ENGHIEN: No, of course not!

THE GENERAL: Then why you tell me ...

BOIS-D'ENGHIEN: Look – try and understand. She's a woman – so she's got her vanity. Now you tell her I said she loves herself more than she ever loved anybody else, and she'll never want to see me again. She'll be all yours. Understand?

THE GENERAL [*delighted*]: Ah Bodégué, I understand! Bodégué! Fernando! Gracias, gracias! Muchas gracias!

BOIS-D'ENGHIEN: Good! That's settled then!

THE GENERAL: I go to her! I run! Adios, Fernando! Una buena sante! Now I no keell you no more, Fernando! [*He runs off downstairs.*]

BOIS-D'ENGHIEN: Good! Fine! And I keell you no more, either! [*He leans over banisters, watching him go.*]

BOUZIN [*appearing through door of dressing-room, left*]: I can't hear anything! Anyway I can't stay in there all day!

BOIS-D'ENGHIEN [*still looking over banister, he turns and sees* BOUZIN *coming out of the door*]: Wait! Don't shut it!

BOUZIN [*unable to stop the door closing*]: Oh!

BOIS-D'ENGHIEN [*at the door*]: You silly idiot! I told you not to shut it!

BOUZIN: I couldn't! It was too quick for me!

BOIS-D'ENGHIEN [*moving forward*]: So now I'm still locked out!

BOUZIN [*laughing*]: What are you doing dressed like that out on the landing?

BOIS-D'ENGHIEN: What am I doing! If you think I'm doing it for fun . . .

BOUZIN: But it is funny!

BOIS-D'ENGHIEN [*furiously*]: You think so, do you? It's all right for you, of course. You're fully dressed! [*He sits on the chair right, without seeing the revolver under him. He jumps up exclaiming*] Oh! [*Seeing the pistol, to himself*] Aha! [*He picks up the gun and, holding it behind his back, goes over to* BOUZIN; *very pleasantly*] Bouzin! . . .

BOUZIN [*smiling*]: Monsieur?

BOIS-D'ENGHIEN [*still very pleasantly*]: You are going to do me a great favour!

BOUZIN [*smiling*]: Me, Monsieur?

BOIS-D'ENGHIEN [*still very pleasantly*]: Give me your trousers.

BOUZIN [*laughing*]: Ha, ha, ha! You really are funny! Quite mad!

BOIS-D'ENGHIEN [*changing his tone and advancing on him*]: Yes, I am mad! Quite mad! You've said it. So off with your trousers! [*He points the revolver at* BOUZIN.]

BOUZIN [*terrified, backing up against the centre dividing wall*]: Oh, good heavens! Monsieur! Please!

BOIS-D'ENGHIEN [*threateningly*]: Give me your trousers!

BOUZIN: Oh, please, Monsieur! I beg you!

BOIS-D'ENGHIEN: Come on! Be quick! Your trousers, or I fire!

BOUZIN: Yes, Monsieur! [*Terrified, he begins to remove his trousers, huddling against the dividing wall.*] Oh, my God! What a situation to be in! In my underpants! On the stairs of a strange house!

BOIS-D'ENGHIEN: Hurry! Be quick about it!

BOUZIN: Here you are, Monsieur, here! [*He gives him his trousers.*]

BOIS-D'ENGHIEN [*taking them*]: Thank you! Now your coat! [*He points the revolver again.*]

BOUZIN: But I won't have anything left!

BOIS-D'ENGHIEN: You'll have your waistcoat! Hurry, your coat!

BOUZIN [*giving his coat*]: Yes, Monsieur, yes!

BOIS-D'ENGHIEN: Thank you!

BOUZIN [*huddling pitifully against the dividing wall, holding his hat with both hands against his stomach*]: Oh, why did I ever set foot in this place!

[*Meanwhile* BOIS-D'ENGHIEN *has gone over and sat on the bench with the clothes, put the revolver on the bench on his right, and puts on* BOUZIN*'s trousers. Once they are on, he gets up and moves right to fasten them, standing with his back to the audience.* BOUZIN*'s face lights up as he sees the revolver on the bench.*]

BOUZIN [*to himself*]: The gun!

[*Putting his hat on, he tiptoes over and picks up the revolver. Tipping his hat to a jaunty angle on his head, he approaches* BOIS-D'ENGHIEN *full of self-confidence, holding the revolver behind his back.*]

BOUZIN [*very pleasantly*]: Monsieur Bois-d'Enghien?

BOIS-D'ENGHIEN [*as he finishes buttoning the trousers*]: Yes?

BOUZIN: My trousers, if you don't mind.

BOIS-D'ENGHIEN: What? [*He turns and laughs.*]

BOUZIN [*pointing the revolver, his voice as menacing as he can make it*]: You are going to give me back my trousers or I will kill you!

BOIS-D'ENGHIEN [*putting* BOUZIN*'s coat on*]: Yes, old chap, you do that.

BOUZIN: You'll find out I'm not joking! My trousers or I shoot!

BOIS-D'ENGHIEN [*fastening the coat*]: Go ahead! Go ahead!

BOUZIN [*pulling in vain on the trigger*]: What the ...!

BOIS-D'ENGHIEN: No, no! Not like that. Look. You do it like this. [*With the ends of his fingers, and under the horrified gaze of* BOUZIN, *he pulls the fan from the barrel of the revolver which he leaves* BOUZIN *holding.*] You don't know how to use these things, old chap.

BOUZIN: I've been tricked! [*He throws the open fan on to the bench.*]

BOIS-D'ENGHIEN [*laughing*]: Poor old Bouzin!

[*He picks up the revolver, pushes the fan back in, and puts it in his pocket.*]

CONCIERGE [*coming up the stairs*]: This way, gentlemen.

BOUZIN [*leaning over the banisters*]: Look! There's someone coming! [*He rushes up the stairs, two at a time, to the floor above.*]

BOIS-D'ENGHIEN: That's all right! Ah! It's good to feel fully dressed. Even if they are somebody else's clothes!

CONCIERGE [*coming up on to the landing, followed by two policemen*]: That's right. This way. [*He leads the policemen past* BOIS-D'ENGHIEN.]

BOIS-D'ENGHIEN: Policemen? What's going on? Who are you looking for?

CONCIERGE: A man who was seen in his underclothes on this staircase.

BOIS-D'ENGHIEN: In his underclothes? [*To himself*] Oh, poor Bouzin! [*Aloud*] I've not seen him!

CONCIERGE [*about to go up the stairs*]: It was the Brugnot wedding people who made the complaint. That's why I've had to fetch the police. [*Continuing up the stairs after the policemen*] Go on up. He must be up there somewhere. He can't get that far. There are only five floors. [*They disappear up the stairs.*]

BOIS-D'ENGHIEN [*who has accompanied them up the first few steps*]: Poor Bouzin! He really doesn't have much luck!

[VIVIANE *appears on the landing from below, followed by* FRÄULEIN BETT. *She holds a roll of music in her hand.*]

BOIS-D'ENGHIEN [*descending the stairs two at a time*]: Viviane! You here?

VIVIANE: Yes, me! Me! Who's come to say to you: 'I love you!'

BOIS-D'ENGHIEN: What? You mean ... even after what has happened?

VIVIANE: What does that matter. I know one thing ... that's that you really are the husband I've always dreamed of!

BOIS-D'ENGHIEN: I am? [*To the audience*] That must prove something!

FRÄULEIN BETT [*interrupting them*]: Ich bitte um Entschuldigung. Aber wer ist es?

VIVIANE [*to* FRÄULEIN BETT]: Ja, ja! [*Introducing them*]: My companion who teaches me German. Fräulein Bett: Herr Capoul!

BOIS-D'ENGHIEN [*astonished*]: Eh?

FRÄULEIN BETT [*nodding to him*]: Oh, ja, ich kenne Monsieur Capoul.

BOIS-D'ENGHIEN [*completely at a loss, to* VIVIANE]: What are you talking about? Who's this Herr Capoul?

VIVIANE [*in a low aside to to him*]: If I'd told her I was coming to see you, she'd never have brought me. I had to say I was going to Monsieur Capoul – for my singing lesson.

BOIS-D'ENGHIEN: But she'll soon realize ...

VIVIANE: No, she won't! She doesn't understand French! [*Becoming all romantic*] To think you have all those women always running after you!

BOIS-D'ENGHIEN [*protesting*]: Oh, now, really ...

VIVIANE: Oh, it makes me love you all the more!

BOIS-D'ENGHIEN: It does? Well... yes... as a matter of fact... I've almost lost count ... there's been so many!

VIVIANE [*delighted*]: Really? Perhaps there've actually been some who have wanted to kill themselves for you?

BOIS-D'ENGHIEN: Fifteen! Yes, you've only just missed seeing one of them. Here's the pistol I had to take from her.

VIVIANE [*with ecstasy*]: A pistol? And to think I'm in love with a man like that! Ah!

BOIS-D'ENGHIEN [*trying to take her in his arms*]: Ah! Viviane!

VIVIANE [*quickly*]: No! Not in front of her!

BOIS-D'ENGHIEN: Damn!

[VIVIANE *smiles at* FRÄULEIN BETT, *who smiles back without understanding.* BOIS-D'ENGHIEN *joins in and they all grin at each other.*]

FRÄULEIN BETT [*stopping smiling*]: Aber warum bleiben wir auf der Treppe?

VIVIANE [*laughing*]: Yes, she's got something there!

BOIS-D'ENGHIEN [*laughing also, without understanding*]: What did she say?

VIVIANE: She wants to know why we're staying out here. Let's go in!

BOIS-D'ENGHIEN: We can't. My door's locked. I'm waiting for somebody to fetch the key.

VIVIANE: But ... my singing lesson ...

BOIS-D'ENGHIEN: Tell her it's the custom ... that great artists like me always give their singing lesson on the stairs ... There's more room.

VIVIANE [*laughing*]: All right! [*To* FRÄULEIN] Monsieur Capoul immer auf der Treppe singe!

FRÄULEIN BETT [*astonished*]: Nein?

VIVIANE: Ja!

FRÄULEIN BETT: Oh! Wie seltsam!

VIVIANE [*she leads her to the bench right and sits her there*]: There! [*Loudly*] And now, Mama's only got to arrive on the scene!

BOIS-D'ENGHIEN: Your mother! But ...

VIVIANE: Now, now! Don't worry – you'll see!

BOIS-D'ENGHIEN: Look – what are you up to?

VIVIANE [*unrolling her music*]: This is supposed to be my singing lesson. If you want to say anything, sing it!

BOIS-D'ENGHIEN: What? You want me to ...

VIVIANE: Of course! She'll get suspicious if you don't! [*She gives him a sheet of music and takes another herself.*] Here you are! [*She gives another sheet to* FRÄULEIN BETT *and comes back to him.*] Now, what were you saying?

BOIS-D'ENGHIEN: I was saying what on earth will your mother say when ...

VIVIANE [*softly and quickly*]: Sing it! Sing it!

BOIS-D'ENGHIEN: Oh, all right! Hum! Hum! [*He sings to the tune of 'Home to Our Mountains' from* Il Trovatore]

But your dear mother, what will she say?
When she knows all, she won't like it!

VIVIANE [*continuing singing the same tune*]:

For my dear mother, I've left a note
In which I've said: 'If you want me
You'll find me with my dear Fernand!'

FRÄULEIN BETT [*speaking*]: Oh, sehr nett!

BOIS-D'ENGHIEN }
VIVIANE: } Yes, isn't it?

FRÄULEIN BETT: Ja! Ja! [*Wanting to show that she knows the aria*] Il Trovatore!

BOIS-D'ENGHIEN: Quite right! Il Trovatore!

VIVIANE [*to* BOIS-D'ENGHIEN]: Go on singing!

BOIS-D'ENGHIEN [*singing the same tune*]:

But your dear mother, in her anger,
Will she not refuse, to let you marry me?

VIVIANE [*singing*]:

Oh, yes, she will – be very angry,
But if she thinks – I am compromised
She'll let us have our way,
And give in!

MADAME DUVERGER [*rushing up the stairs*]: Viviane! What are you doing here!

VIVIANE: Why, Mama!

FRÄULEIN BETT [*coming over to her*]: Guten Morgen, Madame!

MADAME DUVERGER [*turning on her*]: And you! What d'you mean by bringing my daughter here! You ought to be ashamed of yourself!

FRÄULEIN BETT: Was bedeutet das?

MADAME DUVERGER: Oh, never mind! I should know better – her and her German!

BOIS-D'ENGHIEN: Madame, I have once again the honour of asking for your daughter's hand in marriage.

MADAME DUVERGER: Never, Monsieur! [*To* VIVIANE] You poor child, who will ever marry you after a scandal like this!

VIVIANE: He will, mama! Anyway, I love him and I'm going to have him!

MADAME DUVERGER [*taking* VIVIANE *in her arms as if to protect her from* BOIS-D'ENGHIEN]: Him? The ... 'I don't-know-what' – of Mademoiselle Gautier!

BOIS-D'ENGHIEN: But I'm not the ... 'I-don't-know-what' ... of Mademoiselle Gautier any more!

MADAME DUVERGER: Really, Monsieur! After what happened last night?

BOIS-D'ENGHIEN [*taking the bull by the horns*]: That's just it, Madame. You jumped to the wrong conclusion! Mademoiselle Gautier and I were saying good-bye forever!

MADAME DUVERGER: In your underclothes! Don't talk nonsense!

BOIS-D'ENGHIEN [*impervious*]: Exactly! I had just said to Mademoiselle Gautier: 'I don't want to keep anything that will remind me of you . . . not even these clothes which you have touched!'

MADAME DUVERGER: What?

BOIS-D'ENGHIEN: And, suiting the word to the deed, I began taking them off. If you'd come two minutes later I'd have had nothing on.

MADAME DUVERGER [*shocked*]: Oh!

VIVIANE: So you see, mama, it will be quite all right for me to marry him now.

MADAME DUVERGER [*resignedly*]: If it's what you want, my child! If you're sure you'll be happy.

VIVIANE: Oh yes! I will be!

BOIS-D'ENGHIEN: Ah, Madame!

JEAN [*entering through door at back of dressing-room*]: Oh, dear, where is he now? [*He opens the door on to the landing.*]

BOIS-D'ENGHIEN: There you are, at last! [*At the door*] Will you all come in? Madame? Viviane?

[*As they are all about to enter the dressing-room, a commotion is heard up the stairs to the floor above.*]

ALL [*turning*]: What on earth is all that? What's the matter? Who is it?

THE CONCIERGE [*descending first*]: We've got him! We had to chase him all over the roof first though!

[BOUZIN *appears, in a state of complete dejection and discomfiture, dragged by* THE POLICEMEN.]

BOIS-D'ENGHIEN: Bouzin!

MADAME DUVERGER: That clerk, now! In *his* underclothes!

VIVIANE: Oh, how shocking!

FRÄULEIN BETT: Entsetzlich!

[*The three women rush scandalized into the dressing-room.*]

THE POLICEMEN: Come along, you!

BOUZIN [*dragging back*]: No! No! Wait! Monsieur Bois-d'Enghien! Please! I beg you!

BOIS-D'ENGHIEN [*at the door of his room*]: Really! I don't know what people are coming to!

[*He goes into his dressing-room shutting the door on* BOUZIN.]

BOUZIN: Oh!

THE POLICEMEN: Come on now! To the station with you!

BOIS-D'ENGHIEN [*inside his dressing-room, to himself*]: That was a rotten trick, I suppose. Still, I know the Commissaire. I'll soon have him out again.

BOUZIN [*struggling*]: I'll appeal! To the Chamber of Deputies! To the State!

THE POLICEMEN: To the station!

[THE POLICEMEN *drag* BOUZIN, *still struggling, down the stairs.*]

CURTAIN